GREYCOURT

GREYCOURT

Tommy Nocerino

Copyright © 2015 by Tommy Nocerino.

Library of Congress Control Number:		2015913602
ISBN:	Hardcover	978-1-5144-0016-6
	Softcover	978-1-5144-0017-3
	eBook	978-1-5144-0018-0

All rights reserved. No part of this book may be reproduced or transmitted in any form or by any means, electronic or mechanical, including photocopying, recording, or by any information storage and retrieval system, without permission in writing from the copyright owner.

This is a work of fiction. Names, characters, places and incidents either are the product of the author's imagination or are used fictitiously, and any resemblance to any actual persons, living or dead, events, or locales is entirely coincidental.

Any people depicted in stock imagery provided by Thinkstock are models, and such images are being used for illustrative purposes only. Certain stock imagery © Thinkstock.

Print information available on the last page.

Rev. date: 08/27/2015

To order additional copies of this book, contact:
Xlibris
1-888-795-4274
www.Xlibris.com
Orders@Xlibris.com
701482

ACKNOWLEDGMENT

Special thanks to the wonderful work of Michelle Kaup for the book cover and also to Lindsey Frye and Pam Riggs for their diligent editing.

"With strength and greatness often comes folly.
Let the United States of America never forget the
strength of this nation's ability to compromise."

The author

CHAPTER ONE

The small dank windowless room was stuffy. No pictures on the wall; three hard, uncomfortable chairs; and two small tables with oil lamps sparsely lit the room. Two men, both in their late twenties and dressed in expensive dark suits, took their jackets off revealing fancy vests and pistols in their waistbands. Another man, also in his late twenties, sat in a chair staring at the opposite wall. The man, exhausted, his sides pained from hunger, gently rubbed the stubble on his face. He hadn't said much, frustrating his captors. Sitting on the chairs backward leaning forward, the two men, agents in the Federal Secret Service, were about to try questioning him again, but their prisoner would give them nothing.

The night before, hell had broken loose near the President's House, later named the White House. President and Mrs. Lincoln were entertaining members of his cabinet and their wives after the news of the day and had no idea what was occurring outside. The war was over. General Robert E. Lee's line was broken at Petersburg, and there was further word that Confederate President Jefferson Davis and his cabinet had fled the capital in Richmond, Virginia. The important news was the fact that Lee surrendered to General Grant the day before prompting Lincoln to call for his cabinet to meet. The war council that afternoon had been in a heated discussion about how the nation's mending would begin immediately, much to the displeasure of Secretary of War Stanton. President Lincoln was adamant that there would be a peaceful transition to bring the South back into the Union, and he wanted to quietly celebrate their success with a dinner. The large second-floor dining room was brightly lit that evening; the moonlight breaking through after a rainy day created a clear path to the white building.

Agent Oscar Geiger curled his brown handlebar mustache and squinted his beady eyes. His wide forehead made him look like a newspaper cartoon drawing, and his squeaky voice made him even more comical. He leaned back holding the chair's back rest, stretching his neck. Looking at his partner, Agent Bill Morse, Geiger shook his head and let out a sigh and smiled. They will break their prisoner, no matter how long it takes. Both agents hated Rebels and considered them traitors, and this one was as despicable as they come. They both got up and left the room to discuss their next tactic—beat what he knew out of him.

Agent Bill Morse was a lanky fellow who walked with a distinct limp. A veteran of the first two years of battles as a Union infantry captain, Morse suffered his left leg wound at Antietam from a Rebel bayonet. He was appointed to a post in the Secret Service, first analyzing spy movements and then on Allan Pinkerton's staff. His long face and round chin were accented by his thick light brown sideburns. He didn't want to beat their prisoner, but he was also an impatient man and knew Pinkerton was just as impatient.

Geiger took out his corncob pipe and packed tobacco in it to enjoy a smoke. The agents stood in a small office outside of the interrogation room and discussed the situation, knowing well that Pinkerton would be down shortly to end the questioning and get a military order to hang the spy after a brief trial. Geiger wanted to do the roughing up before Pinkerton got there and, though Morse was against it, agreed to a beating. The men went back in the room staring down their prisoner.

Morse brought a pair of hand shackles with him, and as he approached, their captive jumped out of his chair in a defensive stance. Geiger took his revolver out of his waistband and pointed it. The man reluctantly sat back down. Morse slowly put the shackles down, but Geiger slammed the revolver against the prisoner's head sending him reeling to the floor. Morse, annoyed at his partner, got up to assist the man; but in a rage, the man jumped up and punched Morse and grabbed at Geiger, knocking the pistol from his hand. Just then, a soldier appeared at the doorway and pointed a breach-loading rifle at him. The man stopped and put his hands up. The soldier, a husky square-jawed sergeant, motioned with the rifle for the prisoner to move and sit down. The soldier stepped aside, and in walked a well-dressed bearded derby-wearing man with a half-smoked cigar clutched in his fingers. Geiger and Morse both straightened to attention as their boss stood eyeing the room and shaking his head, disappointed at the situation. Morse rubbed the side of his face where he had taken the blow, and Geiger felt embarrassed about the whole thing. The soldier saluted and left. The boss told his two agents to leave, much to their protests. The prisoner kept his eyes on their bearded boss as the agents left, the agents only moving to the office next door to listen.

Ten Union cavalrymen rode up in front of the President's House and waited as a carriage sauntered leisurely to the entrance. Two elderly Negro servants waited to escort Vice President Andrew Johnson to the coach. The vice president thanked the servants and got settled before instructing the coachman to drive off. A minute later, five more cavalrymen rode up, followed by a carriage. This continued until two more detachments arrived to pick up Secretary of the Treasury Hugh McCulloch, and Secretary of War Edwin Stanton. Apparently, Lincoln called another meeting early in the evening to further discuss the peaceful transition to unite the country again, only this was followed by a dinner with their wives. Lincoln also summoned General Grant to the President's House for the meeting, but the general missed it, much to their disappointment, running late because of his own officers' meetings.

Secretary Stanton, always the one to know what was going on everywhere, especially at the President's House, noticed some of the commotion as he was leaving. He inquired about it and was told that Allan Pinkerton just returned from Chicago and was in the basement on an urgent matter. Stanton asked to be kept informed, with details, and scribbled a note asking a courier to deliver it to a telegraph office to be sent—but specifically not to use the War Department's telegraph room. The secretary of war seemed edgy over the past few days, and this didn't make him feel any more at ease. The lights in the rooms at the President's House were snuffed out one by one as Stanton's carriage rode away.

The basement room of the President's House was tense. There was a prisoner being held, and he wasn't talking or cooperating. The man with the derby hat and stogie took off his jacket and smiled. "You know who I am?" he asked. The prisoner nodded. "Well then, you'll know that there's no bollocks here," he said, trying to ease the situation. The prisoner noticed a slight Scottish burr in the voice as he listened and began to relax. "I know my boys got a little rough, and they shouldn't have. How 'bout a smoke?" he asked, offering a cigar. The prisoner shook his head, refusing, remaining quiet.

There was a knock at the door and a slight scuffle outside the room. The man went over and opened the door to see three agents pushing a young army officer back, attempting to keep him from going into the room.

"I have a message for you, Major Pinkerton, from Baltimore," he said nervously.

The major nodded, read the message, mumbled a cuss word, and crumpled the paper, tossing it in the corner of the room. He then shut the door. "When was the last time you ate? Probably yesterday, right? I'll have a tray sent in with some coffee. I could use some coffee myself." The prisoner just nodded. The major got up and asked that food and a pot of strong coffee be brought down. They both sat and waited for the food.

"You know, there's a very good possibility you're gonna hang, don't you?"

The prisoner finally spoke. "Hang? Maybe so. Why don't you hang me now?" he asked.

Allan Pinkerton, the chief of the newly formed Secret Service, finally got a response and had to keep the dialogue going. As he was about to answer, Agent Geiger entered the room after knocking, bringing a tray of food. He stood staring at the prisoner, and Pinkerton, annoyed, quickly dismissed him. Pinkerton poured two cups of the steaming coffee. "The president's cook is on call twenty-four hours a day. She's pretty good too," he said, taking a bite of boiled and buttered potatoes. He slowly chewed, sipped at the hot coffee, and placed the fork down. He wasn't hungry but thought that attempting to eat might cut tension. The prisoner held the porcelain cup and breathed in the aroma and then sipped.

Pinkerton smiled. "You know, things are hard. The war is hard. Hell, most of the time, it's hard to know who's on which side. It'll be for your benefit if we can talk." The prisoner looked at the tray. "Go ahead. It's good Yankee food, right from Abe's kitchen," Pinkerton said jovially.

Taking a piece of meat on a fork, the prisoner slowly placed it in his mouth and chewed just as slow. The major looked at the prisoner up and down: mussed up long hair, stubble beard, dirty disheveled clothes. The cut from Geiger's pistol had caked blood on the right side of his forehead. The rugged, narrow face and mustache couldn't hide the fact that this man was a soldier. Pinkerton knew this man was valuable.

"Why don't you tell me everything? I mean, about yourself. Where you from? Family, you know, your history."

The prisoner sipped his coffee, looked down, and then rubbed his face. "Does that matter, Major?" he answered.

"Yes, it does. To me it does," Pinkerton said.

The prisoner let out a sigh. "Where do I start?"

Pinkerton sat back and responded, "How about your name?"

CHAPTER TWO

Norris James Greycourt III rode in the carriage south from Richmond to his family's plantation near the town of Atkinson. He had business there, and he thought it would be a quick meeting, but the after-meeting discussion took a shape of its own. He was looking forward to enjoying his home and visits from his eldest son and new grandson. But the long meeting was disturbing and might change many things, not only in the Greycourt house but also for the entire country. With the last few puffs of his ivory pipe, he gazed skyward and thought about his family. They had an old, strong, and respectable family, mostly because of his stature as a former county judge as people addressed him as "Judge." His wife, the former Eugenia Colton, was a gracious hostess, and the soirees at the Greycourt plantation were usually the events of the seasons.

Both youthful-looking, Norris and Eugenia were strict about appearance, promptness, and protocol and instilled those attributes on their three children. Norris was always well dressed, neatly groomed, with sandy blond hair with a bit of gray at the temples, clean shaven, and narrow cleft chin, and he could be intimidating when he entered a room. Over six feet in height with broad shoulders, he filled the room whenever he entered. He had to use spectacles which hurt his vanity somewhat.

Eugenia, slim with dark hair and sharp features, would make one think that she was from Spain. She was also impeccably dressed— usually in the latest fashion; she made frequent trips to New York for private showings. Even when the couple went riding, they looked as if they were going to a church social. To her, appearance was everything, having come from a large Episcopal family on one the biggest plantations in Virginia. She was always the first to greet the Judge whenever he returned, and they made sure to always spend time alone together. The carriage was now entering the long tree-lined road as it passed the entrance gate; the plantation called Greycourt Manor was aptly named by Norris James Greycourt, a veteran of the American Revolution and Norris the Third's grandfather.

Three house servants waited on the steps of the very expansive house, the white-painted porch encompassing it entirely. As each one assisted the master entering the house, Eugenia waited at the door; with her were their two Irish wolfhounds. As he approached, he didn't understand the troubled look on her face.

Eugenia hugged her husband and, without saying anything, led him to the large living room off to the left of the sprawling staircase that led to the second floor and, much to his surprise, saw someone standing there. Colton James Greycourt or Colt, as he was called, twenty-three years old and the second of their three children, leaned on the fireplace watching his parents slowly enter and close the door. Eugenia poured her husband a whiskey and sat down on the bright red and gold couch. Norris looked at his son. He sipped the drink and stayed standing. Colt faced his father and put out his hand to greet him. Norris took the hand reluctantly, slowly and without enthusiasm, and stepped back. The young man knew what he was in for. He knew his father well; if he wasn't glad to see someone, it showed, and he'd get either the cold shoulder or a lecture. Colt was about to get the latter.

Norris looked around the room gazing at the ceiling and then at the walls, trying to gather his thoughts. He was about to begin his tirade when Eugenia brought up the exciting festivities about to occur in the next few weeks. She went over to her husband's ornate cherry wood desk and reached for one of the four fancy pipes in a tray and packed it. She then handed it to Norris to be lit. Not paying attention to the mention of parties and guests, Colt's father puffed and leveled a steely look at his son.

★★★

Little Eugenia or Genie, as she was known by in the Greycourt house, sat slowly, swinging on the back porch swing looking out waiting for her beau, Jonathan Miles Hale. He visited Genie every afternoon for their usual refreshment, lemonade, and activity, hand holding under the watchful eye of Tessa, the house slave and manager of the Greycourt household. The tall, slim black woman, about sixty years old, had been with the family since her birth; her mother and grandmother were also slaves in the service of the Greycourt family. Tessa sat in a rocker and appeared to doze off occasionally, but she had the unique sense to feel if the young couple sat too close or Jonathan attempted to sneak a smooch on the girl's cheek.

Genie's beau rode up on his brown thoroughbred as Tessa watched Genie jump up at his approach and greet him with a hug. It was just two weeks earlier that young Hale, from a plantation-owning family a few miles east of Greycourt Manor, asked the Judge for Genie's hand, which he gladly consented to. The wedding was to occur two months before Hale was to begin law school at the University of Virginia. Hale was excited this day as he and his family were to be guests that evening at the Greycourts' with another family to discuss their nuptials, but most of all, he had an announcement to make.

Colt, out riding around the grounds most of the day, saw Hale, so he galloped his mare through the pastures and meadows over two rail fences to the white back porch. Tessa smiled at Colt's approach as she always secretly endeared him as her favorite of the three children. Colt dismounted and hopped the white porch fence as Hale got up to shake his hand.

Genie looked at Colt with concern. "How are you today?" she asked.

Colt smiled. "I'm well. I guess you didn't hear much about yesterday."

Hale was curious. "Aren't you graduating next week?"

Colt, in a rather good mood, only acknowledged the question and didn't answer. He turned to his sister. "I listened some, but I said my piece. I spoke to Commandant Reynolds when I made my decision, and he understood. I told the Judge that, and he didn't. No matter what I do, things are never right."

Colt never had a problem discussing things with his sister. Although she was three years younger, she was always wiser in thoughts and actions. He liked young Hale also. He knew that her choices could always be trusted to be sound and right. He wasn't like the rest of his family who usually boasted about their cotton crop and the amount of slaves they owned. Jonathan was quiet at times and just about the kindest gentleman that you'll ever find.

Genie never talked back to the Judge whenever there was a problem with her out-of-the-ordinary ideas or her decision to go to school in Boston where the women of the family always went to The Quaker Finishing School in Philadelphia. She gave in to Philadelphia without a protest; but always admired Colt's penchant to stand up for himself with their father. Colt was one of the very few who did not fear the Judge. Genie knew the wrath Colt could receive by being home and not graduating from the West Point Military Academy.

"What will you do now?" she asked.

Colt smiled, felt his sister's genuine concern. "I know what I want to do or, better, what I have to do. It won't be back to law school or to New York to learn banking. The Judge has lost all hope for me to be the things he wants me to be," he answered, looking at Tessa, noting her wink in approval as she poured a glass of lemonade for him. Colt sipped the drink and then hopped the fence and rode away.

The wide dining room, with the long table and chairs imported from France, was lively with conversations of weddings and the warm spring weather. Norris and Eugenia sat at opposite ends of the table and kept the talk alive with their sixteen guests, Colt, and Genie. Colt sat at his mother's right side at one end and Genie at the Judge's right at his end, with Jonathan sitting across from her. The Lelands and the Greycourts are friends going back three generations and often spent holidays and special occasions together.

They had a friendly competition for many years, usually over horses, but it was billiards that was the real rivalry. Norris prided himself on his prowess at billiards, and Ulric Remsen Leland was the same age as the Judge. Both graduated from Virginia Law and set up their own firms in Richmond with the Judge's firm flourishing while Leland's struggled. Their billiard matches were very popular events among the local inhabitants, but their private matches were more intense with high stakes. Both families enjoyed each other, so this evening was another "small" Greycourt event.

After dinner, the men retreated to the Judge's den for brandy, cigars, and pipes and the ladies to the small parlor across the large bright foyer in front of the grand staircase. The lively talk in the ladies' parlor paled in comparison to the talk in the Judge's den. The Judge dominated the conversation about secession and the violence to come as the others listened intently. Colt stayed quiet, paying attention to every word spoken, as Leland remarked about how the North's failure to compromise was setting the stage for a fight, and the lines were drawn years ago, not just with the election of the new Republican president.

The Judge agreed as he smoked his ivory pipe and then walked over to the wall with the large map of the states and territories. He explained his fears of an embargo as he outlined the East Coast with the end of the pipe and spoke of the possibility that the president might prevent a war by letting the states leave the Union. The lecture caused a stir in the room, and Colt carefully watched each man's reaction to the spoken words. Paul, a distinguished-looking tall elderly half-white, half-black house slave, gently knocked on the door to let the Judge know that dessert was being served in the rear parlor. The men placed their brandy glasses down and joined the ladies.

Jonathan walked into the room with a big grin and put his arm around Genie. The men went to their wives; their children stood together waiting for parents to be seated. Colt looked across the room, eyeing a tall statuesque girl about his age, her long blond hair combed down. There was something about her narrow face and hazel eyes that jogged Colt's memory. He went over to stand next to her, and she smiled at him as he approached.

The protocol was the Judge would begin the room's conversation, but Jonathan spoke first, surprising everyone and, most of all, annoying the Judge. With great joy and pride, he began to speak as Tessa and Paul went around the room with small trays of petite chocolate cakes, honey pudding, and coffee. The room fell silent, and everyone was astonished as they listened to Jonathan's proud announcement.

Colt, unfazed at the sudden turmoil in the room, quietly slipped out unnoticed to the garden at the east end of the house, which hooked around to the rear and sprawled out into three paths. The clear April moonlit sky cast a pleasant light as he walked. He missed the house of his birth and found that hardly anything had changed in his four years away. As he casually walked, he was startled by someone following close by. He turned and saw her.

Colt had been eyeing Victoria Leland all evening, sometimes straining to get a look at her at the other end of the dinner table. She noticed his glances and even winked at him once. She smiled and apologized for surprising him. He bowed slightly and smiled back. They walked and talked and reminisced about their childhoods, recalling how they played together in the fields with their siblings. They even recalled an incident where she fell and skinned her knee, and only Colt and little Genie comforted her, with Colt pressing his blouse against her wound to stop the bleeding. A house servant came out to tell the two that their presence was requested back in the house but not before they agreed to go riding together in the morning.

Jonathan surely knocked the Greycourts and guests back with his announcement. The Judge was annoyed and a bit insulted that he wasn't consulted first by his young son-in-law-to-be. The remainder of the evening was quiet, and the guests left earlier than usual.

★★★

Colt liked to ride early each morning, a habit he had as a young boy and continued as a cadet. He was taught how to ride by Paul, Tessa's husband. Although the Judge bragged that Colt was his pupil, it was Paul who taught Colt the skills of a seasoned horseman. That tutorship got Colt high marks at West Point and the reputation of being one of the finest cavaliers the academy had ever seen. Commandant Reynolds even rode with him one morning. This morning he was excited to ride with Victoria.

Victoria Gail Leland was twenty-three and already a worldly woman. Schooled up North in Boston, she studied the cello in New York City. Vee, as she was called by family and intimate friends, had just completed a successful audition for the New York Philharmonic, which was about to tour in late May. She was a very good horsewoman whom Colt admired. He met her about a mile north of the Leland plantation, and they casually trotted their mounts about the countryside in the clear April morning. Colt, wearing his cadet trousers, black riding boots, a wide-brimmed black hat, and gloves, rode close to Vee, catching the scent of a perfume of wild flowers. The statuesque girl was in tan riding pants, brown boots, brown jacket, tan hat, her long blond hair combed to a bun in the back of her head. Colt couldn't stop staring at her long face and hazel eyes.

"I'm glad you asked me to ride this morning. I wanted to spend some time with you," she said, smiling. Colt smiled back. She continued, "What did you think of last night?"

Colt responded, "I guess I wasn't very surprised. Mostly everyone's going to volunteer sooner or later, Jonathan's no different."

Vee raised her eyebrows. "But with the South Carolinians? I would've thought he'd wait until Virginia left the Union."

Colt was impressed with her knowledge as they slowed their cantering to a halt to rest by a clump of shade trees. "Southern states are leaving almost daily. I would guess that Virginia will go too. What is odd though—why is it taking so long for Virginia to decide? When South Carolina fired on Fort Sumter, it was the signal for the other states to follow. Virginia has to decide," he said.

He was about to continue when he heard a shout in the distance from a rider galloping toward them. It was Scipio, Tessa and Paul's son whose duties consisted of tending to the Greycourt horses and stables. Two years younger than Colt, he was an expert horseman, and his diminutive stature made him a perfect jockey for the Judge's forays into horse racing. With his dark eyes and pointy-shaped face, Scipio was fast to smile and always eager to lend a helping hand. He was thrilled that he was recently granted permission by the Judge to wed, and the nuptials were to be held within the next two weeks. He had an important message for Colt.

"Massa Norris wants you home right away. He say you goin' to Richmond with him." Colt nodded and told Scipio to ride back and tell the Judge he'd be there shortly. The young slave smiled and swiftly rode off.

Vee looked at Colt oddly. "It sounded urgent. Let's ride back now," she said.

Colt paid no mind to her suggestion. "It makes sense for Virginia to secede, even though we don't stand a chance in any long fight. We have to make concessions—both sides do."

Vee hung on his every word and again suggested they ride back. It was obvious to her that the Judge's orders meant little to him. Colt smiled. "I've had the pleasure of riding with you and hope that we can go riding again when I get back," he said very dashingly and took her left hand and kissed it.

She lowered her bright eyes and smiled. "Yes, yes. I accept." They rode back together at a leisurely trot.

They were about five miles away from Richmond when the carriage slowed to a stop. Colt had ridden most of the way on his horse, and the Judge rode alone in the fancy coach driven by Paul. The Judge insisted that Colt ride the rest of the way into the city with him in the lush carriage; although Colt agreed he made a point of showing his displeasure with his father. The Judge read the newspaper, the Richmond Examiner, the rest of the way without speaking. Colt was somewhat puzzled why his father wanted him there. He felt that he was more of a soldier, not a statesman. His brother, a lawyer in Richmond, was better versed in the politics of the times.

Dressed in his best navy blue suit and red tie, Colt struck an imposing figure as he got out of the carriage in front of the upscale Jefferson Hotel on Franklin Street. Paul got the suitcases and waited to follow the two men in. The front desk clerk knew the Judge and had his favorite room, a corner room on the third floor, ready and also informed him dinner was to be served within the hour.

Paul placed money on the desk for the clerk and brought the bags up to the room while the Judge stopped to speak to some acquaintances. Colt surveyed the surroundings and was bored right away. Paul came down and, with a short nod, indicated that their clothes were put out—meaning, he would then retire to the slaves' quarters provided in the back of the hotel. There, the slaves ate better and were allowed to socialize as they were all body servants to their masters and considered the higher echelon of the slave order. Paul was always up as late as the Judge needed him and would arise every morning at six to have coffee and the newspaper ready and, of course, clothes set out. Many times Paul would be a sounding board for the Judge's ideas and also the brunt of his raging vents, usually about politics. The tall, lean, silver-haired slave just nodded and never spoke in these instances.

After washing and changing, the Judge and Colt had dinner in the elegant dining room. The Judge did all the talking about states' rights, while Colt wolfed down his meal of smoked venison, rice, and steamed celery. He didn't pay much attention to the conversation. Only when a heavyset man came over to their table to greet them and whispered something to the Judge that made Colt's ears perk up.

CHAPTER THREE

Pinkerton loosened his tie and unbuttoned his plaid vest or waistcoat, as it was called. He had a pistol in the waistband of his trousers and tapped the metal coffee pot to see if it was still warm. It wasn't, so he got up to order someone outside the room to get a fresh hot pot for them. His prisoner, Colton James Greycourt, was in need of a basin to wash and a razor for a shave. It didn't matter where he was or what the situation was; Greycourt made sure he washed and shaved. He kept his mustache and sideburns neatly trimmed and didn't like beards. Pinkerton stood up and placed his foot on the chair and leaned toward him. The chief of the president's Secret Service knew the man he was questioning was a tough, battle-hardened soldier, and his approach to get information from him had to be calm and, most of all, cautious. If he lost Greycourt's confidence, he'd lose a chance to acquire vital information on the Confederacy's clandestine operations.

Greycourt rubbed his face, gently scratched his stubble, and tilted his head slightly to the right looking at Pinkerton. He was exhausted but would never show it. He took a breath and sat up in the chair. Pinkerton went over to get the door as the coffee and washbasin were brought in by one of the waiting detectives. Two cups were poured. Greycourt got up to wash his face; the cool water felt good on his neck and brow. He asked permission to shave, and the detective nodded, keeping an eye on the straight razor. Pinkerton calmly placed his right hand on the pistol in his waistband. Before shaving, Greycourt gently placed the towel on the side of his head where the agent's blow struck him. The small cut had dried, but it still stung. The prisoner would remember that cheap shot.

Pinkerton watched Greycourt closely. He noticed the careful precision of each stroke of the razor. He recalled that men in the field would shave as quickly as they could, often leaving stubble. Greycourt meticulously guided each move and made sure he didn't miss a hair. Maybe it was the fact that there was no hurry to shave like being in camp, but there was something about the simple task of shaving that held Pinkerton's attention. Greycourt carefully trimmed around his dark mustache and then washed the remaining soap away and toweled off. The detective, being very cordial and patient, placed his foot on the chair and leaned forward as Greycourt sat down with the coffee. Pinkerton again probed.

★★★

The Judge sat in the hotel room, smoking his pipe and staring at the ceiling. He should have felt humiliated from the day's events but knew that his colleagues and neighbors recognized his strength to let some things go. The session of senators and congressmen, with the addition of some men of status in the legislature hall, was as raucous as ever. Several times a call to order was shouted out, and the threat of the sergeant at arms physically tossing members out finally got the charged room to be civil. Motions were voted on regarding Virginia's secession and its articles, and after nearly three hours of debate, it was decided that the entire voting population would decide the fate whether to secede or remain with Lincoln and the Union. Then it got intense.

Congressman Sanford Zollicoffer, a very opinionated wealthy planter, held the floor discussing Jefferson Davis's ascension to the presidency of the Confederate states. He felt Davis was weak and suggested that he was better suited to lead the new government. The Judge, taking offense to this monologue, stood up to be recognized.

"Sir, Honorable Congressman Zollicoffer, I appreciate your zest for leadership, but I must ask what real qualifications you have. From what I hear, you've only attended a handful of sessions here and abstained in a majority of the voting. You've spouted about leadership and all, but I feel it's more about power and not Virginia or the future. You never once brought up the mere fact that we might be engaged in a real fight—a war. What is your plan to lead that? You have no military experience. The Honorable Jeff Davis is a West Point man, veteran soldier, and former secretary of war. I stand by those qualifications."

The room, hanging on each word, waited as light clapping was heard in favor of the Judge's brief speech. Zollicoffer's face tensed in anger.

"Sir, Most Honorable Judge Greycourt, I have to ask you, if there is to be a fight, whose side would you favor? It's well known of your past association with Mr. Lincoln. Whose side would you favor, sir?"

The charged room was aghast at the accusation of the Judge opposing Virginia and the South, calling him a traitor. Most members present knew of the Judge and Lincoln working side by side in Congress on various tariff issues. Colt, sitting next to his father, was about to leap up and challenge Zollicoffer when the Judge placed his right hand hard on his arm, keeping him seated.

The Judge wryly smiled and shook his head. "Sir, right now, my allegiance is to the United States of America. As everyone in this room knows, if Virginia secedes, I will go with her." Zollicoffer, waiting for the challenge, slowly sat down. Colt, staring at the congressman, clenched his fists, hoping to make eye contact to no avail.

The Judge sat and smoked, and Paul entered the room to remind him that dinner was to be served in half an hour and he should change. There was a knock at the door, and Colt entered. He stood in front of the fireplace.

"I'm leaving in the morning," he announced. "I find this whole thing useless and a waste of time." The Judge was annoyed. As it seemed, everything Colt did annoyed him. The Judge puffed and stared at his son. Colt continued, "Virginia will secede, it's well known, yet we have to have this nonsensical protocol. What's the debate tomorrow? What will our battle flag be? What color uniforms will be worn?"

The Judge didn't like such talk. "You are ignorant to government and its workings. Gentlemen discuss and debate issues, not draw conclusions and make decisions on whims. You have a lot to learn. That's why I brought you here."

It was Colt who was now annoyed. "Learn? Certainly, an insult is to be addressed, yet it wasn't."

The Judge took his pipe away from his mouth and looked at the intricate paintings on the wall of swans and doves. "Is that what this is all about? A challenge? Do you realize why I stopped you and didn't allow myself to get drawn into a duel? A challenge would have been the talk and focus of the session, not Virginia. Besides, dueling is outlawed in this state, and any combatants would be arrested unless, of course, the duel is done in secret. This would have been no secret. You are ignorant to these things."

The Judge then got a bit louder. "You know nothing! You couldn't even graduate West Point! The governor is already appointing officers, anticipating war. Make no mistake. The fight will start here in Virginia."

Colt shrugged. "A fight? Up North there's talk of settlement. Lincoln wouldn't want a fight. He'll negotiate a settlement."

The Judge pursed his lips. "Lincoln? Settlement? His election is the cause of war. There will be no one for him to negotiate with." Colt was puzzled. He thought his father, a sensible sage, would lead the charge to make peace to avoid war and bring reason to both sides.

The Judge got up to change his clothes. "I want you there tomorrow to meet the governor. By the eternal, if you couldn't graduate West Point, then at least you'll get in front of the governor, and he'll see you're officer worthy. That's what I want." Colt looked at his father with disdain like never before.

The next day Paul put out the Judge's clothes as he usually did and made sure breakfast was served promptly. On instinct, Paul went to the next room to look in on Colt and wasn't surprised to see the boy dressed with his bag packed. Paul leaned down to pick up the grip and stopped. "You'd like me to tell the Judge you're gone?"

Colt turned to him before opening the door. "No. I was just going to leave and say nothing."

The distinguished-looking slave smiled. "Before you leave, you got to know you'd be disappointing him. He wants success for you. Someday, and that may be soon, I'll tell you a few things about the Judge." Colt turned from the door, took his jacket off, and sat on an easy chair to wait for his father.

Just days before this decisive meeting of the Virginia gentry, shots were fired on Fort Sumter, South Carolina, sending Southern states in a frenzied firestorm of war. Level heads tried to prevail as the Judge eloquently spoke during a cold February morning of the hardship of war and, most of all, the fact that they were all Americans and should reason with one another. His words were convincing enough that it resulted in a vote not to secede when they reconvened in early April. But this April morning was different.

Colt came to realize what Congressman Zollicoffer's challenge was all about. The Judge's speech not to secede weeks ago made him out to be a Northern sympathizer and disloyal to Virginia. After all, he himself was a planter, and siding with the North was treasonous. The chamber buzzed with talk: young boys ran in and out of the room with newspapers and dispatches for the delegates; pipe and cigar smoke filled the air as animated talk dominated. It got loud, louder until the chamber sergeant at arms slammed his thick hand on the high front bench calling for order. As he got their attention, John Letcher, governor of Virginia, slowly walked into the robust chamber, nodding to many of the attendees. Honest John, as he was known for his modest way of living void of extravagance, was bald and spectacled with a long face and thin lips. He stood in agreement with Judge Greycourt on his points not to secede and even at one time supported a measure to end slavery in Virginia, which he later repudiated. Now this was his meeting.

As the room finally came to order, Governor Letcher stood at the high wooden court bench, firmly grasped his jacket lapels, and, with his head held high, began, "Friends, fellow Virginians, as you all know, Abe Lincoln has called for seventy-five thousand volunteers. It's obvious that these people will invade our lands. I ask you, where do we stand now?"

The chamber erupted with shouts of 'SECESSION! SECESSION!' and delegates began standing, shaking their fists, cursing Lincoln.

Governor Letcher glanced over at the Judge who was sitting, smoking his pipe. He glanced back at Letcher and nodded.

★★★

Colt couldn't get back to Greycourt Manor fast enough. The delegation voted to put secession out to a vote for the Virginia-voting populace, and he knew the sham vote would be for secession. Before he bolted out of the chamber, he was approached by Governor Letcher's aide and told him that Colonel Robert E. Lee accepted an offer to command all Virginia's troops. The governor, knowing Colt's West Point training, was about to appoint him captain and wanted him to meet Colonel Lee, who was in attendance in the chamber. Colt agreed, and there was an exchange of introductions and brief talk of the place that was so dear to both men.

Swiftly riding back, he never stopped to hear his father's elated approval. Determined, he would quickly outfit himself at the ready and wait for orders. After over an hour of riding, Colt stopped at an inn to get refreshed and rest his horse. He slowly walked in and was greeted by a short portly man with a bald head and thick brown mustache. "Welcome, sir. Take any table. We'll help you presently," he said, smiling.

Colt removed his hat, bowed, and took a table in the far corner. There were six tables and a bar in the dark establishment, with four men standing at the bar drinking and two tables occupied, three men at each one. The patrons all watched Colt as he sat at a table and stretched. A young man came over for his order and told him that they were serving lamb stew today and he'd bring over a tankard of their homemade applejack. Colt declined the stew and asked for a loaf of bread and butter and the applejack.

As he sat and rubbed the back of his neck, two men walked in, eyeing the place up and down, and one loudly asked, "Who's got that red roan outside?"

Colt sat up and lifted his head. "That's mine. He all right?"

The man, thin with a shadowy growth above his face and a dark brown hat pulled down, covering his eyes, smiled. "He's fine. I wanna buy 'im."

Colt shook his head. "Sorry, friend, he's not for sale."

The man made a sour face and looked at his companion. "I didn't ask if he was for sale. I said I wanna buy," he said, looking away from Colt.

The two men, smiling, approached Colt's table, and he noticed a revolver in the man's waistband. The young server came over and placed a plate of fresh bread and butter and a jug of the homemade beverage on the table. The two men looked at the server with disdain; they felt disrespected by him walking in front of them to serve him. Colt said nothing as he began to butter the bread.

"Well, well, we got a real dandy jay sitting here," the man said, commenting on Colt's attire. "I'll give ya $5 for 'im. Real cash, Yankee money," he said, smiling.

Colt had no patience for this. "Sorry, not for sale. Buy another horse," he answered and started eating. The entire room was now fixed on the confrontation, and the owner and the young server slowly walked over.

"I gotta try 'im, see how he's broke."

As the server got closer, he was grabbed by the man's companion. Colt jumped up, grabbing the revolver out of the man's waistband and hurling him against the wall behind him, pressing his hand against the man's throat. "I said not for sale, friend," Colt exclaimed, gritting his teeth. Looking at the server now, Colt noticed a pistol against the youngster's head held tightly by the other man, the owner pleading not to harm him. Colt placed the revolver against the man's head hard. "I'll blow your brains out, friend. Tell your friend to let the boy go. Tell him. I said tell him!" he said, staring directly into the eyes of his captive.

The man shook his head. "He ain't lyin', Noah, let the boy go," he demanded. The young man pulled away and stood next to the owner.

Colt then dragged the man across the room, out the door, and threw him on the ground. Noah, the companion, stood behind, not raising a hand as the owner now had a shotgun aimed at him.

"Git, both ya. Git," Colt said sternly as the men mounted their horses and slowly rode off. He placed the revolver in his waistband and walked back to the inn.

★★★

The Judge got back to Greycourt Manor late in the evening and, before he could take his shawl off, barked out a demand to see Colt right away in his study. Mrs. Greycourt ran to the front door and said she didn't know where their son was but would fetch him. Tessa nodded and said she knew where he was. She had seen Colt and Scipio walk out to the barn to look at the new foal that had recently arrived. As Tessa ran out to the barn, to her surprise, the Judge was close behind her.

Colt and Scipio were checking on one of the horse's hoofs when the young slave saw the Judge enter. He took his cap off, bowed slightly, and quickly left the barn. Colt stood up, faced his father, and before he could say anything, the Judge, with the back of his right hand, slapped him across the right side of his face. Colt, stunned, clenched his fists to retaliate but held back. The Judge squared himself. "I know you'd like to but won't," he said, knowing that his son wanted to physically strike back. Colt relaxed and didn't answer. The Judge then looked at his right hand, almost sorry, and then looked at Colt. "Why? Why is it that in all my attempts to make you successful and obtain prestige and position, you withdraw and seem to work against it? What are you afraid of? I ask you, what in all damnation are you scared of?"

The young man let out a short sigh and pursed his lips. "I don't know what I want. I do know I don't want you making me successful or prestigious or anything else. I have to do it. Me. I have to do it for myself."

The Judge shook his head. "You can't. Everything you've ever done is wrong."

Colt wasn't shocked at this. He knew, since he was very young, that his father didn't think much of him. He always criticized. The slightest, most minute activity or idea would be met with ridicule. His time at West Point was more than a learning experience—it was time away from the Judge.

The horse nearby fidgeted and jostled in his stall and Colt turned to go. The Judge got annoyed. "That's what I mean, no attention to what I'm saying. You see, I wanted you to personally meet the governor, shake his hand, and present yourself as a good Virginian. He would have appointed you a major, for sure, not captain. I wanted him to meet you. But no, you had to rush out!"

Not about to let the Judge get the last word this time, Colt lashed out. "Meet me? Major? Just like that, a major? If I'm earning anything, it'll be because of me, not you, Judge, because of *my* efforts. I should be a private. Hell, a major? No, sir, no. Whatever I do from now on is on my own. And get this: that will be the last time you put your hand on me, ever. I swear it."

Outraged at his son's insolence, the Judge clenched his fist and was about to lash out again when Colt bowed and left the barn. Standing alone, the Judge slowly shook his head in disbelief.

★★★

Activity at the Jefferson Hotel was teeming with servants scurrying about with fresh linens and pillows, readying the rooms for the rush of guests about to converge to vote on secession. Only men were allowed to vote, and the hotel's wealthy guests came from around the state to get their vote counted faster than casting in their local county office. Slave quarters were on the rear grounds, and the number of slaves in the city of Richmond swelled to nearly three slaves to every one freeman. The hotel guests, mostly planters, took over the dining room, the gardens, and the parlor rooms, all discussing the upcoming monumental decision. The wait for breakfast in the dining room was over half an hour. Local residents came to the hotel to mingle and maybe get inside information about cotton prices. But the talk was all about secession.

Colt Greycourt toweled off his face and bare chest and looked out of his hotel room window watching fancy carriages and high-stepping thoroughbreds saunter on the street below. He shook his head and mumbled something.

Victoria came into the room from the bedroom, still wearing a silver-and-blue robe and stood next to Colt. "You said something?" she asked with a smile.

Colt looked at her and gently kissed her forehead. "Oh, not really," he answered as he felt her place her left arm around his waist and tug him close. "These fools. They're so cocksure of themselves that Lincoln will just let them leave. They just don't know," he said.

Victoria's eyes widened. "Know what? Shouldn't they want Virginia to follow the other states?"

He looked at her and sighed. "This whole thing is about the territories. Lincoln doesn't want slavery expanded to the territories. He knows slavery will eventually go away, not right away, but eventually. Besides, why would you need slaves on the frontier? You can't grow cotton there. I know. I spent one summer patrolling Western Missouri. This is wrong. It'll be a real shootin' war."

Victoria got a sudden chill. "Shooting war? You mean fighting, battles?" she asked timidly.

Colt nodded. "I'm glad you're leaving to tour with the symphony, hopefully out of the country," he added.

Victoria coyly smiled. "I have to leave for Philadelphia right after breakfast. We have to get ready now."

After saying good-bye to Victoria and paying his room bill, Colt headed to the northern part of the city to visit his brother. He enjoyed his night with Victoria. After running into her in the hotel lobby and learning that she had no room reserved, he offered to let her stay in his room, which she gladly accepted. Their friendship became intimate. A groom held his horse outside, and without acknowledging the courtesy, Colt rode off through the throngs of people.

Reginald James Greycourt was somewhat successful. He was the youngest partner in the firm of Simmons, Manfry, and Reed, a prestigious Richmond litigation business. Colt's elder brother was not as athletic or physically built as Colt. His niche was books and studies. He married right after graduating University of Virginia Law School and started a family, which included three daughters, all a year apart in age. His wife, Sandra, was from a wealthy planter family in Northern Virginia, and they made a home in the finest part of Richmond. Reginald, clean shaven to his father's liking, was of slim build with light brown hair and hazel eyes. Always well dressed, he greeted his brother who had been waiting for him on the rear porch overlooking a healthy garden with newly planted bushes and flowers.

As the brothers shook hands, a house slave brought out a tray with two glasses and a whiskey bottle. The slave placed the tray down, poured two glasses, and left. Reginald downed the whiskey in one gulp as Colt looked on. Pushing his glass toward his brother, Reginald obliged and downed that one also. Reginald smiled. "Great to see you, fella," he said, wiping his mouth with a cloth napkin.

Colt nodded. "You're doing well, eh? Business agrees with you. How long has it been? Two, three years?" he asked, noticing a bit of arrogance in his brother's attitude.

"Yes, too long, brother."

Reginald poured himself another drink. "How did playing soldier treat you?" he asked. Colt took that question as a usual put down. "You know the Judge was counting on you to graduate. I guess you did it again," he casually added. Colt, not expecting anything different from his pompous brother, didn't want to be there any longer but wanted some answers. He watched his father's actions and reactions while in the chamber meetings and had the sense that there might be something else going on.

Reginald sipped the whiskey as the house servant came over to announce dinner in one hour; Colt tried to explain he wouldn't be staying, but his brother wouldn't hear of it. Just then, the three little girls ran out to greet their uncle. Sandra was right behind them and, smiling, welcomed her brother-in-law. She asked about his plans and was very pleased to have him for dinner. Colt enjoyed the girls climbing onto his lap. Dinner was served.

Fancy dinnerware and European crystal adorned the table as they ate roasted lamb with jellied yams and a pickled corn mix that

Colt had never eaten before, liking it very much. Reginald did all the talking about his work, and Sandra hung on his every word, frequently asking questions. Colt was bored and would occasionally nod and wink at his nieces, causing them to giggle. Dessert was to be served in the large family room right after dinner. Sandra obediently brought her husband a fancy goblet and decanter of brandy and placed a thin cigar on an end table covered with an intricate doily. She also offered a goblet to Colt, and he politely declined.

As the children left to get ready for bedtime, Colt stood up and leaned on the fireplace. He looked around the elegant room and wondered how long this would last when war broke out.

Reginald watched his brother's movements. "Well, tell me, boy, what are your plans?" he asked with a smile.

Colt turned and cleared his throat. "Cavalry. I've been appointed captain."

His brother nodded. "I see. Too bad, if you had some real education, you could've been with me in the War Department as an advisor to Jeff Davis. The Judge got me the job."

Colt shook his head. "War Department? What do you know about the military? This isn't a Virginia Reel. It's gonna be tough. You'll have to know battle tactics and leadership. Where do you come in?"

Reginald got annoyed and stood up. "I know. I didn't go around playing soldier for the last few years like you, but it won't be about that—"

"About what then?" Colt interrupted. "You keep saying I was playing soldier. Well, I'll tell you, War Department man, while you were having tea every afternoon and discussing nonsense, I was spending summers fighting off malaria, mosquitoes, and the Seminoles all the while patrolling Northern Florida. Hell, I even spent one summer in Missouri trying to keep the peace on the border. Playing soldier? You might think twice about that job in the War Department. There'll be many a man playing soldier soon, very soon."

Colt squared himself, facing his brother. "Sure the Judge got you a cushy job. What's he gonna do?"

Reginald got angry. "You don't know much. The Judge knows how to play it. He'll be in the Office of Diplomatic Affairs. He'll be lining up countries abroad to invest in our government."

Colt shook his head. "Well, well, I should have known. Anything to escape the bullets. Where is he gonna live, London?"

Reginald smiled. "Now you're catching on. And Richmond, of course."

Colt had enough and was about to say good-bye when his nieces ran in to say good night, and he lovingly hugged and kissed them. Sandra offered him one of the guest rooms, but he declined, saying he had to get back to Greycourt Manor, even at this time of the evening.

As he walked out waiting for the groom to fetch his horse, Reginald put his hand on his younger brother's arm. "You know, when you get some wartime in, come see me. I'll get you a post with me. Maybe by that time, the war will be over."

Colt shook his head and said, "There'll be many dead men that played soldier before all this ends."

Reginald looked away and then at Colt. "When this ends, we'll be rich. You come along with us and you'll be rich too," he said.

Colt's eyes narrowed. "Rich? What do you mean by that? How?"

Reginald didn't answer as he turned and walked away.

CHAPTER FOUR

Secretary of War Edwin Stanton sat in his rocking chair in his upstairs bedroom. His servant just placed a glass of warmed milk on the small table next to the chair. He took a sip and then dismissed the elderly servant before mentioning to him that he'd most likely be needed in a short while.

Stanton, still in his suit coat, sat and slowly rocked. He was disturbed at not knowing what was going on in the basement of the President's House. His note went unanswered. The evening had been cordial—the president gathering his cabinet and their wives to celebrate the eminent end of the war. He was at odds with Lincoln over the entire plan of reconstruction—Lincoln wanting a smooth welcoming back of the Confederate states "without malice"; Stanton wanted to punish the traitors, as he called them.

He got up, unwrapped the shawl his servant had placed around him, and went to the desk in the corner of the room to write two notes. He scribbled one note, looked it over, scribbled another, and tugged the pull cord for his servant. He looked toward the door and, being an impatient man, became irate waiting for his servant. Two knocks at the door, and Stanton answered to enter. Getting up, he instructed the servant to personally bring one note to the War Department's telegraph office, the one Lincoln and Cabinet members use, and the other note to the basement of the President's House and to wait for a reply. The elderly man, a faithful servant to Stanton for many years, nodded and left the room.

Lincoln's secretary of war let out a sigh and checked his watch again. It was almost midnight.

★★★

As Colt walked alone through the magnificent gardens of his host, Miles Washington Hale, he couldn't help but notice the sweetness of the air and the vibrant colors along the winding paths of flowers and hedges. The gardens rivaled his mother's meticulous work as a gardener and felt the hosts tried extra hard to show off their grounds. The wedding ceremony had ended about thirty minutes earlier, and Colt didn't feel like gathering with the men for brandy and talk, while the ladies and children were getting together to discuss fashion and the new bride's gown.

A well-dressed house slave approached Colt to offer a cordial drink, and he declined. Continuing walking and admiring topiary of deer and rabbits, he caught the scent of perfume. He turned and saw Victoria standing behind him. She smiled, reached out, and firmly took his right arm. Colt smiled back, glad to see her, and gently hugged her. Victoria looked around and dabbed at her forehead with a lace handkerchief as he took her arm to continue walking and admiring the grounds.

"I didn't think you'd be here. I'm glad you showed," he said.

She smiled. "It's really hot for late June. I might be overdressed," she said, tapping her fingers on her long-sleeved dress.

Colt looked at her up and down. "You look exquisite."

The aroma of barbeque wafted in the early summer air. Colt and Victoria walked back toward the mansion when they noticed about twenty slaves led by an elder, all dressed in their "Sunday" clothes, march toward the large circle at the rear of the house and form a semicircle with the elder standing in the middle facing them. Mr. and Mrs. Hale came out on the second-floor balcony and waited.

The elder began conducting the serenading slaves as the guests came out on the large back porch to enjoy the singing. House slaves served drinks and provided cool cloths to wipe guest's foreheads. The songs were gentle hymns, a gift to the new bride and groom who then came out and stood with the Hales.

When they were finished, they all bowed; and the elder, a man of about seventy, turned from the singers and smiled a wide smile and bowed as well. He then motioned for two children, a boy and girl about ten years old, to come forward and recite a short poem about this joyous wedding day. The elder got a bit annoyed when they both stumbled trying to pronounce the word *matrimony*. The entire crowd applauded. They all bowed, excited as they were promised earlier that they would have no work the rest of the day and could celebrate in their slave quarters. As they turned to march away, Colt looked up to see his father standing next to Reginald, both looking at him trying to get his attention. Colt made out as if he didn't see them. Victoria waved to some people she knew and took Colt's arm and walked toward them to visit.

The bride and groom went around thanking each guest at the conclusion of the barbeque and retreated to change clothes for dancing at the evening ball. A fifteen-piece orchestra was set up on a specially built bandstand in the ballroom on the third floor. The elegant room, taking up the entire floor, was surrounded by a balcony so guests can walk out for air or to chat. House slaves set up tables around the room for the guests, and bartenders were placed in the corners of the room.

Colt was to give a toast to the bride and groom and was a bit nervous about doing it. He had a short prepared speech, which he was to give after the first dance. His speech went over very well offering luck and a long fruitful life together sparking delightful applause. After a waltz with Victoria, she asked that they go out on the balcony to talk. To his surprise, she asked questions about his first days in camp with the First Virginia Cavalry, particularly the size of the camp and amount of men there. At first, Colt wondered why there was so much interest; but after talking, he came away impressed that she would care so much about him.

★★★

The cavalry camp, set up a few miles west of Richmond, was lively and unusual. So unusual that Colt couldn't walk about the camp without hearing the rousing tunes of banjo players and fiddlers and glancing at an occasional reel by a group of soldiers. Music and frolicking were encouraged by the senior officers, especially the one in command, James Ewell Brown Stuart, the dashing devil-may-care Virginia cavalier.

Colt was given a very modest send-off in late May. His mother prepared a trunk filled with socks, two coats, undergarments, two pairs of thigh high boots, and a dozen of blouses. She had a gray tunic made with yellow captain's stripes and a long dark gray coat. His sister gave him two pairs of dark gray gauntlets and a black felt hat. The Judge gave him two Navy Colt .44 revolvers with a case of ammunition. His saber and scabbard were West Point issued.

The Judge toasted the cause and a quick resolution to the conflict, and hoped all returned home safely, and all present, little Genie, Mrs. Greycourt, and a few close friends, agreed.

Colt didn't say much as the Judge held the floor most of the evening discussing the new "country" and how prosperous it would be. The more the talk went on, the more Colt got agitated.

Before the guests arrived, he and the Judge got into a difference of opinion about the entire subject of secession and imminent war. He felt his father was very casual about it and that men fighting and dying was some kind of glamorous fairy tale. Colt told him about serving three tours with the cavalry, one in Missouri where he did little as an orderly but two tours in the Northern Florida swamp fighting Seminoles and seeing men maimed and killed. Although he saw limited action, he was in one engagement and felt lucky he wasn't killed himself.

Spending time up north, Colt got a good sense of the way of life there, especially his trips to New York City and Boston. He hoped the Judge would reason with the others and negotiate for peace before fighting. The Judge dismissed the thought and said a good fight once in a while was good for the country. Colt vehemently disagreed.

As the guests were leaving and offering Colt luck and safe keeping, he couldn't help but feel slighted once again. The Judge never toasted his own son.

★★★

Hordes of men, young and old, from all over the South, came to Stuart's camp to join up with him. The sprawling acres with its pitched tents, campfires, long stockade, and miles of wagons filled with food stuffs like flour, coffee, corn meal, and smoked meats easily accommodated the multitude of cavalrymen. Banjo music was heard throughout the camp, and the levity was addictive. Would-be cavaliers passed through the entrance, but some were stopped by the brawny sentinel standing on a huge boulder watching all that came. Thick armed, barrel-chested Barnard Ward stood tall, all six feet six inches of him. With his huge arms folded on his massive chest, Ward, wearing a red shirt with the sleeves folded, dark blue trousers with suspenders, and knee-high boots, had his slick black hair parted down the middle.

A blacksmith for the Baltimore Fire Department, he was also a champion bare-knuckle boxer, winning all thirty-one of his fights by knockout. A Virginian by birth, his family moved to Maryland when he was an infant but declared his allegiance to his birth state. Leaving a wife and nine children behind, he put some money aside to take care of them while he was gone. He planned on being away for six months, the amount of time he figured the war would last.

He looked up and down everybody that passed through. One middle-aged man riding a Morgan mare, finely dressed in a light gray tunic and gold braids up and down the sleeves, short-cropped blond beard and mustache, stopped to speak to Ward. Leading a group of thirty mounted men and boys, he dismounted and approached the huge sergeant major.

"My good man, I demand to see the commander," he barked.

Ward looked down from the rock and stared at the brazen peacock. "Keep movin'," he barked back.

"My good man, I am Major Emory David Dawes of the Eastern Kentucky Riding Rifles, appointed by the governor himself," he boasted.

The sergeant looked straight ahead. "I don't care if you were appointed by King Solomon himself. Keep movin'," he barked again. The dandy major huffed, turned to his men, and slowly rode through.

A thin man wearing a worn straw hat and riding a gray thoroughbred slowly approached Ward, and the sergeant stopped him. "Where you think you going, rube?" he bellowed.

The man smiled, showing few teeth. "Gonna ride with Jeb Stuart," he proudly answered with his head held high.

Ward smiled back and said, "Well, you're about the ugliest-lookin' sorry ass I ever did see."

The man smiled a wide smile and took off his hat. "Well, I guess I'll be scarin' them Yanks to death, I guess."

Ward reared his large head back and let out a guffaw some said was heard all the way back to Richmond. "Get movin', rube, you're in," he said and motioned the man through.

Sergeant Ward then squinted a bit and looked at the next new volunteer. This one had his boy with him.

Colt got within a few feet of Ward, stopped, dismounted, and approached the sergeant. "Captain Colton James Greycourt reporting for duty, sergeant," he said and saluted. Ward, impressed with the courtesy and professional presence of the young man, saluted back. "Sir, captain's quarters on the right on officer's row. Colonel Stuart's tent in the middle, sir," he answered and eyed the young slave with Colt.

Colt saluted back and motioned for Scipio to follow with their two horses plus one pack horse with Colt's belongings. His heartbeat rose as he continued through and saw the excitement of horses being led by wranglers around the camp—wagons unloaded; teamsters driving wagons to all corners; scores of men, young and old, forming up to look regimental in case the colonel walked around; banjo music was heard within the hustle of activity.

Colt's adrenaline heated his insides at all the sights and sounds. *If there was ever going to be a fight, this cavalry command would be victorious,* he thought.

CHAPTER FIVE

Pinkerton listened intently as his prisoner told of his first experience in the camp of the First Virginia Cavalry. The detective, an astute judge of character with a keen eye to one's body language, watched Greycourt with a keen intensity. He had gotten the wrong information at the start of the war many times, sometimes hindering or derailing a campaign. He was ashamed of his intelligence-gathering skills when he had given General George McClelland the incorrect troop strength and movements of Confederate forces during his Peninsula Campaign. It wasn't the only time he had reported incorrect information early in the war.

As the war went on, he became much more careful in detail and the reliability of his staff. He checked and confirmed all reports. Now, with this prisoner in front of him, he took no chances. By finding out the background and history of this man, Greycourt, he might uncover much more than just the goings-on of the recent activities around the President's House.

Pinkerton checked his pocket watch and eyed the time—one thirty in the morning. This man had his ear, and the detective wanted more. A knock at the door interrupted them, and Pinkerton gave a call to enter. Morse and Geiger both entered, and Morse handed him a note. Pinkerton read it, shook his head, and crumpled it. The two men asked if they could stay and were obliged. Greycourt looked at Geiger and Morse with scorn and thought he'd make a point of busting them both in the face if he ever got out of this mess.

★★★

Captain Greycourt slowly rode through the sprawling camp and was greeted by a young orderly leading him to his officer's tent. Scipio was to arrange his bunk and gear while he paid a call to Colonel Stuart and properly introduced himself.

In front of a very large tent sat two officers at a table under an awning, looking at a roster filled with names and ranks. Greycourt stood at attention, waiting to salute. Once acknowledged, he was led in to meet the commanding officer. Jeb Stuart was looking over a list and making marks next to lines when he glanced up at the young captain and smiled. He stood up and put his hand out to shake, but Greycourt stood at attention to salute. Stuart smiled, winked, and saluted back. He again put his right hand out to shake, but the captain was waiting for the command to be "at rest." Stuart, impressed with this man's protocol, gave the command and then put his hand out again to shake. Greycourt gladly shook hands, and Stuart laughed out loud.

"Captian Colton James Greycourt, Virginian by birth. Welcome. I'm a Virginian too, as you know," he said proudly.

Colt nodded. "It was your father that wrote the letters of recommendation for my entry to West Point. I am grateful."

Stuart smiled. "I know your family, good people, your folks, and mine fought the British, fought them twice. And we won both times," he said, laughing.

Colt looked at the imposing figure in front of him—about six feet two inches in height, thick head of russet hair with an equally thick russet beard, clean-pressed cotton blouse with gold cuff links and a simple plain gold wedding band on his finger. His blue eyes lit his face as he spoke. It was easy to see this man had that unique aura about him that people just gravitated toward. He exuded confidence, optimism, and positive attitude rarely seen. People liked being around him.

"I'll be relying on you, Captain, to get some things in order. I like your cut, and as a West Point man, well, you have the leadership most here lack. I'm glad you're here," he said with a slight drawl and placed his hand on Colt's shoulder.

The captain nodded. "Sir, I'm honored to be under your command and will do everything in my being to make this cavalry successful, sir."

Stuart looked at him. "I believe you will, Captain. I really do."

Colt's quarters were three tents down from Stuart's. There were three cots and four chairs with one fold-down desk. Scipio made Colt's bunk and set his trunk at the foot of the cot, took care of the horses, and then set himself up in the slave quarters at the very rear of the camp. There were about sixty slaves, both men and women, put up in tents. They were to do the cooking, attend to the grounds, and most of the men were to be teamsters for the wagons. Some wealthy officers, like Colt, brought their own slaves to attend to their needs. The women were there as laundresses. Strict orders were given by Stuart that no soldier was to enter the slave quarters for any reason.

On his cot waiting for him was a duty roster written out by Stuart himself. A tall, lean man with a large carpetbag came into the tent and looked around as Colt eyed the paper and then looked up. The man nodded as he placed the bag down, and Colt got up. "Captain Colton James Greycourt," he said, smiling and putting out his hand.

The man, about the same height as Colt, smiled back and removed his hat., "Captain Dion Ettienne du Seine," he said, shaking hands. Du Seine, long-faced with an olive complexion and long straight very black hair, was sharply dressed over a wiry strong body. He chose his cot and began to set up his space. The first item he removed was a picture that he placed on top of the desk.

Colt looked at it. "Your family?" he asked.

Du Seine turned and smiled. "Yes, my wife and son," he answered proudly.

Colt took the picture and examined the photo of du Seine sitting with his son on his lap and his wife standing next to him with her hand on his shoulder. "That's a very pretty photo, beautiful family. Why would you leave them to come here?" he curiously asked.

Du Seine, not offended at the question, smiled. "I have to be here. That's all I have to say to that." Colt took the hint that it was not to be discussed. "I'm from New Orleans," he continued as he unpacked.

"I'm a Virginian," Colt answered.

Du Seine nodded. It was obvious that du Seine was an easygoing person, and it was going to be good to share the tent with him. They talked about the camp and the unusual happenings with its excitement and energy as they organized their places.

After a few minutes, another tall, lean man entered the tent. "Captain's quarters?" the young man asked as he came in. Colt and du Seine both stood, facing the newcomer. They introduced themselves, and the new man proudly took his hat off and slightly bowed. "I am Captain Enrique Innocencio Gonzalez Gonzalez Hegan Ortega," he said with a wide grin.

Colt and du Seine looked at each other.

"Say that again, Captain," Colt asked, and the tall Mexican recited it again, adding that his father is Mexican and his mother is Irish. "We'll just call you Ortega, all right with you?" he asked, and they all laughed.

The three captains, all the same age and very similar in physical makeup, got along well. They had their assignments and took them very seriously. Colt drilled his men three times each day in attack formations, close-order fighting, and most of all, discipline.

Recognizing bugle calls, his men were not going to be dismounting and fighting; they were going to attack and fight on horseback. Stuart's cavalry would not use muskets or rifles but were to be mounted fighters with swords and pistols.

Du Seine and Ortega learned cavalry tactics from Colt and followed his every move. Colt even fenced with both to hone their skills. They were excellent horsemen, but mounted fighting was more than galloping and charging. After three weeks, the three captains had the finest, sharpest cavalry brigade in the entire First Virginia Cavalry. Stuart was more than pleased with his young captains.

Two nights each week, the entire camp had a big soiree. Wagons of citizens, mostly women, came and joined in the music, dancing, and jovial atmosphere. Food and drink, not alcohol, flowed abundantly as the men danced and sang. Stuart always sat in a large chair at the center of everything.

Some nights, Ortega's two younger brothers, who were privates, played the flutes and guitars along with six other men from Ortega's county in Texas. They played traditional Mexican songs and dances, enlightening the crowd. Ortega, always charming, led the dancing usually with the prettiest young lady. Colt seldom attended these activities as he was more concerned with studying and letter writing.

Colt, du Seine, and Ortega became close friends and confidants. Du Seine was the eldest of nine children and made sure he wrote to each of them. He wrote to his wife every week. His father, Marcel Jean-Paul du Seine, was born in France and came to America as an infant. His grandfather bought the land on which the vineyard and estate stood. Their main crop was rice. The plantation was north of New Orleans, but the family lived in a spacious townhouse in the city.

The community, old French families that came to the colonies to start new lives and seek opportunities, prospered in the rich soil and climate. Du Seine proudly and frequently spoke about his family. Colt noticed that he didn't speak much about his father though.

Ortega was an exceptional horseman and was very tough with his younger brothers regarding their riding skills, and Colt got a kick out of watching him reprimand them. In Spanish, of course. Ortega, the son of a proud Mexican family that fought for the independence of Texas, carried his darkly handsome good looks from both his father and Scotch-Irish mother. The Ortegas were highly respected by their neighbors and friends and often looked to for counsel in matters of water rights and cattle. The Ortegas had a huge spread running as many as five thousand head of cattle at times. Señor Victor Ortega, a very serious man, ran it with an iron fist. His ranch hands were disciplined wranglers, and he brought up his six sons the same way. Enrique, the eldest, was taught every part of the cattle business as he was to be the next in line to run it. Enrique's grandfather, Don Miguel Ortega, at seventy-three years old, still rode but was retired from the family business.

Their spread, twenty-five miles north of San Antonio, was considered the jewel of the territory. They frequently had big gatherings, especially when the neighbors paid their respects to Don Miguel or when word got around that the Ortegas helped a family in need. Their generosity was well known for miles around. Señor Victor, like his father, taught charity, which was expected of the entire family. Colt saw that in his young Texas friend in that, he was always assisting others, whether they were officers or privates. He was very moved by that.

Ortega also proudly spoke of his family and beautiful fiancé who he hoped to marry when he returned to Texas. Colt felt fortunate to have such fine and upstanding friends. He didn't speak much about his own family.

All their hard training and discipline was about to be put to the test. Colt had received a letter from Victoria telling him that she was staying in Baltimore for a few days before she left with the Philharmonic. Excited, Colt was granted three days leave.

Being careful as he traveled by railroad, Colt knew that Baltimore was under Union control as the result of the riot of April 19 when the Massachusetts militia marched through the streets getting pelted with rocks and debris and firing on the mob killing twelve civilians.

He made his way to the Camden Hotel, just a few blocks from Camden Station. There he met Victoria in the hotel dining room where they had supper and talked. He was overjoyed to see her, and they talked of good times and especially her travels with the Philharmonic. They talked, and all the while, Colt noticed a well-dressed young man sitting at the table to their left staring at them constantly. Colt casually asked if she knew him, and she responded she didn't, asking if he was the one being stared at. Colt thought he might have been found out to be a Confederate officer.

He noticed the man lighting a cigar, then placing money on the table, and then getting up. He walked to their table. "Pardon my interruption, but I can't help to notice that perhaps we've met?" he asked, looking at both smiling.

Colt looked up and politely responded that they were never acquainted and continued eating.

The man then introduced himself. "I'm Clive G. Dalrymple." He smiled. "The 'G' is for Gregory, but I never use it."

Colt looked up and noticed the impeccably dressed man might be an actor or something like that. The tall, lean man, about thirty years old, had a thin black mustache and deep-set dark eyes. The man stood there waiting for an invitation to sit, but Colt wasn't offering. "I didn't get your name, sir?" he asked.

Just then, Victoria interrupted, "We're just passing through this fine city, Mr. . . . Mr. . . . what was it, Dalrim . . . ?" She was not able to pronounce his last name.

"That's Dal-rim-pal. I know. Everyone has trouble with it," he said with a chuckle.

Colt thought this man to be a silly oaf.

Victoria smiled. "My friend is here on business and quite frankly . . ."

Colt stood up. "My name is Greycourt. Thank you, sir," he said. Dalrymple took the hint and graciously bowed and walked away.

Colt was concerned. "What do you think of that?" he asked her.

Victoria shrugged. "I don't know. He didn't look like a soldier. Maybe a politician or actor or something like that," she answered.

Colt nodded. "I guess so," he said as he saw Dalrymple walk over to the cigar stand and buy cigars. Dalrymple glanced over at them again and smiled, tipping his walking stick slightly forward toward them and left the lobby.

After dinner, they went up to her room, but she did not let him in. She kissed him good night and wished him well and hoped to see him again soon, maybe in New York or Philadelphia. He thought what she said was odd and was disappointed.

As he sat waiting for the train to depart from Baltimore early the next morning, he kept thinking about the tavern he had visited the day before. Earlier than expected to meet Victoria, he stopped at the tavern a block away from the hotel for a cold ale. He stood next to a counter that had some hard cheese, salty meats, and soda crackers left from the free lunch hour they provided each afternoon. He checked his watch and sipped the ale.

Two Union officers walked in and got their steins of beer and picked a few of the items on the counter. Without paying attention to Colt, they freely discussed some things that caught his attention. Being within close earshot of their conversation, he heard very clearly.

He had *The Baltimore Sun* newspaper on his lap glancing at the articles. As the conductor yelled out for all to board, a woman walked into his car. Seeing the seat next to him was empty, she asked if the seat was free. He got up and slightly bowed and nodded. She sat, stared straight ahead, and unbuttoned the top button of her fancy black dress. Colt asked if she preferred the window, and she declined. She commented on his chivalry, and she remarked he must be from the South. Colt smiled, didn't answer, and the conversation went to cotton and horses and whether he was married with children. He said he was not, and she commented that she had just lost a daughter but had two other daughters to care for. He conveyed his condolences, and she was taken by his sensitivity.

Colt proved to be a very comfortable traveling companion on the trip south. As the train pulled into Richmond Station, he assisted her and asked if he may help with her luggage; she declined but told him her name was Rose as she left the car. He watched her walk along the platform and go directly to a waiting carriage without so much as a travel bag. That seemed odd.

As he left the train, he walked out through the depot and spotted Scipio waiting with his horse; and without saying anything, they swiftly galloped to the camp. Without stopping, Colt rode right up to Stuart's tent and requested permission to see the commanding officer. His request was granted. Stuart exchanged pleasantries, but Colt was anxious to tell him what he had learned. Showing him the newspaper articles from *The Baltimore Sun*, Stuart's eyes widened. Grabbing Colt's arm, he called for his horse as they rode a few miles north to General P. G. T. Beauregard's headquarters.

Colt, Stuart, and three of Stuart's aides entered the camp after the picket's escort and found the general in his tent having tea with a visitor. Beauregard got up and greeted Stuart and was introduced to Colt. Colt noticed the visitor, a lady, sitting with her back to them, not turning around. Stuart, the ever gracious and chivalrous cavalier, turned to the lady and introduced himself before the general could speak up. She turned to Colt and smiled.

"This is Mrs. Rose O'Neal Greenhow," Beauregard said with a smile. "She comes here as a friend to our cause and has some vital information."

Colt recognized her as the lady he sat next to on the train.

Stuart smiled. "That's why we are here, sir."

Beauregard tilted his head toward Colt and listened as he described the conversation he had overheard of heavy troop masses in Washington and an imminent invasion of Virginia. Beauregard, in an attempt to test the validity of the information, asked when and where it would take place.

Stuart let Colt speak. "Sir, General McDowell plans to invade across the Potomac from Washington with about sixty-five thousand troops toward a railroad line. I think it's called Manassas Junction. They will be invading around July 20 or 21. They plan to take the railroad line and then march south to Richmond."

General Beauregard smiled and looked at Mrs. Greenhow. "That's exactly what Mrs. Greenhow conveyed, only she did not know troop strength, and she was close to the date. Captain Greycourt, you've provided us with vital information. I am extremely grateful," he said.

Stuart was overcome with pride that one of his men had procured such information and impressed his superior officer. Beauregard called an emergency meeting in Richmond with President Jefferson Davis and General Joseph E. Johnston, encamped in the Shenandoah Valley. Stuart was ordered to stand by and be ready to move out at a moment's notice.

Colt had just finished his dinner meal in the officer's tent with Dion and Ortega when they were summoned to Stuart's tent, along with other officers, and told to form their brigades and wait for instructions to move out. Excited, the three captains hurried back to their tent as bugles sounded for recall, and all twelve hundred cavalrymen sprawled out in rank and file watching Stuart, accompanied by Sergeant Major Ward, walk among the troops shaking hands and exchanging pleasantries with most of the men, many he didn't know. Colt, astride his charger, stared straight ahead next to his direct, Major Lengen, waiting for Stuart to walk past. As he passed, the commander of this powerful cavalry looked at Colt and tipped his hat, and Colt acknowledged with a slight nod. The troops were given orders to move out at dawn.

★★★

The three captains sat on their cots and were quiet. Scipio came in and asked if he could fetch something for the men, and they declined. Du Seine and Ortega were uncomfortable with Colt's slave and always politely declined his services. Ortega was worried about his brothers and went out to find them.

Du Seine wrote a short note and placed it in an envelope with his chain and religious medal and handed it to Colt. He asked Colt to make sure his wife got the envelope if something should happen to him. With the utmost assurance, Colt told him he'd deliver it to her himself in that event.

Ortega walked in with his two brothers, asking to have them present in the tent; Colt and du Seine quickly agreed. They spoke little, anticipating what was forthcoming.

CHAPTER SIX

The two Secret Service agents stood against the wall as Colt Greycourt described his early days in the cavalry camp. Geiger and Morse hung on to every word, their interest growing as he continued.

Pinkerton now felt he had his prisoner close to where he wanted him. Still in his hand, he unfolded the crumpled note and reread it. He let out a short sigh and looked at Colt. "Ever been to New York?" he asked.

Colt looked at the two men against the wall and then at Pinkerton and didn't answer.

"New York?" he asked again.

Colt shook his head. "Why do you ask me about New York?"

Pinkerton looked at Geiger and Morse and then back at Colt. "Nothing really. I just thought I'd ask," he answered. He then got up and poured another cup of coffee for Colt.

"You were a West Point guy before you turned traitor, weren't you?" Geiger asked.

Colt clenched his fists and didn't answer.

"Didn't you ever go down to New York City while at the academy?"

Colt looked at the agent and then at Pinkerton. "I've been to a lot of places," he casually said as he sipped the brew.

Morse then leaned forward. "Yeah, but did you—"

"All right, maybe we'll get to that later," Pinkerton interrupted. "How did you get to Washington? I mean with all the roads and bridges picketed, it would be almost impossible for a Reb to get by."

Colt smiled a half smile and looked down. "How would you know? Can you spot a Reb? There might be hundreds of Rebs here, now, right now."

The three men stepped toward Colt and, at once, all jabbered, "Where? Who are they? Where are they? What are they going to do?"

Colt put his hand up. "I said might be. Might be. Are you fellas that bad at your jobs?"

Morse got angry and attempted to grab Colt, but the prisoner stood up and managed to catch the agent's chin with his palm, shoving him back. Pinkerton got between the men and settled things down.

Calmly, Colt sat back down, smiled at the men, and asked for a fresh pot of hot coffee.

★★★

The July heat wasn't as bothersome as the flies that seemed to mingle at the tent opening. General Jackson sat, hatless and sipping on lemonade, his favorite drink, while listening intently to the talk of the other officers' light and jovial banter of the day's fight. Jeb Stuart's tent, always the most spacious and never void of comfort, was the spot chosen to discuss what had just occurred. Generals Beauregard, Johnston, Lee, Longstreet, Early, and Jackson stretched their weary legs; while Stuart, the able and sure-minded commander, happily poured drinks and refills as he described his cavalry's success in assisting in turning the tide of the first battle against the invaders.

That morning, July 21, started rather smoothly as the Confederate cavalry took their position five miles south of the Bull Run River after setting up camp the day before. Stuart, instructed to standby with his nine hundred mounted fighters, was ready to support the infantry.

As the fight began at five thirty in the morning, cannon fire filled the air as troops on both sides scrambled to get into position south of the town of Centreville. Confederate officers sensed that there was confusion on the Union side as troops scurried in opposite directions and artillery posts set up very late, seeming to be out of position. Confederate infantry moved swiftly but buckled under fire as federal riflemen dug in and formed a skirmish line, forcing the gray men back, as if retreating. General Jackson stood alone, urging the men to stand fast and then ordered them to charge the lines and batteries. Union troops, surprised at the rally, fled, leaving rifles, ammunition and abandoning cannons.

In a flanking maneuver, Union troops moved to hit the Confederate's rear but were attacked by the troops under the command of General Joe Johnston, which raced into action by rail. Stuart's cavalry charged into action as Union artillery, occupying Henry Hill, saw Jackson's men attempt to take the high ground.

Greycourt, leading his one hundred troopers away from the fray, rode in sight of a line of Zouaves, a regiment in the dress of French infantry with bright red trousers, red-and-blue-colored fez hats, and short blue-and-red jackets.

Greycourt, squinting to see exactly what was about fifty yards in front of him, took off his hat and waved, yelling, "Hey, boys, there's our own Loo-siana Tiger Zouaves! Let's cheer 'em on!"

Just then, a volley of rifle fire whizzed over their heads as the line in front of them was actually the Eleventh New York Fire Zouaves. Greycourt, eyes widened, yelled out to retreat and regroup; in their haste, they ran head long into a horde of Union troopers fleeing in chaos.

Stuart then appeared with three hundred riders hacking away, seeking out the New York Zouaves with Greycourt, Ortega, and du Seine next to him. Charging relentlessly into their enemy lines, slashing with sabers and with pistols drawn, firing, and killing many of the fancy dressed infantry. Stuart, seeing Hampton's Legion led by Confederate commander Wade Hampton, crested a hill on the northeast securing their advance. The orders then were to chase the blue army all the way back to Washington. But what stood out most, especially to General Jackson, was Captain Greycourt's charge into a Union battery that was preparing to fire on his advancing infantry.

Greycourt, before running into the New York Zouaves, ordered his cavalry to charge the cannons, bearing down on Jackson's men. The swift riders not only overran the Union artillery, but it also enabled Jackson's men to take the cannons and the high ground.

Stuart, proudly retelling these exploits and even chuckling a bit at the Zouave incident, was going to call for his three captains and personally congratulate them. Jackson didn't see any humor to the mistake, but the look on his face told everyone in the tent something different.

Dion du Seine sat at the small desk in the tent writing a letter to his wife about the morning's action. He wasn't describing the fight but more that he was safe and unharmed, not even a scratch. Ortega was on the edge of his cot listening with amusement as his two younger brothers sat on the floor boasting about their actions and exploits. Captain Colt Greycourt sat on the edge of his cot holding his black hat, poking a finger through the hole at the top. He thought about his mortality—the fact that he was a good half inch from getting his skull blown through. Even more, he felt a sense of invincibility in that he escaped getting killed in such a furious fight.

His thoughts grew heavier as he was aware that his blunder on the field would get a serious reprimand and maybe even a bust down to lieutenant after his report is submitted and read.

Scipio then came in and offered the men plates of smoked ham and fresh fruit taken from the fleeing Washington civilians who were watching the battle as if it were a stage play. Picnic baskets filled with breads and meats, and even bottles of sarsaparilla, a peppery-flavored soda pop, were gladly scooped up by the pursuing gray riders. Greycourt declined; du Seine and Ortega never looked up to respond.

Scipio noticed a small wound on the right side of Greycourt's forehead. As he attempted to treat it, the captain put his hand up, moving him away. He hoped that the visible wound could ease the reprimand. He then stood up, excused himself, and left; the others smiled and nodded. One of Stuart's staff, a major, appeared and ordered the captains to report to Stuart's tent at once and then inquired about Captain Greycourt. The major was told he had just left and went off to find him.

It was night as Jeb Stuart sat behind his desk in his tent glancing down at the three notes in front of him. Du Seine and Ortega stood nervously at attention for a minute, waiting for Stuart to address them. He was concerned that Greycourt was not present, and after asking the men about their families and how they are faring as a stall, the major appeared with the captain. He stood next to Ortega at attention, not apologizing for his lateness.

Stuart gave the order to be "at rest" and proceeded, "Captains, you've performed in an extraordinary way. I must say I am very pleased." The three captains stood, staring at Stuart as he continued. "Captain Greycourt, why were you not available when the major came to fetch you?"

Greycourt looked at the commander. "Sir, I was at the hospital tents looking in on some of my wounded men. There were only a few, thank heaven," he answered.

Stuart nodded. He was pleased at the action of a true officer. Stuart glanced down at the notes and looked up. "Captain Greycourt, your error on the field has caused a great concern for our generals." *Here it comes*, he thought. "Captain, what occurred out there?" he asked.

Greycourt tensed. "Sir, I approached a detachment of what I thought was our own Loo-siana Tiger Zouaves. To my utter surprise, they were New York Fire Zouaves. Luckily, we suffered no casualties."

Stuart chuckled slightly. "Captain Greycourt, your blunder on the field has caused great concern with our generals. They're upset that this occurred. General Jackson, General Longstreet, and General Lee himself have briefly studied the situation and concluded that the Confederate Army must adopt its own colors and battle dress. They've petitioned President Davis to adopt gray as our color and a design of our own battle flags as well as our new nation's flag."

Stuart smiled at the young men and looked at Greycourt. "Captain Greycourt, sir, you've performed admirably, and General Jackson has commended you for your gallant charge at the Yankee battery saving lives of many men. Your charge enabled the general to take a vital position routing the enemy. Your action is worthy of the West Point training I know you've received. Gentlemen, I am pleased, very pleased with your valor and actions. I am grateful and proud to have you men in my command." The commander then stood up and shook each of their hands and dismissed them.

Newspapermen from Richmond and Baltimore swarmed all over the camp. Stuart was more than happy to accommodate any reporter eager for an exclusive interview, and two photographers roamed the grounds setting up their bulky and odd-looking boxes on legs, taking photos of men on horseback, groups of cavalrymen posing, and even cooks and orderlies. The camp was as jovial as it's ever been. For Captains Greycourt, Ortega, and du Seine, it was work.

Reports were due that day, and the captains, always the obedient servants of duty, didn't want to be tardy in their work. Ortega and du Seine followed Greycourt's lead all the time in his actions, manners, and conduct. The three men bonded as brothers in a short time. From different places and upbringing, they shared a unique brotherhood that was noticed all over the camp and added to the overall free-spirited atmosphere on the grounds. They were always available to help out, whether it was riding instructions or the art of swordsmanship, and Colt was always there to write letters for the boys that couldn't read or write. Their reports were reviewed and ready as they were summoned to Stuart's tent.

As they were led in by one of the commander's staff, the three captains saw Major Dawes standing in front of Stuart's desk complaining about his treatment at Manassas. Complaining about not getting orders to attack and join the fray, Dawes sternly lectured the commander of his appointment from the governor of Kentucky; not being engaged in the fight was an insult. Stuart listened and almost broke out laughing at the ridiculous rant.

Sergeant Major Ward, a huge presence with arms folded over his massive chest, stood and stared, seething at such disrespect. The three captains stood silent, and Stuart got up to greet the men while Dawes continued. He then turned to Dawes and told him he appreciated his vigor and enthusiasm and was honored to have him in his command. The next time, the Eastern Kentucky Riding Rifles will lead the charge. Ward, about to toss the major out by the scruff of his neck, breathed out a huff and escorted Major Dawes out.

Stuart let out a laugh. "That major, well, he's good for parades and reviews, but I don't know about a fight. Gentlemen, I'm very glad you have your reports with you, early I might add, and I'm grateful. Now, I'm granting you all two weeks leave. The Yankees are regrouping, and I understand they've appointed a new commander, George McClellan. He'll be tied up overhauling and this and that, so we'll be expecting no action. I guess there will be more men coming in, but I think you men deserve to see your families. On that note, I want to again thank you for your dedication and service to the cause. Be safe."

Stuart stood up, shook their hands, and saluted as they were dismissed. Outside the tent, the three shook hands. Colt, in the middle, put an arm around each of his friends, and they walked jovially together.

★★★

The plan was to spend the night at Greycourt Manor, get the train out of Richmond to Atlanta and then a train to New Orleans to visit with du Seine's family. Scipio was also to go home during the furlough. The two-hour ride to Colt's home was swift as Scipio lagged behind, driving a buckboard wagon with their carpetbags. Ortega and du Seine were at awe taking in the sweeping landscape as they approached the large white-columned house through a tree-lined road leading up to the house. Three dogs ran out, barking and jumping in excitement, scenting Colt and Scipio, and curiously eyeing the two visitors. Colt smiled at the dogs; one, a wiry wolfhound, leaped on the wagon, smothering the young slave.

As they approached the beautifully landscaped circle in front of the house, four house slaves stood at attention smiling happily to see Colt, their favorite, and his visitors. Scipio waved and smiled as he brought the wagon to the back of the sprawling house. Mrs. Greycourt stood at the doorway and eagerly waited to see her son. It was a pleasant surprise for all, and she welcomed the guests.

Three grooms ran out and took the horses to the stable. The men took off their hats and dusted themselves off. The slaves bowed and curtsied to the guests; Mrs. Greycourt, smiling warmly, hugged her son. She let him go, eyeing him up and down, checking his appearance. She smiled again and greeted the two young men, noticing how similar they were—about the same age, height, and build—and they all had long dark hair.

They left to wash the dusty road off and dress for dinner. Colt was expecting the Judge to appear. His mother took his arm and explained that the Judge was in Richmond. In a way, Colt was relieved.

After hot baths and a change of clothes, dinner was served in the lavishly decorated main dining room with its paintings and brightly lit candelabras. Roast duck, rice, vegetables, and hot biscuits were served with a cool white wine. Mrs. Greycourt was eager to hear about the guests' families, paying close attention to their every word. Ortega and du Seine were impressed. Not knowing what to expect at the huge plantation, they were surprised at the calm and organized demeanor of the surroundings. Mrs. Greycourt made them feel at home. The three retired to their rooms after briefly sitting on the back veranda with glasses of brandy.

Colt was up early, ready to depart for Richmond, and went into his father's den to wait for his mother. He stood by the desk and noticed the unopened mail from various places like New York City, Atlanta, and Richmond, since he did business in those places frequently. The letter from New York was from a bank, and the others had return addresses of different businesses. There was an envelope at the bottom of the pile that caught Colt's eye, and he nudged the pile a bit to glimpse the return address. Oddly, it had an address but no person's name or business name, just an address. The envelope was from some little known town in Pennsylvania.

Colt stood, staring down at the large mahogany desk as his mother walked in.

"Your friends are fine gentlemen. I'm pleased," she said with a smile. Colt nodded and smiled back. "I know you're disappointed that the Judge isn't here. He's been in Richmond assisting President Davis," she said apologetically.

"I know I've disappointed both of you," he answered.

Her eyes welled. "No, you've never disappointed me. Ever. You know how the Judge is," she said, wiping a tear from her left cheek and dabbing at her eyes. "We'll be moving to Baltimore the beginning of next year. The Judge said it's better for us. He has a house picked out."

Just then, Ortega and du Seine came down the huge staircase and waited in the atrium-like foyer. Breakfast was being served.

★★★

As the train pulled into the station in New Orleans, du Seine's eyes widened at the sight—a throng of family and friends were eagerly waiting his arrival. Du Seine sent a wire notifying his family of his homecoming, causing excitement for a rousing and anticipated visit of their favored family member. He was the first to exit the train into a rush of family. His father made sure Dion's wife and child were the first to greet him. Hugs, kisses, tugs, hand shaking were all around the train platform as Colt and Ortega stood on the train car steps waiting for room to disembark. Colt, especially, was taken by the affection these people were showing. Not just for Dion but also for each other as they all hugged and embraced at his arrival.

Dion's father, Marcel, made the sign of the cross upon hugging his oldest child as Father Richard, a priest and family friend, blessed the young man. Dion then turned to his companions and beckoned them down as he was anxious to introduce them. A black train attendant took a horsehair brush and wiped their suits as they were being warmly greeted.

Colt and Ortega immediately felt at ease and at home as Dion's family greeted them with the same affection. Dion put his arm around his wife and one-year-old son as they walked to the carriages that would transport them to the estate. There was a big soiree planned for the evening.

The du Seine estate was big yet modest. Gardens sprawled on both sides behind the columned house with oak trees and weeping willows flanking the home. The air had a magnolia aroma about it. Marcel Jean-Paul du Seine was a man of short, stocky stature. With a thinning, receding hairline and pencil-thin mustache, he didn't quite look his fifty years of age. His father purchased the land right before the second war with England and fought on the front line at the Battle of New Orleans, defeating the invading British.

General Andrew Jackson personally thanked him for his courage. The sugar and rice crops were profitable and bountiful. Marcel assumed control of the plantation after his father's death five years earlier since his three sisters—two that lived in France and one in New York City—had no interest in it. He also had a modest vineyard on the grounds that he was proud of. Marcel was a good neighbor, patron of the church, and always helped the downtrodden. Marcel and his wife of twenty-five years, Marie, were dedicated to their children. But there was something hidden in all of it.

Marie du Seine was tall, slender, and ten years younger than her husband. With long black hair and black eyes, she posed a strikingly beautiful sight. They were inseparable, and each evening, they took walks in their gardens as a ritual, just the two of them. Their seven children, four boys and three girls, were well mannered and popular with the other families in the parish.

Dion was the oldest and favorite of the du Seines. It was obvious to everyone that he had the physical traits of his mother with the same hair, eyes, and cheekbone structure. What was it that he got from Marcel?

Colt was shown to his room by a house servant assigned to him as a body servant during his stay. His bath would be prepared and his clothes set out, pressed, and ready to wear. Ortega had the same treatment—they would want for nothing. The backyard was being readied for the guests to have a place to mingle and have drinks as they arrived.

Dinner in the spacious dining room was being prepared with the finest meats and Marcel's wine. An orchestra had just arrived and was setting up. As Colt was dressing, he'd occasionally step out onto the porch outside of his room to watch the activity. Dion's two young brothers, Jean-Paul and Martine, ten and eight years old respectively, came into his room to see what he was doing. The boys took an immediate liking to Colt as soon as he got off the train. They asked him question after question about horses, fighting, and battles. It was obvious that Dion had written to them about him. Dressed in a navy blue suit and yellow-and-blue tie, Colt was groomed and ready for the party.

As he left his room with the boys, Ortega happened to leave his room at the same time to walk downstairs. Waiting at the bottom of the long staircase was Marcel, Marie, and Dion's sisters, Yvette and Marcella. The young men were not to go unescorted for the evening. As the men came down the stairs, Yvette's eyes locked on Colt as she lightly nudged her younger sister, pushing her out of the way so she would reach him first. Marcel greeted them and asked if they were attended to their satisfaction; they replied most positively.

Marcel introduced his daughters to the men. Marcella, at seventeen, smiled widely at Colt but took Ortega's arm; and Yvette, twenty years old with dark hair and eyes, stared at Colt as he stood on the lower step. She took his arm and immediately walked him out of the house into the fresh summer air. Marcel and Marie looked at each other.

Yvette didn't say anything as they walked into the garden. As Colt tried to initiate conversation, she interrupted with questions about him. Colt was amused. As they stopped, Colt looked up at the second balcony at the corner of the house and saw a young woman standing and watching them. Tall and almost an identical twin of Mrs. du Seine, she was wearing a dark blue dress and seemed to be holding a string with beads of some kind. Yvette noticed him staring up.

"That's my older sister Marie. She won't come down," Yvette said, disappointed that he was paying attention to her sister. Colt's eyes met Marie's, and the young woman turned and went back into her room.

By now, the guests had arrived; about forty family and friends crowded the grounds with wine flowing and plates of cheese and fish cakes circulating. Father Richard, conversing in French with Marcel about the hot weather but mostly how good the wine tasted, was asked to do the blessing before dinner. Ortega had a captive audience with Marcella, even though he told her that he was taken and hoped to marry his sweetheart soon. Colt's mind was on the other sister, Marie.

Dion was the main guest of honor, never leaving his wife Annette's side and holding his son. Marcel then broke away from some of the guests to speak to Colt. The diminutive Marcel took Colt by the arm and led him away from the crowd along a garden path.

"My son writes about you in every letter to us. You are his brother. I am grateful he has you as a friend and brother," he said. Colt listened, aware that he was to listen and not speak. "You see, I did not want my son to leave and fight. His responsibility is here with his family, not fighting. We are Catholic. We don't believe in taking lives, yet my son feels he has to do this. He has nothing to prove, yet he says he does," Marcel said solemnly. "I know you are a good man. My son says you are. Will you do something for me, for his mother, for his wife and child?" he asked. Colt nodded. "Will you make sure my son returns home safely? Can you, with the power God bestows upon you, bring my son home?" Colt was taken aback. "I can't bear the thought of my boy being away to fight."

Colt felt the utter sincerity in his voice, and the grip on his arm got tighter as he spoke. Colt nodded and placed his hand on Marcel's hand, and they walked back to the guests.

As dinner neared, the guests were surprised to see young Marie walk out into the crowd to greet people. She had been a recluse staying in her room for months, only leaving it occasionally for meals. Her dark eyes spied the crowd. She saw her father and Colt emerge and went directly to them, annoying Yvette. Marcel, glad that his oldest daughter joined in the celebration, introduced them and left to greet other guests. He took her hand and kissed it.

Young Marie was twenty-one and could have been an artist's model. Her statuesque presence was attention grabbing wherever she went, if she did go anywhere. She immediately latched onto Colt as his tall solidly built frame excited her, an excitement she hadn't felt for many months. Colt glanced over at Ortega who was practically consumed by his escort. Yvette joined them, and the three went around, speaking to all the guests, a sister on each arm. Colt's gentlemanly charm was captivating. It was time for dinner.

Seated first near the head of the long table next to Mrs. du Seine, Colt had young Marie and Yvette sitting on his right. Ortega sat opposite Colt with Marcella to his left. Servants glided in and out of the huge dining room, tending to the thirty guests with trays of meat and rice and shrimp made into three different dishes. Three servants held wine bottles, filling glasses throughout dinner. Children and young adults sat in a smaller dining room next to the kitchen.

Dion and his wife sat in the center of the table, enjoying every bit of the conversation, some in French. Father Richard sat next to Marcel at the other end of the table, and their boisterous conversation often got looks from the guests. Marie just sat and smiled, clearly enjoying the evening.

Colt sat on the edge of the bed shirtless, just his trousers on. His suspenders hung down as he slipped his boots off. The evening was a wonder, and it reminded him very much of the balls he attended in New York City as a cadet. Wealthy families requested West Point cadets as escorts for their daughters, and Colt always obliged dancing and dining with the elite of the big city. The evening, with its elegant dinner and dancing to a twelve-piece orchestra, went well into the early morning hours. The first dance was strictly for Dion and his wife, and then Marcel and Marie joined.

To thunderous applause, the orchestra continued playing as the guests were invited to waltz. Marie beckoned Colt to the floor, much to the dissatisfaction of young Marie and Yvette. He danced every turn as all the ladies positioned to get a dance with the dashing tall Virginian. Ortega was busy most of the evening talking cattle with some men, and Dion and his beautiful wife disappeared early. He stretched and rubbed his eyes and heard a faint knock at the door.

As he got up to see who it was, the door slowly opened. Barefoot and wearing a light blue robe stood young Marie. She put her finger up to her lips and pointed to a chair in the corner. Colt glanced at it as it was clear she wanted him to sit as he put his blouse over his shoulders. He preferred to stand and leaned against the desk next to the chair. Young Marie, standing tall, fluffed her thick dark hair with both hands. Colt noticed the robe open at the top, exposing parts of her cleavage. She looked at the door and then at the window.

"I wanted to speak to you alone. You danced all night. I can't blame the ladies though," she said, smiling slightly and glancing down.

Colt relaxed as she continued. "They want me to go to France, to a convent. I don't want to go."

Colt looked directly into her dark eyes, and she became a bit unnerved at his sincerity. "Don't go. You can make your own decisions. Why France?" he asked.

Young Marie was glad to hear him say that and felt very confident that she could talk to her brother's friend. "I was married for only three months. My husband was killed, and I still haven't gotten over it. I've stayed in my room for months. Tonight was the first time I've been out of the house since he was killed."

Colt didn't want to pry but was curious. "Your husband, how did he die?"

Young Marie lowered her eyes and then looked at Colt. "He was killed in a duel," she said.

Colt stiffened. "A duel? Was he defending your honor?" he asked.

"No," she shot back. "No. My family's honor."

Colt was surprised to hear that. A man upholding the honor of his in-laws when there are men in the family still alive?

"They want me to go away. I've been a widow for over a year's time. My family thinks it will be better for me to live with nuns in France. I don't want to go," she solemnly said.

Colt noticed her taking a step toward him, and he could smell a light perfumed aroma.

"My home is here. My life is here with my family. My life is to have a husband and children. Not in a convent, not in France." He was trying to catch on with what she was saying and what she was actually inferring. "A husband would keep me here with my family," she said apologetically. She then took a step closer toward him and with her right hand, grabbed his trousers over the belt buckle, pulling him to her.

Horses were brought to the front of the impressive house. Each of the three grooms led two horses as Marcel invited the guests and two daughters to ride on the grounds to tour his plantation. It was just before sunrise; Colt and Ortega were excited to ride. When they saw such magnificent mounts, they quickly jumped into the saddles. Marcel led the way as they trotted off—Colt, Ortega, Dion, and two daughters, Yvette and Marcella—breathing in the warm morning air. As they rode past the workers in the rice paddies and sugarcane fields, another horse galloped up to join them. It was young Marie, and she positioned her mount next to Colt's. He smiled as she half smiled back.

Marcel took them about a mile from the fields to an area with a group of two and three room cabins. Women hung washout to dry as children played out on the dusty road. There was a general store at the end of the road. Marcel waved to the women and children, and they happily waved back. Colt thought it odd—they were white people.

Young Marie leaned over to Colt. "We have no slaves here. These are the families of my father's workers. They are all free to come and go as they please."

Colt stared at the dusty road and didn't respond.

Ortega showed off his riding prowess with jumps and tricks around the saddle, much to the delight of the du Seine family members as they all rode back to the house.

Young Marie stayed close to Colt, and he even escorted her to the breakfast table. The hot chicory smelled very inviting as they walked along the long table filled with bacon, scrambled eggs and sausages, a sweet rice dish, and loaves of different kinds of breads. Ortega filled his plate, and the young sisters chuckled at the sight. Dion came into the room with his elegantly dressed wife, and Marcel went to get Marie and the other children. Colt took a scoop of eggs and bacon as a servant poured a hot cup of the chicory. Young Marie sat next to Colt with an almost empty plate holding just a little rice.

The entire family ate together, including the youngest child, five-year-old Marianne, who sat next to Dion's baby boy just brought in by his nanny. Marcel was overjoyed at the sight of the table, especially young Marie joining. Servants hurried, filling cups and placing the sugar bowls in different areas of the long dining table. The conversation was lively; the children were teasing each other, and all were poking fun at Dion's habit of shining his boots before leaving his room each day. Colt and Ortega had also noticed that habit and listened to the laughter and light banter. Two Great Danes trotted into the room and sat next to Marcel waiting for a table scrap or two.

They all wanted to go riding again after breakfast, but Dion, feeling as if he was a poor host, asked if it was all right for him to spend the time with his family instead. No one had any problem with that. After riding, Marcel was taking Colt, Ortega, and Dion to a popular tavern in the French Quarter of New Orleans to show them the fancy courtyard-style houses and fancy restaurants.

A carriage took the men into town and to Le Versailles, a tavern frequented by many of the planters in the area. The talk was usually of horses and crops. There were boisterous greetings as Marcel and the young men came in and went right up to the bar. Dion, Colt, and Ortega shook hands with the many friends of Marcel at the establishment, all but one.

The crowd swelled, and the talk shifted to the war. There was fear that New Orleans would immediately get sealed off by the coming Union blockade, choking them off from the rest of the Mississippi River, their lifeline to the rest of the country. Surely they might all go bankrupt.

An elderly man of about seventy-five years reminisced aloud about the pride he took as a boy in defending America against the might of the British as they attacked a rag-tailed force of backwoodsmen, a handful of regulars, local men, and pirates under General Jackson. How distraught he was at the thought of that very flag he fought for was now his enemy. He's lived too long, he thought.

Moving to the bar from his usual table in the back was Henri Louis Sevard, a wealthy planter that kept close friends nearby at all times, buying them drinks in exchange for listening to his rants about taxes, tariffs, and slaves. Tall and slim with a long-pointed face, his thin black mustache and short-cropped beard made look sinister to people. Impeccably dressed with top hat, gloves, and cane, he made his way next to Marcel.

"I've not been introduced to those young gentlemen, my friend, Marcel Jean-Paul du Seine," he said sarcastically.

Marcel looked up and then looked away. "My son's friends, Messrs. Greycourt and Ortega."

Sevard smiled. "You can see my friend Marcel Jean-Paul du Seine cannot look me in the eye when addressing a gentleman. You young men must know who you are with."

Dion went to confront Sevard when his father grabbed his arm, stopping him. Colt and Ortega tensed.

"Allow me to buy these young men a drink. I'm sure you haven't been properly treated by your host," he said, Sevard's friends smiling. Colt turned to face this despicable person. "Certainly with a wife much younger, taller, and much more handsome as your host . . ."

He was about to continue when Colt slapped him across his face with the back of his right hand. Startled, Sevard adjusted his hat and put his hand up to his face as the entire crowd gasped in surprise at this sight. Angered and rubbing his cheek, he turned to Marcel. "My second will call upon this cockerel this evening to meet tomorrow at sunrise. His choice of weapons, I hope it's pistols."

Marcel said nothing as Sevard and his friends left the tavern.

The crowd gathered around Marcel and the young men. Dion felt ashamed that his friend got drawn into the feud. "Colt, that should have never happened. He's been goading my father for years only to find his insults falling on deaf ears."

Ortega placed his hand on Colt's shoulder. "If it wasn't Colt, it would've been me," he answered.

"No. It would've been me," Dion responded.

Marcel looked at the three men and shook his head. "They are words, just words. There's been enough killing because of words. I'll not have it again." Then they left the tavern.

CHAPTER SEVEN

Secretary Stanton sent another cable to New York City. He was growing more agitated, not knowing what was going on in that basement. His notes went unanswered, but he couldn't go and see what it was all about without disturbing the president. Quickly a cable came back to him. He shook his head. His man in New York might know about what was going on in that basement room.

Detective Pinkerton grew more curious as Colt told his story. The prisoner seemed more relaxed but continued to glare at Morse and Geiger with disdain. Their reactions were evident as Colt spoke, annoying him. He even asked if he could get a few minutes alone with them to perhaps teach them some good Southern manners. Morse and Geiger were quick to oblige, standing firm as Colt stood up. Pinkerton intervened and declared this was a civilized investigation, and all were to act accordingly.

Colt sat back down and glared again at the two agents. Looking at Pinkerton, he said, "I haven't been charged. You can't hold me without charges."

The detective smiled. "Boy, don't you know, President Lincoln suspended Habeas Corpus. Didn't you know that? It simply means we can hold you for as long as we want without a court order or even charges. We don't have to bring you in front of a judge either."

Disappointed, Colt let out a sigh, and Pinkerton poured him another cup of coffee.

★★★

A crack of thunder came from the distance just north of the camp. It had been mostly dry in the early summer, and the rain would be welcome. Scipio shined Colt's boots as the three captains reviewed their written orders—the next group of recruits were expected within a week and would need to be trained. All had been quiet during their absence; the Union Army was under reorganization headed by the new general in chief. Stuart was glad to have them back, a day earlier than expected.

Mail just arrived in the camp, and an orderly brought in letters for the three men. Dion and Colt's stack were about the same size; Ortega got his usual three letters. Colt noted his envelopes were from New Orleans and from Baltimore. First, Colt read a letter from young Marie. She noted her appreciation at his gallantry to turn her away and send her back to her room when she practically threw herself at him. She also told him she had demanded not to leave the family for France, and they had agreed. She was grateful to him and hoped to see him again soon.

Dion hastily opened his first letter and quickly read it. His head sunk down into his chest. Ortega looked at him and tapped Colt on the leg.

Dion looked at them. "This letter is from my sister Yvette," he said slowly. Both men looked at him eagerly. "She says that my father met Sevard at sunrise after we left."

Marcel had quickly arranged to put them on a late train the evening of the incident to get them out of town, much to Colt's protests. He had explained that Sevard was a dead shot, killing his challengers. He had been trying to get Marcel to duel for many years—insulting his family, his appearance, and, mostly, his wife.

Sevard's jealousy of the du Seine plantation, especially the fact that there were no slaves, added to his ire. He tried many times to pit the other planters against du Seine without success. The last person to uphold the family's honor was young Marie's husband. This had caused a rift and was the real reason Dion joined the Confederate cavalry. He had to prove that cowardice was not hereditary.

Marcel did not believe in dueling. It was outlawed in Louisiana, but it was an old-world method to settle disputes, usually insults.

Dion looked at the letter and then at Colt. "My father shot and killed Sevard and was brought in front of the magistrate that day. The case was dismissed because of a ruling of self-defense. My father is not himself. He's ashamed of his great sin." Dion got up and left the tent.

Colt and Ortega sat quietly and watched their friend leave. A bad feeling engulfed Colt as he felt personally responsible for the events that caused so much pain. He felt he should write a letter to Marcel but changed his mind when he read the second letter from young Marie. This letter expressed her gratitude for his gallantry in defending her family. They hadn't known anything about the insult or duel and found out about the matter when Marcel sat at breakfast with all of them. He couldn't eat, and he spoke slowly, explaining what he had done.

The parish sheriff arrived, taking Marcel to court. Within hours, neighbors were showing up to congratulate him; it was very obvious that killing Sevard was celebrated. The name du Seine was no longer associated with cowardice.

Young Marie again wrote that she looked forward to his next visit. Colt read the letter from Victoria. In it, she expressed her concerns for his safety and was glad to hear he had gone to New Orleans during his leave. The New York Philharmonic was preparing to tour the New England states and was engrossed in rehearsals in New York City. She was eager to hear about his leave, and she was curious about his next assignments with the cavalry. What were the plans for him and the regiments?

Colt was excited to respond back, proud that someone was genuinely interested in him and his position as captain.

★★★

Colt sat in the dining room of the Baltimore Arms Hotel having breakfast and reading the newspaper. He was enjoying the very strong coffee and the meal of eggs, bacon, grits, and toast, savoring it as he had gone almost an entire day without food. A waiter came and cleared the table. Asking if he wanted a fresh pot of coffee, Colt accepted.

Dressed in a dark blue suit and red tie with thin white stripes, Colt was on an information-gathering mission. He was to spend two days in Baltimore and then travel to Washington and bring back as much information as he could memorize. Colonel Stuart got the idea from the patrols that were sent out along the Potomac River set up as small outposts north of the camp. Colt, Ortega, and du Seine led these patrols, but Stuart wasn't satisfied with just serving as guardians. He wanted information, and he knew how to get it. Captain Greycourt was just the man.

He read about the streets of Washington swelling with recruits and thousands of supply wagons. Not yet completed, Colt wanted to see the capitol dome for himself. He sipped and folded the paper. Looking up, he saw a face he really wasn't too pleased to see—Clive G. Dalrymple. Holding his gray top hat and smiling, Dalrymple waited for an invitation to sit. "Good to see you again, Mr. . . . ?" he asked.

Greycourt looked away from his paper and nodded. "Hello," he answered.

"Here on business, Mr. . . . ?" he inquired.

Taking a sip of the coffee, Greycourt just looked at him.

Smiling, Dalrymple sat down, knowing he wasn't getting an invite. "Where's that lovely creature you were with the last time? Your wife, maybe?"

Annoyed at all the questions, Greycourt motioned the waiter for his check. Still with a smile, Dalrymple got up. "The next time you're in Baltimore, you must be my guest for dinner, Mr. . . . ?"

The waiter came and was paid with a generous tip.

"My card, sir. Have a nice day," Dalrymple said as he left.

Greycourt looked at the card. "Clive G. Dalrymple, Esq.," it read. He placed it in his vest pocket and left the hotel.

The train station in Baltimore was jammed with people coming and going, selling peanuts and newspapers, and porters carrying baggage across the platforms. Greycourt looked forward to the short ride to Washington and got a window seat as he took his jacket off to hang it on the hook next to him. Glancing out of the window, he thought he saw Victoria. It sure looked like her.

"Victoria! Vee!" he yelled out. But the young girl walked into the train depot. Even the bonnet looked like hers. Troubled, he sat down and closed his eyes.

After checking into the National Hotel, Greycourt changed his suit and took a carpetbag with him. He walked around under the guise of a salesman and tried to memorize all he could. The streets were filled with soldiers, horses, and wagons; tents were set up all over, and a stable on every corner with pigs and chickens scattered around. He noticed the construction of the Washington Monument underway and the unfinished dome of the capital building. Whatever open fields there were had regiments of troops marching and drilling. There were Union troopers by the thousands. After walking the city, he decided to stop into a tavern a block from his hotel to have a drink and a cigar and, most of all, to eavesdrop on conversations.

★★★

Most College of New Jersey graduates went into banking, business, the law, or politics. Clive G. Dalrymple, a native of Newark, New Jersey, spent two years at his father's law firm in New York City when he befriended slick-talking private detective Lafayette C. Baker. Right before the war started, Dalrymple had no desire to enlist, so he took Baker's offer to work for him as an investigator under contract with the federal government. With an unlimited expense account and practically free reign to operate as he saw fit, Dalrymple mastered the art of gathering information, traveling between New York City, Baltimore, Washington, and Richmond. He reported directly to Baker.

He sat and scribbled a few notes of the day's observations. He didn't trust anyone in Baltimore, didn't like the city at all for that matter, but it was a wealth of information regarding Rebel news. He also had the authority to hire anyone he deemed useful to him. He jotted a few notes about Greycourt and his suspicions about this sharp-looking rogue.

He glanced at this morning's telegram from Baker, which lay open on the desk. General Winfield Scott was about to be relieved of duty but had recommended Baker for a promotion to the rank of captain of intelligence. With this salary increase, he would make sure Dalrymple was also paid more. Strict orders were given to watch anyone suspected to be a Rebel spy.

★★★

Stuart's camp now boasted about twelve thousand cavalrymen. Now promoted to brigadier general, Stuart was equipped and prepared to seek out and destroy Union troops, disrupting any campaigns. Captain Greycourt came back from Washington with important information regarding Union troop movements.

During his last night in Washington, the captain overheard three Union officers discussing their imminent orders to form their troops for an invasion of Virginia. George McClellan was planning an assault on Richmond early next spring, and from what he heard, it was going to be a mammoth undertaking, utilizing all 125,000 Union troops.

Greycourt was able to accurately describe where the artillery was stored; thousands of cannons bunched together less than a mile from the President's House. He also brought back newspaper articles with interviews of officers, even Lincoln himself. There would be no fighting as autumn approached, enabling the new Southern government time to raise funds and stockpile supplies and foodstuffs. Stuart saw the opportunity to keep training and, especially, have frequent meetings with Generals Lee, Jackson, Longstreet, and Johnston. The information Greycourt relayed to the generals through Stuart was invaluable, and the officers were extremely grateful.

CHAPTER EIGHT

Allan Pinkerton was getting tired, but the thought he was close kept him going. He had a strange feeling all along that there were going to be attempts on the president's life and was sure this captured Confederate officer was the key.

"Tell me about New York. You liked it? How many times you been there?" Agent Morse shouted at Greycourt. There was a pause as Colt looked at the three men.

"I liked it, liked it very much," he answered.

Agent Geiger leered. "Liked it? Liked up north? Then why'd you turn traitor?"

Greycourt calmly turned to Pinkerton. "I'd like to ask a favor."

The detective smiled. "Depends. What is it?"

Colt looked at Morse and Geiger and then at Pinkerton. "Leave me alone for ten minutes with these two here. I'll knock on the door for you when I'm finished with them."

The men looked at each other and laughed.

Pinkerton wasn't so amused. "Now let's be civil here. There's no need for that. We're getting away from what's important," he said.

Colt Greycourt's thoughts went to his times in New York City. As a second-year cadet, he'd gone to the city with two other classmates for a weekend. They stayed at the Fifth Avenue Hotel, a fancy place not too expensive. After an evening of going from tavern to tavern, they got the address of a posh whorehouse on the east side of Manhattan to round out the night. Colt had never been with a woman, and he had been anxious, but the experience had been educational. He had gone back to New York on three more occasions, alone, to walk around the city as he enjoyed its energy with restaurants, theaters, and bustling crowds.

When he was in his third and fourth years, he was chosen as an escort to attend the New York Cotillion, a formal ball for young ladies of wealthy families in New York State. A request was sent to the commandant who selected the cadets. The tall, dashing Colt Greycourt was one of the first the commandant had chosen. The formal soirees took place at the Astor House—one of the most opulent hotels in the city, if not the entire country. The chosen cadets stayed at the Astor, all expenses paid for the weekend. He got to know the city fairly well.

Pinkerton had gotten the room settled and thought about dismissing the two agents but felt their presence might jog this Confederate's memory and maybe break that tough shell.

★★★

The camp had been unusually quiet for some time. Tents were adjusted, campfires started, and volunteers were needed to set up a huge hospital tent. Most of the slaves were rounded up from their camp to do the heavy work, and large cauldrons with hot water steamed to wash the clothes of the returning men.

The heat of the day had to hit ninety-nine degrees, some thought. Orderlies, sweat streaming down their brows saturating their blouses, scurried about from tent to tent delivering cold fresh water. The troops had been out riding for three months felling trees, obstructing roads, sniper firing at different times, gathering information, and then smashing regiments of Union troops and capturing wagons, taking prisoners, and deceiving the invaders into thinking a force greater than theirs, lay waiting between their path and Richmond.

General George McClellan was able to get his huge force of about one hundred thousand men up the James River onto Virginia soil to march on the Confederate capital to end the war in one large swoop. It took weeks to get the plan moving; he began in early March when the weather was still in between snow and chilling rain, hindering their movements.

Trudging through mud up the Virginia peninsula, McClellan's men would inch their way north, buying time for Confederate forces under Robert E. Lee to form and repel any attack. The lusty cavaliers, molded into the image of their commander, were weary and now serving many sleepless nights, relentless pursuits, and short, quick hit assaults on the long train of wagons and infantry. The word was a lively soiree was planned after a day or so of regrouping.

Captain Colt Greycourt was just finishing a letter to Victoria when he was summoned to Jeb Stuart's tent. His report to the commander would be a long, detailed one and thought Stuart would want to talk about it. As he approached the tent, he noticed a thick-haired, dark-mustached man strumming on a banjo sitting on a stool just to the right. Sampson "Sam" Sweeney had come on board as part of Stuart's staff solely for his banjo playing and was a delightful addition. Sweeney's brother, Joel, was said to have invented the banjo, and the Sweeney family was known for putting on minstrel shows. Sweeney nodded at the captain as he approached. The major at a table in front escorted him in.

Stuart, promoted to brigadier general of cavalry almost a year earlier, got up from his chair, his blue eyes and thick rustic beard glowed as he exuded pride and confidence. Greycourt saluted; it was returned, and they shook hands as the major left. The sound of the banjo playing in the background was relaxing as he was offered a chair. A map of Virginia was hung behind Stuart and some documents in front on his desk. Stuart, having endured the same rigorous schedule and action, looked fresh and spry, ready for another jaunt; his light blue blouse looked like it was just laundered.

Stuart smiled. "Captain Greycourt, you've performed exceptionally well once again. Your action maneuvering your corps behind enemy lines and forcing Yankee reinforcements away from our main force was vital in our attack on their Sixth Cavalry, although it was rather odd that they were aware of our approach from the northwest of the capital. Regardless, your leadership and academy training served us very well over this campaign. The information you acquired from up north was very beneficial to our success. I've recommended you for promotion to major, which I'm certain will be approved within the next day. General Lee, now commander of all the armies of Northern Virginia, will sign off, that I know."

Greycourt stood at attention, listening as Stuart continued. "I am proud to have you in my command and particularly proud that it was my father that sponsored your appointment to the academy."

Stuart smiled, telling the young captain to be at rest and to sit. He did. An orderly came in with two glasses of lemonade. "I have an important job for you, and it's a job for a most trustworthy person," Stuart said.

Greycourt was curious and excited. The commander continued, "I'll tell you all about it."

★★★

The Judge sat at his desk in his office in Richmond and finished writing a report regarding the pending contract with Great Britain to purchase rifles and ammunition. He also recommended himself as the agent to negotiate the contract at a meeting to take place in Baltimore the following week. He felt confident and stared at the document for a moment. Reginald walked in and sat down. The Judge pushed the contract toward his son and waited for his reaction as he lit his pipe and leaned back. Reginald nodded and put it down. Puffing out a billow of smoke that had a crisp, rich tobacco smell, the Judge then pushed a white envelope in front of him.

Reginald tapped the thick envelope with two fingers and looked at his father. "Just come in?" he asked.

The Judge nodded. "Take your cut now. I'll take care of my man when I'm in Baltimore."

The young lawyer took four bills, $200 of Yankee greenbacks, not Confederate money. He folded them and placed them in the billfold in his right breast pocket of his jacket. He took a cigar from the desk and lit it. "This contract, will it cause any trouble for us?"

The Judge shook his head. "Not really. If anything, it will prolong the war."

Reginald smiled. "And prolonging the war benefits us." They both smiled.

★★★

Captain Colt Greycourt, soon to be Major Greycourt, was exhausted. He had new orders that came directly from General Stuart on recommendation to the Confederate commander of the army of Northern Virginia, Robert E. Lee, and would have to rest up before undertaking it. Both du Seine and Ortega were fast asleep in their cots; their snoring seemed like the culmination of their tireless efforts to stifle the invading army and contributing to its retreat.

Colt found it difficult to sit and write a letter in the tent, so he grabbed a pencil and paper and found a spot in the shade of a tree. He was writing to Victoria to tell her the good news about his pending promotion and, most of all, the daring ride around McClellan's army.

He described the enthusiasm throughout the camp as the companies, rising before dawn, readied themselves quickly and in a quiet, ghostlike fashion. Colt, du Seine and Ortega were to move out first and head south to the James River and shadow the Union Army as they disembarked from Alexandria to Fort Monroe and then headed up the river. The captains were amazed at the tremendous amount of wagons filled with provisions—over 120,000 men, herds of horses, artillery batteries, and tons of hardware.

Teamsters vigorously moved at the officers' commands as boats slowly approached to land. A steady drizzle made movement of the convoy difficult as they observed from a distance. A report was received that there was also a land approach flanking the river. Colt sent word back to Stuart of the huge force heading to Richmond. Colt remarked to du Seine that it looked as though this push was to take Richmond and end the war right away. They were to rendezvous back with Stuart sometime the next day to report and get further orders.

As Lee, Jackson, Johnston, and Longstreet positioned their corps between the invaders and Richmond, Stuart, with twelve hundred horsemen, set out to disrupt the Union advance by getting behind the blue army slugging through the muddy roads. McClellan's poorly planned assault had mistakenly been launched in the rainy Virginia spring. Stuart's cavalry circumvented the entire Union Army after discovering that the right flank was uncovered, enabling them to attack the long wagon train—capturing wagons, over two hundred horses, tons of provisions, and three hundred prisoners with minimal opposition. His main adversary leading the Union cavalry was none other than his father-in-law, Colonel Philip St. George Cook.

Stuart returned without a single casualty. Greycourt mistakenly got caught between two corps of infantry and was surprised by Union cavalry that quickly engaged in a furious mounted melee. Sabers clashed, pistols fired at close range; Greycourt's men were tangled in the fury but were able to cut through by flanking both the infantry and cavalry. Greycourt's men then regrouped north of the fracas. The lightning-quick battle stalled the Union advance as McClellan's camp got word of the engagement and surmised that the Rebel attack was coming from the flank. There had been no movement by the Union Army for days.

Those actions from the spring to early summer was known as the Peninsula Campaign, and though outnumbered, the Confederate Army claimed victory and turned McClellan back to Washington.

Greycourt's long, detailed letter to Victoria ended with his proud announcement of his promotion and his new temporary assignment. He sent it to her at the Baltimore Hotel, her address while touring with the New York Philharmonic.

★★★

Clive Dalrymple sat in the dining room of the Fifth Avenue Hotel in New York City and began eating lunch without waiting for his lunch companion who was twenty minutes late. Dalrymple was not a patient man, even if it was his boss. Roast beef, potatoes, corn, and warm bread were served along with a bottle of wine.

Lafayette Baker walked in and saw Dalrymple eating. He was a bit annoyed but let it go. He sat down and ordered the same lunch with coffee. Baker, thirty-six years old with dark, deep-set eyes, wanted up to the minute information on what the Rebels were up to. He knew Dalrymple had something.

The waiter set down the plate of food and poured the coffee. After looking around the crowded dining room, Baker leaned forward. "We didn't do so good in Virginia again. Hell, it took McClellan so damned long to move. The Rebs just sat and waited. Pinkerton gave McClellan some bad information, mostly about troop strength, and he didn't do so good for us at Bull Run either."

Dalrymple slowly chewed and listened as Baker continued. "The meat's tough. Anyway, I intend to get command of all military intelligence, and now's the time. What have you got, my friend?"

Dalrymple swallowed and sipped some wine. He wiped his mouth and leaned forward. "The northwestern counties of Virginia are going to join the Union—"

"Look, my popinjay young friend," Baker interrupted, "everyone knows that. Give me something no one knows."

The well-dressed young man smiled. "All right, boss, how's this? Since you rudely interrupted me, there's going to be a strong Rebel presence in Northern Virginia and a push further north, probably into Maryland. We have some time though. There's a Rebel scout up there now."

Baker sat back and grimaced. "The next time you have something like this, get it to me as soon as you can. Don't sit your ass on it!"

Dalrymple adjusted his necktie and collar. "I just got it. You said no wires with this kind of thing."

Baker cleared his throat. "I'll get someone from the War Department on this right away. Oh yeah, your envelope is at the front desk. If you're taking on any more help, let me know. Mr. Secretary is generous with me and spares no expense for information."

The waiter came over with the check, and Dalrymple pointed to Baker, getting a dirty look in return. "I think the two I have now are all I need," he said.

★★★

Colt Greycourt received his commission as major about an hour before he left on his assignment. With a compass, two Navy Colt revolvers, some dried beef and coffee, and a good memory, he set out before dawn to ride north and gather information of Union activity along the Maryland and Pennsylvania borders. He was given two weeks to complete his mission without raising any suspicion. Dressed in civilian clothes on his reliable and sturdy mount, Greycourt was to pose as a liquor salesman if he was ever accosted.

Heading northeast, his intention was to stop in as many towns and county seats as he could and to watch for Union troop movements and then to go to Maryland. After three days, he didn't observe anything to report. On the fourth day, he did. Eating an early dinner in a tavern in the town of Berryville, the county seat of Clark County, he contemplated turning around and going back. Aside from the known Union outposts in the North, he really didn't find anything unusual of importance to report. There were no cavalry movements or troop buildup, only sentry outposts.

He finished his meal and drank the last of the strong coffee; the proprietor came over with a bottle and glass and asked if he wanted a shot of whiskey. The owner, a portly man of about fifty, smiled through his red-gray beard and poured. He stood and watched as Greycourt first sniffed the glass, looked up, and slugged it down, wincing, feeling the burn all the way. The owner nodded and offered to pour another. He put his hand up to stop him, unable to speak because of the fire in his chest and throat. The whiskey was obviously a homemade rotgut brew, and the smiling owner waited for a reaction. He walked away bringing back a pitcher of cold water.

Three well-dressed men walked in, all with black mustaches, sporting the new rave in men's grooming—sideburns. A young girl went over to their table and quickly brought them tall steins of ale and told them that the meal served for the day was venison stew with cornbread and cherry pie. One of the men tried to make small talk with the girl and earned dirty looks from the other two. They sat at a slight angle to Greycourt's right. The three men faced him. What caught his attention was the voice of the man speaking to the server. He had a distinct northern accent, maybe from Boston, he thought. He had heard that voice before.

After a minute, he remembered it was two days ago in another town. Odd that he was in the same tavern now with two other men. Greycourt adjusted his necktie as the proprietor came over with his check. He stood up and placed 30¢ on the table and then dug down for another nickel as a tip. Wearing a greasy apron and smoking a pipe, the rotund man smiled and bowed in thanks for the gratuity.

One of the men at the other table looked up. "I see you pay with good Yankee coins, sir."

The man, sporting a dark brown mustache and nattily attired in a gray suit and riding boots, smiled and waited for a response. After a minute of silence, another of the three asked, "Are you an American or a traitor, sir?"

Greycourt observed that they couldn't possibly see what kind of coins they were. He turned and put on his hat. "Sir, I am a salesman," he answered.

Another of the three, of slight build, wearing spectacles and thin black mustache, smiled. "Salesman, eh?" he asked.

Greycourt said nothing, nodded politely, and turned to walk away when the man he recognized said aloud, "Sir, what's that? You haven't rallied 'round the flag'?"

The others in the tavern now looked over at Greycourt as he stopped and turned. It was now obvious that this was a Yankee establishment.

"I'm a salesman. I'm loyal to my employer," he answered and asked the proprietor where he can get a room for the night. The three men watched him leave and commented to each other how he had the look of a soldier.

The small room on the second floor of the Berryville Inn was just enough for the night. For 25¢, he got the room, a shot of whiskey, and breakfast the next day. It was similar to the other places he stayed, but this one had a large American flag outside and a picture of Abraham Lincoln prominently placed in the foyer. The other inns weren't so blatant with their allegiance to the Union. He had to be careful in any conversation he had.

He took off his jacket and tie, went over to the window to open it, and saw three riders slowly approach and tie their mounts in front. They dismounted and waited outside. He slumped down as not to be seen by the window and placed his right hand on the pistol in the right side of his waistband. The inn's proprietor, an elderly man smoking a corncob pipe, came out and nodded as the slight man with the glasses seemed to have been giving him instructions. He then heard footsteps on the first floor, some low talking, and then someone coming up the stairs. There was a knock at the door next door to his room and more low talking. Two people hurriedly left the room and went downstairs. He went back to the window, and although he couldn't see much, he surmised that he was the only person inside. He went over and got his other revolver out of his carpetbag and stood off to the right of the door.

It was quiet, just some rustling and snorting from the horses outside. Greycourt's heart raced, and his palms got sweaty. Beads of sweat saturated his forehead and ran down his face. He grabbed a small towel on the dresser and wiped his face. His white blouse was now soaked with sweat. He heard footsteps enter and slowly come up the stairs. His hands had to stay dry as he gripped the two revolvers.

The footsteps came up to his door; to his ears, the sound of someone trying the locked door sounded as if it was amplified in a theater. There was a knock, three quick taps on the door, his heart racing to near explosion. He felt the urge to pee himself but held it. Just then, three blasts ripped through the door around the doorknob, and a kick sent the door flying open. Two men bumped each other as they rushed in, and Greycourt squeezed the triggers, getting off ten shots, hitting the two men entering first, killing them instantly; the third man fired his pistol twice but missed and then ran down the stairs fleeing quickly on his horse.

The dead men were from the tavern. He rifled through their pockets. He didn't realize that he was hit twice; a bullet went through his blouse, wounding him on the right side and a shot, wounding the right side of his forehead. Blood trickled down the side of his face, mingling with his sweat. He winced in pain as he felt his side. The inn's owner came running up and looked at Greycourt and shook his head. He then reached for the towel on the dresser to treat the wound. Greycourt waved him off as he tried to grab wallets and anything else he could get his hands on but had trouble bending down and slumped to one knee. The innkeeper helped him up.

Though angry, Colt nodded thanks and gathered his belongings, giving the innkeeper a twenty-five-cent piece and riding off.

It all happened in seconds. His intuition saved him from being murdered. These men were not roving businessmen; they were assassins out to get him.

As his eyes opened, he was startled to be in very unfamiliar surroundings. He tried to sit up but was sore and lay back down. As he tried to move to get out of the large bed, the door opened, and a girl about twenty-six years old came in with a tray. She maneuvered very easily, opening the door and holding the tray which had a cup, a pitcher of milk, and a small plate of meat. She stood at the foot of the bed and smiled. "You're awake. That's good."

Greycourt looked at her up and down and rubbed his eyes. "Who are you? Where am I? How did I get here?" he asked, clearing his throat.

The girl smiled and said, "Well, you're about ten miles east of Berryville. The dogs were barking last night, and I came out to see, and there you were. My eldest boy helped me get you up and in bed. My name is Belinda Hunnicutt. This is my place." She poured the milk in the cup after placing the tray on a table next to the bed and handed it to him.

"Got any coffee?" he asked.

She smiled. "Drink that first," she ordered as if he were a child.

"Did you dress my wound?" She nodded. "Did you wash me also?"

She nodded and then said, "Not to worry. I have three sons. I know what's there."

Greycourt's face got red from embarrassment. "Where's your husband?" he asked.

She looked down. "Dead."

After three days as a "guest" at the Hunnicutt farm, Greycourt was anxious to leave. He had gotten most of his strength back to at least chop some wood, much to Belinda's ire. She had to constantly scold him. He was to rest and not lift a finger. Her three sons—ages nine, seven, and five—all pitched in to help their guest, listening to every order and demand made.

They sat and talked each night after the boys went to bed. She was fascinated with his life growing up on a plantation with its elegance and parties, something she could never imagine. When he told her that he's useless repairing things like fences and the window shutters, she was surprised as she was under the impression that all men knew those chores. He admitted to know only one or two things, not very much.

On Greycourt's last night, he asked her about getting married again. She shrugged. "Maybe, then again, who is there to marry? All the men have gone to war. Mr. Olsen down the road, he's a widower and older than my father. I guess there'll be a time."

He looked at her; her willowy full figure was attractive as the moonlight hit her long light brown hair; her dark eyes were a glimmer in her world of toil and despair. Yet she was cheery, positive, and full of hope. She took good care of her boys, taking time each to teach reading and writing, as she seemed to be educated enough.

"Your husband, did he die recently?" he asked.

Belinda looked at him. "Last summer, two men came and said he should join up with them to fight. They said Mr. Lincoln was gonna take our land if he didn't fight. He was a good man. He worked long hours in that factory in Pennsylvania, you know the one that makes gun powder and things like that. He made enough to buy this farm and then got killed last summer."

Greycourt felt a tightness in his stomach. "Where was he killed?" he asked.

Her youngest boy came and sat on her lap. "He does this a lot. I'd sit here alone each night, and he just gets out of bed and falls asleep in my lap," she said with a smile as she stroked his blond hair as he nuzzled against her. "He was killed somewhere in Virginia last year in July. I guess he was shot, I don't know, I never got details. I got a letter from the War Department in December telling me he was killed. They even sent money to me, $5. I never believed those two men."

Greycourt felt terrible for her. "But you came through it. This farm, it's wonderful," he said, trying to cheer things up.

"Came through it? I think of my husband every day, how we were going to have more babies, make the farm bigger, raise a good Christian family," she answered.

"I'm so sorry. I didn't mean to . . .," he replied.

She smiled. "No matter, don't apologize. You never told me, why you aren't married?"

He knew the conversation was turned back to him, so he felt a little better, still cautious. "I don't know, with school an' all, been too busy, I guess."

She smiled as she stroked her young son's hair. "You should never be too busy to get married. I have these boys, and I wouldn't trade anything in this world for them or time I had with my husband. You're a kind man," she said.

He smiled back.

"I noticed that my boys haven't left your side since you've been here. They love your horse too," she said as her face brightened.

He turned and faced her squarely, looking directly into her dark eyes. "More reason why you should be married again. Those boys want a man in their lives. They're good boys, obedient. I'd like to have them with me . . ." He then caught himself.

"With you where?" she asked.

"Oh, out riding, that kind of thing," he answered, almost slipping about the cavalry.

She smiled. "They'd like that, even this little one here," she said gently, tapping the boy's leg. She got up and carried the sleeping boy back to bed. She came out, stretched, and looked up at the starry sky. "If you get cold tonight, you can come into my bed, if you like."

Greycourt was taken by surprise and felt awkward. He got up, took her right hand, kissed it, and walked inside to go to bed. Belinda stood there looking at her hand, feeling tingling sensations all over. She looked out at the farm, smiled, and went inside.

★★★

Three men sat around the small table in the room at the National Hotel in Washington. There was anger in the room, and the bottle of whiskey was almost empty. One lamp was lit as they talked about the botched job.

Lafayette Baker scratched his head and cleared his throat. "Three men. Three men," he angrily repeated. "Could it be any simpler? You get this guy right where you want him and can't finish him. And he gets away to boot!"

Clive G. Dalrymple sat and pushed back on his chair. He had two too many whiskeys and felt very loose. "Nigel, Nigel, Nigel," he said, shaking his head, "you're a smart man. Didn't you set it up the right way?"

The third man, Nigel Blaine, adjusted his spectacles and rubbed his left shoulder that had been nicked by a stray bullet in the quick melee. "I set it up better than anyone could. That son of a bitch was waiting for us. It's as if he knew what we were there for in the first place. Besides, I'm a negotiator, an accountant. I'm no gunman."

Dalrymple got angry. "Set it up better than anyone? If it was, he'd be dead. You should've stayed and finished the job. Maybe got killed too."

Blaine leaned forward. "If I'm dead, how ya gonna know things? You know, things about certain deals and activities in the South?"

"We have another source, better than you," Baker interrupted.

Dalrymple corrected his boss, "I don't know. He has good sources. I have a very good source. We need them all."

Baker got up and left the room.

Dalrymple poured Blaine another whiskey and looked at him. He knew Blaine was working both ends—hired spy for him and contact agent for a wealthy Southern businessman. He could only trust him as much as he wanted to, which was very little. But this job to kill a Southern spy seemed to be an easy task since they knew their target and his moves. The Union agent was determined to get this Rebel spy by any means. Blaine wasn't done with this assignment, he thought.

Nigel Blaine was a slightly built, spectacle-wearing Harvard graduate that got caught embezzling from his employer, the Bank of New York. Avoiding jail time by paying back the money, he even had some left over because of his unique accounting skills. He went to work for a brewery in Brooklyn as their bookkeeper, which was where he met Dalrymple. The brewery was being represented by Dalrymple's law firm for tax evasion and bribery charges. The two became fast friends, both being sneaky, snarly people. A New Yorker from the west side of Manhattan, Blaine, with a short-pointed nose and thin eyebrows, was usually the brunt of jokes and pranks growing up. But his wit and quiet, mean streak made revenge easy. Now he was going to use his smarts and savvy to beat both sides.

★★★

The banjo was playing outside the commander's tent, and the camp was very lively readying for the special event of the evening—a bare-knuckle boxing match between Sergeant Major Ward and a big strapping Arkansas razorback named Karl "King" Kirby. Bets were being negotiated. People from around the county were coming out to watch. Both combatants were undefeated, and the company of riders from Arkansas was bragging all day about their fighter, much to the chagrin of the Virginia boys.

Major Greycourt sent word to Stuart that he was back. He was anxious to share his report of the mission and the one important fact he obtained. He sat in his tent, and du Seine and Ortega came in, jubilant that their friend had returned and the three of them can again be cavalrymen. He didn't miss much, just patrols and some skirmishes with Yankee infantry. A stack of letters was on his cot next to his pillow. He looked forward to reading them. Writing back would have to wait until he checked the duty roster that he was sure to be on.

Scipio came in and told him that he curried his horse and would get him bowl of mutton stew, hot biscuits, and coffee. He undid his tie and top buttons of his blouse and stretched. He noticed the letter on top was from du Seine's sister, young Marie. He would read hers first.

As he read the letters, he would stop in between and think about the family that showed their generosity and benevolence in taking care of him; their evening conversations about many things and how Belinda's boys followed him and the times he put them on his horse. Before he left, he placed $3 on her kitchen table. He knew she wouldn't take it from him but left it anyway. He would never forget them.

Officer's Call. Greycourt jumped up, scrambled to wash his face in the basin next to his cot, and fixed his blouse and tie. He didn't have time to get into uniform and was prepared to get a reprimand as he quick-stepped to Stuart's tent. He saluted the major at the front of the tent as Stuart stepped out. The meeting was held outside under a tree behind his tent. Standing next to Stuart's chair was Sergeant Major Ward, and next to him was a giant of a man with an unusual long sword. The man had a long, thick black mustache and a very large head and thick neck. Heros von Borcke was a Prussian cavalry officer that made his way to America by running the blockade from Bermuda and joining up with the Confederacy. For his gallantry and military prowess, he was assigned to Stuart's cavalry where he quickly became a confidant of the commander and now his chief of staff.

Greycourt was introduced to this colorful individual with a hearty handshake and beaming face. This gray giant made fast friends with his broken English and boisterous ways. Ward took roll call and noted Greycourt's attire, which Stuart quickly dismissed as he knew he had just arrived back from a mission. The officers were advised of a plan to invade the North through Maryland on information provided by Colonel John Singleton Mosby and additional information expected from Major Greycourt.

General Lee needed to know Union strengths in Northern Virginia, Maryland, and Southern Pennsylvania and ordered Stuart to ride north. Greycourt, without any warning, was asked to give a briefing of what he saw north regarding enemy strengths and civilian sentiment. A map was brought out and stretched on three sticks so the major could show where he rode and what he observed. The information was fresh, and he had details of the terrain and which towns to avoid. With Greycourt and Mosby's information, Stuart felt confident that the raid was going to be a spectacular success.

★★★

Clive G. Dalrymple was in Baltimore to meet his contact from Richmond. Baker, still angered at the failure to kill a spy, now stressed the importance of his trip to gain information of Rebel troop movements. His contact always insisted on meeting in Baltimore as it was primarily a pro-Confederate city where they can be safe and not raise any suspicions, even with a heavy Union Army presence. He sat in the dining room of the City Hotel, located a few blocks from the railroad station, and read the newspaper waiting for his contact, a high-ranking official in the Confederate government.

Wiping his mouth after taking a forkful of eggs, he looked up and saw his contact standing there staring at him. He waited and nodded as the man then sat down. A waiter came over and took his order for breakfast. Dalrymple took an envelope out of his breast pocket and placed it in front of the nattily dressed man. Checking his plate, he took another fork full of eggs and slowly chewed.

"This seems to look thicker than usual. Is that so?" the man asked.

Dalrymple nodded. "The new contract was a good one. With more recruits and volunteers streaming into Washington, the supply of guns and ammunition have to keep up. The factory is working seven days a week now."

The well-dressed man sitting across Dalrymple put three teaspoons of sugar in his coffee and slowly stirred. He looked at him. "Tell me, what do you tell your friends in the North? There has to be someone you work for up there? This $50 I'm giving you can't possibly sustain you with your expensive suits and fancy shoes. You've got to be working both ends?" he asked.

Dalrymple smiled and lowered his eyes. "Believe me, I give them nothing. It's usually obvious information that could be read in any newspaper."

Sipping the coffee, the man smiled. "Makes no difference to me or my partner what you do. We're grateful we have you. Besides, the longer this war goes on, the better it is for us. You too, sir." Adjusting his tie and then wiping his nose with his cloth napkin, Dalrymple smiled and nodded.

The waiter came over to pour more coffee, and the man told him to leave the pot. "I guess I'll see you in three weeks?" he asked.

Wiping his mouth and slowly looking around the dining room, Dalrymple nodded.

★★★

It was about an hour until sunrise, and Greycourt lay awake on his cot. He had trouble sleeping, his mind going in all directions. He was excited about the new orders but kept thinking about other things: young Marie du Seine, the Hunnicutt family, his sister and brother-in-law, and Victoria. He rubbed his side as the wound still ached at times. He didn't have time to see the surgeon to maybe repair the stitching of the wound done by his kind caretaker.

The last time he had seen his family was last Christmas. He had gotten a three-day leave, and he went back to Greycourt Manor to celebrate the holiday with his family, the Lelands and the Hales. He felt it would be the last Christmas together for a long time and wanted to hold tightly to every minute. His brother-in-law Jonathan proudly wore his gray uniform with its captain's stripes and gold braids on the tunic sleeves, a gift from his in-laws. His brother and family carried on without a care in the world, showing off the latest fashions while prancing around the house. The Lelands and the Hales, stylishly dressed, talked of cotton prices and the plight of slavery as well as plans to travel to Europe.

As the families gathered in the great parlor room with drinks and small snacks, Colt leaned against the fireplace, sipping a glass of wine. He noticed the Judge eyeing him up and down with a disturbed look on his face. Colt, not in uniform, wore a black blouse unbuttoned at the top, gray trousers, and no tunic. His black mustache and long hair about an inch beyond the nape of his neck made him look like an outlaw or desperado in the Judge's eyes. He looked hardened, his face matured with its sharp features accenting his blue eyes.

As he listened to the talk, Victoria was standing across the room sipping a cherry cordial and was setting her eyes on him. His rugged good looks and quiet demeanor stirred her insides as she too noticed his physical maturity from the last time she saw him. She noticed the change in his appearance as dashing and devil-may-care.

As the conversation got around to the war, Paul came into the room, glanced at Mrs. Greycourt, and she nodded back. He proudly announced that dinner was now served in the main dining room, and guests were to take their seats for the holiday feast.

Dinner talk was mostly about the new home that the Judge and Mrs. Greycourt bought north of Baltimore while large oval platters of beef and roasted pork were served along with vegetables, biscuits and ale, and cider to wash it down. Colt was quiet during dinner, listening to the conversation, and puzzled why the war was totally shut out since all their lives were being affected. He ate, enjoying every bite, noticing Victoria's glances. She was sitting directly across him, but the glances he paid more attention to were those from the Judge sitting at the head of the long table. It was as if the Judge was ready to pounce on anything Colt said. He knew his father's ways and purposely stayed quiet.

After dinner, men retreated to the Judge's den for brandy and cigars and the ladies to one of the side parlors for fruit cordials. A plentiful dessert table was set up with sweet cakes of all kinds, liquors and cordials, almond cookies, and rice pudding. Coffee was poured by the house slaves. It appeared to Colt that these people had no idea that the war existed outside of these walls. In only the first few months, the South had whipped Lincoln and the northern invaders, giving them a very brazen sense of optimism and confidence. The desserts were very sweet and tasty, and the conversations were louder and more boisterous as liquor took effect in spite of the strong coffee served. Around midnight, the guests retired to their rooms.

As Colt lay in his bed, the bed he slept in since he was a child, his mind kept going to the looks his father was giving him. There was to be a confrontation of some sort tomorrow, and he had difficulty figuring what it would be about.

He sat up and gazed at the floor of the room. The large area carpet hadn't been changed, and the charcoal pictures of horses that he drew when he was a young boy were still on the walls. He was a bit crude but was proud of his work, even though he wasn't a very good artist. That rust and yellow rug had many a battle on it: Colt had been given a large set of lead American and Redcoat soldiers as a gift when he was ten years old. He had spent many hours alone setting up battles of the American Revolution. With hundreds of these lead figures, he'd reenact the battle of Saratoga, Yorktown, the Cowpens, as told to him by Paul's grandfather who fought for the colonies yet remained a slave for the Greycourts. He got up to look for the large red-and-blue box tucked away in the bottom of the closet when a soft knock was heard at his door. Standing there in a pink robe was Victoria, barefoot, and her strawberry blond hair wildly waved about.

Colt stood looking at her as she closed the door and looked at him. "I thought maybe you'd be coming into my room?" she asked. Colt didn't answer.

Six o'clock Christmas morning and the house was already active—the banging and clanging of pots and pans in the kitchen, the hot coffee aroma seeping throughout the huge house. Tessa and three other house slaves were shining silverware; fancy Wedgwood dishes were so delicately made that you can almost see through them.

Paul was upstairs, getting the Judge's clothes ready, and brought him a cup of coffee. Just a few hours earlier, Paul, Tessa, Scipio, and three other house slaves, under the supervision of Mrs. Greycourt, finished decorating the twelve-foot-tall Christmas tree. Presents were put under the tree.

Mrs. Greycourt gave each slave a present when they were done and made sure no one, not even the Judge, saw her do that. Paul got a white linen shirt and bow tie, Tessa got an ivory comb and brush set and a can of ladies talcum powder, Scipio got a pair of boots, and the three other slaves, all female, got new shoes. Functioning on less than three hours of sleep, Mrs. Greycourt got her bible and nodded for Paul to go down to the slave quarters and make sure all were awake.

With Tessa, Scipio, and the three other house slaves, Mrs. Greycourt walked down the winding road behind the house and gardens to the shacks to read scripture and sing hymns. All the 146 slaves gathered in front of the quarters of David, the well-dressed elderly slave with white hair and slim build. He stood next to Mrs. Greycourt as snow flurried about their bare heads. The slaves knelt and bowed in her presence. She was always very cordial to all the slaves, personally congratulating them when there was a birth or seeing that the sick were properly treated.

Their overseer, Matthias Waxmann, a quiet man of forty-five, never attended the prayer services on Sunday morning, but he did this Christmas morning, hoping to get a gift. Mrs. Greycourt read the disciple John's rendition of the birth of Jesus, gave a brief lecture about obedience and sacrifice in the name of the Lord, and then told them they had the day off. They sang two hymns so robustly that the guests up at the house could hear. She made sure that they all would have enough to eat with special sweet treats as part of the holiday. As she turned to leave, some of the children ran up to her, bowing and kissing the hem of her dress. Old David smiled and bowed and began to start a sermon, as he usually did each Sunday morning. On holidays, Mrs. Greycourt was in charge.

Colt, only wearing a white nightshirt down to his knees, went to the water basin set on his dresser to wash. A house slave placed the fresh water there while he was still asleep so he could wash up. Victoria had left his bed about two hours before to go back to her room as not to arouse any suspicion. There was a knock at the door, and it was Paul. He had a message from the Judge that Colt was expected to be in the den promptly in ten minutes. Colt nodded and got dressed.

The Judge was standing next to the large mahogany desk near the roaring fireplace, looking over his spectacles as Colt walked in without knocking, irritating his father. They exchanged good mornings, and Paul asked Colt if he wanted coffee. The Judge quickly answered, declining for him. Colt waited for the scolding to start.

"Look at you," the Judge said in a low voice, shaking his head. "You look like an outlaw, a desperado." Colt, standing there in a dark gray blouse, black trousers, and black boots, said nothing. "You're an officer in the First Virginia Cavalry, boy, not a militia leader. Look like an officer. Get your dress uniform on today, Major," he scolded. Colt, annoyed at this, looked at his father.

"Do you know what I've done? Where I've been? Do you know what my assignments have been?" he asked angrily. The Judge never liked his young son's retorts, especially when they were questions. Colt continued, "I'd like to know what you've done for 'the cause'. What risks have you taken?"

With his feathers ruffled, the veins in his neck popping, the Judge clenched his fists. "You stupid boy. What your brother and I have been doing is all for the Confederacy. I'm trying to negotiate deals with British emissaries to coordinate munitions and equipment disbursements. I'm a direct advisor to President Davis. When this war is over, we'll be set for the rest of our lives."

Colt was puzzled. "Set?"

The Judge nodded. "Yes. There's always a profit to be made from war. This would concern you also."

Annoyed, Colt folded his arms and shook his head. "Me? What are you doing to make this profit?"

The Judge took his pipe from his desk and packed it. "What's this with you and that Leland girl? You were in her room last night, weren't you?" he asked. Colt shook his head.

"She's a good girl. She helped us months ago getting plates to print money. She did well." Colt was puzzled.

"Getting plates? How?"

"She was in New Jersey and was able to get these plates. That's all I know." A person just doesn't walk into the New Jersey mint in Trenton and get money printing plates, he thought.

The Judge lit his pipe. "We owe a lot to her for that. We have Confederate money now. Please, son, for me, wear your dress uniform today. It'll make me look good. There are some very nice gifts out there, and we should be with our guests."

The orchestra was setting up at the back of the ballroom. The entire third floor was a ballroom, chairs lining the walls and a servant's station set up for refreshments. The floor also had a balcony all around it so guests could walk outside. The large holiday meal was served and consumed by the eighteen guests at six o'clock in the cool December evening. Now the celebration was to continue with an additional twenty invited friends and relatives, dancing to the music of the sixteen-piece orchestra.

Waltzes and reels were the dances of the day, and Colt, a most popular dancing partner to all the young ladies, got a waltz with Victoria and graciously spun her out of the ballroom and onto the balcony under a clear starry Christmas night. He had a question that needed answering.

Victoria folded her arms, leaning up against Colt. "I might need my shawl, that elegant Christmas gift you gave me."

Colt took off his dark gray tunic and placed it around her shoulders. "This should be better," he said, placing his right arm around her. He noticed a honeylike scent from her long hair.

"I had a talk with my father this morning. Well, he tried the usual lecture, but I wouldn't give him the satisfaction," he said as she interrupted.

"I don't know why you have to debate with the Judge. He means well."

Colt continued, "He told me you were able to get mint plates to print our currency. How were you able to do that?"

She smiled. "Well, I have a few friends up north that are, shall we say, sympathetic to the cause and were willing to help. I asked some questions, got the right people, and was able to deliver the plates to Richmond. That's all that is."

Colt looked at her. "You're a cellist with the New York Philharmonic. How are you able to do it? I'm curious," he said.

Victoria smiled and kept the conversation to a casual exchange. "Colton, my love, the many patrons of the arts have various interests and views. I happen to be acquainted with such people that feel Lincoln is wrong, and the South has every right to break away. That's all that is. I was doing a favor."

Colt was still puzzled and was about to continue questioning when his mother came out with her arms open and smiling.

"The entire evening and the most dashing young man in the house hasn't asked me to dance. Vee, my darling, may I borrow my son for a waltz?" she asked.

Victoria nodded and smiled as she returned the tunic to him, and they went back into the ballroom.

CHAPTER NINE

Secretary Stanton got up and paced, took his spectacles off, and shook his head. He checked his pocket watch and decided to go to the government telegraph office and communicate directly with New York. He was tired. He had a lot of work ahead of him and needed some sleep, but this new situation was puzzling. President Lincoln had certain definitive ideas on how to treat the South. Even though the army of Northern Virginia surrendered and Richmond was in shambles, the Confederate Army of Tennessee was still intact, and the latest word was that it had no intention of laying down its arms. Stanton had words with the president before the party broke up, and although Lincoln made light of it, Stanton was disturbed. He called for his servant to get his carriage.

The War Department telegraph office, three blocks from the President's House, was a twenty-four-hour, seven-day-a-week operation with soldiers manning the telegraphs and the messengers at the ready to deliver messages and responses. There had been thirty to forty operators during the day and night, but this night had three. The president had his own telegraph in his office, and many times Stanton and Secretary Seward would sit with him as messages came in about troop movements and the results of battles.

Stanton walked into the office, a black shawl wrapped around his rotund frame, and he looked at the three operators sitting around idly waiting. He walked over to a table with envelopes and paper and quickly scribbled a note to be sent. Before he was able to give the note to the young operator, a message was coming in. Stanton stood behind the operator as he was transcribing and raised his eyebrows as he squinted to read the message. The operator finished, folded the paper, and placed it in an envelope marking it "President Lincoln, Confidential" and called out for an orderly who was waiting outside the building. The secretary took the envelope from the operator's hand and, to his surprise, attempted to open it. The operator, a private, shook his head and appealed to Stanton's honor of respecting the envelope and also his own job.

The secretary, ignoring the operator's pleas, took the envelope and gave it to the orderly. The orderly, a boy of about eighteen and also a private, froze at the sight of Stanton. Saluting, he took the envelope. As he slowly turned to leave, Stanton grabbed his arm and walked out with him. Before going outside, Stanton took the envelope and broke the wax seal. He read the message: *Just arrived in Phila. Heard about trouble. Stay where you are. Waiting for the first train to Wash. Ward.*

The wire was from Ward Hill Lamon, Lincoln's very good friend and also his chief of security. Pinkerton had gotten word to Lamon somehow and yet did not notify him of these events, whatever they were. Stanton got angry. He placed the message back in the envelope and handed it to the orderly. Stunned and now terrified at having to bring the message to the President's House in an open envelope, the private froze. Stanton looked at him sternly, took the envelope, and rubbed the wax to make it look as if the seal was never broken. The private then leaped on his horse and galloped to the President's House.

★★★

General Stuart got his orders directly from General Lee in a private meeting about the new plan to draw the army out of the Potomac. Stuart was to take his cavalry and ride north into Maryland to scout the area. He was also to cause as much havoc as he could to draw attention away from Lee's advancing army. Stuart would take twelve hundred riders north and reconnoiter, gather information, and disrupt any federal movements. With Greycourt and John Singleton Mosby's information, Stuart knew exactly where he would lead his men without being noticed.

The camp was restless in the hot August night, and most of the troopers were outside their tents smoking and talking, anticipating an early start on a most perilous and exciting campaign. These men were battle-hardened horsemen resting after a spectacular raid a few months before in June.

The Chickahominy Raid, which boosted Southern morale, established Stuart as a Southern hero, making the bold cavalier a household name and scourge of the North. His exploits were chronicled in all the newspapers in the South and even some in the North. That successful ride gave more confidence to the general, who not only was already confident but also had the feeling of invincibility.

Colonel Fitzhugh Lee held a briefing meeting of his officers, one of those was Major Colton Greycourt. The major liked being under Colonel Lee, the nephew of General Robert E. Lee. Greycourt had been adjutant to Lee. It was his plan during the Northern Virginia Campaign, where their daring raid at Catlett Station swooped into Union Major General John Pope's camp and took his tent and dress uniform, presenting it to Stuart. Now Stuart reassigned Major Greycourt to his command, and under the cover of dawn, they were to embark north, scout the land, and disrupt Union activity.

In the quiet of the very early morning, General Stuart led his twelve hundred riders out of camp and northward hoping to inflict damage on Union forces. The dashing cavalier with his chief of staff, Heros von Borcke riding next to him, exuded confidence in the entire troop as they trotted out to rendezvous and support General Stonewall Jackson's brigade of foot cavalry, as they were called. His mounted riders screened or provided protection for Jackson, moving north in the heat of late August; Stuart, having no engagements as his scouts reported no federal troops or cavalry nearby, decided to turn east and seek any Yankee activity, while Jackson's infantry continued northward. He decided to bivouac about five miles north of the town of Urbana, Maryland, positioning his troopers between Jackson's infantry and Washington itself. Camp was set up, and Greycourt, with Ortega and du Seine in his brigade, led the first patrol into the area.

With five riders, the young major was responsible for the eastern sector, where they were most likely to find Union troops. Greycourt's patrol found something that he thought the general would be very interested in. It wasn't a Yankee camp.

Stuart and three of his staff were invited to dinner at a local planter's home. Upon his return to camp, about to make his rounds through the camp as his usually did, he was approached by Greycourt returning from patrol. Stuart, always glad to see his young officer, returned his salute and listened to the report. Eyes widening, Stuart called for horses and his chief of staff, von Borcke, but was told cannon fire couldn't wake him as his snoring made the tent walls tremble. Stuart let out a loud laugh.

Six riders went off into the night, and about two miles from their camp, they came upon a welcome sight. They approached the grounds and mansion with its six huge columns and three floors; the general, taking a lantern from one of his aides, went right up the three steps and opened the front door. The lantern cast a pooled light as they entered the large foyer with its grand staircase. Off to the right of them was a huge room.

Stuart slowly nodded. "I am very pleased, Major," he said, looking about the room as a mouse scurried across the floor.

"Sir, there's been no enemy occupation, at least from what I've seen. This would make an ideal headquarters," Greycourt observed.

Stuart, looking the room over, nodded and mumbled something that sounded like a yes.

★★★

Just before sunrise, Sergeant Major Ward stood with his huge arms folded, watching a detachment of men gulping down their coffee and mounting up to ride out. Twenty-five men under Heros von Borcke's supervision were to clear out shrubs, fallen tree branches and clean the large garden behind the mansion. A major and three others were to go into the nearest town and recruit painters and carpenters for work. A wealthy planter nearby sent a dozen of slaves to help. By late afternoon, the entire estate looked sharp and very presentable. The mansion was ready.

Major Greycourt, with a detachment of five riders that included du Seine and Ortega, rode out east of the camp and came across an unusual sight—a Union cavalry camp with men wearing bright blue uniforms and carrying lances instead of rifles or sabers. These men, with their fancy lances, looked more like honor guardsmen created to ride in parades. Hiding in thick brush about twenty yards from the Union camp, Greycourt noticed their banner, the Sixth Pennsylvania Cavalry. There looked to be about a hundred mounted men as they fell into formation, getting themselves ready for a review, a parade, or a drill. Oddly, there was no picket around their camp.

Ortega and du Seine quietly moved toward Greycourt and reported. "That's a *bonita*-looking troop, if I say so myself, Major," Ortega said, smiling.

Du Seine nodded. "Dandy looking. Looks like a color guard," he said. "No pickets either."

Greycourt's eyes kept moving about, cautious. "That's a might purty-lookin' bunch, hey, Major?" a trooper said, crouching behind the three.

"Yeah, pretty all right. No pickets, no sentries. There's got to be a regiment of some kind nearby. Infantry? I'm guessing it's cavalry. Let's get movin' east a bit," Greycourt said, and the patrol left.

The Landon House, built in 1846, was a magnificent mansion. Used as a school at one time and known as the Landon Female

Academy, the sprawling estate was a gem in the countryside, with a two-story galleried porch and ballroom. Its Greek-style interior woodwork was unsurpassed in design. The completed renovation by Stuart's men and local townsfolk brought out its magnificence. Things were all ready; a large soiree would take place on a warm September evening.

Greycourt returned to camp only to find it moved to the Landon estate with its grounds as a bivouac site and the mansion for the gala ball. Wagons and carriages of people came from all around to partake in the festivities. Roses by the dozens from Baltimore adorned the ballroom at the east end of the mansion alongside Confederate flags and garland. The bandstand was all polished and sturdy as Stuart requested the services of the Eighteenth Mississippi Cavalry Band camped only a few miles to the south.

Stuart, dressed in his sharpest tunic, shiny spurs, and gold buttons, cut a dashing figure as he welcomed Anne Cockey, whom he dubbed "The New York Rebel" because of her fierce loyalty to the Confederacy. A relative of Mr. Thomas Cockey of Urbana, Anne was beautiful in her pink-and-white ball gown, auburn hair, and elegant necklace. She was immediately smitten with the general after having dinner with him the night before.

Wagons stopped at the finely manicured shrubs at the estate entrance, and the guests got into carriages, which took them to the mansion's impressive front door. Stuart stood at the threshold to greet each guest with von Borcke presenting a rose to the ladies. Each of the ladies that came alone were greeted by one of Stuart's finely dressed officers and escorted into the magnificent ballroom first and then off to a room across the wide foyer filled with tables of finger foods, roasted pheasant and chicken, pickled okra, platters of corn, and a wide table full of apple pies and desserts. A well-dressed slave served the finest port, elderberry, Madeira wine, and apple cider.

After eating, the guests standing as they ate, the entire group of about sixty people went outside to the front of the mansion and waited for instructions from another well-dressed, white-gloved slave. The elderly man called out to choose partners for the Grand March.

The Grand March, a tradition to begin gala balls, started with couples parading, then fours, then eights—all to the sound of a magnificent melody played by the orchestra. Stuart, with Miss Cockey on his arm, and von Borcke, with his lady fair, led the march with great enthusiasm. Upon completion, the entire throng went into Landon House to continue the dancing and revelry.

To the right of the bandstand in a fine-looking high-backed chair sat General Stuart with Ann Cockey on his left. The general got much enjoyment watching von Borcke dance and cajole with the guests. Wagons filled with ladies from Urbana had just arrived as the sun was setting, and the ladies hurried into the mansion. Dressed in their finest gowns filling out dance cards, the ladies danced to a polka at the insistence of von Borcke, which sent the entire room into a joyous fair. A reel, then a waltz.

Stuart, a fine dancer, twirled Miss Cockey around the room, much to her delight. Von Borcke, the Prussian mercenary—dressed in his sky blue tunic filled with fancy medals on the left breast, dark blue trousers with bright red and gold piping, and shiny boots—held the floor with his boisterous conversations and didn't miss one turn when the music commenced. The broken English he spoke was very entertaining. Stuart engaged everyone, as the bold cavalier was the center of attention and the pride of the South.

Dancing continued, officers in their fine tunics and shined boots, with the band never missing a beat. Stuart, sitting a reel out and conversing with the enamored Miss Cockey, looked up to see a captain hurry toward him with an urgent message.

Excusing himself, Stuart and the captain went outside to see Major Greycourt standing next to his mount, the bright September moonlight shining on him. Removing his gauntlets and dusting his trousers off, he stood at attention as the general approached.

"What is it, Major?" Stuart asked.

Greycourt saluted and took off his hat. "Sir, Union cavalry, about fifty riders less than five miles from here, sir."

Stuart nodded and looked around the grounds. "I'll guess those are Buford's boys. Heh, that's one tough cuss."

Ann Cockey came out of the house walking up to the men. Greycourt bowed at her presence and looked at Stuart, the general taking the lady's hand.

"Major, I suggest you get dusted off and grab a few dances. We'll take it from here," he said with a smile. Another young lady walked over staring at Greycourt, her eyes fixed on the rugged and dashing major. She was about twenty years old with reddish hair and wide green eyes. Her light makeup accented her eyes, small nose, and thin lips.

Both Greycourt and Stuart bowed as the major responded. "Sir, no, sir," he said.

Stuart was perplexed as the major continued. "Sir, I request to lead the expedition because I know exactly where the Yankee cavalry is right at this very minute. There is a ravine in the woods, and they'll have trouble getting through. They should be approaching it about now. I can lead us on their left flank, and if we can get behind them, trap them in a fish hook. Sir, I—" He was interrupted by Stuart.

"Major, get a fresh mount," Stuart interrupted and then turned to von Borcke who also came out. "Sir, assemble the men. We leave in ten minutes," he called for an orderly for Virginia, his horse.

Major Greycourt kept du Seine and Ortega next to him as they prepared to ride off. Stuart, now mounted, was handed a bright red rose by Ann Cockey, and he gallantly doffed his plumed hat. Greycourt, next to the general, adjusted his hat as he noticed the young red-haired maiden looking up, presenting him with her handkerchief which he tied around his right arm. One hundred riders were in their saddles, pistols loaded and ready to follow Greycourt into the moonlit night to seek out the Yankee patrol. The gala guests stood on the balcony and porch waving as they watched Stuart leading, riding east to seek out their enemy.

Ortega and du Seine rode out ahead and, within minutes, came back and reported that the Yankee raiders were just outside of Urbana. Stuart, irritated that the enemy would dare enter the town that was so gracious to them, took off at a gallop; the thunder of hooves behind him erupted the night. Major Greycourt took a troop of thirty men further south as Stuart hurried to meet the Yankee raiders head on.

Just east of the town, pistols drawn and lightning quick, the Southern cavalry surprised the blue riders, gunshots firing into their ranks, creating mayhem as the melee began. The Yankee force was more than Greycourt had reported, and Stuart, in the lead with two pistols firing, was overwhelmed at first as the enemy riders turned around and attempted to flank his men. In an instant, Stuart was in the middle of the fray firing and hitting men.

The blue cavalry were surprised again with Greycourt's thirty riders flanking them, overwhelming the enemy. Leading his charges, Greycourt fired his pistol and hacked with his sword; the Yankee cavalry, at the disadvantage and now viciously trying to break away from the entire fray, were pinned in with blue riders falling from their horses and the wounded pushing to escape the wrath. Some who rode off to the east were chased; the main body, enveloped in a hooklike vise, tried hacking their way out. But the gray riders, pistols firing, would take the field. Major Greycourt, emptying his revolver, frantically hacked at the enemy with his saber as he whirled and spun on his mount, bullets flying by, horses screeching in the eerily lighted field.

As Stuart and his victorious horsemen approached the still illuminated Landon House, he noticed Ann Cockey and a few guests standing on the front porch anxiously waiting for their return. It was quiet. A rider met him and told him that wagons filled with guests had just left to go back to Urbana thinking the gala had ended. Surprised and irritated, he ordered the rider to go out and fetch them back as the party was to resume with even more vigor and spunk. Luckily, the band was still there. Stuart dismounted with the rose firmly tucked in his sash just the way it was before riding off. He then kissed Cockey's hand and went into the house, the band playing "Dixie" when he walked in.

Greycourt, exhausted and sore from a blow to the right shoulder, was dismounted as an orderly took his tired horse. Standing watching his every move was the red-haired girl, eager to comfort him. With a glass of cold lemonade, she smiled as he wiped his face with the back of his dirty gauntlet, bowed, accepting the glass and drinking it in one long gulp. She took his arm and waited as he looked at the huge house. He then led her in as two wagons filled with the ladies of Urbana returned to the soiree.

★★★

The Judge walked over to President Davis's modest home and lit his pipe, which kept going out. He finally got a good flame and savored the smoke as he puffed. Three emissaries from Great Britain were arriving in two days, all according to how they would run the Yankee blockade. As the Confederate president's special assistant, the Judge was asked to meet with President Jefferson Davis to discuss the proposal for weapons, powder, money, and perhaps, troops. Davis trusted the Judge's ideas and insight but also admired his way of negotiating in a very warm and friendly manor.

Mrs. Davis met him at the front door as a well-dressed house slave, a tall man with gray temples stood erect and ready to take his hat. After exchanging pleasantries with the Confederate first lady, Varina Davis, a gracious and somewhat quiet woman in her early forties, he was led upstairs by the slave to a small office.

Davis was standing, looking out of the window with his hands behind his back. He turned and greeted the Judge. "How are you, my friend? I hope you and your family are well," he said.

The Judge nodded and asked the same of Davis. "Your son, is he well?" he asked. The Judge nodded and added, "He's with General Stuart. My son-in-law is with the Tenth Virginia Infantry, a captain. He's a very capable officer."

Davis got up and went over to the window, looked out, and turned to the Judge. "You know, it's good day to go fishing. When this is all over, my time will be by the river. I would like you to join me when that time comes. Do you fish, sir?"

The Judge tapped his pipe in his left hand and nodded. "I did a long time ago. I'd be delighted to go fishing with you, Mr. President," he replied.

Davis, looking gaunt and troubled, sat back down and leaned back in his high-backed chair. "Tell me, sir, what will be your strategy when meeting with our friends from Great Britain?"

The Judge nodded. "It's about cotton. The British are concerned about the blockade. My thought is to assure them that the blockade will not hinder shipments."

Davis slowly nodded, pondering. "You'll have to thoroughly convince them that we are committed to the cotton trade. How will you do that?" he asked.

The Judge gently tapped his pipe in the palm of his left hand. "I can guarantee monthly shipments, first out of Texas, that's been the most successful route so far."

Davis looked puzzled. "So you think blockade runners can get tons of cotton out through Texas? That would mean moving it through the South to say, Galveston?"

The Judge nodded. "Once we're successful from Galveston, the Yankees will concentrate their efforts there, and it will open up other ports. The shipments get to Cuba where British ships pick them up."

Davis placed his index finger on his forehead and tapped it, thinking. The Yankee blockade had a stranglehold on them, and although blockade runners were fast with some able to get through, cargoes carrying tons of cotton would require bigger ships. "Our ports from Charleston to the Keys to the Mississippi are blocked. I fear we'll be starved to death over time. Are you sure we can get cotton out and supplies in?" Davis asked.

The Judge nodded. "My thought is to go to London and appear before the court and make the alliance. I'm very positive that I can make agreements for weapon shipments and also, perhaps, naval assistance. Their shipyard in Liverpool is capable."

Davis got up again and went to the window. Turning to the Judge, he said, "Varina would like to invite you and your lovely wife to dinner soon. I would also like that." The Judge sensed that the president was disturbed and wasn't very focused on their meeting.

Lightly tapping his pipe in his left palm, the Judge had to ask, "What seems to be wrong, Mr. President? You seem, well . . . distant."

Davis half smiled. "The war seems to be going well, but I'm troubled by people in the northwestern part of Virginia. If they become part of the Union, it may very well cut off our resources like iron ore, coal, lumber. Yankee occupation can choke us as much as the blockade. I've discussed this with General Lee, and we've got a plan. General Stuart will take control of that region and disrupt all Yankee activities. Stuart is sending a courier here today."

The Judge thought for a moment. "The factory has been working almost twenty-four hours a day, seven days a week. No resources, no vital supplies. Can our plan work, sir?" he asked.

Davis sat down with a somewhat puzzled look. "That's the only tactic. It has to work."

There was a knock at the door. Davis called out to enter, and a house slave placed a folded note on the desk. Davis read it, nodded, and crumpled the note. The Judge got up and put his hand out, and Davis took it. "I'm looking forward to dinner with you and your wife soon," the president said, smiling.

The Judge smiled. "I will give you my date of departure for England. I know we can make alliances, and this war will soon end in our favor."

Davis nodded, patted the Judge on the back, and walked him to the door.

Davis went back to the window and watched the Judge get in a waiting carriage. Gaunt, tired, and worried, the Confederate president placed his hands behind his back and stared into the night.

Also watching the Judge get into the carriage was Major Colt Greycourt, Stuart's courier. As he approached the Confederate President's House, he noticed a familiar-looking man get out of the same carriage and say something to the coachman. Greycourt stopped, leaned against the corner of the building, not wanting to be seen.

CHAPTER TEN

Allan Pinkerton and his two agents stood outside of the room. Pipe and cigar smoke filled the air as they looked at each other. Geiger, irritated at the entire questioning session, shook his head as Pinkerton was briefly recapping their prisoner's story. Geiger shook his head.

"Where is this going, Chief? He's taking a long time to tell us nothing," he said. "I say we rough him up, beat whatever it is out of him."

Pinkerton relit his cigar. "Beat it out of him? That guy is tough. You can't get to him that way."

Geiger shook his head and looked at Morse. "We can get it out of him, right, Morse?" he asked his partner.

Morse slowly nodded. "He's not so tough."

Before Pinkerton and his men went back into the room, he stopped and turned. "That guy isn't infantry. He's cavalry. He rides headlong into a fight. He doesn't hide behind a tree and shoot his rifle. Look at his hands, there were some broken fingers there. He didn't get those writing prose. And his face, he caught a hard one to the nose a few times. That guy is a battle-hardened soldier that's been in tougher spots than this, much tougher." Pinkerton puffed on the cigar, and a thick billow of smoke rose. "I'd guess that he'd put up a pretty good fight if we went at him. That's no flubdub sitting in there. Let's keep on him. I think we're close," he added with a wink.

The three interrogators entered the room and saw Greycourt standing, stretching, pressing his palms together, and leaning back, his tall, solidly built frame an imposing sight as he stretched. The Confederate major, clean shaven, his dark hair shorter than he'd ever worn it, looked at his captors with disdain. Pinkerton motioned him to sit. Hesitantly and in a defiant way, he sat.

The chief of the president's Secret Service sat in his chair backward, leaning forward. Looking at his unlit stogie, he threw it on the floor. "Greycourt . . .," he began, only to be interrupted.

"That's Major Greycourt to you," the fiery Confederate answered. "We don't acknowledge Rebel traitors," Geiger charged, only to have Pinkerton raise his hand and stop his agent. "Yes. He's right, Major Greycourt."

The room calmed, and Greycourt relaxed a bit. Pinkerton smiled. "West Point graduate, heh? Ya know, you'd be a big man in the Union army if ya stayed. Probably General Greycourt."

Looking around the room, Greycourt put his hand up and slowly rubbed his temple. "I couldn't stay, I would be letting my—"

Morse leaned in, interrupting, "Too bad." He said it sarcastically as Geiger chuckled.

"General Reynolds, he was the commandant then, wasn't he? Didn't get along with him?" Pinkerton asked. The three men waited for the answer.

"General Reynolds is a good man. We used to ride together some mornings. He said I was one of the finest horsemen he'd ever ridden with," Greycourt answered.

"Was. He's dead. Killed by you, Rebs at Gettysburg," Geiger said.

Pinkerton got up, shook the coffee pot, and told Morse to get another fresh strong pot. The Confederate major felt remorseful at hearing of Reynolds's death. He had admired and respected him, later finding out that Reynolds gave him a kind of "legitimacy."

Geiger got right up to Greycourt's face and spat. "What is it? Honor, duty, country?" he asked gruffly.

"No, it's duty, honor, country, mister," he answered back.

Geiger smirked at the answer and looked at his boss.

★★★

Major Greycourt's brief meeting with President Jefferson Davis was uneventful as he dropped off the reports written by Generals Lee, Jackson, Longstreet, and Stuart describing the Maryland campaign. Davis didn't say much as he took the leather pouch, shook his hand, and led him out. Greycourt was to meet his father at the Richmond Hotel for dinner and start his new assignment the next day—ride with Colonel John Singleton Mosby and his Partisan Rangers.

Major Colton James Greycourt sat in the plush dining room of the Richmond Hotel waiting for his father. In civilian clothes, a blue suit and vest, crisp white shirt and red print tie, and shined button-down shoes, he looked like an ordinary businessman, except the dark mustache and long black hair, which set him apart. People were drawn to his chiseled facial features and blue eyes. The war gave him a hardened look. The waiter came over and placed a pitcher of ice water and a dish of warm rolls with butter. He ordered a whiskey.

As he waited, he noticed a slim, well-dressed man sitting by himself across the room to his right. He stared as the waiter brought the drink, then catching himself, acknowledged the old gray-haired waiter. He sipped and began to stare again. That was the man who got out of his father's coach and spoke to the coachman. Knowing he had been stood up, he got out a piece of paper and pencil to write a letter to Victoria, telling her about his experiences in Maryland and the new assignment. He decided to approach the man sitting alone after he finished his letter.

He walked past the table and stopped and turned. "Excuse me, sir, do I know you?" he asked with a smile.

The thin man looked over his glasses and slowly shook his head, surprised to be approached.

"You sure? I could swear we've met," he asked again.

The man once again shook his head and continued to read his newspaper. Then it came to him—this looked like one of the men that tried to kill him at the inn, the one that got away.

"Too bad," he said.

The man looked up. "Huh?" he answered.

"If you want another chance, I'll be here in Richmond overnight, then going north," Greycourt said sarcastically. He then walked back to his table to order dinner.

He finished the whiskey as the waiter brought his dinner of smoked venison, sweet corn, and boiled potatoes. He began to eat as the Judge walked in. A different waiter scurried over to take his hat and his order for a whiskey, assisting him with his chair. Major Greycourt kept eating, looked up, and nodded, acknowledging his presence. The Judge, annoyed at the disrespect, lit his pipe and began lecturing him on the ways of a gentleman, especially grooming as he still disapproved of the length of his son's hair.

The Judge sipped his drink and continued on about how the new government was slowly taking shape and the gallant efforts of men fighting to save their way of life. Major Greycourt just listened as he ate. The Judge again began to admonish his son for never completing anything, particularly not graduating from West Point. He finished his lecture suggesting he visit his mother at their home in Baltimore. The Judge grew silent as the major asked about his relationship with the man sitting at the table to their right. Although he pressed him three times, there was no answer.

Finally, in an effort to end the inquiries, the Judge sternly answered that he had never seen the man. When Greycourt pressed again, asking what the man had been doing in his carriage, the Judge got further annoyed. Changing the subject again, reminding his son to visit his mother, the conversation ended. They said their farewells coldly and left. Greycourt made a point of paying the check.

★★★

John Singleton Mosby was a Virginian. A lawyer by trade, his exploits as a soldier were admired by many. He escaped from a Union prison early in the war and then was a valuable scout for General Stuart. An expert gatherer of information, he was promoted to colonel of his own unit of riders to patrol the northwestern part of Virginia, seeking out Union camps and Union sympathizers. His "Partisan Rangers" of about two hundred men were to wreak havoc and disrupt any and all Yankee operations. They were also permitted to harass the local civilians—within reason. Major Greycourt was to join them in January as an observer for Stuart and to dispatch vital information.

After a brief meeting with his mother outside of Baltimore, he was brought up to date on family things. She arranged to have him visit her cousin, a surgeon, to repair the wound he sustained at the inn, which never healed properly. While getting cut and stitched again, a reporter from the Baltimore Daily Gazette was waiting to get a boil lanced and started asking Greycourt questions. When he found out that he was an officer under Jeb Stuart, he sat next to the gurney, pressing Greycourt for information while the stitching began.

The reporter was curious about the last campaign in Maryland and was excited to get a firsthand report. Greycourt began by telling the story of the sabers and roses ball and the subsequent skirmish with Yankee cavalry. But the real story was the action at Sharpsburg. Stuart's cavalry, making up for lost time to support Stonewall Jackson as Yankee infantry, engaged Confederate forces as Lee's command was moving north from Harper's Ferry. Stuart, late and without vital information about McClellan's troop strength and movements, screened Jackson's movement north. Greycourt was assigned to Fitz Lee's Third Virginia Cavalry.

In the September heat, Fitz Lee's men smashed into Union cavalry that was unleashed when Union infantry lines opened, to surprise Lee's men. Greycourt, commanding B Company, rode into the Union rear flank and pushed the blue riders away from the main body as Fitz Lee's men slammed into the fray, driving their enemy back into the infantry. Pistols firing, sabers hacking, soldiers falling, wounded or dead, and the shrieks from the horses were deafening.

Major Greycourt, in the middle of the chaos with pistol firing and saber swinging, inspired his charges with his tenacious vigor, giving them confidence in battle. The horse artillery pounded the Yankee flanks, enabling Jackson's troops to advance and though outnumbered, holding the field as frantic fighting went on around the stone bridge over Antietam Creek. Yankee Generals Burnside and McClellan seemed to have miscommunication as Jackson engaged General Hooker's corps with continuous flanking movements.

Stuart, now joined by Fitz Lee and Hampton, rode north to get between the Potomac River and the infantry as the battle raged from skirmishes to heavy fighting. Stuart took a position on Nicodemus Hill observing the action as General Lee gave orders to protect their flank in order to allow safe passage across the Potomac. Greycourt, leading B Company, dismounted with their pistols, peppered Hooker's corps in the woods and made it appear as if a stronger force of Confederate troops were on his right. The entire battle subsided around five thirty in the afternoon while the September sun was still simmering.

Lee gave orders to retreat across the Potomac, with Stuart guarding their rear. To his surprise, McClellan did not pursue. The Union forces withdrew from the area heading back to Washington, proclaiming victory. The Confederates also proclaimed victory. Exhausted and fearing their horses would drop from lack of water and food, Stuart cautiously regrouped. Major Greycourt, with Captains Ortega and du Seine riding next to him, took a small company south toward the town of Sharpsburg along Antietam Creek. What he saw had a lasting, horrifying effect to his entire being—bodies, hundreds of bodies strewn about in the road to the east and west. Blue, gray, butternut, and blood, a lot of blood.

Greycourt drew back at the scene. There were Union soldiers poking about the bodies looking for their dead comrades. The redness of blood was so thick it was hard to distinguish uniform colors. It seemed that the blood was ankle deep. The soldiers, waiting for wagons to come for the dead, were too engrossed in their task to even notice the Confederate riders. Feeling sick to his stomach, he motioned with his head to ride away as he heard a bugle call, for assembly, in the distance.

Stuart waited for his officers to join their troops. They were to embark for Williamsport on the Maryland side along the Potomac River with his horse artillery and a small infantry detachment. He made sure the small troop of Yankee cavalry across the river saw his presence, hoping they would attack. After a day of waiting, the Union Army sent a division of infantry to dislodge Stuart, but the skirmishes could not budge the Confederate general, and they eventually withdrew.

The Confederate cavalry and their horses got a well-deserved rest when scouts reported no Union activity or sightings. There was no grazing pasture for the horses until an unusual solution presented itself. A local farmer showed up with a loaded shotgun wanting to see the "feller in charge of this whole shebang." The farmer, a man of about seventy, was angry that one of his stray cattle was shot and was now being roasted on a spit.

Heros von Borcke met the man and won over the farmer with his boisterous, jovial manner, even inviting him to eat. The farmer figured that since the steer was his, why not, putting his shotgun down. He told them where there was a decent-grazing pasture less than a mile north. The camp became very relaxed as banjo and fiddle music was heard, and the aroma of strong coffee began to fill the air.

Ortega and du Seine went to fetch Greycourt at the medical tent. He had been looking in on the wounded from his company. His friends wanted him to join them as they dug into three big steaks. The camp feasted on the beef and venison, rabbits, and quail, and the young major enjoyed a full plate of steak and corn.

A rider with three sentries came trotting through the camp looking for General Stuart, carrying a message from General Lee's headquarters. The bugle sound for Officer's Call cut through the camp, and Greycourt, annoyed at the interruption, put his plate down and walked briskly to Stuart's tent.

The rest would be short as Lee approved Stuart's plan to again circumvent the Union troops heading back to Washington to wreak havoc with their wagons and maybe buy Lee and Jackson some time. They were to start out early in the morning.

As Greycourt was about to go back to his food, Stuart stopped him and relayed what Fitz Lee told him about the young major; with noble gallantry and keen senses, Major Greycourt performed in an exemplary manner. His daring leadership was worthy of the knights of old, slaying the dragon and infidels. The major's flanking maneuver, striking the enemy cavalry causing disarray among their ranks, was a distinct part of winning the field. Stuart was most pleased with Greycourt's actions on September 17 and told him he was proud to have him in his command.

The report for the entire Antietam battle was three killed and forty wounded. Wagons were sent to transport them back to Richmond, and supply wagons were loaded with provisions. Scipio rejoined the teamsters and other slaves and was abruptly told that the brigade was moving out at dawn.

The next morning Stuart's daring ride with his entire cavalry command rode around McClellan's retreating army about fifteen miles from Washington, capturing supply wagons, horses, and twenty-five Yankee infantrymen.

The Southern horsemen surprised the enemy as they hit the supply train hard. Communication went all the way up to the Union general that they were under attack by a large force. Instead of engaging in a fight, McClellan made haste back to the safety of the capital, losing men and supplies. Once again, Greycourt's daring charge with Ortega and du Seine created a diversion, making it seem like an attack was hitting the flanks, bringing Union infantry up to face them. Stuart and Fitz Lee attacked the rear guard, and Hampton's brigade peppered the column with pistol shots from the nearby woods. Stuart's horse artillery rained shells around the column.

★★★

Back at the camp, Greycourt was very glad to see Scipio but was saddened to tell him that he'd have to go back to their main camp near Richmond.

As the young slave quickly brought out a carpetbag with Greycourt's clean blouses and undergarments, a captain shouted for him to stop. "Halt, a Negra doesn't run unless he stole somethin', boy," he called out.

Scipio stopped and looked at the captain.

"He's my boy, Captain. No concern of yours," Greycourt said casually and took the bag.

The captain, with reddish beard and moustache and what looked like a once broken nose, stood erect, all six feet five inches of him and scowled at the major. "Major, why is this Negra boy here? We had orders that no Negras were to be at camp," he said.

Greycourt squared his body, facing the big-boned captain, and tilted his head slightly to the right. "Captain, I am addressed as 'sir.' Don't you ever question a superior officer, ever! Do I make myself clear, Captain?" he asked.

Scipio was afraid. He knew that he would catch the wrath of this boisterous captain when Greycourt wasn't around and tried to quietly step away. The captain was irritated at being scolded. "Major, sir, we have orders . . . Don't move, boy!" he shouted to Scipio.

"Maybe the major did not receive those orders?" Greycourt looked at Scipio and nodded for him to walk away.

"Captain, you're on report for questioning a superior officer. What's your name, and who are you assigned to?"

The captain stared at Scipio as he walked away, not looking at the major. "Captain Lamar Gratton, First North Carolina Cavalry, Hampton's brigade."

The North Carolinian was regrouping in Stuart's camp. Greycourt was not impressed. "If this were the time, I'd demand satisfaction," he said, looking right into the man's grayish eyes.

Gratton stared right back and responded, "Someday, Major, someday. I'd gladly accept. We will meet again."

★★★

Victoria sat in her suite at the Hotel Astor in New York City. She had a stack of letters from her beau, Major Colton James Greycourt, to read. Tonight, she was to meet with the traveling manager of the New York Philharmonic and then have supper at Delmonico's. She had been a very busy girl, but now with a longer residency in New York, she was excited to see Broadway shows and go to the many fine restaurants. She opened the first letter after stacking them in order of postmarks. The Baltimore Hotel was forwarding her mail to New York so she wouldn't miss any of his letters. As she began to read, there was a knock at the door. Annoyed at the disturbance, she got up to answer it.

The handsome tall and well-dressed man walked in and tossed his hat on the fancy chair next to the desk. He smelled as if he just finished chomping on a scallion, much to her displeasure, and further annoying her.

"I expected to see you later. Why the visit now?" she asked. The man, with his ever-present arrogance, didn't answer. Uncomfortable with the silence, she said, "I like this hotel." The man slowly looked around the front sitting room and nodded.

"A sitting room and a separate bedroom in the most expensive hotel in New York, I can see why you'd want to stay here. But you'll stay where we put you," he said callously.

She picked up the letter and started to read again when the man snatched it from her hands.

"I should read these first. I need all the help I can get," he said, smiling.

She got up and took the letter back. "You get plenty of help. What did Baker say?" she asked.

The man took out a long thin cigar from his breast pocket, lit it, tilted his head up, and blew a billow of smoke. "He's all right. He's pleased so far. He favors you. I favor you," he said, smirking. He got up and put his hand on her left shoulder, pulling her toward him and bending to kiss her.

"Stop! Didn't you have enough last night? I have a meeting in half an hour, and you've ruined my schedule. Get out now," she scolded, shrugging him off.

The man smiled. "All right. Delmonico's with Baker later. Don't be late. Let's see if those letters have something for us," he said. He put his hat on and went to the door. "Remember, don't be late, ever," he said and left.

Victoria went over to the window and watched the carriages pulled by prancing horses along the busy street and wiped a tear from her eye.

★★★

As Greycourt sat at the window seat on the Richmond Flyer heading south, his thoughts went to his friend, Ortega. He thought of the camp right after their daring ride around McClellan's retreating Union Army. The three—Greycourt, du Seine, and Ortega—sat, patiently waiting outside a makeshift hospital tent with seven cots. Ortega's youngest brother, Manuel, was one of them. Charging the Union rear, his horse took a tumble when it was shot out from under him, and he landed on his head. Ortega's nerves were on edge.

After a few minutes, the doctor came out. The physician, a man of about seventy-five years old wearing a long white coat and dirty spectacles, looked at the three. "Which of you is the brother?" he asked.

With a worried look, Ortega stood up and took his hat off. "I am, sir. Is he . . ."

He was about to continue when the affable doctor smiled and said, "He's lucky, just a bump on the head, that's all."

Ortega looked at his friends. "A bump on the head!" he said and chuckled. Ortega then went into the tent and began scolding his brother in a combination of English and Spanish. Relieved, Greycourt and du Seine both burst out laughing.

Winter furloughs were common: sometimes it was too cold to fight; roads were muddy and difficult to move troops and wagons;

men were given permission to see their families and to spend the holidays.

General Stuart was invited to a Christmas celebration with Generals Lee, Longstreet, Jackson, and Early at the Richmond House, a popular hotel and dining room. The general, always the family man, would then join his wife and children at the home of an old family friend of his. Ortega was granted a three-week furlough to return home and marry his longtime sweetheart, Lydia Suarez. Major Greycourt got two weeks furlough to attend. Du Seine was invited but chose to go home to be with his wife who was expecting their second child.

Ortega and his two brothers could not be still on the train. They went from car to car, pausing to look out of the windows and annoying some of the passengers. They were amazed at the speed of the huge train and its engine. The younger Ortegas tried to board the locomotive itself but were cursed at by the engineer and fireman. Two days on trains, Richmond to Atlanta, then onto New Orleans, then a half day's ride by stagecoach to the small Texas town of Gibbs Station north of Dallas.

Waiting for them was a buckboard driven by an old Ortega family friend and ranch wrangler, Santos. The Ortegas whooped and hollered seeing their old friend and introduced Greycourt to him. Santos, about fifty-five, his thin moustache on a thin-weathered face, was beaming in delight to see the boys in the bright December sun. Two horses were tied to the back of the wagon for Ortega and Greycourt to ride out to the ranch. There was a lot of laughing and jovial banter as they rode, mostly making fun of Manuel's fall. Greycourt laughed along with them and had the feeling that his stay was going to be filled with joy and celebration—not only the wedding but for life itself.

As they crested a hill, Ortega saw the ranch in the distance and took off his hat, waved it, and let out a loud yell. Motioning Greycourt to race him to the gate, both riders took off in breakneck speed. Ortega waved his hat at the sight of his family that was all waiting standing on the front porch of the expansive house with its columns majestically tall. His father, Don Miguel Ortega, was the first to greet them. He embraced his eldest son and hugged him tight, a tear rolling down.

Next to him was Mrs. Ortega, slim with strawberry blond hair, who cried tears of joy seeing her son, hugging and kissing him. His three elder sisters and their husbands and babies gathered around him. His three younger sisters joined in. He grabbed Greycourt's shoulder and introduced his best man. They all pulled and tugged at their beloved brother's friend, the younger sisters stretching to kiss his face. Ortega scanned to see where his bride-to-be was and saw her standing inside in the huge foyer. He pushed everyone aside and went to her, hugging her tightly as he kissed her on the lips.

As he held Lydia tight, he looked up and saw a man slowly walking down the wide stairway from the second floor. It was his grandfather, Don Victor, the sixty-six-year-old patriarch of the sprawling ranch that had been in the family for three generations.

A cane in hand and dressed in a black suit and blue tie with a slim build, pencil-thin black moustache, and chiseled features, Don Victor Ortega was a well-respected man among the community of ranchers and neighbors. A fair horse trader and cattleman, he shared his numerous watering holes with all his neighbors and taught his son to do the same. A fierce defender of Texas, he fought with tenacity against the tyranny of Santa Ana, and his Mexican army had been cited for bravery at the battle of San Jacinto defeating the Mexicans. Don Miguel was his only son among his six children.

The thought of his grandson about to marry warmed his heart to carry on the Ortega name. He proudly went to his grandson, hugged, and embraced him. The entire family was now in the huge foyer, all laughing and embracing. Greycourt was in awe at the sight of such warm affection.

The wedding was two days away, and two days after would be Christmas. A tailor was coming out to the ranch later in the day to fit the Ortega men and his best man with new suits and shoes. With time to stretch out and shake off the travel, Greycourt, their most honored guest, was given the finest room in the house. From his room on the second floor at the rear of the house, Greycourt viewed the acres and acres of land where hundreds of horses and thousands of cattle grazed and roamed, truly a magnificent sight. Other guests were provided comfortable rooms, but none as spacious as his.

People were coming from all over the territory—friends, family, wealthy and not so well off, even local politicians. Three hundred people were expected at the Ortega ranch for the nuptials. Ranch hands and neighbors rode out to assist in preparing for the biggest fiesta in the territory. Chairs and an altar were set up on the northeast section near the house, and the entire house and grounds were prepared for the guests. Barbecue pits were set up to cook the many sides of beef, and wagons with barrels of beer and wine were rolled in.

After an early ride on one of the ranch's fine Morgan horses, Greycourt sat for a breakfast of steak and eggs, biscuits, and hot coffee. At the long dining room table sat Don Victor, Don Miguel, and his strikingly beautiful wife Eileen of the Riordan family that owned a large spread about ten miles from the Ortega ranch. Mexican servants poured coffee as they asked Colt about his family and background, his religion, and his upbringing. Two more guests sitting at the table were interested in the young Virginian. Ortega came in and sat down. As he was served, he began talking about their last adventure with Stuart's cavalry. But those at the table wanted to hear more about Colton James Greycourt.

The December morning was brisk, but the day was expected to be sunny and mild. Ortega's three younger sisters stayed close to their guest from Virginia most of the morning, receiving flirtatious winks and smiles from the handsome cavalier. The youngest little sisters, ages twelve and ten, giggled at the attention. The ceremony was at one o'clock in the afternoon. The guests began to arrive about an hour before.

The groom, in his new dark blue suit and bright red tie, was nervously pacing when his best man, Greycourt, dressed in his new dark gray suit, blue tie, and new button-down shoes, tried to calm him with stories of their exploits and experiences. Ortega looked out the window of his upstairs room and saw the buckboard wagon with the priest, Father Arturo, and a wagon filled with the boys' choir right behind. The wedding mass was less than an hour away.

The rows of tables were filled with family and guests. The bride and groom walked around visiting with each and every person. A twelve-piece band played lively Mexican music as the revelers danced and laughed and celebrated this much honored day.

In a wheelchair sat Ortega's elderly grandmother. Dona Maralba, confined mostly to her room because of arthritis in both her hips, was able to attend the nuptials in the wheelchair with her husband next to her. Father Arturo, with white hair, thin white mustache, and thin tan face, always with a smile, sat at the immediate family's table and enjoyed the wines and delectable foods. Greycourt danced the first dance with the bride's cousin, Maria Elena, a tall, dark-haired, and dark-eyed sultry girl of twenty-one. She was immediately drawn to the dashing, gallant Virginian and made sure he was comfortable and introduced to everyone. Don Miguel got up from his table and sought out Greycourt and asked Maria Elena if he can borrow the young man.

Walking toward the house, Don Miguel expressed his respects expressing how glad he was that his eldest son's best friend was able to stand up for him on his wedding day. He took his arm as they walked, asking about his family, looking out to the distance.

"Colton, my eldest son is our joy as you can see. Of all my children, Rodrigo is our most favored. We know he will carry the name honorably," he said softly. "I will ask that you stay close to him . . . and my other sons. You see, I did not want him to go and fight, but my father reminded me of a time years ago when we fought against the dog, Santa Ana, and his army. We fought for our right to live and work our land. We fought hard. I lost two brothers fighting for Texas. We are proud of them. Rodrigo and his brothers are fighting honorably as we did."

Greycourt listened intently as the distinguished man spoke.

"Weeks ago, three men came to me and asked that we sell them ten thousand head of cattle for the Confederacy and offered to pay with Confederate money. I did not trust them and told them so. They came back the next day with twenty men and guns. I was ready for them. My ranch hands had their guns drawn on them, and they left without a shot. My fear is they will come back with more men. I need my sons here. They are not cowards or deserters. I need them here."

Greycourt feared that he would be asked to have his sons discharged, which would be difficult.

Don Miguel went on. "In three months, I will be driving twenty thousand head of my cattle to Kansas City, then on a train to Sioux City, then to Chicago. These Confederate rustlers will be watching. I need Rodrigo and my sons."

Greycourt did not know what to say but tried to be diplomatic. "Don Miguel, with all my respect, I can try to speak to General Stuart for their discharge for family reasons. I can try, although it will be difficult."

The older man took the young Virginian's hand and squeezed. "Gracias, mi amigo. Thank you," he said with a smile. As they walked back to the festivities, he stopped and turned to look at his guest. "I will also ask that while staying close to my sons, you will see to their safety. I know that is much to ask, but my sons write to us about you and how you are very . . . very caring to others. I can only ask that my sons return to me very soon or with God's help, when this war is over."

Greycourt assured him that he would keep close to his sons as best he could.

★★★

Major Greycourt was less than two hours from General Stuart's main camp west of Richmond. Although the winter months were usually filled with preparations for the spring, he was not very anxious to begin his new assignment.

His mind was on the last few days with Ortega and his festive, jovial family—no talk of war or problems or any strife during the wedding fiesta and Christmas celebration. Laughter and merriment ruled the household. Greycourt noticed the stark contrast of his own family and the similarities of du Seine's and Ortega's. He looked at the fine silver pocket watch with the carved stallion on the cover that was a Christmas present from the Ortegas.

Rodrigo and Lydia gave him a pair of black cavalier boots made of the finest leather. He thought hard about the personal task given to him by Don Miguel—the exact same task the elder du Seine had burdened him with. Keeping himself alive and healthy and to keep his troops alive was always the order of the day. Now it was personal—make sure his friends returned home.

CHAPTER ELEVEN

Pinkerton poured Major Greycourt another cup of coffee and put two heaping teaspoons of sugar into the cup.

"You know how much sugar costs today, Major?" he asked.

Greycourt stirred the coffee with his right index finger, licked the warm coffee off of it, and nodded. "Expensive. Only the President's House can afford it I guess."

Pinkerton smiled at the remark. "You never had to worry about prices or cost or anything like that? You just walked into a room and someone put food in front of you, poured your coffee, like I just did, practically chewed your food for you," the gruff Pinkerton said.

Greycourt tilted his head slightly to the right and squinted a bit. "Have you been listening to anything I've told you? Have I told you about privileges? Is that me, a privileged person?" he asked.

Geiger interrupted, "You own slaves. That's privilege enough. How did it feel owning another person?" he angrily asked.

The Confederate major smiled. "I never owned anyone. That's how it felt," he shot back and got angry at the question as he immediately thought about Scipio.

"You're gonna hang, Rebel," Morse countered.

Greycourt didn't pay attention. "Let's stop the nonsense now and just tell us where your friends are," Morse demanded.

Pinkerton put his left hand up for the talk to cease as he leaned forward and relit his cigar. "Tell us about the River Queen."

★★★

Even with the cold and snow flurries, the camp was still lively with banjo music as Sweeney sat outside General Stuart's tent strumming away. Fiddle and Jew's harp sounds also could be heard throughout the camp mingling with the fine aroma of bacon and coffee. Greycourt had to leave Texas the day after Christmas and get back to camp as another campaign was being planned. The train ride back gave him time to contemplate the last few days with the Ortegas. After a victorious Fredericksburg campaign where Stuart's cavalry protected General Jackson's flank with his horse artillery of just two cannons, the leave to Texas was welcomed.

It was unusual for a campaign to occur in the winter, as the weather had a tendency to create problems when moving troops and wagons on the muddy roads. The Union Army, under their General in Chief Ambrose Burnside, attempted a late fall offensive to take Richmond and met Confederate troops under General Lee, at the town of Fredericksburg, Virginia, on a cold and overcast morning. Fog made it difficult for the armies to see each other. Stuart's cavalry came into the forefront as they rode out, locating the Union infantry and reporting movements of pontoon crossings at the Rappahannock River, which gave Lee and Jackson time to position their brigades in wait.

Fierce fighting back and forth occurred as Jackson's men positioned south of the town, faced Union General Reynolds, flanking attempts only to be kept at bay by Stuart's horse artillery and quick attacks with his horsemen. This kept Jackson's flank cleanly protected, enabling him to best Reynolds. The outcome of the Battle of Fredericksburg on December 13 was a Confederate victory in spite of heavy casualties. Burnside had to turn back to Washington.

He intended to go straight to Stuart's tent to request a discharge for Ortega and his brothers. He thought it very odd that Scipio wasn't at the train station in Richmond to meet him with a wagon, so he had to rent one. He approached his tent to put his bag down and expected to see Scipio shining his boots or just waiting there for him. He placed his bag down on his cot—no Scipio?

Greycourt left his tent and walked down to the slave quarters on the north side of the camp. The slave quarter was off limits to all but the sergeant major or the general's chief of staff, von Borcke, but he went there anyway getting odd looks from the inhabitants. All the slaves stopped what they were doing and watched the major slowly walk around looking. An elderly slave about sixty-five, tall and lean with graying hair, approached him

"Sir, I can bring you to him," he said in a low voice as he was careful to address the officer. Greycourt nodded. The old slave led him to a tent at the end of the camp. They walked in.

Lying on his stomach, his head turned to his left, his back covered with strips, was Scipio. Greycourt closed his eyes, his stomach tightening at the sight. He looked around the tent. "Who did this?" he blurted out. There was no answer. Scipio was fearful of speaking up. The old slave shook his head. "It was that captain, wasn't it? Wasn't it?" he asked aloud. The old slave looked at Greycourt and lowered his eyes. The major left the tent.

Going straight to the camp doctor's tent, he just barged in as the doctor sipped coffee and smoked his pipe while reading a newspaper. The doctor looked up over his spectacles. "Well, can I help you, sir?" he asked sarcastically.

Greycourt nodded. "Come with me, please, Doctor. There is someone I'd like you to see," he said.

The doctor, not moving, sipped the coffee and knew all about what he wanted. He blew smoke from his pipe. "He'll be fine. No need to worry," he answered.

"So you knew what happened and did nothing? Doctor? Doctor of what?" he angrily asked.

Annoyed, the doctor looked up. "I don't know who you are or give a tinker's damn. I wasn't going to get in the way of some darkie getting what for by a captain," he shot back. "My services are not for them."

Greycourt got closer. "You'll come with me, Doctor, right now. Get your bag," he demanded.

The doctor smiled. "What happens if I don't? I don't answer to you. My skills and service are for the Confederacy."

Greycourt smiled back. "I'm Major Colton James Greycourt of the First Virginia Cavalry. You'll come with me now. You know why? 'Cause it's hard to be a surgeon or doctor with two broken hands and broken fingers."

The doctor grabbed his bag and went with the major as Stuart's chief of staff Heros von Borcke passed by and went with them.

All the slaves in the camp, about forty of them, now gathered around outside the tent as they saw the three men rapidly approach. The men took off their hats, and the ladies curtsied as they passed and went in. The doctor took off his jacket and rolled up his sleeves and examined Scipio. "Who treated this boy?" he asked out loud.

No answer. He repeated the question, and a thin young light-skinned slave came into the tent. "Sir, I did, sir," he answered.

The doctor, on one knee, turned to see the young man standing at attention. "Who might you be, boy?" he asked.

The young man looked at the old slave to get his approval to speak. "I am called Job, sir," he answered.

"Job? Like in the Bible?" the doctor said. "Well, Job, where did you learn how to dress wounds and, wait a minute, even set this boy's shoulder?"

Holding his hat in his two hands in front of him and again looking at the old slave, Job answered, "I was born on Dr. Jonah Clay Simpson's plantation in South Carolina. I was his helper and assistant, sir."

The doctor stood up. "Dr. Simpson, heh? Excellent physician. Good family of doctors too. Why are you here, boy?" he asked.

The young slave stood tall and at attention. "Dr. Simpson died two years ago, and his son in-law brought me. He is with the cavalry, sir."

The doctor took a jar of salve out of his bag and handed it to the young slave. "Take those strips off and dress the wounds with this. Apply clean strips over it and in a two, maybe three days, he'll be fine. Can you read, boy?" he asked.

The old slave slowly nodded, and Job answered, "No, sir, I can't read."

The doctor stood up and rolled his sleeves down and puffed his pipe. "That swelling over his left eye will go away too. Don't worry about that. Job, after you dress the wounds, get your things and come to my tent. I'll have a word about you to the surgeon general and Simpson's son-in-law."

As they left the tent and walked back to their quarters, von Borcke stared out. "I should have stopped it. That captain—he wasn't supposed to be here—just grabbed that boy and tied him to the spare wheel of the limber. He gave him ten lashes. When the boy didn't flinch or make a sound, he gave him ten more. From what I know, the captain just rode into camp, found the boy, and dragged him for the camp to see. He had two other men with him. I did nothing."

Greycourt looked at von Borcke a bit disgusted and said nothing.

Du Seine was in the tent and was surprised to see Greycourt still in civilian clothes and quickly strapping on his gun belt. Greycourt yelled out for an orderly to get his horse. Du Seine followed and went with his friend.

The camp of General Wade Hampton's brigade was less than two miles from Stuart's, and they rode hard to get there. Upon arriving, they slowed up and asked where Captain Gratton's tent was. A private spit his chaw on the ground and pointed to the third tent on the right. They rode a few yards and gave their mounts to a private sitting by. Greycourt barged in to see Gratton sitting on his cot with three other captains laughing and joking smoking cigars.

Gratton looked up. "You need permission to enter, Major. You're not in uniform either," he barked, the smile coming off his face.

"STAND UP," Greycourt barked back loudly. The conceited captain looked up and slowly stood up. Greycourt threw his right glove down hard on the floor as Gratton chuckled. With that, a quick blow from a hard left fist caught Gratton on the right side of his face, sending him reeling to the floor. The three other captains jumped up to see du Seine's revolver out aimed at them.

Gratton wiped his face and growled, "I'll have you court-martialed, hung in Richmond Square, whupped like a nigga boy yourself."

With clenched fists, Greycourt stared. "Your choice. Have it to my second within three hours. We'll meet before dawn tomorrow one mile south of this camp at the two oak trees." He picked up his glove, and they left the tent.

★★★

Victoria stretched and relaxed in the fancy suite in the Hotel Astor. As she looked over at the cello resting in the corner of the room, she began reading the letters from Major Colt Greycourt. Each letter, dated about two weeks apart, was warmly written and intimate. Colt described his assignments and the plans of Stuart's cavalry, always answering the questions in her letters.

After she finished reading the letters, she stacked them in date order with a piece of blank writing paper in between each one. She was going to respond to each one and date her letters one week apart. What she really wanted was to see him in person and spend time with him—it would be much easier.

The carriage would be outside waiting for her in about an hour, so she had to get ready. Dinner at Delmonico's and then at the Winter Garden Theater for a performance of the popular-drawing room comedy, *Our American Cousin*. The evening would end with friends at the Saint Nicholas Hotel for drinks. She wasn't very enthused about the evening as her usual escort wasn't the kind of man she'd envisioned being with, even though she knew him a long time and had been to Delmonico's many times before.

She wasn't looking forward to the gathering after the theater either; a local politician, a few city officials, and a newspaper reporter from the *New York Herald* were the frequent guests of their host Lafayette Baker. She wasn't sure what Baker did for a living but knew what she had to offer, in terms of information, was very beneficial. There were a lot of political jokes against the president, some bawdy, but the talk was always about the war.

Victoria put on a stylish blue gown with a white waist sash, pearl necklace, wrist bangles, and the latest black leather button-down shoes with a matching black purse. Refreshed and dressed, she went out to the waiting carriage, stopping at the front desk to tell the manager that she'd need a card in order to have her mail forwarded to the City Hotel in Baltimore, Maryland.

★★★

Major Greycourt had to meet up with six of Mosby's riders at Leesburg and, from there, report to Colonel Mosby himself. He had some time to think during his ride from Fredericksburg. He had to see General Stuart immediately after his challenge at Hampton's camp, an appeal to get Ortega and his brother's relief of duty to return home.

As the two cavalrymen rode back to camp, they noticed Sergeant Major Ward standing outside Stuart's tent, his huge arms folded and eyes straight ahead. It started to drizzle as they rode up to the tent. Dismounting, they saluted, but Ward stopped them. He explained that the general wasn't to be disturbed as Generals Jackson, Longstreet, and Hampton were in a strategy conference at the request of General Lee. It was imperative that Greycourt see Stuart, but Ward would not budge, suggesting he see him in the morning. With no choice but to wait, he went back to his tent and began writing a letter to Victoria.

Gratton's second appeared at the tent's entrance about an hour later. The well-dressed captain informed du Seine that the choice of weapons would be rapiers. This was accepted, and they agreed to meet at dawn the next morning. Du Seine then went to von Borcke to request his presence as the referee. In the event of any cheating, von Borcke was to shoot the culprit.

★★★

There would be no duel.

As Greycourt began writing, an orderly came to fetch him, taking him to Stuart's tent. An officer's meeting was about to begin. The generals had left, and the officers were to be briefed, conveying plans for the entire brigade to move out before dawn to rendezvous with Hampton's brigade near Fredericksburg. Mosby had supplied information that the Union Army was again on the move, heading toward Richmond, which was less than a day away from Fredericksburg. The plan was to have a scouting party, led by Major Greycourt, observe the movements and report back to Stuart who would be waiting about a mile south. Wade Hampton's cavalry would shadow all infantry movements by Generals Lee and Jackson from the North, heading toward the Chancellorsville crossing. Greycourt had to be up well before dawn with his squad to get a head start, du Seine at his side.

The overnight drizzle had gradually turned into a downpour, and the mild temperatures saved the weather from becoming a severe blizzard. An orderly woke him with a cup of hot coffee before three the next morning and was brought a leather poncho to wear over his dark blue frock coat and cape. The long cavalier boots he was given as a gift would come in very handy. He had two Navy Colt .44 pistols, one in his holster and one in the waistband of his black trousers with his saber. He also had to pack extra clothing; he was to meet up with Mosby in Northern Virginia after the rendezvous and act as Stuart's liaison in the operations of Mosby's Partisan Rangers.

The scouting squad, six exceptional riders, rode out in the rain through woods and unmarked roads to hastily get to the Rappahannock River just south of Fredericksburg. Of the six, Greycourt was not familiar with two of the riders, apparently Mosby's men. They made their way through the driving rain, slow footing for their mounts. About ten miles north, Greycourt's binoculars caught movement.

Teams of engineers had pontoon bridges lined up in order to make four, maybe five ways to cross the river due north of the Chancellorsville crossroads. Mosby's report had them crossing the Rappahannock at Fredericksburg, but that had changed. Greycourt also noticed something odd—some infantrymen staggered about and were kind of rowdy and disheveled even though in uniform. It was almost as if they were drunk. He spied the troops along the banks, most still in the woods as the rain poured down. He wiped the field glasses with the handkerchief stuffed in the right sleeve of his coat and ordered one of the riders to go back and relay the message of the new movements to General Stuart.

Du Seine took the glasses from the major and shook his head. "Colt, that doesn't look right. There's no order over there. What do you think?" he asked.

Greycourt took his glasses back and looked at one of the riders that he didn't know. "Hey, trooper, what's yer name? Who are you with?" he asked.

The trooper, wearing civilian clothes with a black porkpie hat and black overcoat, which was sopping wet, looked up. "Thomas F. Harney, sir, of the Torpedo Bureau under General Rains. I'm with Colonel Mosby for a while, sir," he proudly answered.

"Torpedo, heh? You're an explosives man then?" Greycourt asked.

"Sir, yes, sir," he replied.

The third pontoon got across as the infantrymen began crossing with cannons and had wagons waiting. Still dark, the scouts slowly rode about two hundred yards to the north to get a closer look. The first to come across was a rather portly officer on horseback with odd-looking whiskers. The rustic hair started on the sides of his round face and then hooked down and up to his moustache.

Du Seine squinted and chuckled. "Hey, Colt, that's General Burnside. Look at those whiskers," he said and took the field glasses again for a better look.

Immediately, the scouts saw that the trudging was difficult. The rain turned to drizzle again, and the wagons had gotten stuck in the mud, backing up the entire division. The pontoons of wagons, cannons, and troopers were in muck up to the ankles; horses bucked as teamsters placed planks under the wheels to gain traction. Cannons, with sunken wheels, had stalled the march across.

A cavalry troop from Fitz Lee's brigade came up behind the scouts. They howled at the spectacle of the mud march as they began heckling. Not caring if they were seen or not, much to Greycourt's displeasure, he ordered the troop to flank him to the south. The drizzle was steady, and the horses, their whinnies screeching in frustration, jumped and bucked while Burnside barked orders to keep moving and to get those horses moving.

Stuart rode up next to Greycourt and asked for a brief report but put his gloved hand up as he watched the comical show.

"Yeah, they got all the smart ones," he said under his breath as he chuckled. Stuart advised they were bivouacking about three miles south to get out from the rain as Hampton's brigade continued north. Stuart thanked Greycourt for his service and asked that he continue to monitor the situation, even though it looked like Burnside was not going anywhere.

There were some shots fired over the heads of the Union soldiers as they tried to move. The Confederates were teasing and scaring the men in blue. Hours went by as the marchers and equipment couldn't budge, stalling in the sunken muck. Greycourt, du Seine, and the other scouts couldn't believe what they were seeing. After futile attempts to move, Burnside gave the order to turn around and return across the river.

The heckling and catcalls stopped as the last of Fitzhugh Lee's men left, and Greycourt was left to watch the retreat. He could not understand the Union leadership attempting movements over that quagmire, in bad weather, and no regard for the soldiers that were in ankle-deep mud.

After Harney made a pot of coffee and the scouts ate some dried beef and hard biscuits, they decided to head back. Du Seine was to report back to Stuart, and Greycourt was to continue north to meet up with Mosby. Upon saying their farewells, du Seine handed the major a small stack of letters addressed to him from his family. The du Seine family had taken a fondness for Greycourt, especially du Seine's sister Marie. Along with the letters from Victoria and his sister, he would have plenty to read and write in the days ahead.

★★★

The Judge sat in the living room with his daughter and lit his pipe. She was about two months from giving birth; the anticipation and eagerness in the house was overwhelming. Mrs. Greycourt and Tessa didn't let the young girl lift a finger and made sure she was always comfortable and calm. Her husband Jonathan was trying to get a transfer to General Lee's staff, and the Judge said he'd write the necessary letters to Lee and President Jefferson.

As he read the newspaper, *The Baltimore Sun,* he heard a carriage come to the front door. Paul, with an umbrella in hand, went out to meet the unexpected visitor. A tall well-dressed man came out of the carriage, and Paul led him into the house, asking him to wait in the foyer. After a minute, the Judge walked to greet the visitor. Both men went into the den to the right of the foyer. Paul brought in a decanter of brandy and two glasses.

The tall visitor lit a cigar and handed an envelope to the Judge. "They're thinking of a seven-day week at twenty-four hours and three shifts. The addition of munitions is going very well. We can't keep up," he said, sipping the brandy.

The Judge nodded and puffed. "I thought it would. What else is there?" he asked.

The visitor placed the cigar down on an ivory ashtray. "There's going to be some trouble in Northern Virginia. It seems like a brigade or some kind of troop will be operating up there."

The Judge's eyes widened. "Near the border? We can't have that. What are you going to do about it?"

The man looked around the fancy room. "We have a good idea about some things. We have good sources," he said.

The Judge leaned forward. "Get them. Get them out of there. We can't have anyone or anything stopping that factory. Get them. Kill them all if you have to."

***

John Singleton Mosby was thirty years old. Lean, with a long face and thick brown hair, he was a lawyer before the war and from an old Virginia family. He joined the cause as a private and advanced to second lieutenant, then major, then colonel and was being recognized as an expert gatherer of information. Captured early in the war and part of a prisoner exchange, he immediately obtained vital information for General Lee just after being released. Seen as an important man in reconnaissance, he was dispatched to Stuart and then formed his own battalion to operate in Northern Virginia. He was to disrupt federal movements, obtain information, and recruit new men. He formed the Forty-Third Battalion of the Virginia Cavalry with forty men which would operate from the Shenandoah Valley to the Potomac River.

The success for these "Partisan Rangers" was to melt into the civilian population when not raiding. Gradual recruitment would see his battalion grow to six companies and one artillery unit, about four hundred men. Under the Confederate Partisan Ranger Act of 1862, General Lee gave Mosby total control and free reign of the territory. Greycourt and Harney met up with Mosby in the town of Middleburg.

With snow falling in the early February night, Mosby greeted Greycourt and Harney as they shook the snow off their frock coats and hats and were immediately handed cups of hot coffee by a young orderly. Mosby was glad to see them having heard about Greycourt's prowess as a spy and daring as a cavalry commander. He had met Harney before and welcomed the explosives expert. The heat from the fireplace felt good as Greycourt sipped the coffee and listened to the colonel's plans for operations and what they were to accomplish. The key was disruption in that they were to attack and stifle all Union movements and also gather as much information as possible to drive the enemy from Virginia all together. Greycourt was excited about it. As they talked, two men walked in out of the snow.

Dusting themselves off, they looked around the room, saw Greycourt, and smiled. "Well, lookee here, Noah, don't we know'd this one?" he asked his companion, pointing.

The other man, slim with a choppy russet beard and smelling badly, took off his hat and smiled. "Hey, Chan. Yup, we knows 'im. Didn't he have that roan a time back? He's different now with that mustache," he answered.

Chan chuckled as he was handed a cup of coffee as Mosby watched intently. Both men leaned forward, getting in Greycourt's face. "Still got that roan, popinjay?" Chan asked, smiling.

Greycourt stood up. "Yeah, wanna try to take him again?"

Mosby then stood up and put his hand out. "Men, we have things to accomplish. The enemy is out there," he said, pointing. "Not in here."

Greycourt sat down as Mosby described their mission, which was a raid on Thompson's Corner, and Greycourt was to ride alongside Mosby as he was not assigned to command a company. The colonel made arrangements for Greycourt to stay with him at a nearby farm owned by an elderly couple just outside of Middleburg.

When their scouting was over and Greycourt had to continue on to meet Mosby, he made his farewell to du Seine, making a point to tell him to be careful and that they'd meet again soon to resume the impending duel. The decision of rapiers pleased Greycourt as he was one of the best fencers in his class at West Point. His fencing foe at school, who had just as much prowess with the sword, was his classmate and friend, George Armstrong Custer. Angry and disappointed that the duel was postponed, he made it a point to tell du Seine to extend his compliments to the captain and that the duel will still be on upon his return from Mosby's mission.

★★★

With success of the raid on Thompson's Corner disrupting Yankee movements and stealing horses and supplies, Mosby received word of enemy activity again and called a meeting with his officers. In a tent outside of the barn at the Reiser farm where the two officers were staying, Mosby had a table set up with a map of the counties in Northern Virginia and Maryland. The six officers stood leaning over the table looking at Loudon County, northeast of Middleburg. The day before, a Yankee cavalry troop raided Middleburg looking for Confederate forces.

They had received word that Rebels were occupying the town and wrecked the tavern, hotel, general store and threatened to burn the church and adjoining schoolhouse. The Yankee raiders were sure that Mosby was hiding in the town but couldn't find him. They then left, finding nothing, and headed east. Mosby got word right away but had to wait until his men could be summoned. The officers knew that they could be a day or so behind and that pursuit with a surprise attack would work. Mosby's plan was to start out in the middle of the night. They could get about twenty-five men in the saddle in about an hour, and the muddy roads would surely slow the Yankees down, and Greycourt was to ride into Middleburg and get details on the enemy's strength.

The night ride wasn't difficult as one of their men knew the paths through woods and back roads. After three hours riding, they stopped to rest with one scout riding ahead. Coffee, dried beef, and hardtack satisfied them, but there was no grazing for the horses in the wooded area, and the little grain they carried had to suffice for the time being.

Greycourt found out that it was small patrol of about fifty men from the 18th Pennsylvania, as one of their officers dropped his calling card when a boy pushed him away from his parents. The card said, "Captain Edward A. Sheppard, 18th Pennsylvania Cavalry." Mosby knew he could get the better of them with a surprise attack. They would move out at dawn.

About three miles east of the town of Aldie in the northeastern part of Virginia, Mosby's raiders came upon a camp of Yankee cavalry that was well protected by sentries and stockade. Greycourt was able to get a closer look and saw that it was the 18th Pennsylvania with the First Vermont. Most likely patrolling the same territory, they linked up and were probably going to raid Aldie when the townsfolk were just rising to start the day. Getting the information back to Mosby, they surmised that the First Vermont had about fifty men; and along with the fifty or so with the 18th Pennsylvania, that would make it two to one against them.

The Partisan Rangers rose before dawn and made their way to the western part of the town out of sight, waiting. They were right—the First Vermont rode in as the people came out to open their shops. As the Yankee raiders very casually dismounted, Mosby's men took off with screeching, hideous yells frightening the horses and catching the Vermont men completely by surprise. All twenty-eight of Mosby's riders rumbled through the muddy street firing pistols and killing their foes as they tried scrambling for cover. The Vermont men fled in retreat as the 18th Pennsylvania galloped straight for Mosby, and in the frenzy, the colonel lost control of his horse and was forced to jump off, losing it in the fray. Greycourt, two pistols firing, saw this and forced his mount toward Mosby who was now staring at a Yankee captain's pistol. About to shoot, the captain's horse was shot out from under him as Greycourt was jostled in his saddle. The horse pinned the captain as another raider was about to shoot the wounded captain, but Mosby stopped him and took the captain prisoner.

The 18th Pennsylvania, being overwhelmed, retreated east along with the Vermont men. Mosby ordered five men to keep watch as the aftermath was sorted out. In all, nineteen Yankees were captured along with twenty-three horses and twenty-four Yankees killed. There was only one wounded rider for Mosby. The townspeople, waiting for the end, came out into the street, waved their hats, and cheered Mosby's Rangers as they taunted the captured men. Hot coffee was brought out. Greycourt tipped his hat in thanks but saw a disheveled Yankee with blood trickling down his cheek and gave him the hot drink. Among the captured were two captains who were going to be interrogated intensely by Mosby using his sharpest attorney-like questioning.

After a hearty breakfast prepared by the hotel's proprietor, the rangers regrouped and sent a wire to Richmond about the fight and to pick up the prisoners being held in the local courthouse jail, and a doctor was also summoned to treat the wounded. The brief interrogation was very eventful for Mosby and Greycourt as they found maps in the captured horses' saddlebags showing routes to Middleburg and specific instructions about Fairfax. At first, the captains didn't answer any questions, but Mosby threatened to hang one Yankee every half hour if they didn't give up information about their patrols. After thinking about it, they talked. They locked up all the prisoners and tended to their horses. Mosby was already planning his next move.

★★★

As Mosby and his victorious men rode back west toward Middleburg, Greycourt, riding next to the colonel, was silent. He was thinking about a few disturbing things; one was how did the Yankee patrols know they were in northern Virginia, and how did they know, specifically Mosby, was the officer in charge? Also troubling was that he thought a shot was fired at him during the melee from one of his own men. He couldn't quite tell. He just had that sense.

CHAPTER TWELVE

The three corporals sat nervously as Secretary Stanton paced in the telegraph room of the War Department. They usually played cards or dozed off during the midnight shift, since watching for messages was very slow. Stanton, with a blue-and-white shawl around his rotund body, paced waiting for a wire. He grunted a few times as he looked at his pocket watch. As he looked around and saw how nervous the corporals looked, he decided to leave. As he reached the door, he heard a wire coming through. His eyes widened. He hurried over to the desk, and two of the corporals silently chuckled at seeing the heavy-set man move so quickly. He grabbed the message, as it was just barely written out. He adjusted his spectacles and read, mumbling and rubbing his chin.

Just then, another wire came through, and Stanton leaned over, looking at the writing. He attempted to take the message when the corporal, a young man from Illinois, placed his hand over it. The secretary got irate. "Young man, I'll have that please," he demanded.

The corporal slowly turned and looked up and shook his head. "Sorry, sir, this is to be delivered to Major Pinkerton by order of the sender," he said in low voice.

Stanton bristled at the insolence of the young man. "I shall take it," he said with a smile.

Now shaking, the young corporal shook his head. "Sorry, sir. A War Department courier must do it. It's orders."

Stanton tensed. "Ordered by whom?" he shouted.

A response came from one of the other corporals. "You, sir."

★★★

The general store in Middleburg had a lot of activity. The owner, a man of about sixty-five, just got in two barrels of sugar and one barrel of crackers. He had hoped there would be flour also, but it wasn't on the wagon. Sugar, from New Orleans, went for $30 a barrel, and the townsfolk came in to get at least one or two cups each week, as they understood the luxury of it. The winter brought more baking, as farming would be limited to tending the livestock. Greycourt bought a couple of cigars and lit one. The people in the store knew who he was and politely acknowledged his presence. They were careful as not to divulge his identity in the event a Yankee spy was in town.

Greycourt walked around the busy store and went over to the post office desk. Oddly enough, although the Confederacy now controlled its own mail, it still went interstate to the North by way of mail smugglers since mail exchange between the North and the South was forbidden, although mail to Baltimore was allowed. As he gave a letter addressed to Victoria to the postman and the 5¢ for postage, he looked up and saw announcements and posters. Two posters caught his eye.

Mosby was talking to old man Reiser behind the pigpen when Greycourt rode up and asked to speak to the colonel. Obliging, they went into the barn. Leaning against the stall where his horse was, Mosby smiled. "What's so important? What have you got?" he asked.

Greycourt took off his hat. "Those two with us, Chan Goode and Noah Beaudry, are wanted in three states. Bank robbery, murder, and one of those states is Virginia," he said with urgency in his voice.

Mosby shook his head. "Major, those men are important to us. You think I have time to go over the personal history of each man? Sure my men had some trouble, but it's different now."

Greycourt did not like the answer. "Can we relieve those two men?" he asked.

Mosby lowered his eyes and then looked up. "No, Major, we cannot."

Plans were set to raid the Union Army at Fairfax Courthouse in two days. By now, seventy more men had joined up with the Confederate Forty-Third Battalion as the result of the Middleburg and Aldie raids. Scouts returned and advised Mosby of the coordinates and position in Fairfax County, which was in the hands of Union forces under the command of Brigadier General Edwin H. Stoughton. They would be deep in Yankee territory, and the raid would be as daring a ride ever attempted. Greycourt liked the strategy.

Taking twenty-nine men with him, Mosby began the raid around midnight. Surprisingly, there were no sentries posted or any guards around the courthouse. Slowing their gallop to a trot and then to a canter, the rangers quietly swept in and began rounding up the sleeping Yankee soldiers, rousing them from their slumber with hardly any force. Mosby and Greycourt went into General Stoughton's quarters and noticed he was asleep, uncovered, lying on his stomach naked. Mosby drew his sword and gently spanked Stoughton on his bare behind.

Startled, Stoughton turned and saw the two men standing over him. "What's the meaning of this? Who are you?" he asked, rubbing his eyes.

Mosby smiled at Greycourt and then at Stoughton. "Ever heard of Mosby?" he asked.

The general perked up. "Yes, have you caught him?" he asked.

Both men smiled. "I am Mosby," the colonel replied.

"General Jeb Stuart has control of the courthouse. Now get dressed and be quick about it," Greycourt added.

The rangers gathered up their spoils: a Yankee general, two captains, thirty enlisted men, and fifty-eight horses, all without firing a single shot.

As weeks went on and Mosby's raids were more successful at each attempt, his reputation grew, and a price was put on his head by the Union command in Washington. Mosby and any of his rangers, if caught, would be hanged immediately. More men came to Mosby to enlist also. Yankee patrols continued scanning the countryside, harassing the local farmers and townspeople searching for Mosby and any one of his rangers. Difficult as it was, they easily melted into the various populations.

The spring would come early as the beginning of April was warmer than usual; getting farming started and more people outdoors. Chan Goode and Noah Beaudry went to Mosby and asked if they could scout the Maryland-Virginia border as he thought it a good idea and was impressed with their initiative. Upon hearing this, Greycourt, disturbed, requested to go with them, as he just a bad feeling about their motives. Mosby granted permission for him to go and observe and to bring back information. Five men, Chan Goode, Noah Beaudry, Thomas Harney, and a young man by the name of Ab Nevers, with Major Colt Greycourt, rode east toward Maryland with different plans.

Not far from the border, Goode and Beaudry decided to rest the horses before continuing, so they stopped outside of Berryville where there was a farm. Greycourt recognized the farm. Chan Goode dismounted and led his horse to a trough as two dogs came running out from behind the house. Beaudry, Harney, and Nevers stayed on their horses. They noticed Greycourt dismount and go directly to the gray-white stone and dark wood house with smoke billowing out of the chimney. He knocked on the door as Goode watched as a young boy opened it.

Belinda Hunnicutt came to the door, wiping her hands on her apron as two other young boys stood next to her. She looked at him carefully. "I know you. You look different with that mustache an' all. Come in, you and your friends," she said, smiling.

Goode hurried up to the door and pushed in past the three boys.

The girl turned around. "I know you too. You're not welcome," she said with a scowl.

The other three came in as she looked at the five men standing near the table. She stared at Beaudry. "You neither, get out," she barked. She then looked at Greycourt and shook her head. "You're with them—git."

The major was puzzled but remembered what she said when he was there months ago about two men showing up to get her husband to join the Confederate Army. "Hold it. We mean no harm. Water and rest for our horses a bit," Greycourt replied.

She walked over to the wide sink, reached under it, and produced a sawed-off shotgun. "No water, no rest, leave now," she ordered.

Goode and Beaudry laughed as they looked around. Goode took a step toward her, and Greycourt stepped in between, "No. We're leaving right now," he said.

Angered, Beaudry grabbed Goode's arm, and they left with Greycourt standing there looking at her. She put the shotgun back and shook her head.

As the men rode away, Goode was speaking to Beaudry aloud, wanting the others to hear, saying things like "This major is no major here" and "Nobody made this peacock in charge. We didn't invite 'im," angering Greycourt. They decided to stop for the night, but the major turned and rode back.

It was nighttime, and the smoke still billowed from that chimney as he approached the farm. Greycourt knocked on the door as the dogs were barking and fussing.

The young lady came to the door with her shotgun ready. "I said you're not welcome. Leave," she said.

He put his right hand up and asked to come since he was alone. She nodded. He took his hat off and stood there, while her three boys stood by the doorway of their room to watch. "I mean no harm. I'm with those men on a brief mission," he said.

She poured him a cup of coffee. "You're with them. That's all I know." He nodded thanks for the cup. "Those two men came to get my husband. You know what I found out later on, they were paid $10 to bring men to join their army. Hell, they only gave me five when he died," Belinda said solemnly. He then went into his pocket and took out a $10 gold piece and placed it on the table. "I don't want your money. I just want to be left alone," she said, looking at the table.

The five riders found lodging with a farmer about five miles northeast of Berryville. Goode and Beaudry had gotten up early and went to speak to the farmer who was flattered that he could be of assistance to some of Mosby's men.

Sleeping at one end of the barn was Greycourt. He slept away from the others and with one eye open. As Harney and Nevers got up and washed their faces; Goode and Beaudry came into the barn and announced that they'd be heading north to Martinsburg in Maryland to seek out Yankee cavalry reported there. Greycourt, rubbing his eyes, overheard this and asked where they'd heard such information, and they told him their host knew about it as he had been up there recently.

Knowing the terrain and also knowing that Yankee troops were in and around nearby Hagerstown, he thought something about it was odd. It was no secret that there was Union cavalry patrolling along the Maryland Pennsylvania border, and that would include Martinsburg. It would make sense to turn around and head back to Middleburg, back to Mosby, after just obtaining information about troop strength in and around Hagerstown.

Goode and Beaudry would not listen and said just Goode, Beaudry, and Nevers would go north. Greycourt and Harney would stay at the farm. Annoyed, the major abruptly told them that where they go, they all go. The five men set out to the North.

Nevers, the youngest of the five, knew the shortcuts through woods and heavy forest, making their ride faster, bypassing the town of Winchester so they wouldn't be seen. They arrived in Martinsburg before noon and noticed that there were no Yankee cavalry or camps in or even outside of the town. Goode ordered Harney and Greycourt to wait on horseback at the south end of Main Street as they would ride into the heart of the town. Greycourt surmised trouble.

There were shops on both sides of the busy street, a hotel at the corner, and a livery stable at the very north end. The tavern had a large white sign in front displaying its name, "Mary & William's Tavern", that was sure to catch one's eye. Greycourt strained his eyes looking up the street and saw in the middle of the dirt street was the constable's office, and next to that, his eyes stopped—the Bank of Martinsburg. He told Harney to wait as he galloped north directly for the bank.

As Goode and Beaudry dismounted and were about to go in, with Nevers remaining on his horse, Greycourt called out, getting the attention of some people walking on the wooden sidewalk in front of the constable's office. Goode stopped, growled, and sneered at Greycourt as the constable, a gray-haired man of about seventy years old, came out holding his pipe and looking over his spectacles. He looked up at Greycourt.

"Can I help you, young man?" he asked.

Goode, thinking this was Greycourt's way of diverting the old lawman's attention, turned to go into the bank when Greycourt turned to the two men and shouted, "NO!" as they opened the door. The constable, unarmed, was puzzled as he watched Greycourt draw his pistol, pointing it at the men. Beaudry spat on the ground and grabbed Goode's arm as they then mounted up, and the three rode north out of town, cussing under their breath.

That night, the five men took up refuge at a roadside inn north of Boonsboro, which was really a whorehouse. Goode, Beaudry, and Harney welcomed the company of the heavily made-up ladies and had to coax the young Nevers to join them. The ladies teased him about his red face and frail body, joking about his prowess. The husband and wife that ran the house, a well-dressed couple that would look very typical at a church social, tried to relax Nevers by giving him a few shots of their home-brewed whiskey.

Greycourt, not liking the whole scenario, finally went to his defense and told him that he didn't have to do anything that he didn't want to, and they'd both stay out back where the slaves slept until morning. Nevers would have none of it and pulled away, the cheap liquor taking effect, and stayed in the parlor, laughing along at the bawdy jokes about him. Greycourt got a spot up in the hayloft in the barn and dozed off with piano music playing and laughter in the background. They were going back to Mosby the morning.

Greycourt sat on his horse outside of the inn and waited for the others to come out. A well-dressed slave had brought out a cup of coffee to him that he welcomed with a grateful nod as he heard some laughter from inside. Nevers came out, looking as if he went without sleep, and asked the major for money since the four of them could not pay the proprietors, which was causing a bit of a disturbance. Angered by the entire affair, Greycourt reached into the haversack that was hooked to his saddle and grabbed a small purse with some coins. He looked at them and handed them over to the young man who then ran inside.

One by one they came out, Goode, chewing on a biscuit, and Beaudry, rubbing his face as they waited for their horses to be brought out. The inn's owner came out to Greycourt and asked for a few more coins as the ladies usually get extra if men stay overnight. The major told him that the money he got was enough, and if he wanted more, he'd have to get it from his guests. The four men were mounted and ready, except for Harney who wasn't around, and no one knew where he was.

As they impatiently waited, Harney was spotted by Nevers riding on the northern road waving his hat. They paused as he rode up. "Hold on. I have it," he exclaimed.

The men looked at him. "We're going back to Middleburg. The major said so," replied Beaudry.

Harney shook his head. "Not yet. I found what I've been lookin' for," he said with a smile.

★★★

Tessa had packed two large suitcases and one carpetbag for Mrs. Greycourt. Since England abolished slavery many years before, the Greycourts did not want to take Paul and Tessa with them across the Atlantic to London and thought it best that their slaves stayed in Baltimore with their daughter and her new baby. The Judge had meetings with two members of the British Parliament over the past two days and was sure he had them convinced that the Confederacy was an independent country worthy of an alliance and trade agreements. He would join them on their trip back to England and request an audience with Victoria, Queen of England.

The Judge was planning to stay in London for several weeks, hoping that it would take a long time to get on the queen's audience list and also hoping the war would continue. He was confident that he would be received positively and that he'd also get treaties and agreements signed. Mrs. Greycourt was excited to travel to England, mostly to get far away from the war, but she worried about Colt and her son-in-law, Jonathan.

As they had dinner in the hotel dining room, Mrs. Greycourt took a bite from the delectable plate of peppered braised beef and creamed potatoes and leaned forward slightly. "Isn't that Vee Leland with a gentleman at that corner table?" she asked.

The Judge tilted his head as his knife cut through a large steak, took a bite, and turned around to his right. "I'm not sure. I don't think so," he replied.

She took a sip of wine. "I think it is," she said, lowering her voice. "What would she be doing here? Isn't the Philharmonic touring in Canada? That's what the newspaper said," she continued.

The Judge's upper lip tightened. "That's right. That wouldn't be her. She is in Canada," he answered, taking a small bite and then sipping coffee.

A waiter came over to pour more coffee and to announce the dessert menu. She was about to get up and walk over to see if it was, in fact, Victoria Leland, when the Judge quickly suggested chocolate cake or a raspberry tort and rushed her choice. She stood up, annoyed at the discussion for dessert. As she watched the couple get up and leave the dining room, she took the cloth napkin and dabbed around her mouth and hurriedly went out to get a closer look.

A carriage took the couple quickly away, and Mrs. Greycourt stood at the doorway watching, not having a very good look. She returned to the table as the Judge finished his meal and told her that he ordered coffee and the raspberry tort. The dessert was finished, and the Judge left payment with a generous gratuity for the waiter.

He looked at his pocket watch as they walked out of the dining room. At the front desk, there was a small envelope addressed to him. He read the note, nodded, and said he had a meeting in an hour in the dining room.

Sitting in the far left corner of the hotel dining room, the Judge puffed on his pipe as a waiter brought a cup of coffee and the late newspaper. He checked his pocket watch and looked up to see Dalrymple and Victoria enter and walk toward his table arm in arm. They sat, and the waiter brought two more cups and saucers of fancy China with gold inlaid on the edges. The Judge told the waiter to leave the coffee pot and put a quarter in the waiter's hand.

As Dalrymple started some small talk, the Judge interrupted, "What in the hell are the two of you doing having dinner in this hotel? I told you where I'd be. My wife saw the both of you, and I had to convince her that she was wrong. She even followed you out of the hotel but couldn't get a good look," he said, his eyes glaring at the well-dressed young man. "The next time I tell you something, you'd better listen, got me?"

The two nodded.

"Now, what's the situation at the factory?" he asked as he took out an envelope with paper money, Yankee money, and handed some bills to both of them.

Dalrymple looked at the money and lowered his eyes. "I thought I'd get a bit more. After all, I—"

"Did what?" the Judge interrupted him.

"She's done more than you have," he said, pointing to Victoria.

"Now, what's the news of the factory?" he asked again.

Victoria sipped her coffee and gave the Judge an account of the building for the manufacturing of cannon balls and small arms.

The building's new addition was almost finished and would bring in a new three-year government contract. This would be important in order to continue the war they all agreed. Dalrymple and Reginald, his son, can handle the contract; she continued to explain. Although he was apprehensive about it since he'll be in England, he agreed.

The Judge's pipe went out, and the waiter came over with a box of matches.

Dalrymple took out a cigar to be lit by the short, lean waiter. "All letters will be sent to my address here at this hotel, so it's up to the two of you to send them on since there are no mail deliveries to Europe. I trust you to do this Victoria," he said.

★★★

The rain came down a little heavier as Greycourt waited for Mosby to come into the tavern on Main Street in Middleburg. The successful raid on Miskell's Farm routing the Yankees sent more accolades from Richmond and bestowed honors on Stuart as a shrewd strategist. Greycourt placed his hat on the chair next to him and saw Mosby come in, shaking off the rain. Mosby shook Greycourt's hand after they saluted each other, and the tavern owner brought over a bottle of brandy and two small glasses. Their mission was a success, and Mosby was going to recommend a promotion for the young major regarding the daring raid he was in command of. Greycourt wasn't so pleased.

"Sir, Chan Goode and Noah Beaudry must be arrested," he said sternly.

Mosby was surprised and sipped the brandy. "Arrested? They were on that raid with you. Maybe they'll get commendations," he answered.

Greycourt shook his head. "Sir," he said in a low voice so no one else in the tavern would hear. "That whole ride into Maryland was to rob a bank, nothing more. I stopped it. We were in Martinsburg, and they tried to rob the bank," he said.

Mosby, the lawyer in him, took over. "Did you see them rob it? Did they announce it was a robbery?" he asked.

Greycourt lowered his eyes and shook his head. "I stopped them from going into the bank. I knew their intentions," he replied.

Mosby pursed his lips. "So they didn't even go into the bank?" he asked.

"No," he replied.

The colonel wasn't even slightly convinced.

Greycourt wiped his mouth with the back of his hand and sat up. "Sir, let me tell you about that factory. The whole incident, if I may," he said.

Mosby nodded.

"Thomas Harney came riding up to us in front of a whorehouse before we were about to head back home, barking about a munitions factory in Pennsylvania in a town called Waynesboro. He said one of the whores let it slip that sometimes the workers there would make the long trip down to Boonsboro. He rode up there and looked around and saw only one guard for the whole building. Without talking about it, the four took off, so I followed. We had to be careful as there was a full brigade of Union cavalry in Hagerstown, so we had to ride eastward. We almost ran smack-dab into a Union patrol but hid in the woods until they passed. Harney got all the information from the guard during the night. He told the man he was lost and needed to head to Baltimore. The guard told him that the factory closed at midnight and opened at six each morning. We waited until an hour after midnight."

Mosby was very intrigued with the story and leaned back to listen as Greycourt continued.

"The five of us went around to the back of the factory as the guard came out to make his rounds. Goode and Beaudry stopped him, holding his arms behind him and pulling his head back. That guard was all seventy-five years old and had a flintlock pistol for a weapon. He put up no resistance as they knocked him down and held his head against the ground. I knocked them both off the old man and helped him up. I told him we weren't going to hurt him and that we were just there getting gun powder and ammunition, nothing more. We were walking through the place when Harney got a bit excited when he found a huge bomb. The old guard suggested that we take what we wanted and just leave. Goode slapped the guard, and I pulled a gun on them and told them they were on report, young Nevers too. Just then, Harney came running, shouting that he placed a bomb in the hot furnace section at the rear where it looked like they were building an addition. I grabbed the guard, and we ran outside to mount up. As I was pulling the old guard up on my horse, Goode shot and killed him."

Greycourt's eyes narrowed as he described the murder; he choked up a bit as he described how. As he was attempting to get the old guard up onto the back of his horse, Goode turned around and shot him dead. The others rode off. Confused about what to do, he attempted to pull the dead man up but couldn't. The guard fell, and Greycourt had to hurriedly gallop away from the factory. He got about a hundred yards from the building when it exploded in a thunderous blast, sending fireballs and debris into the night sky.

"They rode ahead of me. I caught up with them in Berryville, and I'm glad I did. Nevers doesn't know any better. He's just a boy. Goode and Beaudry are murderers and must be dealt with," he said sternly.

Mosby slowly nodded. "Major Greycourt, so Goode shot and killed a guard, and you want him arrested? Don't you know what we're doing here?" he asked.

Greycourt got angry. "Sir, they're outlaws. It's not the cause, it's *their* cause," he shot back.

Mosby got annoyed at the major. "Sir, I have battalions formed now, good men. Sure, there's some men of, I guess, questionable honor, but I can't interview and question every volunteer. Some of these outlaws, as you call them, are vital to us."

A few men came into the tavern now and flicked the rain off their hats and coats. Mosby poured some more brandy in Greycourt's glass and wiped his forehead with his handkerchief as he listened to the major.

"Sir, they rode way ahead of me. I finally caught up with them back in Berryville and walked in on Goode at a farmhouse."

A few of the men that came in were new volunteers and noticed Mosby and Greycourt sitting in the back in serious discussion. Greycourt noticed them leaning in, trying to listen.

"Goode tried to have his way with the lady of the house, and I busted in on him, with pistols drawn," he said.

Mosby's eyes widened. "You pulled your guns on him?" he asked, surprised.

The major nodded. "Yes, sir, I did. I took him by the arm and threw him out."

Mosby tilted his head. He didn't like what he heard.

The others rode off with Goode, cussing, the dogs barking and Beaudry firing a shot into the night sky. Greycourt stayed with the young girl to make sure she was all right. She was shaking a bit, afraid of what might have happened. She then looked at him and pulled him toward her and hugged him with tears running down her face. Greycourt said nothing as he held her.

★★★

Du Seine and Ortega sat in their tent reading their mail as a horse rode up and an orderly ran over to take the mount. It was Major Greycourt returning from his assignment with Colonel Mosby. The two captains were anxious for their friend's return.

The major went into the tent and saw his friends looking up at him; both seemed to keep from laughing. Taking his hat and gray frock coat off, he looked at the two men and tilted his head slightly to the left. "What is it? C'mon, what?" he asked, smiling.

Du Seine and Ortega broke out laughing, Ortega, with his head back, and du Seine, almost doubled over. "You look like an outlaw, a des-per-a-do," du Seine said. "What happened? Didn't pack a razor?"

Greycourt rubbed his face and noticed the three-day stubble on his face and the red neckerchief tied around his neck. Looking at them, he burst out laughing and swung his hat at them. As they composed themselves, Greycourt flopped down on his cot and stretched. "Oh, I'm sorry I didn't get to speak to the general about you and your brothers," he said as he quickly sat back up.

Ortega shook his head. "I know, Colt. You had to move out. I am to meet with the general tomorrow morning about our leave. I also heard about your duel. I'll be there with you and du Seine. I can't let my friend get satisfaction without me."

The stack of letters waited for him as he took off the red neckerchief and unbuttoned his blouse. He was going to get cleaned up and back into uniform for his report to General Stuart.

An orderly came into the tent with two buckets of water, one warm, one cold, and also left a straight razor on the desk next to his cot. He noticed a letter on top of the stack from Victoria.

Cleaned up and feeling like an officer again, he walked down to the slave quarters and looked in on Scipio who had recovered but was scared to go back to the camp without Greycourt there. Jubilant to see his master and friend, Scipio and some of the other slaves went over to greet him, taking their hats off and respectfully bowing slightly. Word of the impending duel had gotten back to the slave camp, and they looked at Greycourt as their champion. The old slave, looking at the major with admiration, bowed and said they would all be at his beck and call if he ever needed anything.

The major walked with Scipio, and some of the slaves followed. An old woman, taking a break from the large tubs of hot water for laundry, came over and handed him a cup of cold lemonade. He was due at General Stuart's tent in a few minutes.

Sergeant Major Ward stood outside the general's tent in his usual stance with his huge arms folded and standing erect. Banjo Sweeney strummed a tune as Greycourt approached the tent. Mrs. Stuart and their children had just left. The camp was always in good spirits when spouses came to visit. Stuart was especially enthused after seeing his lovely wife and family. The general was glad to see the major and greeted him with a salute and hearty handshake. Stuart got out from behind his desk and sat next to Greycourt as he listened to the description of what became popularly known as Mosby's Partisan Rangers and their exploits.

Describing raids and attacks behind enemy lines in Northern Virginia, Greycourt painted a picture of daring-do in exciting fashion with Stuart hanging on to every word. Then the description changed as he told Stuart the rangers were outlaws, terrorizing good people that were indifferent to the Union or Confederacy. He particularly described the criminal antics of Goode and Beaudry and their youthful lackey Nevers. Greycourt felt that Mosby's operations should be more military-like, and Stuart agreed, but the general felt the Rebel colonel should continue his operations as they were being heralded as a success in the South.

Stuart again thanked the major for his service and was pleased to have a fine officer like him in his command. The general, looking invigorated and as confident as he's ever looked, told Greycourt that this evening, Generals Lee, Jackson, Early, Longstreet, and himself were meeting to plan another strategy to rid the south of the Yankee invaders.

CHAPTER THIRTEEN

"You're gonna hang."

Greycourt kept hearing that over and over for the past hour. Geiger and Morse had taken over most of the questioning, and each time they felt the frustration in his answers, they shouted that phrase, "You're gonna hang."

Pinkerton lit a fresh cigar and offered Greycourt one, which he declined. Loosening his tie and unbuttoning the top button of his white blouse, Pinkerton felt he had to take over. Geiger and Morse were good men, but they were greatly lacking the skills to handle this situation.

The room got quiet for a minute as Pinkerton wiped his face with his handkerchief. "You've been a Rebel major for a long time. How's that? Shouldn't you be a general by now?" he asked.

Greycourt shrugged slightly. "I was promised a promotion to colonel, but it never came about. I was expecting the rank of colonel after Chancellorsville, actually, before that. I guess things got fouled up after that."

Morse leaned forward, shaking his head, looking at Geiger. They both felt that their prisoner was stalling. Pinkerton thought the opposite.

With no sign of wearing down, Greycourt began to describe the excitement of the next campaign—not only a decisive victory for the South, but it was also proclaimed a brilliant battle plan. Pinkerton was very interested. He had heard about Chancellorsville but never got firsthand information from a Rebel. Geiger turned and left the room. Morse leaned against the wall, eager to hear what Greycourt was about to describe. Although the Confederate major could only describe the actions of his company, there was a lot of interest about one of the most talked-about battles in the entire war up to that time.

As Greycourt began to speak, Geiger walked back in with a leather satchel, much to Pinkerton's ire. They all looked at Geiger as he handed the satchel to Pinkerton. Removing a fancy rolled-up item with a ribbon tied around it, Pinkerton handed it to Greycourt.

★★★

The campaign started out with as much excitement as any other in the Stuart camp. Word was circulating of another Union offensive as the result of Mosby's scouting. After the meeting of the generals, all the brigades would be moving out.

Ortega and du Seine were shining their boots when Greycourt walked in and told them the mess tent was ready. Scipio had been there and put out a fresh set of clothes, shined his boots and belt buckle. His letters were neatly stacked, and he looked forward to reading them after the officer's meeting set for an hour after supper. The three went to the large tent together and sat at the end of a very long table at the east end. They feasted on full plates of smoked ham, boiled potatoes and carrots, hot biscuits and sweet butter, hot coffee, and strawberry rhubarb pie.

Du Seine could not stop talking about the birth of his new son, and Ortega was just as excited to get a letter from his wife about the birth of his first child around the month of September.

They finished their hearty meal and answered Officer's Call to meet in Stuart's tent. They were to move out the next morning to support Lee and Jackson's holding of their supply lines across the Rappahannock River in Chancellorsville, as reports were that Union Major General George Stoneman, under Major General Joseph Hooker's orders, was to cross the Rappahannock River and cut all lines and engage the Rebels.

Mosby's information was not only accurate but was also provided quickly enough to give Lee and Jackson time to get their troops in place. They would be up against a much larger force, almost twice their size, but because of the cunning of Lee and Jackson, they had a plan, a plan that would almost defy the odds.

Stuart was to flank Jackson's movements, screening his foot cavalry, as they were called, as to confuse the Union commanders of their troop strength. The First Virginia Cavalry, only two brigades at the ready, was to keep the communication lines open from the Rappahannock River to the Orange Turnpike—spreading his troopers thin. This was to prevent any Union movement around Jackson's flank. Also, at Stuart's suggestion, they were to assist in holding the flank with sharpshooters from the Fourth Virginia Cavalry and, at the same time, protecting Lee's rear.

The first day of fighting saw Major Greycourt take B Company of the First Virginia east to support Jubal Early. Facing a formidable Union force led by Generals Sedgwick and Reynolds just south of Fredericksburg. The railroad was in serious jeopardy of being destroyed. Early, a tough old Virginian, saved the day as he took on Sedgwick, allowing Lee and Jackson to successfully attack Union forces west and save the railroad.

Greycourt kept communication lines open within the ranks, but most importantly, he protected Early's flank from disaster. In the heat of fighting, Reynolds attempted to turn Early in. Greycourt's men, armed with only pistols, were mounted and held Prospect Hill to the south, forcing Reynolds back as the Union general thought for sure he was facing an entire cavalry brigade.

Greycourt, Ortega, and du Seine, with their company, regrouped just outside of Fredericksburg at Marye's Heights, giving their horses a much needed rest and feed. They received orders to stay put and support Early and, at the same time, provide information back to Stuart who was supporting Lee by protecting Jackson's flank. Jackson and Lee devised a plan to split their forces and have Jackson's men surprise attack Hooker at Chancellorsville.

Scouts went out to monitor Union movements, and they got close enough to their encampment that they could hear soldiers snoring as they slept. It looked as if General Reynolds had moved his troops closer to their position at Marye's Heights.

Greycourt, Ortega, and du Seine, on foot, went into Fredericksburg to see if Union troops had taken the town. To their surprise, they had not. It looked as if Reynolds was moving north on the other side of the river, possibly to support Hooker at Chancellorsville, but he was moving at a snail's pace. The three officers quickly got back to their camp and sent couriers to Stuart. With this information, Stuart cleared all roads and paths between Early and Lee, which gave them easy accessibility to reinforce each other.

On the second of May, Jackson surprised Hooker by smashing his relaxed troopers in a frenzied, chaotic run, forcing Hooker into total confusion. Early attacked Sedgwick at the Old Richmond Road; Reynolds was nowhere near Sedgwick and out of position to support Hooker. Early held, and the Union troops, confused and defeated, withdrew back to Washington once again.

The cavalry continued to patrol until the counties were free of Yankee troops and then went back to camp. Stuart was ordered to General Lee's headquarters outside of Richmond for a report and also to pay his gentlemanly respects. However, the brilliant victory was overshadowed . . .

Stonewall Jackson was dead.

Perhaps the greatest military feat ever attempted that resulted in total victory was completely overshadowed by the death of General Thomas J. "Stonewall" Jackson.

Jackson was shot by his own sentries on the night of May 2 as they mistook the general and his staff for a Yankee patrol. A volley was fired, wounding Jackson and killing some of his men and horses. The glory of their victory was empty.

The South prepared for the funeral a few days later. His prayers were met as Jackson waited until his wife came to him before he died.

★★★

Reginald James Greycourt was not himself. He was nervous, sat with a decanter of half-filled brandy, and just stared; he wouldn't pay any attention to his children playing right in front of him. Greycourt Manor wasn't the same, he thought. Of the ninety-seven slaves working the manor and its fields, only forty-five remained; the others had run off. Their overseer had done an admirable job of keeping the cotton and tobacco moving, but the blockade and suspension of trading with the North had badly hurt their revenue stream. He was aware that Union forces would possibly move into the county one day soon and loot anything not nailed down. The continuous invasions to take Richmond could very well succeed.

There were no house slaves, so his wife had been tending to things herself. Reginald was never this anxious. He stared at the envelope that rested on his lap and shook his head in disbelief. In his other hand, he held a note with words he'd thought he'd never read. He had to get word to his father.

★★★

Stuart's camp was a bit more subdued than usual. Banjo Sweeney played a more tepid set of songs, and the fiddle playing around the camp was just as serene. Sergeant Major Ward stood with his massive arms folded, his usual stance, outside of the general's tent listening to the meeting. Greycourt, von Borcke, and the other staff members listened to Stuart's report from his meeting with senior staff in Richmond.

The victory at Chancellorsville gave a huge boost for the morale of the South and heightened England's outlook for the South's credibility. But Jackson's death dampened the entire campaign.

Stuart had never seen Lee so distraught. The general, who took command of Jackson's Second Corps, was commended for his ability to successfully command infantry on the battle's third day. Stuart was to take command of Jackson's troops until a suitable replacement could be assigned.

Once again, Greycourt, Ortega, and du Seine were given commendations for their swift and successful support of Early and keeping the flanks and rears of the army safe and intact. Greycourt's reports of Union General Reynolds's movements were vital to the victory, and Stuart was recommending him for a promotion to colonel.

To keep the morale strong, there was a bare-knuckle match between Ward and a big North Carolina farm boy for the evening. The paymaster had just arrived, and Confederate dollars were bet freely.

Greycourt, thrilled at the word of his pending promotion, requested permission to visit his family in Richmond. It was granted, but he really wanted to see Victoria, even though he knew she was in New York. With Scipio at his side, they rode into the evening for Richmond.

The city was bristling with activity. The Tredegar Iron Works was on a demanding schedule, turning out armor for new ironclads, heavy locomotive parts, and the development of the Brooke Rifle, an enormous railway cannon. The only problem, a significant one, was the growing scarcity of raw materials.

Greycourt and Scipio rode to the Richmond Hotel where his parents lived only to find out that they had left months ago, leaving a forwarding address in Baltimore. He learned that Reginald and his family were also gone. They headed to Baltimore.

Tessa and Paul made sure their guests were very comfortably welcomed; they prepared a hearty meal. Greycourt left to allow Scipio time with his family, even considering letting him stay while returning to camp alone. He decided to ride into the city and drop off a letter to Victoria at her address at the City Hotel, knowing it would be forwarded to her, wherever she may be.

Greycourt noticed Union soldiers patrolling on foot around the city, strolling in the streets with their weapons at the ready. Baltimore was more Confederate than Union; it was feared a Rebel uprising would take the city. Dressed as a civilian, he rode about the city, inconspicuously passing soldiers in blue and then stopping at a tavern to get out of the unusual late May heat.

As he sat with a long, thin cigar and a brandy, three Union officers walked in and began casually talking, sounding upset and irritated, causing Greycourt to lean in a bit. He got up to get a newspaper at the corner of the long bar and overheard one of the officers say that it was folly to withdraw all troops back to Washington in order to regroup under another weak command.

General Hooker was under fire for the debacle at Chancellorsville, and the president wanted to ponder what to do next. The newspaper, *The Baltimore Sun,* had an interesting article about General Stonewall Jackson and the effect his death would have on the South. To his surprise, the article was very positive and as a testament to the late general's skill and leadership. Greycourt saw an opportunity.

★★★

The dining room in the Saint James Hotel had one of the best menus in the city. Their oyster appetizer was the most popular, and the roasted lamb shank had been written about in most of the newspapers. Although she really wasn't very thrilled with the company, Victoria always made sure she ordered a full dinner, selecting the most expensive items. She sat across Clive G. Dalrymple at the very fancy table, and to her right, sat a squirrely looking fellow, Nigel Blaine.

The conversation was mostly about the war and the incompetence of the Union. Dalrymple commented that it was good for business, at least for a while.

Victoria was puzzled. "What do you mean good for business, at least for a while?" she asked.

Dalrymple smirked. "I think the baked flounder with capers looks good. What about you, Blaine?" he asked.

The thin man to his left nodded. "Looks good, with wild rice," he answered.

It was obvious that they did not want to respond. Not used to being ignored, she pressed, "What business? What happened?"

Dalrymple shook his head and sipped his whiskey.

Blaine was beginning to get nervous. He was about to respond to her when Dalrymple spoke up. "The theater tonight will be fascinating," he said with a bit of sarcasm. "Edwin Booth as Shakespeare's *Hamlet* should be a thrill."

Blaine said nothing, and Victoria tilted her head slightly in bewilderment. The waiter came and took their orders and poured another whiskey for the always impeccably dressed Dalrymple.

Blaine took off his spectacles and cleaned them with his embroidered handkerchief and looked at Dalrymple. "Do we have anything new to tell the boss?" he asked him.

Nodding, Dalrymple smiled at the always elegant lady. "Maybe, I don't know. What can you tell us presently, my dear girl?" he inquired.

Victoria slowly shook her head and couldn't decide if she wanted to disclose the new letters she received or not. Victoria reached down for her satin purse to retrieve the letters and then tensed. They had all been opened and read.

Blaine leaned forward to fill his plate as she looked at Dalrymple. *Did he have to be so damned good looking,* she thought?

★★★

About a dozen horses were being driven by three wranglers around the camp as the spring sunrise seemed to invigorate the cavalrymen. Coffee pots on camp fires and the long mess tent for the officers were giving off the sweet aromas of smoked hams, homemade sausages, biscuits, and fresh strawberries, all compliments of the good citizens of Richmond.

Ortega and du Seine had just finished writing letters home and were waiting for Greycourt to return from an early morning horseback ride. The major loved to ride his reliable and impressive mount each morning with Scipio, the best horseman he had ever seen, usually at his side.

The word around the camp was that Stuart was planning a huge cavalry gala for the beginning of June, requesting a review by General Lee. The camp, now located near Culpepper Courthouse, amassed a powerful force of over nine thousand men, not including the famed horse artillery. Stuart felt proud and confident that he could best any cavalry pitted against him by the Union. The victory at Chancellorsville was such a morale booster that Lee had more aggressive plans that he took to Richmond for approval.

Greycourt returned and said he had to get washed up, shaved, and groomed before breakfast, much to his friends' dismay as the aromas were very enticing. They were impatient, so he just washed his face and hands, combed his hair, and put on a clean blouse.

The three sat together; Ortega and du Seine exchanged joyous information from their letters, mostly about the new du Seine vineyard and the Ortegas' drive to Northern Iowa. Greycourt regretted that he never got permission to dismiss Ortega and his two brothers to assist their family, but Ortega, by no means, held it against him. Big, full plates of food rested before them waiting to be devoured with orderlies poring rich, hot coffee and chicory. There was an Officer's Call for noon, the three expecting to be filled in on all the information about the upcoming event.

The meeting took three hours. Not only did they plan for the grand showing of cavalry, but also to screen and protect Lee's army six miles northeast of Culpepper and to set up a bivouac along the Rappahannock River. Greycourt had known about these plans for weeks; Stuart confided in him about an operation that would, if successful, put an end to the war.

Greycourt was to lead a patrol to find an area where they could set up. With Ortega and du Seine riding with him, he found an area that would be large enough to accommodate Stuart's entire cavalry command. The area was called Brandy Station.

CHAPTER FOURTEEN

A West Point education is an honorable and distinguished one.

Military leadership, camaraderie, and most importantly, the study of engineering and artillery are the focal points at the academy. The student-soldiers are all disciplined, serious, and gentlemen. The large fort overlooking the Hudson River in New York is a reminder of the Continental Army and the fight for freedom from tyranny, perseverance and intestinal fortitude fought through hardships to transform the Thirteen Colonies into the United States of America.

Young men apply with a letter of recommendation from prominent citizens, usually politicians or judges. The emphasis is character. Colton James Greycourt was given a letter of recommendation from a friend of the family and fellow Virginian, Archibald Stuart. A revered veteran of the War of 1812, Stuart was a member of the United States House of Representatives and the Virginia Senate. One of his last acts of statesmanship before he died in September 1855 was to write a letter of recommendation for young Greycourt. Even though he presented it to the Greycourt family, the appointment came later in 1857. Greycourt embraced the cadet life of discipline, but most of all, he enjoyed the camaraderie.

His first two years were about getting acclimated to the rigidity of the life of early morning exercise, breakfast, classroom instruction, lunch, field instructions, horsemanship, study, dinner, and free time. Cadets Hugh Judson Kilpatrick, John Pelham, Mathias W. Henry,

Olin Rice, and George A. Custer were good friends, study partners, and frequent engagers of carrying on. Greycourt and Custer were usually challenging each other to friendly bouts of swordplay, boxing, and horsemanship. The skills of both these cadets were admired, especially Custer's fencing ability.

Greycourt had trouble with his engineering courses, as mathematics was not one of his strong areas, but in subjects like military tactics and military history, he excelled. In the spring of 1859, he was assigned to Fort Myers, Florida, in Seminole country.

The battle-hardened veterans of the Seminole Wars welcomed the young cadet as he was given the last bunk at the end of the row in the barracks. He was thoroughly warned about the annoying mosquitoes and bad meals. Nonetheless, Greycourt and four other cadets took their assignment eagerly and with vigor.

There were three Seminole Wars spanning from 1816 to early 1858. The garrison at Fort Myers, on the Caloosahatchee River on the gulf coast, was a strategic location that guarded the passage from the Atlantic waterways from the Seminoles. Weary from years of fighting, most of the Seminoles agreed to move to the Oklahoma territory. Many stayed, moving into the Everglades among new white settlers, causing more conflict. Small uprisings occurred and were put down; there were frequent threats of wiping out the entire tribe there if things didn't stop.

Greycourt was assigned to cavalry duty with about forty cavalry militiamen participating in drills and patrols. The heat, sometimes reaching one hundred degrees, was unbearable at times, and wearing a uniform made of wool didn't help. Malaria was also a problem, keeping the medical staff busy. He had never seen an alligator, and the intriguing animals were frequent visitors. The instruction was just to ignore them and they'll go away, and they did.

Colonel Gustavus Loomis, a tough New Englander and veteran of the War of 1812 and Mexico, was the commandant and commander of the Department of Florida. Gray-brown beard and mustache,

Loomis had little patience for the natives and treated the remaining Seminoles like children, frequently scolding and threatening. He particularly liked Greycourt's demeanor and "regimental" look.

Fort Myers was tough on horses. Grain and hay had to be shipped in almost daily. The cadet from Virginia took extra care of his mount, gaining him the admiration of the militiamen as patrols through the thick bulrushes and swamp required skilled horsemanship. Greycourt mastered that quickly. In spite of the heat, malaria, mosquitoes, and bad food, Greycourt thoroughly enjoyed his two months at the fort. He learned upon leaving, returning to school, that Colonel Loomis would request him the next summer.

★★★

Belinda Hunnicutt worked hard every day. She spent a good part of the day tending to chickens, a few goats, gardening, and some plowing. She also made sure her three sons could read and write well by dedicating each afternoon to learning. As she washed her face and arms after a long afternoon of plowing and working to fix a back fence, she noticed that the postman came to deliver a letter. Her folks lived in Delaware and never wrote; her in-laws never corresponded. The letter, postmarked from Richmond, was from Colton James Greycourt.

Excited, she opened the letter, and a $10 bill, Yankee money, fell to the floor. She scooped it up and held it tight. She read the sweet note thanking her for her hospitality and permitting him to sleep over at her home the last time he was there. The money was something to help get through the difficult times. He wrote that he would come by again. She looked at the note, closed her eyes, and kissed his signature. Dogs started barking as her boys ran quickly into the house to stand behind her. It sounded like three horses riding up.

Belinda quickly went to the fireplace and grabbed the double-barrel shotgun leaning next to it. Already loaded, she stood, pointing it at the slightly opened door as her sons trembled behind her, clutching her apron. Two men stepped in and looked around.

Noticing the weapon pointed at them, Goode and Beaudry smiled as they walked in.

"One more step and I shoot. There's a shot for each of you, and I never miss," she said, scowling.

Goode laughed. "Hell, we just want maybe a hot meal, ya know, feedin' the boys fightin' fer the cause an' all."

She tensed and steadied her trigger finger. "Get out, get out now!" she yelled.

Beaudry looked at her and took Goode by the arm. "C'mon, Chan, not now. We can always come back."

Goode nodded. "Yep, we'll be back. I can tell ya that."

Belinda took a step toward them. "You won't be back, not if Colt can help it," she answered.

The two looked at each other. "Colt, ya mean that popinjay? Yeah, I'll want him here so he can watch me take good care of you," Goode replied.

Angered, she tightened her grip. "GET OUT!"

★★★

It was hot. The May winds gave way to the June heat that wasn't very kind to the horses and troopers that came into camp. There were over 9,500 cavalry troopers in addition to four batteries of horse artillery amassed at the Virginia town of Brandy Station. All were preparing for the giant gala to show off Stuart's entire command. Generals Lee, Longstreet, and Ewell were safely encamped at Culpepper Courthouse, confident of the cavalry general's protection from Yankee attack. Stuart, also very confident, was almost too cocky. He believed that the entire Union Army had retreated to

Washington, licking their wounds, and wouldn't dare mount any new offensives after the debacle at Chancellorsville.

Cold lemonade was passed around in Stuart's tent as his officers gathered to get final instructions for the grand showing. In two days, they would honor General Robert E. Lee's victories with a salute to his leadership. Greycourt was to lead three companies of Fitzhugh Lee's brigade, with du Seine and Ortega flanking him. The regimental band was to continuously play.

Newspapermen from Baltimore, Richmond, and as far as Mobile, Alabama, were already in camp, excited about the showing. The entire event was to be led by Heros von Borcke, wearing his bright blue Prussian dress uniform with orange piping. The troopers were excited at the paradelike atmosphere around camp as wagons of smoked meats and fresh strawberries rolled in. The grand review was all set.

The June morning was hot, but a breeze from the north made it bearable. Orderlies and slaves hurried to get horses ready for the officers. Everyone was dressed in their finest uniforms, with sabers and boots shined. Flags were pressed and finely mounted; buglers were shining their instruments—the pride of the Confederacy. They had a clearing picked out about two miles southwest of Brandy Station that could accommodate the entire review with a hill for the spectators to overlook it. The band got there early, as did the press, with von Borcke directing the set up. A little after dawn the entire camp moved out.

Stuart, astride his magnificent steed, Virginia, rode up the hill and noticed that Longstreet and Ewell were there. Where was Lee? He was informed that Lee had requested to attend an emergency meeting with President Davis and would not be present for the review. Stuart, disappointed, proceeded. Waving his beautifully plumed hat for the band to begin paying "Dixie", he watched his cavalry canter around the field. Giving von Borcke the signal, all nine thousand plus riders charged in battle simulation.

With sabers drawn, the riders charged and turned their steeds with lightning precision, charging in companies, screaming the infamous "Rebel Yell." Onlookers from all around the countryside cheered, the ladies waving handkerchiefs, little boys waving their hats. The members of the press could not get enough of Stuart's continuous bragging about his troops, the "best in the entire Confederacy", much to Longstreet's annoyance.

Greycourt, outstanding in his gray dress uniform with shiny boots and spurs, proudly led his companies in their charges. Even more proud, he represented General Fitzhugh Lee who had to stay back in camp to quell his rheumatism. The major was sure he'd get his promotion to colonel at the end of the day.

The finale was a presentation of the entire cavalry, with Stuart leading the huge procession. Refreshment tents were set up back at camp. Stuart declared a holiday for everyone. Civilians and the press were invited back to help celebrate the South.

At the end of the day, Stuart had gotten word that General Lee was back. He quickly sent one of his staff to invite the general and his staff to a viewing the next day; Lee accepted. Once again, the entire camp rose before dawn and readied themselves for the grand review. Only this day seemed hotter and uncomfortable for the horses. The press was eager to see Lee and gathered around him as he sat on his mount, Traveler, waiting for the review to begin.

Adorned with a colorful garland wreath of the finest spring flowers around his horse, Stuart, with his head held high, led the three-mile-long column of men in a slow walk onto the field. Today there would be no charging, no firing of blanks from their pistols into the air, and no artillery fire.

The band played. Riders saluted Lee upon hearing "eyes right." The splendid pageantry and beauty impressed Lee immensely. He admired his general's control of the gusto and energy so effortlessly. Lee descended the reviewing stand and rode down to review each company and rider on their mounts.

Much to his dismay, he noted the poor condition of the saddles and how the horse needed rest. The carbines were of poor quality, looking as if they were hastily manufactured. He instructed his staff to make notations to better equip this cavalry with better tack and weapons, but that order would have to wait until after their next campaign.

★★★

It was a mess, a complete mess.

After the review for General Lee, Stuart set up his headquarters on Fleetwood Hill, a rise near the small Brandy Station railroad station. His men were spread two miles to the north, stretching another seven miles from the confluence of the Hazel and Rappahannock Rivers to screen Lee's flank upon the trek to invade the North. Little did Stuart know that the grand reviews of the previous days were carefully watched by the Union general of Cavalry of the Army of the Potomac, Alfred Pleasanton.

Greycourt's eyes opened. It was still dark. He sat up, rubbed his face, and noticed he was so tired that he had only taken his boots off before falling asleep. He looked down and saw a hole in his left sock at the big toe. Having none of that, he fumbled in the dark using a glint of moonlight to search for his kit bag. It must have been about four thirty in the morning. Frustrated at not finding socks, he just slipped his boots on and left the tent.

In the quiet of the early morning, he noticed birds flying through a dense fog and sounds of trouble to the east. He ran about twenty yards, heard gun shots, and stopped, recognizing the sound of running horses coming closer. Greycourt instantly ran through the camp, shouting, "BUGLER, BUGLER, SOUND ASSEMBLY! ORDERLY, HORSES! HORSES!"

He ran into his tent and violently woke both du Seine and Ortega, pulling them from their bunks and shouting for them to get their mounts. Yankee horsemen galloped through the camp, firing pistols, forcing men to scurry under cots and to take cover behind anything. The chaotic mayhem bustling all around the tents was causing chaos around their horses that were tied up in the stockade, encircling the camp.

Greycourt was able to grab two of his revolvers and his saber as he hitched up his suspenders and cut behind the tent, heading for the horses with du Seine. Ortega ran out, looking for his brothers. Quickly saddling up, the two officers rapidly rode north toward the sound of the gun, to Stuart's quarters.

Mounted men, only dressed in their undergarments, met up with Greycourt, attempting to get some kind of guidance and direction. The surprise attack had swept through the encampment, scattering the troopers. The sun hadn't yet risen as the riders ran headlong into the rear of the Yankee cavalry with swords flailing and pistols firing shot after shot. Three of Greycourt's men fell dead as they followed him.

At a frantic gallop, they were able to get to Fleetwood Hill. Stuart, also surprised by the charging enemy horsemen, escaped to nearby Auburn Road, looking for a safe post to observe the action. His brigades now scattered, Stuart had to get back to high ground to regain command and keep his men from getting routed. Greycourt and about thirty riders finally approached, much to Stuart's relief.

"Where were Hampton and Fitz Lee?" Stuart asked.

Greycourt shook his head. Suddenly aware that he was dressed only in trousers, white blouse, and boots, without a hat or tunic, he apologized to the general for his appearance. Stuart, also without a tunic, dismissed the notion. He volunteered to take his men south to regroup, but Stuart ordered him to ride out to see how General Rooney Lee, Robert E. Lee's son, was faring against the fierce Yankee onslaught.

Riding off, Stuart waved and bid him good luck. As he watched the riders take off, the sound of guns grew louder, a sign that the enemy was pushing through.

Greycourt and his men reached Grumble Jones's corps and then rode off to get to Rooney Lee who was trapped at Yew Ridge. Outnumbered, Lee kept circling, trying to break the Yankee advance. When Greycourt and Jones appeared, a Confederate bugler sounded the "CHARGE!", and a new wave of riders smashed into the fray. Hacking, slashing, pistols firing, horses screeching, riders fatally falling.

The Union horsemen turned to regroup and headed back toward the Rappahannock River. About eight Confederate riders had fallen, mortally wounded. Greycourt saw du Seine appear through the haze. Riding over to him, he reached out to grab his arm, very pleased to see him. General William "Grumble" Jones, grateful for Greycourt's support, suggested he try to get to his troop; the entire cavalry needed to regroup. Brigadier General John Buford's division had swooped in and caught them off guard; Jones predicted that Buford was regrouping to charge again. Jones had captured two regimental colors as well as some small arms and horses.

The major and du Seine rode south to join their men and to better equip themselves. Riding along Kelly's Ford Road, they noticed the horse artillery firing volleys toward the river. More gunfire was heard to the South. Furiously riding, Greycourt ran into General Beverly Robertson's division that was engaged with a large cavalry force charging from the South. Most of Greycourt's troops were with Robertson. Though outnumbered, they held the field.

The attack was well coordinated; it was almost sunrise, and the Yankees had succeeded in totally disrupting Stuart's cavalry command. Buford attacked in the North, and a very large force attacked from the South, creating a vice. But the Confederate command was spread long and wide, so the attack wasn't simple. Greycourt and du Seine made it back to their camp where they found their men coming out of the woods, gathering their clothes and finding a mount. Almost all the men were in their undergarments.

Grabbing his tunic and filling his pockets with bullets, Greycourt rallied his men to again support Robertson as the Yankee riders regrouped across the Rappahannock River. Out of nowhere, a herd of enemy riders came from the South, the sound of the horses like an earthquake. Robertson turned his division toward the oncoming cavalry when two divisions of enemy riders moved to his flank. Greycourt galloped into action, leading his men headlong into the oncoming Yankees, charging at full force.

With a loud, quaking clash, the two sides smashed into each other; horses and riders fell; swords flashed and slashed; pistols rapidly fired. Greycourt and du Seine collided with a Yankee sergeant. Holding his reins and hacking with his saber, the sergeant showed his prowess with the sword but was still no match for the tenacious Virginian. Horses were so tightly bunched together that Greycourt's legs were getting crushed. More bugles sounded, and the two cavalries retreated to again regroup.

General Robertson was holding his own at Kelly's Ford as the Yankee horsemen rode across the river to again mount a charge. Greycourt and du Seine noticed a large force of cavalry attempting to circle their right flank and headed them off. His troopers, their Rebel yell louder now, turned on their enemy with pistols and sabers, stopping the flanking movement. Somehow, an entire brigade got through and headed north toward Fleetwood Hill. Robertson was under attack again as the Union cavalry charged.

With cannon fire from Kelly's Ford Road to the east, Greycourt, assured of cover, was ordered to gallop toward Fleetwood Hill to the north. There, he ran into the rear guard of his old West Point classmate, Judson Kilpatrick's corps. Cutting through and scattering the enemy, they turned their attention away from General Stuart.

Stuart was engaged in a tough fight alongside Hampton's brigade, facing the powerful tenacity of John Buford. It seemed like thousands of riders were in the mayhem battling, screaming, shooting, and hacking. The engagement lasted about thirty minutes. The Yankee cavalry, once again, turned to retreat; the Confederates doing the same.

Major Greycourt took his troop across the Flat Plank stream to the east and secured shade under a clump of trees. The horses needed watering very badly; their riders stopped and dismounted. The animals needed rest as he could see their sweat and exhaustion. His men were just as worn; most were half dressed and yet were still full of fight.

It was almost noon, and Greycourt bantered with his friend, commenting that he never had a cup of coffee, ruining his day. Du Seine, rubbing his left arm from a saber blow, suggested they move to find an area to graze. A courier suddenly rode up and was brought to the major. He brought compliments from General Stuart and said the Yankees retreated back across the Rappahannock to regroup again. They were barely holding Fleetwood Hill. Just then, a bugle call was heard in the distance. Immediately, Greycourt ordered his men to mount up.

The Yankee horsemen took off north to attack Stuart's rear, but the swift troopers, led by Major Greycourt and Captain du Seine, caught them along the Flat Run and smashed into their flank, hurling horsemen as if scattering a flock of birds. The Yankees had a force twice the size of the Confederate troopers. Led by General David McMurtrie Gregg's division and commanding Kilpatrick and Wyndham's brigades, they had great difficulty taking the field. Greycourt, his mount practically spent and tough to control, kept turning to swing his sword. He caught a Yankee trooper on the side of the head, sending him to the ground. As he tried to get up, the Yankee was trampled to death.

Two mounted fighters wrestled for the Stars and Stripes with such tenacity, their horses banged heads and bodies so hard the riders almost knocked each other to the ground. Greycourt and his fighting men were able to hold the rear with swords and pistols, forcing Kilpatrick and Wyndham to again retreat.

As the hot June sun beat down on the thousands of men and horseflesh, the guns and cannons ceased. General Stuart and his staff sat atop Fleetwood Hill, surveying the carnage in all directions. It was almost three in the afternoon. He lost count of how many times he had ridden into battle, leading every charge. Nine, ten times? He needed a report of all his brigades; casualties, fatalities, and missing. He wiped his face with his handkerchief and shook his head in disbelief. The Yankees got the better of him this day. It can never happen again.

★★★

The camp was wrecked. Tents were down, and the few that were standing were torn to shreds. Greycourt rode over to what was left of his tent to get a few things and realized that du Seine was not with him. Just as concerning, where was Ortega?

He galloped just south of the camp where two huge hospital tents had been erected with the help of many of the local residents. Wagons came in from towns south with barrels of fresh water, clean linens and towels, whiskey, and whatever laudanum they could gather. He dismounted and grabbed an orderly.

"Hey, Captain du Seine? Is he here?" he frantically asked. He looked directly in the young orderly's eyes, about sixteen years old. "How about Captain Ortega? Is he here?"

The orderly shook his head. "Dunno. Dunno any of them," he said as he hurried into one of the tents.

Greycourt, tired, sore, famished, dehydrated—his heart raced as he looked for his friends. Taking a hard look at the huge tent, there seemed to be hundreds of wounded. Orderlies, civilian attendants, and all available doctors scurried about, tending to the casualties. Horrible moans all around, he began looking at every cot and death slab, frantically pulling sheets back. As he turned to leave to check the next tent, he felt something pinch his leg—it was du Seine.

He looked down. "You're alive! Thank God," he said, relieved. He knelt beside the cot, most of it covered with dried blood. He pulled the sheet back and saw his friend's left arm heavily bandaged and bloodied.

"They're taking it off, Colt," he said in a low, weak voice. "I won't have my arm. I can't fight with one arm. Help them, help them keep my arm," he said with a tear rolling down his cheek.

Greycourt's felt tightness in his chest. His friend, alive, with blood caked on his forehead and a swollen left eye, was going to lose an arm.

"The doctor said the bullet is too deep. He can't dig it out. He tried once. I couldn't stand the pain. He didn't give me anything for the pain."

Greycourt held his friend's right hand. "I'll get the doctor. We'll save your arm, my good friend," he said assuredly.

As an orderly ran by, Greycourt demanded, "Get the doctor here now! That's an order."

The orderly stared. "Get him yourself," he shouted back and ran off.

A woman of about sixty, witnessing the exchange, came over and said she'd get one of the doctors right away.

"Thank you," he gently said as she turned, and he kissed her hand.

The doctor, a man of about seventy years old wearing a bloody white jacket and dirty spectacles, came over. Unwrapping the bandage and examining the large wound, blood began to ooze out again. "I don't like this. The arm has to come off," he said to the woman.

Greycourt put his hand on the doctor's shoulder. "We can save it, and I'll help you. You probe, and I'll keep him steady."

The doctor shook his head. "Can't. I probed it already. It's too deep. That arm needs to come off now," he replied.

The woman handed a small amount of the pain killer, laudanum, to the doctor and turned to look for more; the doctor said there was no time.

Du Seine pleaded not to take his arm off. "You'll die if we don't," he replied.

Greycourt knelt next to his friend and said, "I am right here. Alive with one arm is better than dead with two, you foolish man."

Du Seine hesitated a moment and closed his eyes tight. "Have at it, Doctor."

Outside the tent, Greycourt sipped a cup of chicory, the only thing he managed to get into his stomach all day. He sat on a stool, screams and groans from the tent piercing his ears. The sounds distracted him from feeling his own aches and pains.

A woman came outside, the same woman that assisted the amputation, and she placed her hand on his shoulder. "There's some food in a small tent behind here. Please go get something to eat," she pleaded.

He thanked her again for her courtesy and benevolence and told her that he still had another one of his officers to find. "I haven't been to that other tent yet," he replied.

She smiled, gently touched his arm, and left.

The other tent seemed worse. A huge pile of arms and legs were stacked up outside. Four slaves attended to three fires with large cauldrons of boiling water. He went in, walking in on an argument between a doctor and an officer about treating the wounded. It seemed that there were six wounded Yankees in the tent that the doctor was tending to. The officer was adamant that the Yankees could die; their own wounded had to be attended to.

Greycourt looked at the six cots with the wounded Yankees. One, an officer, with his head heavily bandaged, asked for water. The Confederate officer spit on the floor in response. Greycourt approached the two men. "Get out, Captain," he ordered.

Stunned, the captain stared. "I'll have you arrested, Major. I'll kill these Yankees before I get out," he scowled.

Greycourt drew his pistol and pressed it against the captain's head. "When I pull this trigger, you'll need help getting out. Or you can go on your own," he replied.

The captain slowly walked out as Greycourt handed the Yankee his canteen. The doctor tended to the men.

Searching the tent, Ortega and his brothers were nowhere to be found. Relieved, he thought that maybe they got themselves under Hampton's command in the confusion of the battle. As he was leaving the tent, he saw a dozen cots with sheets over the bodies. As he passed the last one, he noticed rosary beads hanging from the dead man's left wrist. Shaking, he lifted the sheet. It was Ortega's younger brother, Anselmo, lying dead. He turned to the next cot and lifted the sheet. It was Ortega's other younger brother, Victor, also dead. He turned to the last cot, and his blood ran ice cold as he pulled the sheet back—it was Ortega.

He sunk to his knees. Covering his face, he slowly shook his head in disbelief and clutched the crucifix at the end of the rosary beads. He was so tired and emotionally drained he just wanted to curl up in a ball and disappear into the ground. What will the Ortega family think of him?

Requesting the three bodies to be under his care, he looked for the officer in charge to get permission to have the bodies sent back to Texas. General Fitz Lee, still in pain from his rheumatism, walked among the wounded. Signing order after order for supplies, he had just received a dispatch from Stuart to join him at Brandy Station for a full report.

Greycourt approached the general. "Sir, permission to prepare and deliver three bodies to Texas," he asked.

Fitz Lee scratched his head. "Relatives? You're from Virginia, Major."

Greycourt nodded. "I promised the family I'd take responsibility for these men, sir," he replied.

General Lee shook his head regretfully. "Sir, we have more pressing matters. I have to meet with General Stuart about this entire incident. Request denied. Join your troop, sir."

Disappointed, he saluted and left the general's tent.

Orderlies were piling the dead in two wagons to be sent to a field about a mile away. Greycourt waited and requested that the three Ortegas be loaded last. He accompanied the wagons to the place of burial. Slaves, older men, had shovels. Their orders were to dig graves for each body.

Greycourt asked an elderly slave to wait a few minutes. He selected a place that would be recognizable apart from the others. He took a lock of hair and a piece of clothing from each brother. He wrapped the rosary beads each had around their wrists, placing their hands on their chests.

He removed his blouse, took the shovel from the old slave, and started to dig a grave big enough to have all three rest together. The slave walked away and returned with a shovel to help, all the while praying in a barely audible low tone. As the shovel cut through the soil, the salty sweat mingled with the tears burning Greycourt's fiery blue eyes. A dog barked in the distance as birds flew by. His body could muster no more energy, but still he dug and dug until the grave was large enough. With the help of the slave, each body was gently placed. He reached down and put his hand on his dear friend. The slave waited; then seeing it was time to cover the dead, he caught the major's attention. Nodding, they both moved the dirt back. When they were done, the slave began a prayer, and Greycourt sank to his knees.

After catching some sleep and finally able to wash his face and upper body, Major Greycourt needed something to eat. Nine hours of battle; the entire battle lasted nine hours. Luckily, his tent wasn't totally destroyed; he was able to get some clean clothes and a badly needed shave. His horse was grazing and given a badly needed rest. Now feeling presentable as an officer—clean trousers, a fresh clean blouse and tunic—he adjusted his black hat and noticed his boots were scuffed and dirty.

Greycourt felt he was in the right frame of mind to write letters to Ortega's parents and his young wife. He wrote two letters to the parents, one about Ortega and one about his brothers. He enclosed the locks of their hair and a piece of clothing from each one. He wrote the letter to Ortega's wife last. His hand shook as he wrote about the bravery of his friend. Most of all, he wrote about how Ortega was one of the finest men he's ever known, a good man. He enclosed the lock of Ortega's hair and a swatch from the blouse worn at the time he was killed. He would get a postman at the hospital tent.

Du Seine was sitting up and dictating a letter to his wife. The elderly lady writing for him smiled as she wrote, admiring the young man's attitude. He had just lost his arm, yet he spoke glowingly and proudly that he was alive and will see her and their sons soon.

Greycourt walked in and saw his friend propped up with two pillows. His hair combed and face clean, du Seine looked up, smiled, and waved with his right hand. The lady put the pencil down as he approached and shook his friend's hand. The lady got up and said she'd be back later to finish. Greycourt graciously bowed and thanked her for attending to his good friend.

"Well, look at you sitting up like the Prince of Wales," he said with a grin.

Du Seine smiled. "Excuse me, you mean like the Marquis de Lafayette?" he said, chuckling. Then suddenly overcome, a tear rolled down his right eye. He grabbed Greycourt and him tightly. "I don't know if I can go home yet," he said.

Kneeling down next to the cot, Greycourt shook his head. "I've written a medical discharge for you, effective immediately." He was lying to get his friend's reaction. "Tomorrow I'm getting you to Brandy Station to get you on your way home."

Du Seine lifted his right hand to touch his left shoulder, but Greycourt stopped him. "Don't. When you get to New Orleans, you can have your doctor look you over."

During the amputation, Greycourt steadily held his friend while the doctor worked on him. With little laudanum given to him, he held Greycourt so tight that it could have stopped the circulation in half of his body. Du Seine tried not to cry out but couldn't control the reflex. Succumbing to the pain, he fainted.

Now his dear friend would have to endure the pain and fear of presenting himself to his family. Du Seine felt ashamed and only half a man. Greycourt kept assuring him that his family would be very happy to have him home with one arm, better than not returning home at all. Du Seine rubbed his eyes and asked about Ortega.

Greycourt's gut tightened. "I couldn't send them home when I wanted to. I should have forced my way into the general's tent and got them the discharge," he said.

Du Seine was confused, and then his eyes widened. "What? You mean—" He was interrupted.

"Yes. Ortega went to get his brothers, and I guess they got caught in the attack right away. I should have had them all with us. I didn't protect them like I was supposed to," he solemnly said.

Du Seine shook his head. "No, Ortega had to get his brothers. There was nothing you could have done."

Greycourt lowered his eyes. "I buried all three of them. I marked the grave. I suppose the family will come get the bodies someday." He placed his hand on du Seine's right arm. "I'm getting you out of here, and we're going to have supper."

The two officers accepted the supper invitation of an old farmer at nearby Paoli's Mill. The old man and his wife provided a very hearty home-cooked meal of roasted chickens, turnip greens, grits, and a very delectable strawberry rhubarb pie with coffee for dessert.

Du Seine felt awkward having to eat with one hand. He was embarrassed as he saw the farmer's wife place small pieces of meat on his plate. Looking directly in the young man's eyes, she placed meat on Greycourt's plate, cut the same way.

The conversation was merry as the couple spoke of their family of six children, only four living past the age of two, that lived up north. The farmer, about seventy years in age, told of how, as a youngster, he fought with Andy Jackson at Bladensburg and then all the way down to New Orleans. He told of when the soldiers and militia gathered to form the skirmish line; as they sat for a minute for chicory and hard tack, they were surprised to have Jackson pass by and sit with them. He assured them that they would kill every blasted British soldier in front of them. That remark boosted their confidence immensely.

Greycourt attempted to leave a few gold pieces for the very courteous couple, but they would not have it. They felt it was their contribution to the cause and were honored to have such fine Confederates for company. Du Seine was due on the train south to go home the next morning.

★★★

It was hot. As he gathered his belongings and was readying to join his troop, Greycourt could not forget the conversation he had with du Seine about the last battle. Apparently, the Yankees were watching them for a long time and knew exactly when to strike. Their own scouts and patrols reported no enemy cavalry anywhere near their encampments; the Yankees waited until after the second review to attack. When they did, it was from two directions, and they knew how far their camp stretched. Yankee scouting was not that good.

When he had put du Seine on the train at Brandy Station, he'd told him he would write him soon. Most importantly, he demanded that he kiss and hug his wife first and then hold his sons tight. They would all be glad to see him alive. They parted as brothers; both were shattered at the loss of their friend Ortega and his brothers. Greycourt still felt remorse at their deaths. He would have great difficulty overcoming that.

CHAPTER FIFTEEN

Allan Pinkerton stroked his thick dark beard. He was getting tired. He looked at his pocket watch and saw it was almost three o'clock in the morning. He expected to wear his captive down, but he was wrong. It seemed that Colton James Greycourt hadn't so much as slumped down in fatigue during the whole interrogation. A military tribunal would convict him as a spy and sentence him to hang; he had no doubt of that. But he felt there was something more here that his prisoner just wasn't divulging. Pinkerton looked at the other two agents and motioned with his head for them to leave the room.

"I say we work him over good," Morse said, rubbing his right fist. Geiger agreed.

Pinkerton, still against it, didn't want to hear it again. "Who's going to hold him down? You think he'll let you slug him around?" he asked. "Like I said before, that guy is tough. There might be three of us, but he'll make sure he gets his shots in. You can believe that. Are you paying attention to what he's telling us?"

Morse, annoyed, looked away. "I don't know why you're letting this go on, Chief. What use is his life story?" Geiger asked.

Pinkerton smiled. "Can't you see? He's leading us right to where we need to be. We're getting there."

The three men went back into the room, finding Greycourt standing and holding onto his chair, stretching his back and arms. He looked at the three men. Pinkerton motioned for him to sit back down. Greycourt picked up his coffee cup; noticing it was cold, he placed the cup back down. The men stared.

"You got slaves, don't ya, Greycourt?" Geiger asked him.

He turned his head slightly and looked at the agent. "My family owns slaves. I own nothing," he answered.

"So you never beat slaves or hung 'em?" Morse asked as he leaned into Greycourt's face.

"Slavery is not something I favor. It's wrong—" he started but was cut off by Morse.

"It's wrong, but you had slaves and used them like cattle or dogs. You treated them worse than your dogs. Ain't that right, Major Greycourt?"

Annoyed at the conversation, Greycourt tensed. "Look, I don't own slaves and never have," he said in anger. He looked at Pinkerton. "Can I get a fresh pot of coffee?"

The detective was a bit surprised. "Not tired? How can that be?" he asked.

Morse, still hot under the collar, shouted, "Maybe your slave can get it for ya, Rebel belly!"

Greycourt sat up straight and shook his head and then looked at Pinkerton. He let out a sigh and looked at Morse. "You want slavery talk? Huh, do ya? Well, pay attention instead of thinking about how much rope you'll need for my neck!"

★★★

General Stuart's camp was deserted, except for the slave quarters. As Greycourt rode through, the old slave waved his hat to get his attention. Every rider, every able-bodied horseman was out with the general on this campaign that may be the turning point of the war. The old slave did not know where or which direction the cavalry had taken off for, but Greycourt knew that they were headed north.

Greycourt began heading northeast, recalling a preliminary plan to screen General Lee's advance toward Philadelphia. He'd have to flank the massive force that stretched out for miles; Greycourt surmised that Stuart would be headed northeast.

He had lost a few days taking care of du Seine and burying Ortega and his brothers, but he was confident he would catch up to the cavalry. He'd have to head toward Washington City. About twenty miles south of Washington City, he came upon a sight so sorry he was compelled to stop.

Greycourt rode up behind a covered wagon that was pulled by two mules. He noticed two Negro boys looking out of the back, and his immediate thought was that it was a runaway family.

As he rode to the front to see who was driving, he was surprised to see a girl of about sixteen with the reins. The girl was startled and pulled a rusty old pistol out from under her seat board. He put his right hand up, and she stopped the wagon. "I can kill you if you move," she said.

Greycourt smiled. "Not with that old piece. You got bullets for that?" he asked.

The young girl lowered her eyes and then placed the rusty old gun down next to her. "No, I can't even shoot," she said in a low voice.

Greycourt smiled and got closer and patted one of the mules. "You hitched them up? Good work," he said.

The girl, on her guard, looked at him. "No, Ezra did that. He got killed days ago when we left."

Greycourt leaned in to see what was in the wagon. Besides the two little boys, there were four girls, ages from eight to three years. Lying on a long flat feathered burlap sack was an old woman. The children saw him, and the six of them huddled together, obviously in fear of this white man. He slowly lifted his right hand and waved hello. The children were scared, but one little girl smiled and waved back. He could hear the old woman breathing very heavily. Turning his mount to the front, he tapped one of the mules and nodded to the girl to "git up." The little girl that had waved came up front to sit as the wagon started moving again.

He rode his horse next to her and told her he'd ride a ways with them. It was getting dark, and they'd have to stop. They were headed north like he was. He decided the next clearing they came to would be their resting place. They stopped about an hour later. The mules were unhitched and left to graze. The girl got water from one of the water barrels on the side of the wagon.

Greycourt started a fire to cook. Rice from another smaller barrel tied to the other side was the extent of their food. He had some dried beef and a few stale biscuits called hardtack, but it wasn't enough for all of them. The old woman would be fed first. As he watched the children devour their rice with their tiny fingers, he got up and retrieved the sack from his saddle. He took out the dried beef and gave it to the young girl to break up and distribute to the children. All eyes widened at the sight of something much different than rice. She gave the wrapping back to him, with a few small pieces left. He handed it back to her.

The children needed washing and hoped to find a stream or river. Greycourt told her that he thought there might be one on tomorrow's ride. With the children now asleep and the old woman somewhat comfortable, the young girl sat under a tree a few yards from the wagon. Greycourt joined her. "You have to be tired. How many days on the road?" he asked.

"I think four days, not sure. I can't count good," she answered.

"Where are you all from?"

"North Carolina. We all from the Calver . . . Calver . . . Calverton Plantation. Soldiers came and took horses, cows, and chickens and burned the cotton. Everybody ran off. Then there was fightin' 'n' loud shootin'. I grabbed the children and ran, but Ezra and Mala saw us and got us in the wagon. Ezra got shot and told me to keep going. He was just dead in the road. Mala was always sick. She's very old." The young girl spoke in soft tones, almost afraid to speak up.

"Do you know where you're going?" he asked.

"I don't, but Ezra said keep going and never look back."

Greycourt looked at the wagon and then at the girl. "What's your name?"

She lowered her eyes and looked away. "Dara," she said, almost in a whisper.

"What did you do before this? I mean on the land?" he asked, turning to look at her.

"I never worked in the fields. I worked with my momma in the house. Clean, get things, take care of babies," she replied.

"You speak very well," he said with a smile.

"My lady, Massa's wife, she wanted no field talk in the house. She slapped me once just for askin' her something. I didn't like her," she explained.

Looking over to the wagon, Greycourt asked, "The old woman in the wagon, she kin?"

The girl, following his gaze, replied, "No, just an old woman that took care of everyone down at the shacks. She took care of me better than my momma."

He looked at Dara as the moonlight touched her face. She was light skinned with a small nose and dark eyes. She appeared angelic, and her straight dark hair was matted in spots.

"I know you not gonna hurt us. I could tell," she said.

Greycourt smiled at her. "You get some sleep. You worked hard today. I'll keep my eyes open for anything."

As Dara leaned back on the tree, a little girl climbed out of the wagon and slowly walked to them and cuddled up against her. It was the little girl that waved to him in the wagon. He got up and fetched the horse blanket and placed it over both of them.

His pocket watch was in his tunic, but he guessed it was well after midnight. He could catch a short snooze and start his journey early in the morning after getting Dara and the wagon headed in the right direction. He heard a rustling and quickly drew his pistol—it was three riders.

As the moonlight cleared some clouds, it shed a very unnerving sight.

"Lookee here, Noah, it's the popinjay. Heh, heh. And he's got hisself a lady and child. Hah, a Negra lady too."

"I told ya, Chan, them fancy clothes an' all get everything." The response came from the dark.

"Whaddya think, Noah?" Greycourt stood up. "Keep going. All of ya, keep going," he said angrily, pointing the pistol at them.

"Now that's not very neighborly, is it? Especially when we're all comrades in arms, you know, Mosby's boys," Chan Goode said, smiling.

"You're all outlaws. Keep going," he barked.

"And you're a deserter," Noah Beaudry responded.

Dara and the little girl cowered tightly together, terrified at the intrusion. The little girl hid her head against Dara's breast.

"We gotta rest our horses for the night. This looks like a good place," Goode said, still smiling. The men dismounted. Greycourt was not getting any sleep this night.

There was a dewy mist as the dawn slowly rose. Not sleeping one wink, Greycourt looked around and saw Dara and the little girl still sleeping. He would get a fire going and a pot of coffee on. There were a few biscuits left for the children and old lady, and the rice would have to suffice until he could get them safely north to the kindness of strangers. He knew just the place.

Dara rubbed her face and back, stiff from the ground. As a house slave, she slept on a feather cot in the attic of the mansion; the hardness of the ground was very uncomfortable. The little girl was still asleep. She would have to get her up so they can get moving at the early light. Dara smelled the coffee and went over to Greycourt. "You know those men. They're gonna hurt us. Gonna hurt me," she said.

He looked at Dara. He saw all the hurt and pain, all her anguish and pain and all the other Negroes in the South. His heart sunk in pity. The three despicable riders, Goode, Beaudry, and the youngster Nevers, were what was wrong with the entire cause. Years of hurt in the institution of slavery. State's rights as they all called out for? No. It was their way of life they were fighting for. In some ways up north, it was no better, but at least there were chances.

Greycourt always knew kindness from Paul, Tessa, and Scipio. He never looked at them as slaves the way the rest of his family did. As a young boy, Tessa looked out for him. She would say, "Eat your meals, drink your milk, sit straight like a young man, and always mind your manners." Paul taught him to ride, not just ride a horse but to ride like a seasoned, skilled horseman. He knew that his horsemanship had saved him many times in battles. His own father never had time for him; he knew that was a scar not easily healed. He was going to get this wagon to safety and in the hands of good, benevolent people as soon as he could.

He washed his face with two palms of water and poured coffee for Dara and himself. Goode came over with that same leering smile on his face and demanded Dara pour him coffee.

Greycourt quickly turned to him. "She doesn't serve you. This coffee is not for you."

Angered, Goode squared his shoulders. "Well, we'll see about that, popinjay. She's a runaway slave, and you're helping her escape. That makes you contraband too. You're under arrest, Major," he said.

Beaudry and Nevers walked over. "We're takin' this wagon and contraband to the county guard and you too," Beaudry said. "We'll get five, maybe $10 for this catch."

Greycourt was unfazed. "We gotta get moving. You outlaws have nothing here."

Goode smiled. "Well, we'll be gettin' with this young Negra. You can bet on that, popinjay. And I'll get that horse of yours too."

Dara quickly went to Greycourt's side as the other children leaned out of the back of the wagon. One boy called out that the old woman needed help. Dara quickly ran to the wagon.

As the late June sun was rising, they got the mules hitched and the children settled in the wagon. The wagon started out. Greycourt rode behind it, making sure the outlaw stragglers didn't get ahead of it. The three riders rode behind, following Greycourt closely.

They were making good time. Greycourt took them to the Potomac River just south of Alexandria. There they could get fresh water and wash. He found a place off the road in the woods to rest the horses. There was still a long journey ahead to get them into Maryland and safety.

Dara bathed the children in the river as Greycourt watched over them, his pistol drawn. The three men lurked nearby. They were following the wagon, waiting to pounce at the right moment, and he knew it. As Dara bathed, he told her she needn't worry. He would keep his back to her, watching for trouble.

They went back to the wagon, and food was getting low, so he and Dara went into the woods to find wild game. She had to stay close to him as the three predators were always close, just itching to get at her. They caught two rabbits, skinned, and prepared the meat for the fire.

Greycourt and Dara went into the wagon with all the children. The little girl also stayed close to him. The old woman tried to sit up but had trouble, so Dara held her head up. She smiled at the young Southerner. "I don't know how long I can go. Dara says you a good man. Help her and the chillin'. I knew some good white folks and not so good ones," she said with a smile. She coughed and looked at Greycourt. "I prayed to the Lawd that I get to freedom before I go meet Jesus. I been prayin' for you, that you be safe," she said and grabbed his hand.

He looked at Dara as she placed the old woman's head back down and fell asleep. The rabbits smelled good; the children were excited to eat meat. He poured coffee for himself and Dara as the children devoured the rabbit. The three riders stood nearby, watching.

As dusk approached, Dara was getting the children ready for sleep, and Greycourt told her that she better get some sleep to stay in the wagon, and he'll be on guard outside. As all slept, Greycourt stood at the back of the wagon, his pistol drawn, watching the three as they ate around a fire they had built nearby.

Goode walked over, his hands up in truce. "Hey, popinjay, we decided that we're taking that wagon and mules after we throw that old Negra in the road. We'll let you and those contraband kids go, but you leave the girl with us."

Greycourt, unnerved, saw the other two standing a few feet behind Goode. "I'm tired. I've been thinking. Maybe you're right all along. Let's get away from the wagon. I don't want anyone to overhear our deal," he replied.

Dara was awake and listening, her heart pounding in fear.

Goode smiled. "Hear that, Noah? The popinjay wants to deal. I might let him keep his horse too."

The four men went a few yards into the woods. Dara wanted very badly to hear what was being said, but her terrified body would not move. She heard two shots, which were followed by the sound of a horse galloping off.

★★★

The National Hotel in Washington City was overcrowded; the streets in the city were just as crowded. There was no trouble getting a table at the popular hotel's dining room with Dalrymple tipping the head waiter as soon as he walked in, his usual practice. He sat with a whiskey and waited for his guests. A boy walked in with newspapers under his arm. Motioning for him to bring a paper to him, he gave the boy a penny for the paper and a penny tip. The newspaper, *The Washington Gazette*, had **"THE BATTLE RAGES ON"** as the front-page headline. Dalrymple turned to the second page to read about the events at a town in Pennsylvania where the two massive armies met. His first guest walked over to the table; it was Reginald Greycourt.

His hair now graying at the temples, Reginald sat and ordered a brandy and a cigar. Dalrymple put the paper down and sipped his whiskey. There was no envelope to exchange this time. Plans were shattered now, so they were meeting to get their next plan underway. Reginald knew that the only way they could get things going again was to immediately build a new factory at the same site as fast as possible. It would take a lot of cash, but he knew where to get it. Dalrymple's second guest arrived, and both men stood up to greet her.

Victoria had just gotten in from New York and was told to meet Dalrymple at the hotel. He had an envelope for her as payment for providing them with vital information. She looked at the well-dressed, clean-shaven green-eyed man and thanked him. He sarcastically replied that it was he that should be thanking her. She began conversing with Reginald about his family and his attempts to find work in Philadelphia or New York. She especially wanted to know if he had heard from Colt recently.

Dalrymple interrupted and said he could get the new factory started, but it all hinged one important factor—the war would have to continue for at least the next five years in order for them to recoup their losses.

Reginald, speaking for the Judge and himself, said that would be fine, and the work should get started right away as he was sure the war would continue that long, perhaps even longer. The waiter came over to take their order and deliver the brandy.

Dalrymple waited for the server to leave before continuing to discuss the factory and how much cash would be needed to start. Victoria said she would invest if she was guaranteed a return of at least 10 percent. The two men first laughed but after consideration, agreed.

Reginald, now confident and feeling better about the whole thing, suggested they should toast the new business. Dalrymple smiled and handed him the newspaper, the headline facing front.

Grabbing it, Reginald rifled through the pages and then sunk into his chair.

★★★

The cavalry camp back in Virginia was as quiet as a prayer service. The three-day battle at Gettysburg had taken a drastic toll on the entire Confederacy. There was no banjo or violin playing; most of the men sat outside their tents solemnly recalling what had happened. A wagon with photography equipment came in and was quickly told to leave as there was no cause for celebratory photographs.

Greycourt sat in his tent alone, staring at the two empty cots. The July heat was almost unbearable. He requested a glass of cold lemonade. As he waited, he went through his trunk. He found some letters that recently arrived, two letters from Louisiana, two from Texas, and one from New York.

Scipio came in with a glass of cold lemonade. He handed it to the young officer and began straightening up, taking his boots off so they could be shined. Clothes were gathered to be washed in the slave quarters. Exhausted, Greycourt only wanted to lie down and sleep. As his head touched the pillow, an orderly and two lieutenants came to the tent. Scipio stopped behind the tent to listen. Greycourt put his clothes and boots back on and went with the men.

They led him to General Stuart's tent, and he noticed that none of Stuart's staff was present, nor was Sergeant Major Ward standing in his familiar stance outside the tent. Inside the tent, sitting behind Stuart's desk, was Lamar Gratton, now Colonel Gratton.

Two captains from Hampton's brigade stood behind Gratton as he eyed the major up and down. The orderly left, and the two lieutenants stood at attention on each side of Greycourt and waited for the colonel to begin. Two other captains came in. The officers in the tent were all from Hampton's brigade. The other person stood behind Gratton—young Ab Nevers—the third outlaw rider with Goode and Beaudry.

"Major, this is about as close to a duel as you're going to get," Gratton said, stroking his tight-cropped rustic beard. "Major, you're under arrest."

"Arrest? Arrest for what? What are the charges?" he asked, completely surprised.

Gratton smiled. "Desertion . . . murder . . . and cowardice in the face of the enemy."

"I'm no coward, and I never deserted. Murder? Who did I murder?" he angrily asked.

Gratton turned and looked at Nevers and then at Greycourt. "This man gave testimony that you shot and murdered two officers under Colonel Mosby's command. You did this while deserting your troop." Gratton placed his hands on the desk and held up a paper. "This is a signed statement from Private Nevers."

Greycourt was stunned. Nothing was as ridiculous as this phony "court." He did, in fact, shoot Goode and Beaudry. He got the three men to go with him into the woods near the wagon and, before anything was said, drew his revolver and shot both men between the eyes, killing them instantly. He lowered the gun, telling Nevers not to feel threatened, and the youngster ran for his horse and galloped away.

With the two outlaws out of the way and no longer threatening them, he kept the wagon moving northeast around Washington City crossing the Potomac River by ferry. He was able to avoid two Yankee patrols by using the thick woods as cover. With him driving the wagon, they made better time heading toward Baltimore. After three days, they made it to a children's home in Catonsville, Maryland, about a mile west of Baltimore.

As the wagon approached the home, a gated area on ten acres of land, the children were afraid that it was another plantation. The large building with its white columns and long front porch was well kept and impressive. Greycourt got down to open the large metal gate so Dara could drive the wagon in. There were children playing in front of the house, and they stopped to watch as the wagon slowly entered. Two women came out of the house, also watching as they approached.

The wagon stopped about ten yards from the house, and Dara jumped into the back to look in on the old woman; the children cowered together, not knowing their fate. Greycourt noticed another woman, older than the other two, coming out of the house; she stood sternly with her arms folded.

Dara held the woman's head up. Her breathing was very faint as she tried to speak. "I can't . . . I can't go on."

Greycourt went into the wagon and knelt next to Dara as she held the old woman's hand.

"You free now, Mala. Free," Dara said, smiling. The old woman looked at Dara and then at Greycourt and, with a faint smile, slowly closed her eyes. The two women outside the wagon came over to ask if they could help, and Dara began handing the children to them.

Greycourt got out of the wagon and looked at the woman still standing on the porch with her arms folded.

The last one out of the wagon was the little girl that clung so close to Dara and Greycourt. As she was handed to him, she dug her tiny fingers into his blouse, not wanting to let go; he carried her toward the house. Dara went back into the wagon to see about the old woman.

The children walked toward the porch, looking at the woman who stood there and stopped at the bottom step.

"Get these babies cleaned and fed. Get milk. Get each one fresh clean clothes," the woman, who was obviously in charge, said in an almost angelic yet commanding tone.

Greycourt walked with the child in his arms to the porch and stopped.

"Come in, sir. We'll take care of these precious babies, every one of them," she said with a smile. "Even the one that holds you so close."

Greycourt walked up the stairs as the woman took the child from his arms.

"I think you, sir, should come in and clean up and have a hot meal. We'll see to that," she said.

He looked at her in her black gownlike tunic covered by a black apron with rosary beads around her neck. She wore a cotton coif or a close-fitting cap. After examining her outfit, he realized she was a nun.

With the children in the house getting settled, one of the women went to the wagon to offer help to Dara. As she went in, she saw the young girl resting her head on the old woman's chest. The old woman was dead.

The other children of the home gathered around their new guests, and oddly enough, all looked similar. There were a few white children, but most were of mixed race.

Large vats of water were being prepared to bathe the children, and the cook began preparing supper for all. A large dining room with a long table big enough to fit everyone was being set. The nun looked at Greycourt's fancy white linen blouse and noticed the gray trousers with the yellow piping. She knew he was a Confederate.

"You've come long way, sir?" she asked him.

"I picked up the wagon in Virginia. I recall Dara, the oldest, said they're from North Carolina," he answered. He rubbed his face and his fingers over the stubble. "This is the only place I could think for these people. I had to get them to safety."

The nun smiled. "You don't have to worry. This place is as safe as can be. You see, we take in all children, even, well, just about anybody that's in need. If there's any trouble, Sheree, our cook, will take a shotgun to them."

Greycourt, exhausted, slumped to the right, and the nun called out for help.

His eyes opened, and he was looking at a pristine white ceiling. The bed he was lying in was as comfortable as any bed he'd ever slept in. He sat up and noticed that he was clean from head to toe—all over, up and down—even his hair was washed. He still needed a shave, though.

There was a knock at the door as it opened, and the two women and the nun entered carrying a tray.

"It's lamb stew. We hope you like it," said one woman with a thin face wearing spectacles, her dark hair pulled back. "Coffee, biscuits, and butter. There's more if you want," she continued.

Greycourt sat up and smiled. "I'll like it. Thank you, ladies, very much."

The two women curtsied and left as the nun pulled up a chair as he ate.

"Who washed me?" he asked.

"Don't be ashamed. Those two ladies did. They scrubbed you good. We'll get a razor for you so you can shave," she said. "I have to ask you. How did you come by that wagon? Were you leaving the war?"

Greycourt took a bite of a biscuit and swallowed. "No, I got behind and tried to catch up to my troop. I thought the wagon needed help. I'm glad I stayed with it. Thank you for taking care of them and me."

The nun smiled. "We've had this home open for a few months. You see, these children have no parents, no place to go. Most of them were dropped off, you know, not wanted." She was referring to the mulatto children. "We care for them and teach them reading and writing and manners, important things. Are you risking your life looking after that wagon?"

He continued eating. "Nothing will come of it. As things are going lately, I felt I had to get them to safety. That young girl, Dara, she's the brave one."

The nun took the cloth napkin and placed it under his chin. "I know. We talked. She said you saved their lives. Too bad about the old woman. We'll bury her this evening when it gets cooler."

The home survived on the produce they grew and sold in Baltimore once a month. Bushels of corn, berries, rhubarb, and barley provided a decent income, and milk was abundant from the three cows they had. The four women worked hard and asked nothing in return. Two of the women were war widows with no children to care for, and the cook was a runaway slave. The nun was from Bayonne, New Jersey, and settled in the area after looking for her younger brother who was with the Forty-Second New York Infantry who she learned was killed at Antietam. Distraught and despondent, she could not go back home, so she bought the land and house with money her folks sent to her. In taking care of children, she was able to see her brother in each one of them.

Greycourt finished eating. After being scolded for not cleaning his plate, he stretched, giving a signal that he was ready to get out of bed. The nun took his tray and said they would be downstairs when he was ready.

With his belly full, Greycourt dug a grave for the old woman under a tree and lowered her into the ground with a pair of rosary beads wrapped around her hands. The nun led prayers and laid a small bouquet of wildflowers some of the children had picked on the grave. Dara cried and leaned against him as he bowed his head.

At dawn, the Confederate soldier in Yankee care shaved with the razor given to him and dressed in his clean blouse that had been washed and ironed for him. His tunic was also brushed clean and his boots shined. The children were all still asleep as he went down to the kitchen to get a cup of coffee. The cook, a wiry Negro woman of about forty, told him to sit as she prepared breakfast. Although he said he had to get an early start, she would have none of it and demanded he sit.

Eggs and bacon were crackling, and a tray of hot biscuits was taken from the oven as the nun entered the kitchen. He slept in her room while she slept in another. She asked about his rest, and he responded he had been very comfortable.

"Leaving this morning?" she asked. Greycourt nodded. "We'll pray for you. Hopefully, this war will be over by the time you get back to your troop."

"I hope so too. I've seen too many die," he solemnly replied.

"Come see us when the war is over. You will always be a welcome guest," she said with a smile.

Greycourt wiped his mouth, got up, and thanked the cook as he adjusted his belt and sash. He reached into his pocket and took out a $5 gold piece, the last he had. Placing it on the table, he thanked her for her hospitality and said he hoped that the money would help. She refused, but he insisted. He asked her name, and she replied, "Sister Isabella."

He went to the barn and got his horse ready. As he saddled it, he noticed the horse was well cared for and rested.

Dara came into the barn. "Do you have to go?" she asked.

He stopped, "Yes. I have to join my troop. I hope they didn't get very far."

She looked at him and then grabbed and hugged him so tight his breathing almost stopped.

He held her at arm's length. "They'll take care of you. They're good people."

A tear rolled down her cheek, and he gently wiped it with his index finger. Dara looked at him. "I don't know what would have happened if you weren't with us. Those men . . .,"she said.

He shook his head. "Don't look back," he said as he mounted his horse.

Three more men came into the tent as Colonel Gratton stared at the suspected deserter. One captain tied his hands behind his back and pulled. "Where's von Borcke? Where's Sergeant Major Ward?" he demanded to know.

Gratton smirked. "The generals are all meeting someplace, probably Richmond. Von Borcke, he got wounded at Middleburg. Ward, well, I guess he'll be buried at Gettysburg."

Greycourt could not believe what he was hearing. He had no one to speak on his behalf, and Gratton, his adversary, was taking charge. "The men I killed were outlaws wanted in three states. They weren't for 'the cause.' They were the murderers and outlaws."

Gratton sat up and looked around the tent. "The charges stand. Major Colton James Greycourt is to be hung tomorrow at sunrise."

Most of the men in the tent looked at each other in amazement that the colonel would make a decision so quickly. The major stood there and shook his head. "No, sir. I cannot be hung without a fair trial, and I demand a military review of my case in front of General Stuart. These are false charges, and I demand my right to defend myself," he said defiantly.

Gratton held his right hand up and placed his left hand on a bible as he spoke, "Demand? Sir, you demand nothing. Put him in a tent with guards."

Three captains led the prisoner away, with his hands tied behind him, to a tent at the end of the camp. Before stepping into the tent, Greycourt noticed a clump of large trees about fifty yards away. His stomach turned at the sight.

The tent had a cot and a chair. One guard was stationed at the back and one in front. He requested a pencil and paper to write some letters, and as night fell, he was brought a plate of beans and a cup of coffee that he couldn't even look at. With his nerves on edge, he slowly paced the tent, thinking about being hung. He began to sweat, and the more he wiped his face and forehead, the more he sweated. If he had received his promotion to colonel as promised before all this, he would stand a better chance of defending himself. His only hope was that General Stuart would return during the night and stop this whole thing before the morning. He could only hope.

★★★

CHAPTER SIXTEEN

Victoria finished writing her letters, one to her family that now resided in Baltimore and another letter to Colt Greycourt. The letter to her family was a short one, but her writing to Colt Greycourt was poignant; she hoped to see him soon and spend time away from the war.

Clive G. Dalrymple was a scoundrel, but she needed him as much as he needed her. With him, it was all business, no matter what she did for him and with him; with Colt, she had true feelings. She knew he was genuine, good-hearted, and loyal. She wrote that perhaps he could get a furlough to meet her in Washington City very soon, just the two of them.

As she sealed the envelopes for mailing, she wondered about all this nonsense: the war, hardships for people but, most of all, how she got so involved in all of it.

★★★

It was time.

The night seemed to go very fast. Greycourt dozed off for a few minutes as he sat in the uncomfortable chair in the tent. He looked out and saw one of the guards sitting on the ground asleep with his rifle resting across his lap. He could have very easily grabbed the rifle to take his chances escaping but didn't. Dawn was just a few minutes away.

The young soldier guarding the front of the tent jumped up at hearing of the approach of a small group of men. Colonel Gratton led the group of four captains to witness the hanging. The guard straightened up and saluted the group as about thirty other men congregated. The other guard from the rear of the tent joined the others and was scolded by Gratton for leaving his post without permission. An orderly hurriedly walked in with a bowl of mush and a cup of coffee for the prisoner. Gratton waived him off, shaking his head, and made a bad joke about the last meal of a condemned man. The captains chuckled nervously in response.

The two guards went in, tied his hands behind him, and led him out. His last chance was to fight it out and be shot. That was better than hanging, he thought. A wagon came to the tent to place him up closer to the noose, and then the wagon would pull away, causing the body to hang. He was helped into the wagon. He sweated profusely and was afraid of soiling himself.

The wagon slowly reached the tree with the rope around a big thick branch as all the men gathered around. Most of the men watching were fond of Major Greycourt, who they knew to be a fair and exceptional leader. Colonel Gratton, attired in his full gray dress uniform with gold sash and orange-plumed hat, nodded to have a blindfold placed over Greycourt's eyes.

"Before we blindfold you, do you have any last words? Last words from a coward and traitor?" he asked the prisoner, much to the other soldier's ire.

Greycourt stared straight ahead. "I am innocent of these false charges. When the generals return, they will want to know who was behind this and all who were involved." He looked out at the woods nearby and then at a young soldier standing next to the wagon. "Can you loosen this rope around my hands?" he asked. "The rope is digging into my wrists."

The young soldier, under Greycourt's command, got up into the wagon and tugged the rope very loose, just enough to keep the hands together. Gratton cursed and commanded that they get on with the execution.

As another soldier got up on the wagon to place the blindfold around his eyes, shrieking horses burst into the crowd. Greycourt pushed the soldier away as he grabbed his sidearm and leapt onto the back of his horse. Gratton ordered the men to fire, but much to his shock, none of their rifles were loaded. In the chaos, he drew his own pistol, and as he was about to fire, Greycourt turned on his horse and fired a perfect shot into Gratton's chest, killing him instantly. The captains scrambled for their horses to give chase while all the other soldiers stood and watched. One captain got a shot off as they rode out of camp in a fury.

Riding through thick woods to get to the main road, Greycourt looked at Scipio next to him. Both were hell bent on getting as far away as possible. The two expert horsemen galloped into the woods in a serpentine route in order to keep whoever was following them off balance. After it seemed that they were no longer being followed, they stopped in the woods a good distance from the camp to rest. Greycourt got off his horse and noticed Scipio slump off his. The shot fired by the captain got him in the back, but he kept riding.

"Lie still," he said.

Scipio's blood soaked his jacket and trousers. Beads of sweat were on his forehead as he tried to speak. "We got away, didn't we?" he asked, smiling. "My back hurts bad, sir, hurts real bad," he said, wincing.

Greycourt looked around the woods. They were in the middle of nowhere with no idea where they were, but he wanted to get him to a doctor. "Rest a bit. I'll get you to a doctor," he said.

Scipio smiled. "Ain't no doctor gonna treat me."

Greycourt wiped his face with a white handkerchief. "You'll be treated if I have to shoot the doctor."

Scipio, breathing heavy, smiled and winced at the same time. "How I gonna be treated if you shoot the doctor?"

There was a canteen on the saddle, and Greycourt got it down to give his companion a drink. He then poured some of the water over his face. "I'm turning you over. Be still," he said.

Scipio lay on his stomach as Greycourt looked in the saddlebag on Scipio's horse and found a small knife. He washed the knife and ripped the shirt apart to get to the wound. After washing the wound, he felt around. Scipio cried out but quickly shut his mouth. Greycourt again probed inside the wound and felt the slug. If he could only get to it, he knew he could get it out.

Tearing the flesh around it, he got under it. In excruciating pain, Scipio appeared to faint. The blood was oozing faster now as he finally got the slug. Scipio was breathing slowly as Greycourt tore his own shirt to cover the wound and stop the bleeding.

Scipio's saddlebags were full of dried pork and a sack of beans. There was another pistol in one of them. Unable to make a fire that would disclose their location, Greycourt propped Scipio up against a saddle he had taken off his horse and saw him come to. There would be a search party out soon if there wasn't one out already, since an officer had been shot and killed by a prisoner. Scipio was too weak to ride, but he could not leave him behind—he'd be hung on the spot.

They ate some of the dried pork and made sure the horses rested for a while. Greycourt got up to saddle Scipio's horse when he noticed that a nick was cut in the back of the saddle. He surmised that the shot from the captain nicked the back of the saddle before hitting Scipio. The saddle had probably saved his life.

Greycourt slowly got his brave companion mounted and wrapped his tunic around him for support. They stayed off the road and rode north through the woods trying to get to Greycourt Manor. They were traveling toward Richmond and estimated they could get to their destination sometime tomorrow.

There was a drizzle during the night, but the woods gave them decent shelter and enabled them to get ample rest before starting out again. Scipio was hurting and started bleeding and again pleaded with Greycourt to let him stay behind, but again, the fugitive officer would have none of it. They swallowed the last of the dried pork and rode away.

They picked up their pace a bit but had to leave the woods to cross the main road in order to go through Atkinson on the way to the plantation. As a precaution, Greycourt took the revolver out of the belt of his trousers as he anticipated the county guards were out roaming, searching for deserters or anything else they could steal. They came to a sign that read, "Atkinson – Five Miles", and knew they had to turn west for about ten miles. Just then, they heard horses galloping up behind them.

Turning to look, he squinted. He could not tell if they were regulars from the camp or county guards, but there were four of them. They took off west, Scipio barely holding onto the reins as they rode back into the woods on the other side of the road to take cover. Shots were fired at them as they rode. The four guardsmen stopped their mounts near the Atkinson sign. They looked at each other and then looked both ways. As one of the guardsmen slowly turned his horse, he was surprised by Greycourt and Scipio aiming their pistols at them about thirty yards away, Greycourt holding two revolvers. As the guardsman yelled out, the other three turned and were hit with a rapid volley of fatal shots, knocking them off their horses.

In a surprise out of nowhere, a patrol of Rebel cavalry rode up behind the two fugitives. As Greycourt turned to shoot at them, the Rebels started shooting, forcing them to ride furiously away from the gunfire. He told Scipio to keep riding as he stopped and turned to confront the Rebel riders. As they got closer, he started shooting and hit two riders, but shots were being fired behind him as he realized Scipio had returned to help.

The Rebel riders backed off, so Greycourt and Scipio rode off, heading west. As they rode, Scipio fell off his horse, wounded once again. Greycourt stopped and was about to dismount to help his companion. Seeing Rebels coming at him, Scipio yelled as loud as he could, "GET OUT. KEEP GOING, SIR!" Then Scipio died.

Greycourt Manor was in shambles. Apparently, there was fighting on the grounds, and the house had taken cannon hits. Most of the front of the mansion was intact, but the east side and most of the rear were blown apart. Exhausted and starved, Greycourt dismounted and entered with his revolver drawn, only three rounds left.

Whatever furniture had been left was smashed. The ruins made him sick as he walked to the sacred room which had been the Judge's den. He looked around and pictured the room as it used to be: the desk in the far west corner; fireplace in the north wall; bookcases on the south and east; walls, couch, and two chairs in front of the oak desk. All the furniture was burned or just taken. He paced out where things would have been among the debris of torn and burnt books, papers, some broken furniture and the ripped carpeting. He got on his knees and felt around. After a few minutes, he found a small hook sticking slightly up in the floor. He located a small stick to pry the hook loose. He opened the small wooden cover.

Greycourt looked around and then reached in and pulled up some papers, bonds, and a doctor's bag. He opened the bag, and there it was —$10,000, Yankee greenbacks!

As a boy, he remembered his father hiding something in the floor. When no one was home, he had gone into the den and opened the secret hole in the floor. At that time, there wasn't much money; but apparently, the Judge had gradually been putting money in that bag. He reached inside the hole again and came up with a LeMat revolver, a fancy pistol with a nine-shot cylinder barrel and a secondary smooth-bore barrel capable of firing buckshot.

There was also a box of cartridges stored underneath. The revolver, used by Generals Stuart and Bragg, was a powerful weapon. He looked it over and saw that it was in very good condition. Making sure he didn't miss anything, he reached down again and pulled up a leather folder. Looking inside, his eyes widened. The folder contained an envelope from the United States Military Academy.

He opened the envelope which was addressed to Judge Norris James Greycourt and took out a letter. He read the letter dated April 12, 1861:

To the Honorable Judge Greycourt:

It is my pleasure to send this diploma of graduation from the United States Military Academy of your son, Cadet Lt. Colton James Greycourt. Lieutenant Greycourt has exhibited the very essence of what this academy exemplifies: honor, bravery, camaraderie, and loyalty. His exceptional leadership skills have graded as one of the highest in this august institution's history. With just two demerits for minor infractions, his is a record to be very proud of. I am proud to endorse this diploma and proud to have had this young man at our esteemed institution.

Very truly yours,

John F. Reynolds, Commandant, U.S. Military Academy

After reading the letter signed by Reynolds, he rubbed his face and took out the sheepskin diploma. He did, in fact, graduate. Why was this fact kept from him? The Judge knew that he had graduated yet never told him? He placed the letter and diploma back into the envelope and leather case, took the doctor's bag with the money, and the revolver. Attempting to go up the long staircase in the foyer, he only got halfway as the upstairs rooms had been destroyed by cannon fire. With nothing left to grab, he was satisfied that he had found what he was really looking for and then some. It was time to head north to safety.

Heading north and wearing ragged, dirty clothes, he knew he had to get by Rebel patrols and the ever menacing county guards. If he was detained, his money would be found and taken from him, so he had to be extra careful in his navigation of the countryside. Once he got around Richmond from the south, he could cross the Potomac River and head to Baltimore. He had to see Paul and Tessa.

After three days of staying in the heavy woods along the main roads, he made it to the house in Baltimore; and to his surprise, his brother and his family were there. He did not want to do any explaining, but he had to tell Scipio's parents what had happened.

The white picket fence out front was well kept, as was the front porch and modest landscaping. He tied his horse in front and went in as Tessa ran to him, hugging the boy she practically raised. Paul had been working in the backyard, and he walked into the parlor, his work apron soiled from his tasks. Paul took off his gloves and shook Greycourt's hand and looked over his shoulder, perhaps to see if Scipio was with him. Tessa remarked that the young man looked as if he hadn't had a meal in weeks, looking gaunt and ashen. A hot bath would be readied and a shave and haircut too. Reginald walked in from the backyard and looked at Colt.

"I didn't read your name on any of the rolls of the dead yet, but I figured you weren't found yet. I'm glad you're alive," he said.

Colt looked his brother up and down. "You look healthy enough. How's your family?"

"Fine, just fine. Out visiting on the other side of town," he answered, delighted that his brother asked about his family. "You hear about Jonathan?" he asked.

Colt shook his head. "He got promoted to major in late June and was transferred to First Corps under George Pickett." Colt was puzzled.

"Under Pickett?"

"He asked and was granted permission for the transfer. He wanted to be nearer to Genie and the baby."

Reginald's eyes lowered. "Him and about a thousand other men made that charge at Gettysburg. It took a few days to find out he was dead. Genie is devastated. She and the baby are with her in-laws in Philadelphia. How did you fair up there? I read where Stuart didn't do so good."

Colt was shattered. His young brother-in-law was dead and his young sister a widow, visions of victories and grandeur for the cause. He'd just seen death and hardship.

Reginald looked at his younger brother; the face was hardened, taut, weathered. There was something about those blue eyes too; they looked angry and fiery.

"The Judge went to Secretary Seddon and got the request granted," explained Reginald.

"The Judge did?" Colt asked, surprised. "Why didn't the Judge get him assigned to the War Department in Richmond? He could have been with you. And why aren't you in Richmond now?"

Reginald shook his head. "Things got a bit confused. I'm taking my family to New York. I've got a job lined up with a law firm there."

"Just like that. The cause you were so strongly for, so sure of. Now you just leave," Greycourt asked, not really surprised. "What about the Rebel government? Just leave like that?"

His brother got annoyed. "Yes. I have to take care of my family first. Besides, the war will drag on, and we can recoup our investment."

Now Colt was really confused. "Recoup your investment?"

Reginald continued, "We didn't want to tell you, but we have 75 percent in a munitions factory in Pennsylvania. Well, it got blown up, so we had to reinvest in getting it built again and running. The Judge didn't want you to know until after the war. We were making money, big money."

Colt took a step toward his brother. "So you and the Judge were making money, blood money! Munitions factory for the North while both of you were representatives of the Rebel government. Just whose side are you and the Judge on? Where in the hell is the Judge anyway?"

Reginald scratched his head. "He's in London negotiating a trade agreement with the British. I'm guessing he doesn't know about Gettysburg yet. That might slam shut any agreements, or anything else for that matter, with the British. But then again, you know the Judge. He can talk people into almost anything."

Colt just stared at his brother. His ire was such that he wanted to physically throw his brother out of the house. "Factory in Pennsylvania? I took part in blowing up that factory," he said. He looked around the room and then at his brother. "I hope you and the Judge are broke."

Reginald was shocked to hear his brother say that. "We're in the process of rebuilding that factory."

Unfazed, Colt folded his arms. "The war will be over soon . . . I hope."

Reginald left the room and told Tessa he would not be staying for supper. Disappointed, she beckoned Colt into the kitchen. He began to tell her that Greycourt Manor was reduced to rubble. Tessa was upset at that but commanded Colt to get out of his clothes so she can wash them and to get in the bath out in the backyard. His supper would be ready when he was clean.

Before he undressed, he called Paul into the kitchen. He told them both about how Gratton whipped Scipio and his challenge to a duel because of it. Paul was irate that Colt would risk a duel over a whipping and scolded him that he wasn't raised that way. Colt stopped him and continued, telling them about Dara and the wagon, how he was considered a deserter and coward for helping his friend and for guiding the wagon to safety. He made a point of telling them that Gratton sought revenge for the humiliation of the slap and challenge. Their son helped him escape a hanging but paid for it dearly by dying as they escaped.

Paul and Tessa looked at each other as a tear slowly trickled down her left check. Paul swallowed and stared straight ahead. He felt a rush of pride for his son overcomes his body as he held Tessa's hand.

The bath water was getting cold.

After two days of rest and good nourishment, Colt had to leave. Before he left, he placed $500 on the kitchen table. He thought about going to the Hunnicutt farm to wait out the rest of the war but thought he would more than likely get arrested for being a wanted man.

He would be safe with Victoria, he thought.

CHAPTER SEVENTEEN

It rained frequently in London.

Mrs. Greycourt got very tired of the rain and drizzle. After three weeks of enjoying tea time every afternoon at three o'clock, she was ready to sail back home. The Judge never spoke about his meetings with members of Parliament and was still waiting patiently for an audience with Queen Victoria.

The Judge had been meeting with Lord Henry Radley and his brother, Sir Arthur Radley, but their meetings involved pheasant hunting, billiards—almost anything but discussions of trade agreements. The Judge sensed that the British government was getting very cautious regarding the South and was stalling.

Vice President Alexander H. Stephens was scheduled to join the Greycourts in London in a week. He was anxious for his arrival. It was late morning, and a courier came to the hotel with an invitation for the couple to join his lordship and his wife at their estate.

The sprawling estate of Lord Radley, located in Wembley, had three large gardens, rolling hills for fox hunts, stables, guest cottages, and three tall fountains. Lord Radley was a tall, thin man with a gray-trimmed mustache and gray hair. His face, pointed at the chin, and his blue eyes gave him an austere appearance. A veteran cavalry officer, he never fought in any battles of confrontations but saw three tours in India by patrolling the Khyber Pass. His reputation was that of a soldier-diplomat, and although he came from an old wealthy British family, he gained entry into the House of Lords for his exceptional demeanor and ability to keep the peace in a foreign land.

The Greycourts were invited to stay a few days at the estate, so they packed for their stay. The Judge hoped that they could talk trade agreements and have things settled before the vice president arrived. Two servants came out to the carriage as it pulled up to the grand oval steps in front of the mansion. After helping the Judge and Mrs. Greycourt out of the elegantly built coach, the servants took the guests' baggage.

Lord Radley came out with a big smile on his face, happy to see his guests. He immediately offered them a cold drink before leading them to a large sunroom to the east of the house overlooking the grounds and one of the gardens. Lady Radley, a thin gray-haired woman that looked much younger than her age, stood in the cavernous foyer with her body servant. She leaned on a cane as her arthritic right hip had given her trouble from time to time. She warmly greeted the guests and apologized for not having them out sooner. Lord Radley escorted Mrs. Greycourt; the Judge did the same with Lady Radley to the sunroom for a lunch of cucumber salad, goose liver, cold pheasant, boiled potatoes, and ginger tea. The small talk was about family and grandchildren.

As grand as the plantations were in the South, nothing could compare to the Radley Estate. The gentlemen were walking about the grounds, and the ladies were to retire to the rear porch to continue the visit.

Lord Radley took the left arm of his guest as they walked. "This is a lot of tea, ol' boy," he said, waving his left hand in a semicircle. "My family has been in the tea business for many, many years, and I might say, it has been very good to us."

The Judge was interested as he could latch onto some similarities between the families, making conversation easier.

"Ceylon, India, those far off places, you know. We lived in India for ten years while I was in Her Majesty's service. I was grateful. It kept me close to the family business, you know."

The Judge listened and nodded. "Yes, Lord Radley. I feel we have many similarities," he said with a smile.

"How so, my good man?" he asked rather condescendingly.

"My family has been in the cotton and tobacco business for many years, and I too have been active in politics. My ancestors were of English descent also," the Judge explained.

Lord Radley smiled. "Were they loyal to the crown in that blasted rebellion?"

"No. My great-grandfather and grandfather fought with the colonists, and my father fought with the Virginia Militia in 1812, the year I was born," answered the Judge.

The elder British gentleman cleared his throat. "Yes, well, I guess they bloody well had to."

Being careful to not get into a political argument about years past, the Judge then complimented the wonderful grounds and garden. He asked if perhaps they could take a horse ride in the morning. Lord Radley responded, saying he'd be delighted, as he did not have many chaps around to ride with. As they walked through the east garden, Sir Arthur Radley, his lordship's younger brother, came out to join them.

A gaunt-looking man with a pointy face and very dark hair, his sullen eyes gave off the impression that he did not trust anyone. He seemed to look from the corners of his eyes all the time. He was not a military man, although he did serve briefly in Her Majesty's army in the diplomatic corps. Sir Arthur was always an argumentative fellow and had never met the Judge. He was anxious to hear what the Judge had to offer.

The three men sat in the middle of the garden to discuss the Confederacy's offer. Sir Arthur's smug attitude was apparent right away.

The Judge began by saying that the Confederacy had a lot to offer. As soon as the war was over, cotton would again make it to England by the boatload as prices would be very reasonable, lowering tariffs. English merchants would also be able to open offices throughout the South the same way their agents are in India and Africa and other parts of the world, overseeing various business agreements. Sir Arthur wasn't impressed.

"So you say we should make business agreements with the Confederacy for your cotton and tobacco? Before your bloody war, we had agreements and a steady cotton supply, but now the blockade has stifled shipments. We get, maybe, three shipments a month now," he said, annoyed at the Judge's weak proposal. "Besides, when your war is over, we can resume trade, and maybe the price would be higher, but we'll be working with a nonhostile government."

The Judge nodded and asked if he could smoke his pipe. "I guarantee, gentlemen, that our government will be open and friendly in trade and very reasonable with the tariffs. You'll find that doing business with a friendly government will reap many benefits."

Sir Arthur was not convinced. He thought the Judge was being very vague. "So before your war, we had trade, reasonable tariffs, and everyone was satisfied. Now you are saying that when you win your war, things will be better? I don't see how. Your government and planters will want to make their money back after a war that's bankrupted them. Don't you agree, my good man?"

A servant came out to the gentlemen with a large decanter of brandy and a bottle of whiskey and glasses. The Judge took the brandy, and he tried to speak, but Sir Arthur kept interrupting.

Lord Radley, sipping his whiskey, asked a question, "I say, my good man, weren't we to discuss weapons and ammunition shipments? That's the agreement we're all interested in."

The Judge became uneasy and puffed on his pipe. "Why yes, of course, Lord Radley. We can say that within six months, that blockade will be gone as the war will be concentrated directly at Washington City. Your ships will very likely have no obstructions to our ports. I'll say we'll require three hundred cases of rifles and six hundred barrels of powder each month. Of course, we'll require at least thirty thousand rounds of ammunition with that. We can start there."

Sir Arthur looked at his older brother, sipped his brandy, and sat back. "Surely, my good man, you can't really think that your ports will be free of the blockade? Don't you know what has occurred a short time ago?"

The Judge was puzzled. "I've had some information. The South has had victory upon victory. Peace may be imminent, Sir Arthur," he answered.

Lord Radley looked at his brother, waiting for his answer. "Sir, England is a proud country. Do you really think we would do business with a country that still believes in the institution of slavery? People chained and whipped to do your chores?"

The Judge was very agitated now and was about to answer when Sir Arthur continued, "Your country has suffered a huge setback. Did you know that your General Lee was chased back home after his attempt to invade the North? And heavy losses in some place called Gettysburg, I think that's how you say it, I might add. It's in today's newspapers. Sir, perhaps we should be speaking with one of Mr. Lincoln's men."

★★★

Paul sat on the back porch of the home that he and his wife kept up so very well. He sat in a rocking chair and slowly rocked back and forth. His thoughts went to his son, Scipio, and how proud he was of him.

Scipio was always with Colton. They usually rode together and even tended to the horses together. When Colton was about seven years old and learning to ride, he had fallen off his horse and hurt his side. He dared not cry as the Judge sternly watched from his own mount. Holding back tears, mostly from embarrassment and a hurt shoulder, young Colton James tried to get up but stumbled.

Paul went over to him and gently lifted him up, brushing him off. Tessa watched from the back porch and stared at the Judge. Paul straightened the boy's clothes and whispered for him to get back on the horse. He knew the Judge was irritated that the boy had fallen. He helped the boy back up on the horse, and they continued their ride.

Paul had never forgotten that day. Although it seemed to be a minor incident, from that time on, young Colton James went to Paul for guidance and help. Colton even told Scipio that Paul was the smartest man he ever knew.

Tessa did not want Colt to leave to find Victoria. She urged him to stay with them in Baltimore until the war was over. She thought that finding Victoria would be trouble for him; he might get arrested or, worse, killed. He was determined to find her and then decide what he should do. The last letter from Victoria was from the City Hotel, so that's where he headed.

The front desk clerk said that she had left two weeks earlier with a forwarding address to the National Hotel in Washington City. Colt thought it odd that she move around so often. Was the New York Philharmonic on tour in the northeast?

With enough cash to keep him going in Washington, he bought a ticket from Baltimore and arrived in the northern capital on a very hot August afternoon. All the windows of the train were open. When it approached the city, a fowl stink permeated the air. The capital was filled with livestock, chickens, and horses roaming the streets. It smelled like a very large rancid latrine. There were thousands of Union soldiers walking about the streets; with poor facilities, they found anywhere available to relive themselves, whether it was against buildings, alleyways, anywhere. With all that, Greycourt tried to look as inconspicuous as he possibly could.

The National Hotel was very classy and clean. President Lincoln himself stayed there when he first got to Washington, so it was obvious to Greycourt that the Philharmonic would stay there. He was able to get a room on the top floor, very pleased that he would not be close to the dirty streets. Before going to his room, he asked if he could leave a note for Victoria Leland and was told she had left a forwarding address to the Hotel Astor in New York City. Disappointed, he washed his face, changed his clothes, and planned to get a shave in the lobby barbershop followed by supper in the hotel's stylish dining room.

He checked his pocket watch as he sat down at a corner table and looked at the menu card. Oysters were recommended as an appetizer, and the venison with wild rice and fresh kale were also popular items on the menu. He gave his food order to the elderly waiter and ordered a whiskey and water. As the raw oysters were served with lemon wedges and a hot pepper sauce, he noticed that the room had filled to capacity, and the large crowd made him feel comfortable. That only lasted a few minutes.

A big burly well-dressed man came over to his table and stood looking down at him. "Sir, might I have a minute with you?" he asked.

Greycourt, wiping his mouth with the white cloth napkin, nodded.

"I don't believe I've ever seen you in this hotel. Are you on leave?" he asked.

Greycourt's heart started to pound. "Who might you be, sir?" he asked in return.

The big man smiled. "Oh sorry. My name is Ward Hill Lamon. I am a United States marshal for the District of Columbia. The appointment made by my good and dear friend, President Abraham Lincoln. And your full name Mr. Greycourt?" he asked.

Shocked at the man's knowledge of his last name, Greycourt sat back and let out a sigh. "I'm not sure why you're asking, sir."

"Well, sir, you don't look like a civilian, not in these times, and you are well dressed in a not-so-thrifty hotel. What is your business here?" he asked.

Greycourt had to think fast. "I'm looking to buy land and thought I'd start here."

Lamon smiled. "I'd take it that you're a spy for the Rebel government. Am I right, sir?"

Greycourt would have to take his chances. "Sir, I am a fugitive from the Confederate cavalry—a wanted man. I am risking my life here in Washington but thought I'd be safe here going unnoticed. Obviously, I was wrong."

Lamon, winding his pocket watch, nodded. "If you are that, a fugitive from the traitors, I might have a proposition for you, a proposition that you will have to accept."

Nervously wiping his mouth again with the napkin, he leaned forward. "Tell me, sir, how did you really come to notice me?"

Lamon smiled. "See that gentleman sitting at the far corner table, the one sitting alone and wearing spectacles?"

Greycourt looked in that direction and saw a familiar face— Nigel Blaine.

CHAPTER EIGHTEEN

Secretary Stanton went to his office. Irritable at the entire current situation, he unlocked his private wooden file cabinet, took out a large ledger book, and looked through the pages. He found the page he searched for and stared at it. In the margins were figures, dollars and cents, indicating the costs of various "suggestions" made to his operative in New York City. As he turned the pages, he noticed that the amounts were higher next to each date. Tired but determined, he read on and noticed something he entered two weeks before about an unsolved incident in New York City. He couldn't help but think there was something related to that incident and what was going on in the basement of the President's House now.

★★★

Greycourt sat by himself at a corner table in the National Hotel. Ward Hill Lamon had just left and told him that the tab for the dining room was on him and to have whatever else he wanted. In front of him was an envelope with $100 which Lamon had left along with a document that would guarantee his safety traveling anywhere in the North.

Lamon suggested that they meet again the next afternoon in the hotel's dining room to discuss the proposition. He offered Greycourt a position as an agent, reporting to him directly. At the rank of colonel, he was to get deep into the Virginia countryside or anywhere else he saw fit and to report of the movements of the newly formed

Confederate Torpedo Bureau. Most importantly, he was to report back of any plans or plots against the president.

"You see, sir, President Lincoln gets many death threats each day. Threats from the very first day he was elected. Mr. Lincoln is my charge to protect. Mostly, he's a personal friend of mine. We go back to our days as law partners in Danville, Illinois. My plan is to gather information on any plots and squash them immediately. I have a brigade of cavalry at my disposal just north of here, and they will be dispatched to go up against any attempts, no matter how small or big."

Greycourt listened and was intrigued by the idea. He was a wanted man in the South, and if caught, he'd be hung for sure. He felt betrayed by his own people, his own family, and realized that the Confederacy was a rogue government.

That morning he was walking the streets of Washington City and noticed a tall gentleman with a young boy, walking hand in hand, talking and laughing and enjoying the new day. The gentleman would tip his hat to a passersby and even stop to chat with a few couples. As he looked closer, he noticed the stove pipe hat, long dark coat and got a look at the bearded face—it was President Abraham Lincoln himself!

Lamon was very direct with the young man. "Mr. Greycourt, I'm offering you the rank of deputy as a United States marshal and a full pardon for any and all your actions as a Confederate. I have a document here that you'll have to sign, denouncing the Rebel government and also declaring your allegiance to the United States of America." It was the Oath of Allegiance—it exonerated all Rebels that signed it.

Greycourt looked it over and looked at Lamon.

The big man nodded. "If you don't sign it, you'll be arrested, tried, and hung. If you sign it and double-cross me, I will personally hunt you down and kill you myself."

A pen and ink was brought over by a waiter, and the document was signed. Torn from the start of secession, Greycourt took up arms against the American flag and its people. Now, he firmly believed the oath taken restored his integrity.

Lamon was pleased. He liked Greycourt, even though he knew him only for a very short while. Both were Virginians, and Lamon was hurt when the state of his birth seceded. With a fellow Virginian like Greycourt now working for him, he felt a sense of pride and a little vindication.

"Here's $100 for you to get outfitted. I'll meet you back here the day after next, drunk or sober."

With an assignment from a man closest to the president of the United States, Deputy Colton James Greycourt started his work in the very city he got a second life, Washington, the capital of the Union.

★★★

Clive G. Dalrymple was disturbed. He had just received a wire from his agent partner, Nigel Blaine. He waited in front of Delmonico's restaurant for Victoria who was at a special fitting for new dresses at Marcelline's on Madison Avenue. He checked his pocket watch and saw that, as usual, she was late. Dressed in a light blue dress, white hat with a blue band, white gloves, and white shoes, Victoria struck a very attractive figure, turning many heads as she casually strolled on a very sunny Friday afternoon. She could tell how annoyed Dalrymple was as she approached him and wasn't fazed in the least.

"Late again, my dear," he said sternly. "You know this place. If a reservation is even a minute late, they'll knock you down to the bottom of the list. That usually costs me $2," he said as they went in.

Victoria didn't pay him any mind and went in to be seated at a table in the center of the room after the exchange of $2 with the maitre d'.

A waiter came over and brought their drinks, beer for him and a cherry brandy for her. They ordered lunch, and both looked around the fancy large restaurant to see if anyone else they know may be dining.

Dalrymple sipped his drink and sat back. "Why do you do this to me? You know I expect promptness, yet you make a point of being tardy each and every time we have to meet. You know how I feel."

Victoria rolled her eyes and took a sip of the brandy. "You get what you want from me, more than you deserve."

"I've never heard you complain, and besides, I've made you a more worthy woman, so to speak."

Victoria was tempted to toss her drink in his face but stopped herself. She composed herself, the veins relaxing in her neck. "Clive Gregory," she said, knowing he did not like being called that, "you're not that good, so don't flatter yourself."

Dalrymple changed the subject to the business at hand. "I'm calling Blaine back up here. He had an opportunity and missed it," he said as the waiter brought their meals and poured coffee for them.

Victoria was curious. "Opportunity? How so?"

"Blaine was dining at the National when he noticed your Colt Greycourt sitting in that very room alone. Instead of waiting and tailing him or, better yet, waiting and shooting him, our Mr. Blaine decided to inform Mr. Ward Hill Lamon who happened to be dining there at the same time. You know who Lamon is?" he asked.

Nodding, Victoria's eyes widened. "So he saw Colt in Washington? What happened? Where's Colt now?"

Dalrymple took a bite of the rare steak and wiped his mouth. "That's another thing. He doesn't know. He followed Greycourt the next day and was afraid of being made, so he left him as he entered the National again. He waited but seemed to have lost him."

Victoria wiped her mouth after taking a bite of a buttered boiled potato. "What do you think that was about? Do you think he was arrested? Colt is not that stupid. There's probably a new Rebel plan. After Gettysburg, well, you know, they could be desperate."

Dalrymple kept eating, chewing slowly as he thought. "No, I'm sure they won't. They're regrouping their forces. My guess is that he was in Washington to try and find out troop strengths and the Union's next moves. No matter, but it would be very beneficial if we can give our man more of that very accurate information you've been getting."

To do that, Blaine would have to stay on Greycourt's tail if he wasn't placed under arrest. For the first time, Victoria did not know Colt's whereabouts.

★★★

Under the weak cover of a realtor from Maryland, Greycourt's strategy was to stay at different rooming houses in and around the city. There seemed to be more and more troops and civilians coming into Washington each day, so he was fortunate to get a room at each place. Keeping to himself yet having a keen ear open, he listened to the chatter of the various guests at these inns. There seemed to be more talk of siding with the Rebels, which made him aware that he was close to any possible plots against the president. With his carpet bag in hand, he sauntered down H Street and came upon a three-and-half-story house at 604 H Street NW. He entered, and a young girl had him fill out a card, and he was assigned a room on the top floor for 15¢ a day.

A basin of fresh water and clean towels were provided, along with a very comfortable bed. The place was the cleanest of all the rooming houses he had stayed in the last three weeks. Supper was at six thirty, and a full table was expected as all rooms were filled.

The guests took their chairs as the lady of the house and owner, Mrs. Mary E. Surratt, greeted each person individually. Seated at the head of the table was a professor of English literature from Kings College in New York City who was in town to give a speech at nearby Columbian College. Next to him on his right was a mulatto seamstress who ran away from her masters in Virginia, looking for work. A thin spectacled man with a thin mustache sat next to her.

Greycourt sat at the other end of the table. Two men sat on his left; one introduced himself as Ted Jones and said he was a patent executive for a Philadelphia company, and the other was his assistant, Bill Ruggles, also known as Tippie. Both Jones and Ruggles looked familiar to him. He hoped that he wasn't familiar to them.

The supper conversation was about the war, of course. The professor, a staunch supporter of Lincoln and speaking about the evils of slavery, drew the ire of the table. Greycourt just listened as the professor cited the evils of man enslaving other men and how Lincoln would defeat the South now that the Rebels were retreating.

Mr. Jones was getting agitated and was about to speak up when a man came into the house, immediately tended to by Mrs. Surratt. The young man took off his hat and jacket and peeked into the dining room as Mrs. Surratt spoke to him. Jones and Ruggles got up and followed the young man into the kitchen.

Greycourt leaned to a young lady on his left and asked in a whisper, "Who is the young man that just came in?"

She whispered back that it is John Surratt, Mrs. Surratt's son.

As Greycourt finished his meal of chicken and dumplings with boiled carrots and cherry pie, he complimented the cook for a wonderful meal and went to his room. As he went up the stairs, he noticed the three men go back into the dining room.

Greycourt was about to go out for a walk when he heard a commotion in the room next to his. He went out into the hallway and burst through the door of the next room. He grabbed the man who was attacking the professor by hitting him with his pistol. Knocking the pistol out of the attacker's hand, Greycourt turned the attacker around and smashed him in the face with a hard left fist, sending him reeling across the room and onto the floor. The attacker saw that he could not take on the powerful guest, so he scrambled for the door and ran.

Greycourt turned to the old professor and placed a handkerchief on the cut from the pistol blow on the side of his forehead. It was odd that no one came in to see what had happened. "Here, let me tend to that, sir," he said to the old man as he wiped the wound.

"Thank you, my good man. That's very kind of you to come to my rescue," he answered in a gravelly voice. The professor sat up and touched the swollen orbit under his left eye. "Be careful here, young fellow. I've been here two nights and heard nothing but Rebel talk at supper, talk of hatred for this city."

"Who were the Rebels? The men sitting at the table?" he asked.

Not wanting to start more trouble, the professor said, "Just take care, young man. That man that attacked me . . ."

"I recognized him from the supper table," Greycourt answered, very upset that an old man was attacked. He was going to seek out those men after seeing to the professor's well-being. "Let me get you to a doctor, sir," he said.

The old man, waiving his right hand, said, "No, no. I must get back home. There's a train leaving for New York tonight, and instead of staying the night here, I'd be better off leaving."

Greycourt got a carriage and assisted him to the train station. They sat in the waiting area; the train was about a half hour late in arriving.

Holding an umbrella and his paisley carpetbag, the professor patted his new young friend on the arm. "Thank you again for your kindness, my young friend. I hope helping me has not put you in a very precarious place now."

Greycourt smiled. "Sir, I think I'm in the right place at the right time now."

★★★

The Confederacy was being strangled by the Union's blockade. Blockade runners tried many times to get past the Yankee warships in order to get goods and supplies through, keeping their lifeline breathing. Some made it; some didn't.

The Anaconda Plan was created by the then Union general in chief, the elderly Winfield Scott, stretched from the Carolinas, around Florida, through the gulf, and up the Mississippi River. This plan was devised to starve the Rebels to death and cut off any supplies. Union warships, manned with experienced crewmen and equipped with powerful cannons, forced the Confederacy to counter those mighty ships. The Confederate ironclad Merrimac, or Virginia, wreaked havoc on the wooden blockade ships, so the Union swiftly built their own, the ironclad Monitor. Their battle, which lasted over three hours at Hampton Roads, Virginia, changed naval warfare— Union shipyards were frantically building these armored ships. The Rebel war department had to come up with another means to defeat these vessels.

The Confederate Secret Service created the Torpedo Bureau. After the Battle of Hampton Roads, the Rebel war department commissioned this division to create and perfect various bombs and incendiary devices to place around the Southern harbors. Led by Brigadier General Gabriel Rains, known as one of the bomb brothers, with his brother George Washington Rains who was a brigadier general in the Georgia Militia, the men of the Torpedo Bureau were experts in explosives and demolition. The best of the bureau's experts was Sergeant T. Francis Harney.

★★★

Greycourt stayed at the Surratt House for a week but kept a room at the National Hotel as his real place. After bouncing around to all the rooming houses in Washington, he knew that the Surratt House was most intriguing. The three-story house had comfortable rooms and a long dining room on the middle floor. The parlor, also on the middle floor, was modestly decorated with oil lamps, comfortable chairs, and a couch. The fireplace mantle had some pictures on it with an impressive photograph of one of the most celebrated celebrities of the time, John Wilkes Booth. Greycourt had asked if the Surratts knew Booth; without giving any details, he was told he was an occasional guest whenever he came to town. The Union's new agent gave this information about the Surratt House to Lamon via a secretly coded note with a special symbol on the envelope that was in the shape of a triangle with a cross in the middle.

Early one day, as Greycourt sat for breakfast, he noticed that it was just him and an elderly couple from Ohio. After exchanging pleasantries, he mentioned how unusual it was that the table only had three guests; it was usually full. The old man, an inventor that was presenting his invention to President Lincoln in a few hours, said that he overheard three men discussing a trip to Richmond. Greycourt thought it odd that the men were so brazen and open in their discussion. He pressed the man further but could only come up with a name that was mentioned few times: Harney.

There was no civilian train service from Washington City into the south. Union supply trains, under heavy guard, did make it into certain areas of Virginia. With his commission papers as a United States deputy marshal, Greycourt hitched a ride on one of those supply trains going to Culpepper to resupply Union troops amassing for a push south toward Richmond.

Greycourt took a seat in the officers' car on the train that was heavily loaded with foodstuffs, medical and camping supplies, and ammunition. Sharpshooters, lying prone, were placed on top of each car. The last car was for livestock as a dozen horses, including Greycourt's roan, were also on the train.

The officer's car was relatively quiet, and the supply officers, three quartermasters and three captains that appeared to have been injured in battle, weren't very talkative. This suited Greycourt just fine. Traveling for about an hour, the train came to a screeching halt as an explosion ripped the tracks up ahead. As the guards stood up to see, shots came out of the woods on both sides of the train; the supply train was under siege.

The guards lay on their bellies again, some firing back as the train was peppered with shots. "STAY DOWN AND GET AWAY FROM THOSE WINDOWS!" Greycourt shouted at the men in the car. He drew his revolver and smashed one of the windows on the north side and began shooting in the direction of enemy fire. Waiting for the precise moment to exit the car, he paused and swung his body through the window. With near misses of the Rebel shots, he scurried up the side of the car and lay down. "Steady boys—just wait," he ordered.

Suddenly both sides of the train were rushed by Rebels screaming the "eeyah" of the Rebel yell. "OPEN FIRE!" he shouted, and the riflemen began firing, hitting the charging Rebels. The third car down and then opened its doors on both sides, revealing kneeling and standing soldiers who started firing on the oncoming enemy, cutting them to pieces. Shots were still coming from the woods on both sides, and Greycourt ordered the men to fire high into the trees in the direction of enemy guns.

A bugle sounded down the tracks, and Greycourt saw a Union cavalry brigade gallop toward the train and then disperse into the woods on both sides to flush out the ambushers. The whole fracas ended with about thirty dead Rebels and ten wounded; the Union had six dead, eight wounded. The engineers and officers got out; Greycourt climbed down to observe the damages.

The tracks were blown up about fifty yards in front of them. They would take weeks to repair. A cavalry officer advised that an empty train was on the way from Culpepper to take the supplies the rest of the way under heavy guard.

Greycourt went down to the explosion site to examine it. He saw a wire led into the woods and followed it. A detonator box lay hidden by a tree. It appeared that there had been four horses, as the ground had fresh hoof marks. He followed the hoofs and noticed that they were headed south. Saddling up and getting a few supplies, including bacon, a small pouch of beans, and some coffee, he set out south on the main road toward Richmond.

★★★

Reginald James Greycourt and Clive G. Dalrymple waited for over an hour. They had gone through almost an entire pot of coffee and were about to get up and leave when she entered the dining room of the Hotel Astor in New York City.

Victoria was stunning in a blue chiffon dress, white hat, and stylish blue button-down shoes. Her purse matched her shoes, and she caught some of the patrons' eyes as she sauntered in. The waiter came over, and she ordered a brandy and a cup of coffee. Dalrymple was irate, wanting to slap her, but didn't.

"Again. This time, not ten minutes, not twenty minutes or thirty minutes. An hour," he barked. "You continue to disrespect me," he said gruffly.

Victoria didn't bat an eyelash. "I hope you have some news for me regarding my investment," she asked him as she sipped the brandy.

Reginald checked his pocket watch and shook his head. "I should have been back at the office fifteen minutes ago. Anyway, I have no information thus far about the factory. Your man Blaine doesn't seem to communicate with me any longer. I'm concerned about the progress."

A waiter came to the table and left a plate of sweet rolls and pastries, and Victoria asked for another pot of coffee. Dalrymple needed information and picked up a copy of the *New York Herald* from an unoccupied chair at the next table.

"Ever since July, it looks like the South's been on the run. That factory is nowhere on schedule. It's not easy now, getting young men to work. They're all in the army," Dalrymple said.

"Look at this," he said, holding up the newspaper, "U.S. General Grant was just appointed commander of all Union armies in the west. Know anything about him? Well, I can tell you, that man is a fighter. How long do you think it will be before he's made commander of all Union armies?"

Victoria and Reginald looked at each other as Dalrymple continued. "I'll tell you sooner than you'd think. When that happens, we can kiss that factory good-bye."

Reginald scratched the top of his head. "So now what do we do, turn the factory into something else?"

Victoria got annoyed. "The war's not over yet. If we can get three, maybe four more years, we could make some money, big money. As the war drags on, we raise prices. But we have to get that factory up and running." She paused and sipped the coffee. "Think. What will keep the war going?"

Dalrymple nodded. "Well, Washington is driving this thing and . . . wait a minute, Lincoln's up for reelection next year. I'd say he'll be hard to beat. He has enemies but a lot of friends too. If Lincoln loses—"

Victoria interrupted, "Better yet, if he's not the president now, Stanton would direct the war, don't you agree? Stanton would make sure the entire South burns in hell. He'll keep the war going to their last man. You can believe that."

Reginald was perplexed. "You mean Hannibal Hamlin. He'd be the president."

The dapper Dalrymple looked at Victoria and smiled and then turned to Reginald. "C'mon, man, Hamlin? You honestly think Stanton would let Hamlin make any decisions, any at all?"

Victoria nodded. "If Lincoln wasn't president, we'd stand a much better chance of having the war continue."

The waiter came and handed a note to Dalrymple. He read it and looked out toward the lobby and saw a man standing there. He then turned to Victoria. "What do you have for me? Make it good though. It will be hard to top the last bit of information you had for me."

Victoria shook her head. "I have nothing now, maybe in a few weeks. Ever since Blaine lost Colt, well, I haven't had contact."

Dalrymple then turned to Reginald. "Where's your brother? You have to know?" he asked.

Reginald took a sip of the coffee in front of him. "I don't know. The last time we were together, he was very sore at me. I doubt that I'll see or hear from him again. Besides, you want me to give up my own brother?"

Dalrymple laughed. "Give up? You, the Judge, and my dear Victoria have given him up all along. You're stopping now?"

Reginald got angry. "I'm telling you, Clive, don't get in my brother's way. He's changed since the war started. He can tear you apart and whoever you send at him. I saw it in his eyes. He'll take on anyone."

Victoria's eyes widened at the talk of Colt. She got all tingly just hearing about him.

Dalrymple wasn't impressed and checked his pocket watch. "Shouldn't you be getting back to your job, my friend?" he asked Reginald.

Wiping his mouth, Reginald got up, left a quarter on the table, bowed to Victoria, and left the dining room.

Dalrymple adjusted his tie and smiled at the stunning lady at his table. He thought for a moment. "What do you suggest? Since you have nothing to give now, maybe you can come up with something that I can give to our man anyway."

Victoria lowered her eyes, looked up, and very casually spoke, "This is for just you," she said, looking around. "Can we get to the president? Remove him office early? You know what I'm saying?"

Dalrymple smiled and nodded. "I think we can do something. We have to keep the war going. You're right. Keep that between you and me. Let me work on it."

CHAPTER NINETEEN

Disappointed in their trip to England, the Judge and Mrs. Greycourt bid farewell to all the people that were gracious and hospitable to them during their month there. Mrs. Greycourt was very much taken by the elegance of the English countryside and the proud aristocratic air of the people. She often remarked how she could live very comfortably in the London countryside. The Judge did not share her feelings and was determined to get back to America, Union or Confederate.

The Judge was disappointed that Vice President Stevens never made the trip, which would have bolstered his bid to get trade agreements. He was embarrassed that he would be going home with nothing. Mrs. Greycourt was disappointed that they were leaving but would not miss the weather. Their ship was taking them across the Atlantic to Nova Scotia and then to New York.

★★★

Now sporting a dark mustache and long hair, Colton James Greycourt was in Richmond. His journey from Culpepper along the main roads was without incident, except for being stopped south of Spotsylvania Courthouse by an old sheriff asking his business. But it was his overnight stay at an inn about ten miles north of Richmond that got his interest. He was sure he was on the right trail.

The Roadway Inn was run by a gray-bearded man and his pretty wife. They lost three sons to the war fighting for the South and buried themselves in their business. The inn was very neat and clean with the smell of cedar when you walked in. The couple stood behind a desk and welcomed him as he entered. One night, including meals, would cost 40¢; he gladly paid.

There was a stable in the rear for horses. For 5¢ extra, a slave would tend to the feeding and grooming of it. He was shown a room on the second floor with a big feather bed, dresser, and chair. A supper of chicken stew, biscuits, coffee, and apple pie was served promptly at seven o'clock, and guests were encouraged to sit in the large parlor to visit or read after eating.

Supper was very tasty and filling. The apple pie was exceptional. Greycourt asked for another half slice. He sat alone in the parlor while two other guests decided to go out on the front porch. The proprietor joined him as his wife cleared the table.

"What's yer business, son, if I may ask?" he said with a smile. "You don't have to tell me if you don't want, but I have to warn you. These roads are full of those county guards and highwaymen. I'd be very careful traveling if I was you."

Greycourt thanked the man for the advice and lit the man's pipe for him. "Any strange or odd-looking men stay here recently?" he asked.

The man narrowed his eyes as he thought and then shook his head. "Not that I recall. There were three men that stayed here a few days ago. They didn't say what their business was, but I overheard them say they had to go to Richmond. One of 'em said somethin' 'bout meeting Seddon and then got kicked for sayin' that."

Greycourt then described two of the men, and the proprietor nodded.

"You know 'em?"

Looking around the room, Greycourt leaned forward. "Yes, I was supposed to meet them near here. Is there another inn close to this one?" he asked.

The man shook his head. "Nope. Next stop would be Richmond. What's yer business?"

Greycourt checked his pocket watch and stretched. It was time for him to retire early for a good night's sleep before his ride into Richmond tomorrow.

Taking lodging across the James River at the Manchester Hotel, Greycourt had a good view of the Tredegar Iron Works and Mayo's Bridge spanning the river. The three men were going to meet the Confederacy's secretary of war, James A. Seddon. That told him that the three men were part of the Rebel Secret Service, which was most likely part of the Torpedo Bureau. It took him some time, but he recalled the men at the Surratt House; Ted Jones was really Thomas Nelson Conrad, a part-time spy for Stuart and a confidant of Mosby. Ruggles was M.B. "Tippie" Ruggles, a courier for Stuart that probably was now in the service of Secretary Seddon. The third man, he wasn't sure of, but if these three were involved with blowing up the train tracks near Culpepper, he had an idea.

In a daring move, he decided to ask to see Secretary Seddon under the guise of working for General Stuart. He was received by Seddon's assistant secretary of war, John A. Campbell, as Seddon was in all-day meetings with President Davis, Secretary of State Judah Benjamin, and Vice President Stephens. Campbell welcomed Greycourt and asked about his family, unaware that he was a wanted man in the South.

The discussion then turned to clandestine operations. Campbell told him that there was a plan directly pointing at Washington and Lincoln himself but was not at liberty to discuss it. He was glad to see him, and his report back to Stuart would be favorable; he sent regards to his family. Greycourt thanked him for his time and left.

An aide to Campbell came into the office and noticed the visitor leaving. A thin bespectacled young man, he tugged at his thin chin and looked out of the window. "That man that just left, sir. Wasn't that Colton James Greycourt?" he asked.

Campbell, reading a directive written on government letterhead, didn't look up. "Yes, it was. Fine young man, that Greycourt," he answered.

The aide got closer to the mahogany desk. "If I'm not mistaken, sir, he's a wanted man. Let me find the papers. He deserted and killed one of our officers. It happened months ago."

Campbell looked up. "You're mistaken, man. Greycourt is from one of the finest families in the South. A commended officer with General Stuart and a Southern gentleman," he answered.

The aide shook his head. "I'll get the report and notice to capture. He's a wanted man."

There was something going on that was pointed toward President Lincoln. Greycourt wasn't sure, but it was most likely a heinous attempt of some sort. He would have to get out of Richmond before heading back to Washington City—before someone lets it out that he's a wanted man.

As he was getting his things together, he left a fifty-cent piece on the dresser in the room as he would just leave and not sign out. There was a knock at the door. He took the LeMat revolver out of the rolled sack and slowly went to the door. With his face up against the door, he asked, "Who's there?"

"Bellman, sir" was the response.

He didn't like it. Even after telling the visitor to go away, the voice persisted. He raised the big revolver next to his left shoulder and opened the door slightly. Just then, two men burst into the room, forcing Greycourt backward. He was able to get a shot off, which went into the ceiling as the men rushed him. Wailing away with the revolver, he slammed the weapon on the head of one, sending him tumbling to the floor. Turning to the other, he pointed the gun. The other man drew his weapon, so Greycourt shot him, blowing a hole in his chest, killing him instantly. He turned to the man lying unconscious on the floor, placed the revolver next to his forehead and pulled the trigger—splattering flesh, bone, brain matter, and hair all over.

He quickly rifled through the pockets of both men and heard footsteps on the stairs. He didn't recognize the two men but grabbed their wallets and his roll bag, and he charged out of the room, knocking over the hotel manager and the bellman as he raced down the stairs. He went around the back to get his horse and galloped away across Mayo's Bridge to the Virginia Central railroad tracks heading east.

Confederate Agents Conrad, Ruggles, Harney, and D. Montjoy Cloud sat in Assistant Secretary Campbell's office and were getting their heads chewed off. Campbell was livid that he wasn't aware of Greycourt's treachery. The two men that were sent to eliminate Greycourt were dead. Their target getting away, Campbell stressed the importance of getting him while also carrying out their orders. Secretary Seddon would have to be apprised of the situation now and would not be pleased. Harney was to join his men at the Torpedo Bureau until summoned, and the others were to go to Washington City and carry out their tasks.

The dining room at the National Hotel was crowded. Greycourt was fortunate to get a table, and a waiter asked him if the young couple standing by the alcove could share his table. He put the newspaper down and looked up; they looked like a decent couple, and besides, the young man was in uniform. He nodded for them to join him.

They sat and, after introductions, thanked him for his gallantry. They offered to pay for his breakfast, which he graciously declined. They were just married the night before and were very lucky to get a room at the hotel. The young officer was about to tell Greycourt of his orders when the Union agent stopped him, explaining that there are some things that a soldier doesn't discuss, and orders are the first thing. Too much talking could decide battles before they are fought, he explained.

They asked his business, and he said he was a railroad agent working for the government, and they accepted his cover. The conversation went to President Lincoln's address at Gettysburg a week earlier and how exciting it must be to see him deliver a speech in person and maybe the war would be over soon. The couple finished their breakfast and again thanked Greycourt for his courtesy. As the young man got up, he just had to mention that he was off to General Meade's corps for a winter campaign in Virginia. Again, Greycourt admonished him.

The waiter brought more fresh coffee as he sat by himself and continued reading the newspaper, *Washington Constitution*. Noticing an article about the memorial service in Harrisburg, Pennsylvania, for Union General John F. Reynolds who was killed on July 1, the first day of battle at Gettysburg. His heart sunk. Reynolds was a decent man, a fine leader and teacher. He was someone that Greycourt respected very much. It had been difficult for him to leave Reynolds's mentoring at the military academy at West Point to join the cause. The war had taken another fine person. Too many men dead; he vowed to himself to do whatever it took to get the war to end. He had a meeting with Ward Hill Lamon later that day, and he was going to discuss his plan to track down all threats against the president.

★★★

Confederate Captain T. Nelson Conrad and his men left Washington City during a snow storm, heading north to a safe house in Baltimore. They were getting too comfortable at the Surratt House but also had to wait for John Surratt's return from Montreal, Canada. Surratt would deliver further orders, which turned out to be the "go ahead" and cash. In Baltimore, they would blend in, and no one would ask any questions or suspect anything.

Greycourt stayed one night at the Surratt House and was able to surmise that the person known as Ted Jones and his friends left the day before. He overheard the young Surratt telling his mother that a plan was in the works. Mr. Jones would be protected by friends just north of Washington City. This told him that Mosby was providing an escort for the agents. He would start out on horseback for Winchester, the most likely of places under Mosby's protection, and leave as soon as possible.

Snow flurries and the winter winds made the ride north a bit treacherous. The remark of a winter campaign by Meade, told to him by the young officer, made him more aware of activity of troop movements on both sides. Since it was likely that the Rebel agents were headed to Winchester, he wasn't very concerned about avoiding the main roads. The temperature was dropping, and he needed to stop. He knew of a safe place a few miles east of Winchester that would take him in, rest his horse, and be a comfort to him.

The young girl came to the door holding a shotgun as the three dogs barked inside. She opened the door and looked up. "I have no food or anything else for road tramps," she said. She looked closer and saw a familiar face. "Come in, get out of the cold," she beckoned, placing the big gun down and getting a blanket. "I'll get your horse in the barn. You sit tight for a minute," she ordered. She wrapped the blanket around Greycourt after he took his blue frock coat off.

The coffee was hot. He sipped it, not saying anything. He watched her scurry around the kitchen, preparing hot corn meal mush and fresh bread. The fireplace was ablaze, crackling and sparking, as she placed log upon log, stoking it and heating the entire house. Two of her sons got up to peek out of the door to their room and saw that it was all right, so they went back to bed. The dogs, lying by the fireplace, were quiet and content. She placed a bowl and a cup at the table and told him the food was ready. She placed a small bowl of sugar on the table, much to his surprise.

"Sugar is about $30 a barrel now. Maybe you'll want to save this," he said.

Belinda Hunnicutt, the lady of the house, nodded. "You left me some decent money, so I was able to buy a few pounds. Use as much as you want," she answered.

He began eating, and she sat with him. She watched as he ate the entire bowl in three big spoonfuls. He ate only a half slice of the bread but drank two cups of coffee. He wiped his mouth and sat back.

"I'll wash all your clothes tomorrow morning, all your clothes," she said, looking at him up and down. "There'll be a bath for you."

"A good night's sleep is all I'll need. The bath and laundry could wait another time," he said with a smile.

She shook her head. "You'll wash now. If you're gonna sleep in my bed, you'll wash now," she said sternly, getting up to clear the table.

It was just before dawn, and there was work to be done, but Belinda wanted to stay in bed a few minutes longer. She hadn't slept like that in years and wanted to keep that feeling as long as she could. Greycourt stood by the door and poured water into the basin on the dresser to wash his face. She looked at the scars and healed wounds on his naked body and wondered what in the world he went through for his body to get beat that way. Both shoulders appeared to have poorly healed wounds, and the lower right side of his back had what looked like an exit wound from a bullet.

In spite of his battered body, the sinewy muscular man still looked magnificent. He could use a haircut and shave, she thought. Her sons would be waking up in a few minutes, so she rolled out of bed and wrapped the bedsheet around her naked body.

As he washed his face and ran water through his hair, she gently kissed his back and grabbed her robe to begin preparing breakfast.

It didn't seem as cold this morning as Greycourt looked out from the front porch. Belinda came out and stood next to him. "I don't want you to go," she said, touching his arm.

Greycourt smiled and looked out. "I can stay today, but I'll have to leave tomorrow morning. I have a job to do."

She wasn't convinced and tried to persuade him to stay longer.

"There's work to be done here, and I can't do it. There's at least two hundred yards of fence that need fixing, and the barn roof needs work. I could use your help." She stood closer to him.

He turned to her. "I have to go, and besides, I'm not much of a carpenter. I know horses."

Belinda smiled. "Then you should stay. My land is rich, just perfect for horse breeding." She lowered her eyes. "Stay here with us. I feel that if you leave, you won't ever be back."

He smiled. "I'll get up on that barn roof and do what I can, but I'll be leaving tomorrow morning." He paused for a moment and looked at her. "I'll be back, plan on it."

The city of Winchester was a Confederate stronghold and was a key strategic point. Union forces tried to wrest control in three battles but had been driven back as the Rebels fought hard to defend the Shenandoah Valley. As a major base of operations for Rebel forces regarding their invasions into the North, Winchester was home to the famed Thirty-First Virginia Militia that took part in John Brown's raid.

Mosby's Raiders also patrolled the countryside, looking for Union movements and anything they could steal. The city had been occupied by Union forces last June but was recaptured by the Rebel infantry. This day, General Joseph E. Johnston's army of the Tennessee was on the outskirts of the city reoutfitting and preparing for a hard winter.

Greycourt rode into the city fully aware that he could be arrested and hung if recognized.

The Winchester Hotel was on Myrtle Avenue, which was away from the batteries that were placed around the city. He got a room on the top floor facing Louisiana Heights and its big guns. He decided to walk to get a haircut and hear what the local barber had to say.

Two blocks away was Pete's Barbershop and Emporium. There you could get a shave, haircut, bath, tooth pulled, in-grown toenails clipped, and elixir for a sore throat. The proprietor, Ol' Pete Coppin, was sixty-six years old with a bald head and thick gray mustache. His blouse billowed on his slim build, and the suspenders were needed to keep his trousers up, for he looked as if he had no derriere. When he spoke, it was as if he was always saying something funny as he chuckled after each sentence. A neighborhood favorite, Ol' Pete usually had three or four old men sitting around, gabbing, and carrying on. All eyes shot to Greycourt when he entered the shop.

Ol' Pete smiled and waved him over to sit and asked if it was a haircut, shave, or toothache. Greycourt said he'd like his mustache trimmed and some lilac oil combed into his hair. Pete asked his business, and Greycourt said that he was a horse trader from Richmond working to get animals for the First Virginia. One of the men blurted out that it made sense being that Company H of the Eleventh Virginia Cavalry was in town to shield Johnston as he moved west. One of the men, a portly man wearing a dark brown coat and trousers sporting a thick rustic mustache, kept eyeing the young man as he spoke.

"Excuse me, son, but you don't look like any horse trader I ever seen," he said with a smile.

Ol' Pete cleared his throat and shook his head. "Stop pressin' the boy, Amos. If that's what he said he is, then that's what he is. Heh, heh."

Another man spoke up, "Yeah, son—"

He was interrupted by Pete. "You too, Zeese, stop pressin'! Heh, heh."

Greycourt smiled. "Oh, I don't mind. I get asked that a lot. My orders are directly from Richmond."

Another man cleared his throat and blurted out that it all made sense and mentioned that some of Mosby's men were in town, most likely to watch out for Yankee troops. Greycourt gave Ol' Pete a quarter and a nickel tip, bid farewell to the gentlemen, and dropped into the nearest tavern.

With the weather turning colder, more men were coming into the tavern. Greycourt ordered a brandy and a cup of coffee. Six men walked in, and they looked all too familiar. Luckily for him, they didn't look over at his table in the corner. There was a bowl of pickled eggs and salted crackers at the end of the bar, so he got closer to the men while he kept his head turned. The men were quiet until another man walked in. Greycourt recognized him right away; it was explosives expert T. Francis Harney.

As he gulped down the brandy and coffee, Greycourt left 40¢ on the table and was about to leave when Harney got up get a glass of beer, looked his way, and looked again more closely. He went over to him and put his hand out. "Major, how are you?" he asked with a smile.

Greycourt was made, so he had to go along.

"C'mon and sit with us. You in a hurry?" Harney asked.

Greycourt, hat in hand, shook his head. "I got a minute," he answered.

The six men sat around the round table and made room for the two. Harney was revered, so if this was a friend, it was all right with them.

"You scoutin' fer Stuart? We heard the Yankees are planning another invasion into the valley," Harney said, looking around the table. "You know, the major here, he's about the best scout we have. He rode with y'all. What was it, a year ago?" he asked, looking around the table.

"We're here to wreck some things, bridges, roads, just about anything." Greycourt was uneasy. He had to think of something fast and get out of there. "Yeah, I have to get close and size up the Yankee strength," he said and looked at his pocket watch. "That reminds me, I have to send a wire," he said, looking at Harney.

Harney nodded and smiled. "If they get too close to you, remember Baltimore. That's as safe a town as you're gonna get. We have some of our guys there now planning, well, something big. You in on it?" he asked.

Greycourt leaned forward. "Yeah, it's big, all right," he answered, watching the other scared- and hard-looking faces around the table. "I've got to meet them soon."

Harney smiled. "So you're in with Conrad and Ruggles? Funny, they didn't mention you when we were outside of Culpeper."

Sitting back, Greycourt shook his head. "No, they weren't supposed to." He then got and shook Harney's hand and nodded to the rest around the table. One of the men was whispering to another as they stared at the man walking out of the door into the cold. He had to get out of Winchester right away and head to Baltimore.

★★★

Reginald James Greycourt was sick to his stomach. It was a week from Christmas, and he only had this time to be in Baltimore. Distraught and despondent, Reginald sat in the living room by the fireplace in the house his parents bought that was being cared for by Paul and Tessa. He had a glass of whiskey in his hand and stared at the fire. There was a knock at the door, and Paul looked through the curtain and smiled; it was Colton.

Paul shook both of Colt's hands and smiled as Tessa ran out from the kitchen to hug him tightly. Reginald got up and went to the foyer and stood, watching how overjoyed the slaves were to see his young brother, and stayed back as not to interrupt the moment. Colt then saw his brother and went to him slowly, putting his right hand out. Reginald shook it, and they both went into the warm parlor. Paul brought Colt a glass of whiskey, and Colt asked for coffee also. Reginald slumped in his chair.

"I'm sure you don't know," he said, looking at the fire. "I still can't believe it."

Colt shook his head. "I'm unaware of a lot of things. What is it?"

Reginald choked up a bit. "They were returning from England and had to stop in Nova Scotia. But the weather was so bad the ship couldn't make it to port, so it turned south, probably for Boston. They never made it."

Colt was shocked. "You mean they're, they're dead?"

Reginald nodded slowly.

"How do you know? Maybe they weren't even on that ship?" Greycourt asked.

"That ship went down, and they were on it. I know," he answered.

Greycourt sighed deeply and bowed his head. "Why are you here?" he asked.

Reginald, still staring at the fireplace, sipped his drink. "I came to free Paul and Tessa."

The room went silent for a few minutes. Colt never thought of Paul and Tessa as slaves. They were with him since he was born and considered them part of the family. Tessa looked after him like a son and Paul like a father. Reginald had the legal power to free them, and Colt was glad he was doing that.

"I've been a sorry sight of a man, Colt. I looked at things like a scallywag, and well, I've realized that this war has made things bad, and I can maybe make some things good. The days of knights and serfs and slaying dragons are long gone. There are two children out in the yard, a boy and a girl. I found them weeks ago as I was leaving Washington. They were contraband from Virginia. I brought them here to be safe until I decided what to do with them, and wouldn't you know it? Tessa and Paul said that they would be welcome to stay as long as need be. You should see them. They're both about thirteen or fourteen years old, and it's like they've been adopted. Scipio is gone. Finding these children was a blessing," he said, looking at his brother. "I have to do good from now on, Colt."

Paul brought the boy and girl into the parlor. Although they seemed scared at first seeing the two white men sitting there, it became apparent to them that they would be safe as soon as they saw Colt smile at them. He asked the boy if he knew horses, and the boy nodded. Colt asked him to take care of his horse, remove the saddle, and give it food and water. The boy ran outside to do what he was asked. Tessa, smiling, came into the room and ushered the young girl into the kitchen.

"Where are you headed? Back to Richmond?" he asked Colt.

Standing up and stretching, he looked at the crackling fire and turned to his brother. "No, Washington. I have business there."

Reginald nodded. "It's true then. You've joined up with the Union."

He paused and looked at Colt. "Good," he exclaimed.

Paul came in and said supper would be in an hour, poured coffee for Colt, and left the room.

Reginald stood up and held his brother's right arm. "Listen, Colt, watch yourself. If you're in Washington, Baltimore, New York, or wherever, keep your eyes and ears open and sleep with your pistol next to you. If you come across someone named Dalrymple, or even anyone associated with him, just go the other way. I don't know what your business is but just stay away from him."

Colt tilted his head slightly to the right as his brother spoke. "There's a plan that, well, I'm not sure what it is, but it's about keeping the war going. I don't like it, and I know Clive G. Dalrymple has a hand in it."

This was crazy. A plot in the South and now one in the North? he thought. *Keeping the war going in the North and ending the war in the South? This can only mean one target, a tall target: President Abraham Lincoln.*

Reginald checked his pocket watch. "There's a guy by the name of Blaine also. Watch him too."

Colt nodded. "Anyone else?" he asked.

Reginald shook his head and left the room to wash his hands.

Colt sat back in the chair and picked up a newspaper up off of the floor. He thumbed through it and came to the society page. As he was about to turn the page, he stopped and read one of the headlines. A lump formed in his throat as he stared at the article.

NEW YORK PHILHARMONIC DELAYED
WILL NOT PLAY WASHINGTON CITY

He read the short article and crumpled the paper and then read again:

> Stranded in Barcelona, the New York Philharmonic will have to extend their European tour that began in June. Rough winter seas are the cause, and it is reported that the symphonic troop would head back to Paris. It is not known when they will return.

Colt cut the article out and stuffed it into his breast pocket.

CHAPTER TWENTY

Secretary of War Stanton got out of his carriage at the steps to the President's House. He was near exhaustion as he slowly ascended the steps and was met at the front door by two soldiers standing guard. They saluted him as he tapped on the front door. The first floor wasn't totally dark, telling Stanton that the President's House servants were still awake. He waited a minute until a tall elderly Negro servant opened the door, bowed to the secretary, and took his hat and wrap.

The servant informed Stanton that the president was asleep, but if it was an emergency, he'd wake him. Stanton said not to bother; he was headed to the basement rooms of the President's House. He was accompanied by another servant as they descended the carpeted steps.

Geiger and Morse stood outside the room where the interrogation was ongoing. They were talking to two soldiers, one of them standing, smoking a pipe, the other with his hat off, sitting on the floor. The servant, also a Negro, came through the hallway first, leading Stanton. Turning a corner, they stopped. The four men looked at the servant and saw Stanton behind him. The men then stood at attention and waited. Stanton went to the door and opened it.

★★★

Washington City still had the stockyard smell. More Union troops were entering each day. Cattle and teamsters driving wagons filled with all kinds of supplies crowded the already crowded streets.

Greycourt divided his time between the National Hotel and the Surratt House. He was convinced that clandestine activity against the Union was evident all around the boarding house. It was a matter of time before Conrad and his cohorts would be back.

One particular character on the Surratt stage was John Surratt, the owner's son. From what he observed and heard, John Surratt would disappear for weeks and return, always meeting someone in the parlor room, whispering conversations, and watching everything. He should be in the Rebel army, Greycourt thought, since he was young and strong. He was someone to keep an eye on.

★★★

Nigel Blaine took a leisurely walk along North E Street, from the Willard Hotel and then east to W. Fourth Street to the jailhouse. He had a letter from the War Department for the sergeant at arms who then led him to the colonel who eyed the letter up and down, holding it very close to his spectacles. The colonel nodded and brought him to a small room with two chairs and a scratched and chipped table. A prisoner was ushered in by two guards and sat down. The prisoner, a gangly built man with a long face and dark beard, didn't speak as Blaine asked him to stand, so he could look him over. He was dismissed and the guards brought a dozen more prisoners in for him to look at, which were all also dismissed.

As Blaine got up to leave, his search in vain, he heard a commotion outside the door. He opened it and saw four guards grappling with a big-boned prisoner, trying to subdue him. The colonel walked over and stood about five feet away from the ruckus, drew his revolver, and fired into the floor. They all froze. Blaine looked at the colonel and nodded.

Now that they were all calmed down, the big brute of a man sat down in the chair in the room with Blaine. He took his spectacles off and cleaned the lenses with his handkerchief and let out a sigh. He looked at the prisoner—wide shoulders and broad chest, thick neck and a few small scars on his face. He was definitely a brawler. Blaine also noticed an earring in his right ear. The big square-jawed prisoner sat back and stared across the table. Blaine nodded slowly.

"What are you in here for?" he asked. The brute didn't say anything, and Blaine repeated the question.

"I hit the sergeant of my platoon. Then I hit the captain, then the major, then everybody else around. The sergeant never got up," the big man answered. His voice was deep.

"Are they going to hang you?"

"Yeah, tomorrow. I thought I'd get in as many licks as I can before the rope."

Blaine smiled. "How would you like not to hang? How would you like to get out of here, maybe for good?"

The big man nodded. "Yeah, what I gotta do?"

"I have the paperwork to get you released now. You'll have a room at the Willard Hotel, and we'll meet in the hotel dining room at eight tomorrow morning. I suggest you be there. If not, you'll be found and shot on the spot. Agree?" he asked.

The big brawny prisoner nodded.

★★★

Washington City was buzzing with excitement. The success of the Union's armies was mainly the result of General Hiram Ulysses Grant's ability to command troops and defeat the Rebel army, battle after battle. That success led the United States Congress to create the position of lieutenant general, outranking the higher position of major general. Approved in both houses, Grant was then nominated for the new position. With unanimous approval, he became commander of all the armies of the Union. President Lincoln was thrilled at this and invited the general and his wife to a reception and dinner at the President's House for a grand celebration.

Sitting in his room at the National Hotel, Greycourt read the newspaper before getting dressed and going to breakfast. The paper said that Grant and his wife were to arrive in Washington about three o'clock in the afternoon. The general was scheduled to review the nearby camp of Negro troops. Mrs. Grant was to go to a tea reception given by Mrs. Lincoln. The streets would be lined most of the day with the masses waiting to get a glimpse of Grant.

Washing his face and putting a palm full of lilac tonic in his hair, he got dressed in one of his finest suits and white blouse with a blue-red print tie. He was about to go to the dining room when there was a knock at the door. Knowing how previous knocks had turned out, he drew the revolver from the waistband of his trousers and asked who was there. A telegram was slipped under the door.

Not wasting any time, he raced through the crowded, dirty streets to the President's House to see Ward Hill Lamon. After some difficulty getting past two guards, he showed his identification to a major who led him to Lamon's office. They discussed the troubling wire.

The afternoon went by swiftly as Greycourt went to the Surratt House to reserve a room for the next night. To his surprise, all rooms would be occupied for the next four nights. Stalling, he sat in the parlor, making it seem as if he was waiting for a room, but he was really listening and watching. Three men that he had never seen there were coming in and out. After about an hour, he left and advised Lamon who then quickly had the three men picked up and held for questioning at the garrison a few blocks from the President's House. Lamon gave his new agent an invitation to the reception and dinner with explicit instructions to observe and even arrest anyone of suspicious intent.

The small parade of carriages and cavalry guard, under the watchful eyes of the enthusiastic crowds, went to the front of the President's House, with President and Mrs. Lincoln greeting the honored couple and guests at the door. Lamon and Greycourt entered together after all were situated in the grand reception room on the first floor.

Politicians and military men with their ladies mingled, and Greycourt noticed that the new lieutenant general was a bit uncomfortable with all the attention. Grant looked like a common soldier, which he greatly admired.

The evening went smoothly as the Grants left early, thanking all in attendance. Lamon then summoned Greycourt to his office about midnight with some information that only a few select people would know. The telegram was in his hand as Lamon spoke.

The next morning the newspapers reported on the gala event at the President's House. The general and his wife were to be leaving that afternoon; Grant was returning to his troops and Mrs. Grant to New Jersey to be with her sons. Greycourt knew otherwise.

Nigel Blaine ate a light breakfast of scrambled eggs, toast, and coffee at Willards Hotel and kept an eye on his charge, the big brawny fellow sitting across the room. Blaine was confident that their job would be successful, thus getting him back into the good graces of Dalrymple.

The night before, Blaine met with his new employee at a slimy wharf saloon near the navy yard that catered to prostitutes and deviant individuals. They quietly talked about their task, and Blaine found that the muscled man was not as dumb as he thought, and after a successful job the following night, he could use him permanently. The big man just gave his name as "Lammy," and Blaine took it at that. He gave him an envelope containing $10 and promised another hundred after the job.

The late morning was bright and sunny as the two men, going separate routes, made it to the wharf at the United States arsenal on the Potomac River in the southern section of the city. There, a one-hundred-foot steam-propelled supply vessel that was waiting for them to board. It would then take them up the eastern part of the river to an area where the huge powder magazines were housed. Blaine checked his pocket watch and boarded.

Lammy was more of a bodyguard than anything else; he was to say close to Blaine but also to position the cargo at the front of the boat. The small crew, including six others, slowly got underway.

It was odd that there were no cargo ships or other boats in the river as they proceeded. As they slowly continued up river, the boat, almost stopping, lowered two small dinghies into the water which had five crewmen board and row away. Blaine, now in the pilot's room watching, counted five, not six. Lammy stood at the front of the boat, positioning sacks and crates at the bow of the boat. *Where was the other crewman,* he wondered.

The new skipper of the vessel had some difficulty getting the boat underway again. Cursing, he felt a gun at his head. He was told to be still and not turn around. Lammy, puzzled, looked up and waved to get going. Squinting, he saw two men in the pilothouse. He raced up to see what the trouble was.

The gunman turned slightly, facing the door, still commanding Blaine to face forward as the big brawny brute shoved open the door and stopped.

"You're both under arrest," the gunman exclaimed. Blaine looked out the corner of his right eye and saw Colton James Greycourt. Just then, Lammy lunged. A shot went off, whizzing by the big man's face. The struggle for the gun began. Blaine, busy, was trying to get the vessel underway but continued to have trouble.

The gun was wrestled out of Greycourt's hand. Blaine stretched to kick it away, sending the weapon out of the door. Lammy dived for it, with Greycourt on his back, and both men went tumbling down the pilothouse steps, slamming onto the deck. Lammy's huge right fist missed as Greycourt ducked and countered with a left cross to the big brute's face, sending him backward but not down. Trying to throw the agent overboard, Lammy grabbed both his shoulders and lifted, but Greycourt head butted the big man on the nose, breaking it. Blood gushed all over. Releasing him, Lammy held his hands up to his face as Greycourt pummeled his body with quick punches and a knee to the groin, finally doubling Lammy over. A hard right jab and then a powerful left caught Lammy squarely on the chin, opening a cut. Shaking his head, Lammy then grabbed Greycourt by the throat; Greycourt frantically tried to get the huge mitts off his neck.

Blaine was able to get the vessel moving, and although it was slow, he got it on its deadly course. Throwing his arms upward, Greycourt was able to free the powerful hands from his neck as the combatants began trading blow for blow, inflicting ugly wounds on each other's faces and bodies.

As the vessel made its way up the river, Blaine saw the target—a 250-foot steamer docked in front of the arsenal. He then increased the speed, heading directly toward it. Leaving the pilothouse and running down the steps, he was about to jump off when the two battlers noticed the boat moving faster. Blaine got the revolver and was about to shoot both men when the boat swayed, and Blaine hurried back up to the pilothouse to steer it back on course.

Lammy tried to leap off the boat, but Greycourt grabbed his shirt and pulled him back. Suddenly an empty barge appeared between the target and the vessel. Blaine, not being a good pilot, had trouble maneuvering away. As the vessel was about to hit the barge, Greycourt leapt off the side into the water; and the vessel, loaded with explosives at the bow, hit the barge, creating a massive explosion. Both the vessel and the barge were destroyed, hundreds of pieces scattered all over the river.

Five United States marines ran to the rail of the target ship with rifles drawn and quickly dispatched a lifeboat to pick up the man having trouble treading water.

★★★

Ward Hill Lamon sat, smoking a cigar, and stared at the young man with a blanket wrapped around him, sipping piping hot coffee. Two of General Grant's aides and three cabinet members had just left the room. Secretary of State William H. Seward was escorted into the room in the hull of the large steamer by two marines. The secretary looked at the young bruised and battered man wrapped in the blanket and then looked at Lamon. Seward inquired about medical attention and was informed a doctor was on the way. Lamon stood up and walked to Greycourt.

"Mr. Secretary, as I explained to Mr. Chase, Mr. Welles, and Mr. Speed that my agent here saved the lives of the president and General Grant and very well may have saved the Union."

Seward, his long face growing ashen, listened to the details of the attempt to assassinate both Lincoln and Grant using a boat loaded with explosives. Tapping his forehead with his left index finger, he looked at Lamon.

"When I heard of their plan to meet secretly on a boat in the river without protection so they would not draw any attention, my response was a definitive no," he said sternly. "There should have been at least a half dozen of gunboats out there."

The objective of the plan had been for the two leaders to discuss how to end the war. Then Grant would stay aboard and travel south to meet up with the army. Apparently, the marines, positioned ashore to watch the river, were not at their posts as the vessel approached. An empty barge that had just been unloaded got loose and floated out.

"Colonel Greycourt here, well, he got word that there might be an attempt against the president and took action. He is a valuable man. Both Mr. Lincoln and the general came down to thank him and congratulate him on a job well done. Our only regret is that the two men that perished in the explosion weren't taken alive for questioning," Lamon told the secretary. "We owe him our sincerest gratitude for his bravery, sir."

Seward walked over to Greycourt, stared at him, and extended his right hand; the two men shook hands. The doctor entered as the secretary left and placed his bag on a table next to Lamon. "What in the world happened to you?" he asked, eyeing the patient up and down. The doctor, his spectacles on the tip of his nose, began cleaning around the cuts over his left eye. Although he couldn't do anything about the bruises and swelling around the eyes and his broken nose, he suggested that he check into the hospital to rest his battered body.

Word came back that the crewmen that were picked up in the dinghies were held and then released as they were not part of the plot. They were just hired hands.

The doctor left. Lamon sat across Greycourt and poured him more coffee. They had to get moving before Grant came back on board to sail south as planned. "Do you have any idea who was behind it?" he asked.

Greycourt slowly nodded. "Yeah, that's what bothers me."

CHAPTER
TWENTY-ONE

It was harder and harder to get a good night's sleep for many months. The reoccurring dreams of the Ortegas dancing, visions of Sergeant Major Ward standing majestically with his huge arms folded, Scipio lying dead in the road, and the horrible screams of du Seine as his arm was being amputated disturbed Greycourt every time he closed his eyes. More disturbing was the news that General Jeb Stuart was mortally wounded at the Battle of Yellow Tavern and died a few days later. Like Union General John F. Reynolds, Stuart was a good man with good intentions and morals, fair minded, and both were strong role models. It was almost unthinkable that Stuart could be killed in battle as he exuded that aura of immortality displayed in the old Arthurian legends. His body trembled as the sorrow of Stuart's death overwhelmed him.

His nightmares always ended with a sharp flash of the image of Victoria standing in a garden, smiling. When that happened, he always got out of bed and read the newspaper clipping about the New York Philharmonic being stranded in Europe. One night, he looked through the letters that he saved and examined the postmarks. How could she write from American cities when she was supposed to be stranded in Europe? He needed to free his conscience. He set out to track her down.

The noon train to New York City was an hour late. Apparently, the Baltimore and Ohio Railroad was under the heavy activities by saboteurs, and the Union cavalry was delayed in providing scouts along the rails. As he sat waiting, he read a novel he intended to read for many years, *Moby Dick*. A train from Baltimore pulled into the station across the tracks on another platform.

A boy came through the depot waiting area selling warm peanuts. Greycourt tossed him a penny, and the boy tossed him a bag of shelled peanuts. As the boy walked away, he noticed the people getting off the newly arrived train. To his surprise, he saw Conrad and three other men; one was Ruggles. He didn't know the other two. He handed the bag of peanuts to an elderly man sitting next to him and hurried out to follow the Rebels.

Their carriage took them to the Surratt House. Greycourt was right behind. He thought about getting support but decided to stay put just in case the Rebels left. He then went into the boarding house to inquire about a room. He was turned away again; there were no vacancies. He sat in the parlor, pretending to read a newspaper when a young girl came over to ask him to leave as their parlor was not a place to loiter; it was only for guests. He apologized and left. He was able to get a room on the top floor of the Kirkwood House that looked out toward the President's House.

Lamon was apprised of the new development via a coded note and quickly dispatched a platoon of cavalry to shadow the president. He also made sure he was now going out with him whenever he was out and about town, which he did frequently.

★★★

Shakespeare's *The Taming of the Shrew,* starring Edwin Booth, had just ended at the Winter Garden Theater to a robust audience that gave three standing ovations to the actors and waited for Booth to personally address them. A favorite of the New York City elite, Booth thanked his audience and recited Hamlet's soliloquy as an added treat received by rousing applause.

Dalrymple and his date for the evening, Victoria Leland, left their box for a waiting carriage taking them to Pete's Tavern on East Eighteenth Street in the Gramercy Park section of Manhattan. The edgy man was anxious for a drink and was still annoyed at Victoria for being late for dinner. The late August night was very hot, and the Friday night streets were crowded. Pedestrians and vendors jammed up the route downtown, further annoying him. He might have five drinks tonight, he thought.

They got a table in the back facing the door. The long bar was to their right in the classy, stylishly decorated saloon with its oil paintings of fox hunts and scenes of carriages on Fifth Avenue. Victoria ordered a cherry cordial and coffee, and Dalrymple ordered a double whiskey with a beer chaser. He gulped the whiskey followed by the beer. Victoria shook her head and sipped the cordial as he motioned for another round. She dabbed at her mouth and was about to speak when he quickly cut her off.

"That's the last time you'll be late with me, dearie. If I have to drag you out by the nape of your neck to be on time, I will," he said, feeling the whiskey. "I don't know what to do now. That bone-headed Blaine couldn't complete a simple job. I guess he got what he deserved."

Victoria glared at him. "What he deserved? You know, I wondered why you didn't do that job yourself. You like giving orders but can't handle the jobs," she said.

Dalrymple became cross and leaned forward. "If we weren't here, I'd slap your face." He took another gulp of the whiskey and beer.

Victoria smiled. "You wouldn't. You'd have someone else do it."

Dalrymple rubbed his eyes and sat back. "It's not going well. I haven't given the boss anything new, and just so you know, I've been covering for you these months. You haven't heard from him at all? You're not just keeping him from me, are you?"

Victoria put two teaspoons of sugar in her coffee and stirred. "I haven't heard from him in months. He might be dead. I do know one person that possibly knows where he is and what he's up to or, if he is, in fact, dead."

Dalrymple nodded. "I just need something for the boss, something small even. Let's get together with Reginald tomorrow morning. I have a meeting with the boss in the afternoon and want to give him something. Get Reginald."

The Surratt House had no vacancies for three straight weeks. Each time Greycourt attempted to get a room, he was turned away but stayed close to observe the activities. Mary Surratt and her daughter, Elizabeth Suzanna, better known as Anna, became suspicious each time he showed up, so after a while, he stopped. He knew that the men staying there didn't look like ordinary working men; they had the look of soldiers. He already knew that Conrad was with Mosby. There was something going on.

Early one day, after breakfast and a horseback ride around the city, he strolled in front of the boarding house. He was just about to check on a vacancy when he noticed something: it appeared that the small group of men was gone.

CHAPTER TWENTY-TWO

Greycourt's most prized and cherished possession was his red roan. The twelve-year-old powerfully built gelding was raised by Paul especially for Master Colton. Scarred from the whirlwinds of battle yet still had the tenacity and stamina, the envy of other horsemen. The roan not only saved Greycourt's life many times but also very well may have saved the Union.

On a hot early July morning, Greycourt took his usual ride, but instead of riding south of Washington City, he decided to ride north. Through wooded paths, he cantered further than he intended, but the bright blue sky was glorious, so he continued his ride. He stopped so the horse could get a drink from a small stream and graze on sweet grass on the banks. He was about to turn around to go back when the roan whinnied and raised his head.

Greycourt tugged the reins again, and the roan jostled and whinnied, shook his head, and began to spin around. When he got the horse under control, Greycourt realized something was not right. Now calm, he directed the roan forward, and it appeared that the horse, now steadied, was eager to go that direction. As he approached a clump of trees near a clearing, he saw what looked like puffs of smoldering smoke. As he got almost beyond the trees, he saw them—thousands of Rebel troops assembling into marching formation. Pickets, about thirty yards away, didn't see him. Slowly and without rustling leaves or twigs, he turned around and galloped toward the city.

At breakneck speed, he made it to Ward Hill Lamon's house on North D Street. As a servant rushed out to take his horse, he sped past him through the front door as Lamon was finishing his breakfast. Alerting him of the impending danger, Lamon quickly ordered his carriage. Greycourt mounted his horse much faster and notified Major General Christopher C. Augur, the commander of the Department of Washington who then alerted Colonel Moses T. Wisewell, the military governor of Washington. Three other generals were alerted and ordered artillery units. Over sixteen thousand men south of the city received orders; all were confused as to who was in charge.

Greycourt rode out to get a better look at the enemy's advance and their troop strength when he ran into Major Charles R. Lowell's three squadrons of the Second Massachusetts Cavalry. Completing a reconnaissance, he advised of the approach. Lowell handed Greycourt his revolver, and both led the cavalry directly at the oncoming Rebels, forming a skirmish line. At first sight, they opened fire, scattering the Rebels. The cavalry tried flanking, but return gunfire was too heavy. Lowell, in command and confident he could hold longer, agreed to let Greycourt ride back to the city with more precise information on enemy strength.

Now twenty thousand hastily organized soldiers, teamsters, cooks, and volunteer citizens manned the northeast part of the entrenchments. A large battery of over five hundred pieces of artillery, including heavy cannons, was set high up to rain destruction on the invaders. There was still confusion on who was in command. Troops were spread in the small forts in the northeast, ready to make a stand and to stall until Grant could leave Petersburg with a powerful force to crush the Rebels.

Fort Stevens, part of the thirty-seven-mile-long arrangement of sixty-eight forts guarding the city was built to guard the northern approach but was manned with just ten cannons. Five hundred men were aware that the position of the Rebel army meant they would sweep from the north, hitting the fort first. Secretary of State Seward was prepared to get to the front and observe first hand.

Greycourt, reporting back to Lamon, requested permission to ride north to join up with the cavalry. Much to his reluctance, Lamon allowed it but was concerned for the president's safety as the attempted invasion might be a diversion to get at Lincoln. The sound of the guns guided Greycourt to Fort Stevens as cannon fire and riflemen aimed at the advancing Rebels but did little to slow them down.

Reporting to Union Major General Horatio Wright, Greycourt took a position on the north wall. The charging of the Rebel cavalry on July 11 was repelled three times. The Union defenders' confidence rose with word that two corps of Lieutenant General Grant's army had arrived south of the city and were prepared to march on the Rebels and drive them from Maryland. The command of the north wall was given to Greycourt as he directed artillery and sharpshooters against the Rebel cavalry.

On the morning of July 12, President Abraham Lincoln arrived on horseback, just as he had the previous day, to observe the fight and congratulate the brave men of the fort. Orders went out for Union troops to clear the area of enemy activity, but they only found wounded soldiers and horses. West of the fort, cavalry engagements caused Rebel horsemen to retreat. By the evening of July 12, the Confederate Army was seen crossing the Potomac River near Leesburg and the invasion was over.

Ward Hill Lamon, never leaving the president's side during the frantic events of the last three days, sat in the parlor of his house sipping whiskey, feeling the effects of no sleep for days. Across him in a high-back chair sat Colonel Colton James Greycourt, the unsung hero of the Battle of Fort Stevens that saved Washington City. Lamon knew his charge was just as exhausted and was proud of the young man he commissioned.

"Colonel Greycourt, you've done a service far beyond anything we've seen. I, the president, the Union, am eternally grateful for your actions and service—" The president was interrupted.

"Sir, the real savior is my horse. I recommend a medal for my horse," he said with a wry smile.

★★★

Confederate troops were massing around Richmond as General Lee was in conference with President Davis and Secretary of State Judah P. Benjamin. Lee had a plan to get the army into the Shenandoah Valley to regroup. Grant couldn't possibly find his way in that thick, dense, winding valley. Besides, his men were badly in need of shoes and food. A long stretch in the valley would buy them some time before facing Grant again.

Davis was against it. The Confederate president felt that if Lee retreated into the valley, Grant would easily take Petersburg. If Petersburg fell, Richmond would be next. Benjamin agreed with Davis and said he'd try to get the necessary provisions. But he also said he had a plan that might force a truce or even surrender by the Union, if accomplished. Davis had an idea what the plan was and assured Lee that he would do all he could to get the general what he needed and was confident that they would prevail.

Judah P. Benjamin suggested arming the slaves, but the government would have nothing of it. The one-time attorney general and secretary of war, Benjamin was a lawyer in Louisiana before the war and was a staunch advocate of slavery. He also supervised the Confederate Secret Service and put up most of his own money to fund it.

In an inn on the outskirts of Richmond, Benjamin met with T. Nelson Conrad and Tippie Ruggles. The two men had the plan all worked out and just needed Benjamin's approval. The timing had to be just right, and the secretary was assured it would be.

Greycourt had just returned to Washington City from Baltimore where he visited with Paul and Tessa and their "adopted" children, with a surprise visit from his sister and her baby. Her in-laws were taking good care of her and the baby, but she needed to see for herself if the Judge and Mrs. Greycourt were, in fact, dead. Reginald wired the report of the dead on the lost ship, and their parents were on it.

Genie wasn't the same person she was before the war. She looked older, tired, and spoke with a cynicism he had never heard from her before. He tried being optimistic. "You have your whole life ahead of you. Good things will happen," he said, holding his nephew.

Genie looked down and shook her head. "Maybe, I don't know. My only purpose now is my son."

"I'll come get you when this war is over. It will be good, you'll see," he said with a smile and then made a funny face for the baby.

"This war! This rotten war. You know what this war did? Do you?" she asked angrily. "It destroyed lives, ruined everything, and for what? What? Jonathan said it was the cause. What cause? Antiquated ways of life run by an antiquated class? Jonathan talked about it so much that I got sick of hearing it. Oh, he was going to be a hero, a real hero. Look where it got him. Look where it got us. The Judge and Momma are dead, and Tessa told me Scipio is too." She slumped down into the large couch and wept.

Colton switched the baby to his other arm and sat next to her. "Things are done for a reason. I realized that the cause was really the other way around. You should see Mr. Lincoln. He walks every day with his young son. The man that has the entire country on his shoulders takes time each day to walk with his boy. That man knows right from wrong, the good from bad. In all this mess, he can see the bad yet knows there's good, and that's what this fight is about. The cause is really the North's cause."

Genie looked up at him. "Then why did he invade us? Jonathan said Lincoln invaded us, starting the war."

Colton smiled. "Look in that room there," he said, pointing toward the kitchen. "Can you ever see Paul and Tessa in chains?"

Genie shook her head. "They were never in chains," she answered.

"They weren't? Maybe not chains and shackles you can see, but they were there, just the same," he said.

He put the baby on the floor to let him crawl around. "There are many reasons for this war, and if anyone can fix this country, it's Lincoln. We should thank God for him."

Genie sat closer to him, closed her eyes, and hugged his arm as she rested her head on his shoulder.

Summer was coming to a close, and the city was still hot and had the foul stink of livestock and latrine. More troops were coming into the capital as regiments were forming and brimming with confidence that the Rebels were on the run and near the brink of surrender. Newspapers touted Lincoln's efforts to recruit another one million men to bring the war to an end. But the Surratt Boarding House was buzzing with news that the famous actor John Wilkes Booth was going to be a guest for a few days. He was going to appear at Ford's Theater in Shakespeare's *Hamlet*. T. Nelson Conrad and his four team members were also guests. So was Colton James Greycourt.

Greycourt had been given a room by a young girl that occasionally worked there. She didn't know that this man frequently requested a room and was not to be accommodated. Interestingly enough, and much to Greycourt's delight, he was given the room next to Booth.

The evening supper table was full of guests, except for Booth who was attending a reception given by the editor of the Washington *Evening Star*. There wasn't much talk as the guests passed the large bowl of beef stew and biscuits. Mrs. Surratt poured the coffee until one of the guests mentioned the failed attack on the city. All eyes and ears went in the man's direction as he spoke of the gallant efforts of the Union Army that turned back General Jubal Early's advance.

Conrad was silent, but Ruggles defended Early and said he hadn't been reinforced as he expected. Conrad was not pleased with those words and tapped Ruggles under the table to be quiet.

The guest, an elderly man with a thick white mustache and eyebrows, was in town with his wife to see the play and was thrilled that Booth was at the same boarding house. He kept the conversation about the Rebel attack going. The man asked Greycourt what he thought about it. He had to watch what he said as he was about to mention that if it was Wade Hampton's brigade, the outcome might have been a bit different. Instead, he replied only that he was not in town and didn't know much about it.

Conrad, continuing the conversation, asked where he was from and what his business was. Greycourt smiled and said he was from Baltimore and was in town on a real estate deal. Conrad nodded, not buying the answer.

Ruggles, with a short-cropped beard and mustache, was a wiry-looking man with thinning brown hair and rather small nose. Again, he began to bring up the Rebels, and Conrad watched Greycourt very closely. As Ruggles spoke, Conrad interrupted him. "Real estate in Washington, sir?" he asked.

Greycourt looked at the man with the round face, dark beard, and mustache. With his hair parted on the side and a fine blue suit, he looked like a schoolmaster. He looked him directly in the eyes.

"Yes, sir, real estate, and I do not wish to bring up the name of my client."

Conrad tilted his head to the right. "Do you reckon the name Mosby, sir?" he asked.

Greycourt shook his head. "Can't say I do. A friend of yours?"

Conrad nodded. "You from Baltimore and never heard of Mosby? Ya know there's a war on, don't ya?"

The guests around the table chuckled at the snide question.

Greycourt sipped the rest of his coffee, wiped his mouth with the linen napkin, and smiled at everyone. He looked up at Mrs. Surratt, thanked her for a very hearty and delicious supper, and excused himself. Conrad tapped Ruggles with his right elbow, and he got up to follow the man outside.

Greycourt anticipated this, so he slowly walked up the street, stopped, and took out a long, lean cigar. Asking a passerby for a light, they engaged in brief small talk. Ruggles, now joined by another in the Rebel coven, Dan Cloud, stopped and watched. As Greycourt thanked the man, he started walking slowly again. He slowed and abruptly stopped, forcing the followers to almost trip over themselves. He turned to them and smiled.

"Excuse me, gentlemen, my cigar seems to have gone out. Do either of you, fine gentlemen, have a match?" he politely asked with a smile.

Ruggles got flustered and fumbled in his pockets. Cloud didn't move.

Greycourt went into his vest pocket and came out with a box of matches. "You mind?" he asked Ruggles, pointing to his foot to use to strike the match.

Ruggles lifted his foot for him, and he lit the cigar. Greycourt puffed smoke at the two men and smiled.

"Was I walking too fast for you, boys?" he asked. He puffed again and then threw the cigar into the street.

★★★

Back at the boarding house, Ruggles, Cloud, and a slave that belonged to Conrad named William, sat in the dining area, waiting. The rest of the guests, all except Greycourt, sat in the parlor, waiting for Booth to return. Conrad had gone out and was expected to return in a few minutes. Booth entered the house after midnight to the eager guests; Conrad was right behind.

Booth went into the parlor and was handed a glass of brandy. Conrad went into the dining room and sat at the head of the table. The three men got closer, keeping their voices down. Ruggles took a match from the match holder on the table and struck it on the bottom of his boot. "That jackanapes is no real estate man."

Conrad nodded. "I know. I've seen that guy before. He's got that hardened look of a convict or soldier, you know that look," he said.

Ruggles and Cloud nodded. Conrad looked up and saw Mrs. Surratt bring a pot of coffee into the parlor for the guests, and he motioned to her for a cup.

"I'm thinking it was with Mosby a few years ago. I don't know."

"Hey, maybe he's here doin' the same thing we're doin', huh?" Ruggles asked.

A cup and pot of coffee was brought over. Conrad put the cup up to his nose and smelled the strong aroma before taking a sip.

"He's either with us, or we're gonna kill him."

CHAPTER
TWENTY-THREE

A tall well-dressed servant came into the parlor room of the modest home of Ward Hill Lamon and delivered a tray with two cups and a pot of coffee. Lamon, the president's big, burly thick-boned bodyguard, got up to pour and asked for a bottle of whiskey.

Greycourt sat across Lamon, his long tired legs stretched in front of him, his body sore all over. Lamon didn't say much but was in awe of the young man sitting across him. He could commend himself for enlisting this gallant man who had done so much. The servant came in and left a bottle of whiskey and two glasses. Lamon got up again and poured a drink for Greycourt who poured it into his cup of coffee. Too tired to even talk, Greycourt wiped his forehead with his handkerchief and stared blankly. Lamon sat and rehashed to himself what had been reported to him by the young colonel and how, once again, the president was saved.

The day before, Greycourt met with Lamon to report information about the movements of a group of Rebel agents in and around the city. The war had been sharply turning in the Union's favor, and the Rebels were desperate to keep it going, hoping for any kind of advantage.

Lamon stayed close to Lincoln at Greycourt's, urging while the president was spending the extended summer in his cottage at the soldier's home just north of the city. Expecting trouble, Lamon placed the Second Massachusetts Cavalry at his disposal as they stayed in Washington City to get reoutfitted after the Battle of Fort Stevens. They would also support in the event of any further attacks on the city.

Greycourt rode out of the city following the Rebels as they left the boarding house before sunrise that day.

Staying a discreet distance behind, he followed the men north into Virginia to Loudon County, which was a stronghold of John Singleton Mosby and his Partisan Rangers. He knew exactly where they would be headed, even though the mouth of the Shenandoah Valley was under heavy fighting, engaging General Early against the feisty and tenacious Union Cavalry General Philip Sheridan. If they were meeting up with Mosby, it meant that they needed cover of some sort.

Turning west toward Leesburg would make sense. Being careful as he crossed a stream, he saw Mosby and about a hundred of his rangers waiting for the Rebel agents under a clump of trees. As he turned his mount around, an owl flew by, spooking the horse. This caught the attention of William, Conrad's slave. Spotted, Greycourt galloped away through the thick woods with Ruggles and Cloud in close pursuit.

Ever grateful for his swift red roan leaping over fallen tree stumps and thick bramble, Greycourt, sweating profusely and keeping just ahead of the two Rebel riders, now had to keep low as shots whizzed by him. Without breaking stride, Greycourt headed toward the Union garrison at Fairfax Courthouse. He got the attention of the pickets by waving his hat as he approached. They let him through. He no longer was being pursued.

Hurrying, he made it to the president's cottage where he found Lamon and alerted him of a possible threat. He raced to the eastern part of the city to Rock Creek where the Second Massachusetts Calvary was camped. Major Lowell brought him into his tent to look at the map of the area. Greycourt quickly dismissed it as wasting time and said he'd take the brigade right to Mosby. Lowell, without question, agreed and commanded the bugler to sound Officer's Call.

The officers, remembering Greycourt from the recent July battle repelling Rebel horsemen, listened to his every word and were ready to follow his lead. Lowell agreed and another bugle call for assembly of the battalion of four hundred riders assembled and mounted up, ready to ride.

Within minutes, the battalion, made up mostly of Californians eager to get into the war, were behind Greycourt and Lowell charging toward Leesburg, frantically racing to catch Mosby idling in the same area. About halfway, Mosby's Rangers were spotted escorting a wagon and riders as they headed toward them. Greycourt ordered a squadron to do a flanking maneuver to catch the Rebels by surprise while the main body struck the center. He wasn't sure of the Rebel strength, but he knew that if it was an escort, there wouldn't be more than fifty or sixty riders.

Halting the troop, Greycourt steadied his mount and drew his revolver. Within minutes, the squadron opened fire, surprising Mosby, forcing them back. At that move, Greycourt ordered a charge right into the Rebel center.

Firing furiously into the rangers, Greycourt, without a saber to joust, took the rifle out of its sheath and used it as a lance, banging and hacking. His sure-footed charger turning and spinning at his every move as the squadron was trying to get behind the Rebels. But their expert horsemanship prevented a rear assault.

Mosby's men were forced back as the Second Massachusetts Calvary pushed harder, rangers falling dead all around, horses screeching and panting in the heat of the fight. Twenty-two Rebels were killed and twelve captured. Three men of the Second Massachusetts Calvary were killed and eleven wounded, though not fatally. Mosby had gotten away with the wagon and riders.

The battle took all about twenty minutes. After regrouping and accounting for the dead and wounded, Lowell set off back to Washington City. After resting his horse, Greycourt rode south on his own, looking for the wagon that got away. If Mosby was escorting that wagon and riders that close to Washington, they were definitely up to something. Tiring in the midafternoon sun, Greycourt dismounted and sat by a stream to rest. He had been hit on the shoulders, and he also noticed blood caked on the right side of his forehead. Then he noticed deer scurrying through the woods, warning him there was movement close by. He got up, stayed low, and saw a wagon and seven riders slowly navigating the narrow path.

It was early evening, and a squadron of cavalry was stationed outside of the president's cottage on the grounds of the soldier's home.

Coming up the road was a man in black wearing a stovepipe hat riding a grey mare. Riding next to the man in black was a big strapping man on his right and a soldier on his left with ten cavalrymen providing escort. Lincoln was retiring for the night from the President's House to the cottage. Nearby, the Rebel group with the wagon watched; Greycourt watched them.

Waiting for the signal to move on the president, the Rebels were ready to spring into action. Their leader, having second thoughts, called off the attempt.

As the Rebel group withdrew and went deeper into the nearby woods, Greycourt followed until they got a good distance from the grounds of the soldier's home. Outnumbered, he thought of going back to get support but did not want to lose their trail. Thinking fast, he pounced. "MAJOR, MOVE YOUR MEN UP! CAPTAIN, FORWARD!" he shouted, startling the Rebels. The Rebel leader turned around; it was Conrad.

With both pistols drawn, Greycourt ordered the Rebels to drop their weapons and dismount. All but one did—Ab Nevers, the young ranger that took up with the outlaws Chan Goode and Noah

Beaudry. "You're all surrounded, so just stand tall and don't move. Son, drop that weapon, drop it," he commanded Nevers.

Conrad, his hands up, smiled. "I thought we were being followed, never thought it was you."

Greycourt looked at Nevers. "Son, put it down. You'll be safe when you come with me. All of you will be safe. You couldn't kill Lincoln. We have him too well protected. It's over."

Conrad shook his head. "We weren't going to kill Lincoln, just kidnap him for ransom."

"Ransom?" questioned Greycourt.

"Yeah, ransom. We get Lincoln, and the Yankees release our prisoners. After that, you surrender. Besides, it's not over until the last man is killed."

Nevers cocked his revolver and pointed it at Greycourt. As he commanded his captives to get in a line, Greycourt pleaded with the young man to drop his weapon. Sweating, Nevers shook and blinked. Greycourt pulled the trigger and shot the young man in the chest, killing him.

Realizing there weren't troops surrounding them, Conrad leaped onto his horse. The others did the same. Greycourt got off three more shots, killing another Rebel.

As he tried to follow, he lost them in the thick dark woods and went back to the wagon. He looked at Nevers lying dead; the other Rebel lying there couldn't have been older than the young man. He went over to the wagon and saw a box that appeared to be a coffin about seven feet long and four feet wide with holes drilled on each side. They were obviously planning to use this to keep the president captive.

★★★

Victoria had grown tired of everything. She was tired of spending money on frivolous things, tired of the boring theater patrons in her circle of friends, and mostly tired of Clive G. Dalrymple. She met him after a recital by the New York Conservatory of Music at Madison Square in New York. He was a cocky young lawyer, and she took to the good-looking man right away. A year later, while in the New York Philharmonic, they met again. Only this time, he lavished her with a fancy dinner and a jeweled necklace. She didn't see him again until two months before the war broke out while performing at a July Fourth concert sponsored by the mayor of New York in the still unfinished Central Park. Knowing she was a Virginian, Dalrymple promised her riches if she took up with him. Bored with the Philharmonic, she agreed.

As she primped, she looked at the envelope on the dresser. It wasn't as thick as it usually was, and she realized that her investment in the munitions factory was a loss. Dalrymple promised her a huge sum of money if she was able to get an important meeting set up that would get him much needed information. She got the meeting. She looked at the watch on the dresser next to the envelope. She had about two hours before her guest arrived.

The train from Washington City to New York chugged slower than usual because of reports of saboteurs on the rail lines. Greycourt, reading a newspaper and munching on peanuts, checked his pocket watch and yawned. Two days before, he received a telegram from his brother Reginald to come to New York City to meet about a family matter, and he responded that he would. Less than an hour after that wire was received, Reginald sent him another telegram with a warning and tip-off of what the meeting was really about. He had planned to go to New York, and the wires from his brother hastened his trip.

The train pulled into Pennsylvania Station by midafternoon, and he quickly got a carriage to the Fifth Avenue Hotel. He looked forward to a good night's rest of his battered body in the big feather bed and a breakfast of steak and eggs which the hotel was famous for. He was unusually relaxed for what was ahead.

Dalrymple was early, expecting extra activity with Victoria as he dropped off the down payment he promised her. Annoyed, she opened the door and let him in, ignoring him. As he tried to kiss her, she turned away. Dalrymple took out a long cigar and lit it, put his right foot up on a chair next to her, and flicked ashes on the carpeted floor.

"You'll put the place on fire doing that," she scolded. "Please don't."

He chuckled and blew out a large billow of smoke. "We're expecting a lot of solid information tomorrow, you know. I'll be looking real good. And so will you," he said.

Victoria wasn't impressed. "Will you be here in the room with me or hide in the closet like a rat in the gutter?"

Angered, Dalrymple puffed again. "I'll be watching your back in case he gets violent. I'll make sure you're safe," he answered.

She combed her hand through her hair and rolled her eyes.

The next day after breakfast, Greycourt went for a walk along Fifth Avenue and enjoyed the early October sun and warmth. The fancy carriages wove in and out among the fish carts and vegetable wagons, and policemen strolled about, making the lively street crowded. In his best dark blue suit, white shirt, blue tie, and newly shined shoes, he freely strolled, well aware he was ten minutes late for the meeting. He arrived at the Hotel Astor, and the elevator operator brought him to the top floor suite. He knocked and was let in.

Victoria was dressed in the finest clothes she had—a pink chiffon dress with a white belt, white shoes, and pearl necklace. She was dressed as if she were going to the theater. She looked at him and got all goose pimply. She hadn't seen him in a long time. She looked him up and down. He had the look of a battle-hardened soldier, his sharp features accentuating his blue eyes and rugged build. She felt weak in her knees.

He came in, placed his carpet bag down, and didn't say anything. Victoria smiled and put her hand out, but he didn't take it. She shrugged. "How are you, Colt? It's been a long time," she said.

He looked around the room, then at her, and nodded. "Aren't you taking chances coming up here? You know you're not exactly—"

He interrupted her. "I always take chances," he coldly answered.

"Tell me, what have you been doing lately?" she asked.

He took out a small stack of letters from his breast pocket and extended them. She took them and just scanned the envelopes. "Look at the dates, the postmarking," he demanded. "Read them too."

She wasn't interested.

"Let's see, check the letter May 1863. You remember what happened then? Me and the First Virginia Cavalry were caught by surprise by Union cavalry. One of my best friends and his brothers were killed. My best friend had to have his arm amputated. A few weeks later, I wrote you about a grand parade we were having for General Lee. Before that, I was ordered to ride into northern Virginia scouting Union camps. It just so happened that men burst into my hotel room and tried to kill me. The week before, I wrote to you about my mission. I remember that squirrely faced scrawny guy with the glasses who tried to shoot me. He was also the low-down scurvy knave that tried to blow up President Lincoln and General Grant. I know 'cause I stopped him."

Victoria never thought Greycourt would know or catch on to what she was doing. Taken by surprise, she tried to deny it. "Colt, you think I'd betray you like that? Those are just coincidences," she answered with a smile.

"Coincidences? Then tell me, how is Europe?" he asked, taking a crumpled newspaper clipping from his other breast pocket.

Her stomach tightened. "I had to leave the orchestra and come back to America—" She tried to explain, but he interrupted her again.

"Stop it. Say no more. You think I'm as dumb as a jackass, but you're wrong," he said, angrily. Just then, the door to her bedroom opened, and out walked Dalrymple.

"You foolish, foolish man. We got a lot of information from you. You think we got you up here to slap you on the back?" Dalrymple snidely asked. "How stupid can you be? You gave vital information to us. What did you expect? We expected to hear about your next moves, but I guess we won't now." He then drew a revolver and pointed it at Greycourt.

Greycourt lowered his head and looked at Victoria. "I trusted the wrong person."

Victoria looked at Dalrymple. "Put that down," she ordered.

Dalrymple continued, "We made a lot of money off of you. The more information, the more we made. Too bad the factory had to get blown up, or we'd be even richer. You know, we laughed a lot about you. Laughed a lot even when we were in bed . . ."

"Clive!" Victoria shouted.

Greycourt tensed as he looked at the pistol resting at Dalrymple's side. Within seconds, the faces of du Seine and Ortega flashed across his mind. He drew the revolver from the waistband of his trousers and, at point blank range, fired one shot into Dalrymple's forehead. Killing him instantly, the bullet forced his head up and his body backward against the wall.

Stunned, Victoria looked at the dead man and then at Greycourt. "Good god, Colt! I thought he was going to kill you. I'm glad you got him," she said, looking at the dead body. "Good. Now we can be together, just you and me," she said with a smile.

Greycourt looked at her and fired a shot that hit her directly between her eyes, sending her body across the room. He picked up the letters and the newspaper article, stuffed them in his carpet bag, and left the room.

TWENTY-FOUR

The Confederacy was desperate. Lack of equipment and food, desertions, and massive death tolls devastated the South, crushing morale, yet they were determined to fight on.

Union General William T. Sherman's march from Atlanta to the sea at the end of 1864 wreaked havoc, driving a stake deeper into the South's heart and forcing the Rebels to concentrate their forces in and around Richmond. The city of Petersburg was under siege, and General Lee was determined to keep the Union forces at bay until he could come up with a master plan and move his army into the Shenandoah Valley where they could hide and regroup for a few months.

Lieutenant General Grant was hell bent on crushing Lee, and both generals bumped heads, smashing their great armies into each other. After starving the Rebels out at Petersburg and choking their rail lines, Grant turned to Richmond with a force of over a hundred thousand fighting men. There was one last gasp of hope for the Rebels.

Confederate Secretary of State Judah P. Benjamin had plans for himself and his family in the event Richmond fell but had another plan that might result in a truce or even a peace settlement. His courier summoned Brigadier General Gabriel Rains and two other men to meet in his office in Richmond to come up with a scheme.

Rains and another man had to be smuggled past Union lines and escorted to Benjamin.

Their meeting in the early spring winds of March was one of desperation. Rains, the expert bomb specialist, and his number one man, T. Francis Harney, had an idea that was sure to succeed. Benjamin listened; it was exactly what he had been thinking. The timing of the plan was of the utmost importance. If they succeeded, it would result in total turmoil in the North, perhaps extending the war and buying Lee more time.

Colonel Colton James Greycourt spent the last few months riding around the northern counties of Maryland, hoping that Conrad and his men would be hiding there. The townsfolk in those areas knew nothing about any Rebel activity and were reluctant to even speak to him. He turned his attention to Virginia where he took off for Loudon County; his first stop was just outside of Berryville.

Greeted by two barking dogs, Greycourt took off his black hat and waved as three boys ran out to meet him. Standing out on the front porch, Belinda wiped her hands with her apron. He rode up and dismounted; the boys gathered around the roan to pet it, and he placed the youngest boy in the saddle. Belinda was giddy at seeing him ride up. As he approached the porch, she ran and hugged him until almost all the air was squeezed out of him.

"Are you all right? Let me look at you," she said, pushing back and eyeing him up and down. She grabbed at his arms, tugging him toward her, and looked at the small scar on the right side of his forehead.

"Is the war over?" she asked.

He looked at her. "No, the war is still on, unfortunately. And I'm fine, more lucky, I guess."

She took his arm and led him inside, and he sat down at the table.

"I was worried. The big fight around here months ago. More toward Berryville, I think. I came the first chance I got," he said.

Belinda poured a cup of coffee for him. "We had the luck. The fighting was south of here. We had some men in blue come, looking for all our chickens and cows, but their officer stopped them and paid me for a few. They didn't take all of them. One of the dogs went at them, so they shot him."

He sipped the strong coffee and smiled. "I'm glad and grateful."

She sat closer to him and touched his arm with her left hand.

"The county guard had been coming around to see about deserters, but they mostly want a meal and anything else they can get. They got just the meal."

He looked at her long light brown hair and dark eyes as he placed his right hand on hers. "How did that barn roof hold up?" he asked.

She smiled. "Pretty good, no leaks."

"The fence is next," he replied. She looked up into his face, getting lost in his eyes. She was just so overjoyed to see him and didn't want him to leave.

"Can you stay long? I mean, how long can you stay?" she asked.

He smiled. "I can stay the night but have to head back in the morning."

Disappointed, she slowly nodded. "I won't ask you what you're doing but just pray to God that you come back."

He smiled, leaned toward her, and gently kissed her on the cheek.

★★★

As reports spread through Washington City of Grant's eminent capture of Richmond and Confederate President Davis's escape from the city, the anticipation of total victory was just a matter of days away. President Lincoln was taking more walks with his son, Thomas, who was called Tad, and even carriage rides with Mrs. Lincoln. Lamon had to leave Washington, which upset him, for Chicago on an urgent family matter and kept a cavalry escort close to Lincoln at all times. But he really wanted Greycourt to take his place at the president's side. Now he was worried about having to leave without knowing where his young charge was.

Greycourt's ride back to the capital was slow, detouring three times to avoid county guards and Mosby's patrols. He hid in the thick woods as the rangers,a force of about fifty riders,stopped to graze their horses.He overheard the men talking about which route was quickest south to Washington.Hearing this, Greycourt rose and slowly and quietly mounted and rode off to the city.

On the evening of April 9th, church bells rangand revelers in the streets shouted "VICTORY, VICTORY, VICTORY" as the news of General Robert E. Lee's surrender to Grant was confirmed. People shouted for President Lincoln to appear and address the crowds, to which he gladly obliged. With the fall of Richmond and the surrender, the war was over.

The president called for an all-day meeting the following day at the President's House with his entire cabinet and a dinner with their wives that evening. Lincoln did not want to waste any time in forming a plan to mend fences and restore the entire country to one whole nation again. The evening dinner was to celebrate all the hard and painstaking work of the cabinet members to achieve victory.

That same evening, 150 rangers of John S. Mosby provided escort for T. Francis Harney and three of his men at the Potomac River across the capital. In Harney's possession was a bomb with enough power to blow up an entire city block. The team was to place the explosive under the floor where the cabinet was to have dinner in the west wing of the President's House. When detonated, the entire

Union would be wrapped in a chaotic mess, and the western arm of the Southern army, under General Joseph P. Johnston, could fight on and revive the Rebels. In all the excitement and utter mayhem, the Rebel rangers and Harney's team went unnoticed.

As the sun was setting on April 10, infantry units around the capital were enjoying the pubs and saloons offering free drinks. Hordes of prostitutes worked the streets, taking advantage of the laxity, and small bands played joyous music. Greycourt arrived earlier that day and went to the cavalry barracks in the Georgetown section near Rock Creek. He showed his identification as United States deputy marshal and ordered the cavalry to stand at the ready, which the colonel promptly obeyed.

Tirelessly, Greycourt rode around the city, passing the President's House three times. He noticed lights on and carriages in front, but no guards or sentries posted anywhere. Anyone could waltz in without obstruction. And Mosby's men were headed for the capital.

Riding over the Long Bridge across Alexander's Island into Virginia, he turned northward toward the aqueduct. Greycourt saw a boat with three men get into the river but ran into Mosby's men. After first going unnoticed, they quickly fired on him. As he was about to turn around to attempt to head off the boat, a squadron of Illinois cavalry on patrol galloped past him and took off after the Rebels, chasing them back.

As quickly as he could, Greycourt made it back to the city and rode north with the city lights on his left and the river glistening in the moonlight to his right. As the boat hit the shore, the three men got out. As they disembarked and looked up, two revolvers were staring at them down. Harney put his hands up, but the others hesitated until they saw Greycourt cock both his pistols. He ordered them to kneel with their hands behind their backs. He retrieved the explosives from the boat. As he placed the bomb on the ground, a detachment of cavalry from Richmond arrived and placed all the men under arrest. Despite Greycourt's protest, he was put under arrest too.

★★★

Secretary Edwin Stanton walked into the room and looked around. Pinkerton stood at attention and saluted as did Geiger and Morse. Expressionless, the secretary just looked at them. He then looked directly at their prisoner. He ordered Morse and Geiger to stay in the room while he and Pinkerton went outside. Near total exhaustion, Greycourt eyed the two agents up and down and knew he could muster enough strength against the two if they decided to work him over just for the hell of it.

Stanton rubbed his face and cleaned his spectacles. "So what's all this about? Who is that in there that you've spent the entire night questioning? It's almost daylight."

Pinkerton wiped his forehead with a white handkerchief. "An interesting lad this guy is. A Virginia Rebel. Says he works for us."

Stanton saw a guard standing near the doorway listening and dismissed him. "Well, does he work for us? What does he do?" he asked.

"He's done everything, quite a story," he answered. "They picked him up during the night with a bomb."

"A bomb!" Stanton exclaimed.

"That's not all," Pinkerton replied and briefly told the secretary what the interrogation was about. Stanton and Pinkerton went into the room and ordered the two agents out. Greycourt stared straight ahead as they came in.

"Young man, do you know who I am?" Stanton asked.

Greycourt nodded.

Stanton continued, "Are you a spy for the Rebels? Because if you are, you'll hang, you know that, don't you?"

Greycourt looked at the secretary and nodded. "I'm United States Deputy Marshal Greycourt."

"So you're a traitor as well as a spy? What do you know about New York City?" Stanton demanded.

Greycourt got angry but kept silent.

Stanton, spent of patience and overly tired, turned to Pinkerton. "Take him to the marine barracks and hang him there. Be done with this."

As Pinkerton called for Morse, Geiger, and two guards, Stanton looked at a leather folder on the table. He looked at the diploma from West Point and an official document indicating his commission as a United States deputy marshal. Stanton placed the papers back in the folder. While they waited for the guards to come, the heavy feet of a big man came rumbling down the steps. It was Ward Hill Lamon. Quickly, everyone returned to the interrogation room.

"I should have been here sooner. Sorry, Deputy," he said, looking at Greycourt.

"What's this about anyway?" he asked.

Pinkerton began to speak, but Greycourt spoke over him, getting Lamon's attention and telling what had occurred over the past twenty-four hours.

Lamon turned to Stanton. "This man is an agent under my direction. If he says he stopped a bomb threat, then he stopped a bomb threat. He's telling the truth. He's been tearing around assisting me in protecting the president and, I might say, has done it exceptionally well. I'm nominating him for a special Congressional commendation. His horse also."

Stanton wasn't impressed but was surprised he did not know of this man. "What about New York City? Two of my agents were murdered in New York City months ago, and I want to know who their killer is. If it's him, he'll hang."

Lamon wasn't fazed. "Tell him, Deputy Greycourt."

Greycourt sat down and squared his shoulders. "For one thing, they had money invested in a munitions factory in Pennsylvania. That factory was blown up. They decided to rebuild it and to make up for their losses, conspired to keep the war going. You know what they thought? They thought that by assassinating President Lincoln and General Grant, the war would drag on. Maybe you heard about it? I stopped that."

Greycourt cleared his throat and noticed Stanton, expressionless, as he spoke. "If they were your agents, Mr. Secretary, then I'd go after their boss. That's what I would do."

Lamon nodded at Greycourt and turned to Pinkerton. "Turn the deputy loose, sir. He's earned a well-deserved rest."

Stanton huffed and abruptly left the room.

Allan Pinkerton stopped and extended his hand to Greycourt. "No hard feelings, sir. You know, I've grown to admire you. You're a very unusual man."

As they were leaving the basement room, Greycourt purposely bumped hard into Geiger and Morse, almost knocking them down.

Lamon ushered Greycourt into a parlor room on the main floor in the President's House and asked if he wanted anything, which he declined. Lamon, exhausted himself, tapped him on the arm and nodded. "I'm very glad I got here. Who knows what might have happened."

Greycourt nodded. "They really wanted to hang me."

Lamon shook his head in disbelief. "I think so too."

Greycourt continued, "You know, if these different offices and agents got their communications straight and actually worked together, we wouldn't have to waste all this time like we did. Wasting time cannot be allowed in our business."

Lamon agreed. "Well, we have work to do. I got the news that the war is about over, but it's not over. Have you thought about what you're going to do after all this? I mean when the war is really over? I need a man like you."

A servant came in and asked if the men needed anything. Lamon thanked him and replied no. Greycourt thought for a minute. He had a lot to think about. Looking back, he hadn't properly mourned his parents' death and was disappointed that he couldn't get an explanation from his father as to why he kept his diploma a secret. He had to see to his sister and nephew's well-being. He wanted to begin a relationship with his brother Reginald who, he was sure, had changed his ways. There had to be a trip to New Orleans and Texas to pay respects to families and see friends. He had to eventually reconcile that he killed a woman he thought he knew well.

Lamon leaned forward. "Deputy, I'm dedicated to the president and will be by his side, and I want you there also, even though I'm sure all threats and attempts are done. We can never be sure, though."

Greycourt smiled. "I'm going to hand in my resignation, sir. I've just about had it."

Lamon sat back and adjusted his jacket. "Deputy, you've performed in a most exemplary and extraordinary manner, one that may never be duplicated. I wish you all the luck in the world, and just so you know, you'll always have a job with me if you need one."

Greycourt smiled. "Sir, I owe everything to you."

They both stood up and shook hands. "Remember, you have a medal waiting for you, and I didn't forget your horse. There's back pay, and I'm throwing in a bit more for you, out of my own pocket. Good luck," Lamon said.

★★★

The easy canter of the red roan was almost silent. Birds chirped in the spring sky as the dogs hadn't noticed him yet. He turned onto the property through a large wooden gateway with an arch in need of repair. He stopped to look at it. He gently tapped his horse, and suddenly the two dogs ran to him, barking, as the three boys came running from the barn. He stopped halfway, dismounted, and hugged the boys, putting the youngest in the saddle as they walked toward the house. He waved his hat to her as he walked.

Belinda Hunnicutt's prayers were answered.

Printed in the United States
By Bookmasters